MURDER
IN THE FAMILY

MURDER
IN THE FAMILY

THE ADAMS ROUND TABLE

BERKLEY PRIME CRIME, NEW YORK

Introduction copyright © 2002 by Mary Higgins Clark; "A Moment of
Wrong Thinking" copyright © 2002 by Lawrence Block; "The Funniest
Thing Has Been Happening Lately" copyright © 2002 by Mary Higgins
Clark; "A Girl Named Charlie" copyright © 2002 by Stanley Cohen;
"The Letter" copyright © 2002 by Dorothy Salisbury Davis; "Tango Is
My Life" copyright © 2002 by Mickey Friedman; "In the Merry Month
of Mayhem" copyright © 2002 by Joyce Harrington; "My Cousin
Rachel's Uncle Murray" copyright © 2002 by Susan Isaacs; "The Grapes
of Roth" copyright © 2002 by Judith Kelman; "Motherly Love"
copyright © 2002 by Warren Murphy; "Cat in Love" copyright © 2002
by Justin Scott; "Ronald, D———!" copyright © 2002 by Peter
Straub; "Hole in the Head" copyright © 2002 by Whitley Strieber.

MURDER IN THE FAMILY

A Berkley Prime Crime Book
Published by The Berkley Publishing Group,
a division of Penguin Putnam Inc.,
375 Hudson Street, New York, New York 10014.

Visit our website at
www.penguinputnam.com

Copyright © 2002 by The Adams Round Table.
Jacket design by George Long.

First edition: August 2002

Library of Congress Cataloging-in-Publication Data

Murder in the family / The Adams Round Table.—1st ed.
    p. cm.
    ISBN 0-425-18335-1 (alk. paper)
        1. Detective and mystery stories, American.   2. Domestic
fiction, American.   I. Adams Round Table (Group)

PS648.D4 M8726 2002
813'.087208—dc21   2002071658

CONTENTS

INTRODUCTION

Mary Higgins Clark

O NE of the hardest problems about being a writer is that
it is, and must be, an essentially lonely way to spend
your days. There you are with your pen and spiral notebook,
trusty old typewriter, or state-of-the-art computer, and all
you have to do is to create a plot, a setting, and characters.
You must strive to make the situations so fresh, the characters so alive that the reader is incapable of turning out the
light until he or she has turned the last page.

Family and friends who were born without the need to
tell a story can be sympathetic, but in truth the writer speaks
a language that only other writers know.

"How's the book going?"

"Just great."

That can really mean that at this moment, the writer is
troubled and tortured, convinced that the book is going
absolutely nowhere, is destined to be a failure, will be
trashed by critics, shunned by the reading populace, and
really, why cut down all those lovely trees to give it birth?

Nearly fifteen years ago, the late Tom Chastain, a gifted
mystery writer and dear friend, and I were joking about the

fact that at some point in the writing process we all feel this way. That led to our deciding that we should gather a group of mystery-suspense writers together once a month for dinner. The purpose would be to encourage each other, share the misery and the fun of being storytellers, discuss our current work in progress, and bring up any problems we're encountering.

Tom and I thought it was a wonderful idea and the Adams Round Table was born, so-called because Adam was the owner of the first restaurant where we gathered. We meet on the first Tuesday of every month on the second floor of a midtown Manhattan restaurant.

There, over pasta or dover sole, we spend a couple of very pleasant and fruitful hours together. I have never come away without feeling encouraged, heartened, and able to go back to the manuscript with new energy.

This is our sixth mystery collection. We hope you, our readers, enjoy it as much as we've enjoyed writing it. And if on the first Tuesday of the month around 8pm EST you happen to give a fleeting thought to the fact that we are gathered at the round table, please be aware that we always are thinking of you.

MURDER
IN THE FAMILY

A MOMENT OF WRONG
THINKING

Lawrence Block

M ONICA said, "What kind of a gun? A man shoots himself in his living room, surrounded by his nearest and
dearest, and you want to know what kind of a gun he used?"

"I just wondered," I said.

Monica rolled her eyes. She's one of Elaine's oldest
friends. They were in high school together, in Rego Park,
and they never lost touch over the years. Elaine spent a lot
of years as a call girl, and Monica, who was never in the life
herself, seemed to have no difficulty accepting that. Elaine,
for her part, had no judgment on Monica's predilection for
dating married men.

She was with the current one that evening. The four of
us had gone to a revival of *Allegro*, the Rogers and Ham-
merstein show that hadn't been a big hit the first time
around. From there we went to Paris Green for a late supper.
We talked about the show and speculated on reasons for its
limited success. The songs were good, we agreed, and I was
old enough to remember hearing "A Fellow Needs a Girl"
on the radio. Elaine said she had a Lisa Kirk LP, and one of
the cuts was "The Gentleman is a Dope." That number, she

said, had stopped the show during its initial run, and launched Lisa Kirk.

Monica said she'd love to hear it some time. Elaine said all she had to do was find the record and then find something to play it on. Monica said she still had a turntable for LPs.

Monica's guy didn't say anything, and I had the feeling he didn't know who Lisa Kirk was, or why he had to go through all this just to get laid. His name was Doug Halley—like the comet, he'd said—and he did something in Wall Street. Whatever it was, he did well enough at it to keep his second wife and their kids in a house in Pound Ridge, in Westchester County, while he was putting the kids from his first marriage through college. He had a boy at Bowdoin, we'd learned, and a girl who'd just started at Colgate.

We got as much conversational mileage as we could out of Lisa Kirk, and the drinks came—Perrier for me, cranberry juice for Elaine and Monica, and a Stolichnaya martini for Halley. He'd hesitated for a beat before ordering it—Monica would surely have told him I was a sober alcoholic, and even if she hadn't he'd have noted that he was the only one drinking—and I could almost hear him think it through and decide the hell with it. I was just as glad he'd ordered the drink. He looked as though he needed it, and when it came he drank deep.

It was about then that Monica mentioned the fellow who'd shot himself. It had happened the night before, too late to make the morning papers, and Monica had seen the coverage that afternoon on New York One. A man in Inwood, in the course of a social evening at his own home, with friends and family members present, had drawn a gun, ranted about his financial situation and everything that was wrong with the world, and then stuck the gun in his mouth and blew his brains out.

"What kind of a gun," Monica said again. "It's a guy

thing, isn't it? There's not a woman in the world who would ask that question."

"A woman would ask what he was wearing," Halley said.

"No," Elaine said. "Who cares what he was wearing? A woman would ask what his wife was wearing."

"A look of horror would be my guess," Monica said. "Can you imagine? You're having a nice evening with friends and your husband shoots himself in front of everybody?"

"They didn't show it, did they?"

"They didn't interview her on camera, but they did talk with some man who was there and saw the whole thing."

Halley said that it would have been a bigger story if they'd had the wife on camera, and we started talking about the media and how intrusive they'd become. And we stayed with that until they brought us our food.

• • •

WHEN we got home Elaine said, "The man who shot himself. When you asked if they showed it, you didn't mean an interview with the wife. You wanted to know if they showed him doing it."

"These days," I said, "somebody's almost always got a camcorder running. But I didn't really think anybody had the act on tape."

"Because it would have been a bigger story."

"That's right. The play a story gets depends on what they've got to show you. It would have been a little bigger than it was if they'd managed to interview the wife, but it would have been everybody's lead story all day long if they could have actually shown him doing it."

"Still, you asked."

"Idly," I said. "Making conversation."

"Yeah, right. And you want to know what kind of gun he used. Just being a guy, and talking guy talk. Because you liked Doug so much, and wanted to bond with him."

"Oh, I was crazy about him. Where does she find them?"

"I don't know," she said, "but I think she's got radar. If there's a jerk out there, and if he's married, she homes in on him. What did you care what kind of gun it was?"

"What I was wondering," I said, "was whether it was a revolver or an automatic."

She thought about it. "And if they showed him doing it, you could look at the film and know what kind of a gun it was."

"Anybody could."

"I couldn't," she said. "Anyway, what difference does it make?"

"Probably none."

"Oh?"

"It reminded me of a case we had," I said. "Ages ago."

"Back when you were a cop, and I was a cop's girlfriend."

I shook my head. "Only the first half. I was on the force, but you and I hadn't met yet. I was still wearing a uniform, and it would be a while before I got my gold shield. And we hadn't moved to Long Island yet, we were still living in Brooklyn."

"You and Anita and the boys."

"Was Andy even born yet? No, he couldn't have been, because she was pregnant with him when we bought the house in Syosset. We probably had Mike by then, but what difference does it make? It wasn't about them. It was about the poor sonofabitch in Park Slope who shot himself."

"And did he use a revolver or an automatic?"

"An automatic. He was a World War Two vet, and this was the gun he'd brought home with him. It must have been a forty-five."

"And he stuck it in his mouth and—"

"Put it to his temple. Putting it in your mouth, I think it was cops who made that popular."

"Popular?"

"You know what I mean. The expression caught on, 'eating your gun,' and you started seeing more civilian suicides who took that route." I fell silent, remembering. "I was partnered with Vince Mahaffey. I've told you about him."

"He smoked those little cigars."

"Guinea-stinkers, he called them. DeNobilis was the brand name, and they were these nasty little things that looked as though they'd passed through the digestive system of a cat. I don't think they could have smelled any worse if they had. Vince smoked them all day long, and he ate like a pig and drank like a fish."

"The perfect role model."

"Vince was all right," I said. "I learned a hell of a lot from Vince."

"Are you gonna tell me the story?"

"You want to hear it?"

She got comfortable on the couch. "Sure," she said. "I like it when you tell me stories."

• • •

IT was a week night, I remembered, and the moon was full. It seems to me it was in the spring, but I could be wrong about that part.

Mahaffey and I were in a radio car. I was driving when the call came in, and he rang in and said we'd take this one. It was in the Slope. I don't remember the address, but wherever it was we weren't far from it, and I drove there and we went in.

Park Slope's a very desirable area now, but this was before the gentrification process got underway, and the Slope was still a working-class neighborhood, and predominantly Irish. The house we were directed to was one of a row of identical brownstone houses, four stories tall, two apartments to a floor. The vestibule was a half-flight up from street level, and a man was standing in the doorway, waiting for us.

"You want the Conways," he said. "Two flights up and on your left."

"You're a neighbor?"

"Downstairs of them," he said. "It was me called it in. My wife's with her now, the poor woman. He was a bastard, that husband of hers."

"You didn't get along?"

"Why would you say that? He was a good neighbor."

"Then how did he get to be a bastard?"

"To do what he did," the man said darkly. "You want to kill yourself, Jesus, it's an unforgivable sin, but it's a man's own business, isn't it?" He shook his head. "But do it in private, for God's sake. Not with your wife looking on. As long as the poor woman lives, that's her last memory of her husband."

We climbed the stairs. The building was in good repair, but drab, and the stairwell smelled of cabbage and of mice. The cooking smells in tenements have changed over the years, with the ethnic makeup of their occupants. Cabbage was what you used to smell in Irish neighborhoods. I suppose it's still much in evidence in Greenpoint and Brighton Beach, where new arrivals from Poland and Russia reside. And I'm sure the smells are very different in the stairwells of buildings housing immigrants from Asia and Africa and Latin America, but I suspect the mouse smell is there, too.

Halfway up the second flight of stairs, we met a woman on her way down. "Mary Frances!" she called upstairs. "It's the police!" She turned to us. "She's in the back," she said, "with her kids, the poor darlings. It's just at the top of the stairs, on your left. You can walk right in."

The door of the Conway apartment was ajar. Mahaffey knocked on it, then pushed it open when the knock went unanswered. We walked in and there he was, a middle-aged man in dark blue trousers and a white cotton tank-top undershirt. He'd nicked himself shaving that morning, but that was the least of his problems.

He was sprawled in an easy chair facing the television set. He'd fallen over on his left side, and there was a large hole in his right temple, the skin scorched around the entry wound. His right hand lay in his lap, the fingers still holding the gun he'd brought back from the war.

"Jesus," Mahaffey said.

There was a picture of Jesus on the wall over the fireplace, and, similarly framed, another of John F. Kennedy. Other photos and holy pictures reposed here and there in the room—on table tops, on walls, on top of the television set. I was looking at a small framed photo of a smiling young man in an army uniform and just beginning to realize it was a younger version of the dead man when his wife came into the room.

"I'm sorry," she said, "I never heard you come in. I was with the children. They're in a state, as you can imagine."

"You're Mrs. Conway?"

"Mrs. James Conway." She glanced at her late husband, but her eyes didn't stay on him for long. "He was talking and laughing," she said. "He was making jokes. And then he shot himself. Why would he do such a thing?"

"Had he been drinking, Mrs. Conway?"

"He'd had a drink or two," she said. "He liked his drink. But he wasn't drunk."

"Where'd the bottle go?"

She put her hands together. She was a small woman, with a pinched face and pale blue eyes, and she wore a cotton housedress with a floral pattern. "I put it away," she said. "I shouldn't have done that, should I?"

"Did you move anything else, ma'am?"

"Only the bottle," she said. "The bottle and the glass. I didn't want people saying he was drunk when he did it, because how would that be for the children?" Her face clouded. "Or is it better thinking it was the drink that made him do it? I don't know which is worse. What do you men think?"

"I think we could all use a drink," he said. "Yourself not least of all, ma'am."

She crossed the room and got a bottle of Schenley's from a mahogany cabinet. She brought it, along with three small glasses of cut crystal. Mahaffey poured drinks for all three of us and held his to the light. She took a tentative sip of hers while Mahaffey and I drank ours down. It was an ordinary blended whiskey, an honest workingman's drink. Nothing fancy about it, but it did the job.

Mahaffey raised his glass again and looked at the bare-bulb ceiling fixture through it. "These are fine glasses," he said.

"Waterford," she said. "There were eight, they were my mother's, and these three are all that's left." She glanced at the dead man. "He had his from a jelly glass. We don't use the Waterford for every day."

"Well, I'd call this a special occasion," Mahaffey said. "Drink that yourself, will you? It's good for you."

She braced herself, drank the whiskey down, shuddered slightly, then drew a deep breath. "Thank you," she said. "It *is* good for me, I'd have to say. No, no more for me. But have another for yourselves."

I passed. Vince poured himself a short one. He went over her story with her, jotting down notes from time to time in his notebook. At one point she began to calculate how she'd manage without poor Jim. He'd been out of work lately, but he was in the building trades, and when he worked he made decent money. And there'd be something from the Veterans Administration, wouldn't there? And Social Security?

"I'm sure there'll be something," Vince told her. "And insurance? Did he have insurance?"

There was a policy, she said. Twenty-five thousand dollars, he'd taken it out when the first child was born, and she'd seen to it that the premium was paid each month. But he'd killed himself, and wouldn't that keep them from paying?

"That's what everybody thinks," he told her, "but it's

rarely the case. There's generally a clause, no payment for suicide during the first six months, the first year, maybe even the first two years. To keep you from taking out the policy on Monday and doing away with yourself on Tuesday. But you've had this for more than two years, haven't you?"

She was nodding eagerly. "How old is Patrick? Almost nine, and it was taken out just around the time he was born."

"Then I'd say you're in the clear," he said. "And it's only fair, if you think about it. The company's been taking a man's premiums all these years, why should a moment of wrong thinking get them off the hook?"

"I had the same notion myself," she said, "but I thought there was no hope. I thought that was just the way it was."

"Well," he said, "it's not."

"What did you call it? A moment of wrong thinking? But isn't that all it takes to keep him out of heaven? It's the sin of despair, you know." She addressed this last to me, guessing that Mahaffey was more aware of the theology of it than I. "And is that fair?" she demanded, turning to Mahaffey again. "Better to cheat a widow out of the money than to cheat James Conway into hell."

"Maybe the Lord's able to take a longer view of things."

"That's not what the fathers say."

"If he wasn't in his right mind at the time . . ."

"His right mind!" She stepped back, pressed her hand to her breast. "Who in his right mind ever did such a thing?"

"Well . . ."

"He was joking," she said. "And he put the gun to his head, and even then I wasn't frightened, because he seemed his usual self and there was nothing frightening about it. Except I had the thought that the gun might go off by accident, and I said as much."

"What did he say to that?"

"That we'd all be better off if it did, himself included. And I said not to say such a thing, that it was horrid and sinful, and he said it was only the truth, and then he looked at me, he *looked* at me."

"What kind of a look?"

"Like, See what I'm doing? Like, Are you watching me, Mary Frances? And then he shot himself."

"Maybe it was an accident," I suggested.

"I saw his face. I saw his finger tighten on the trigger. It was as if he did it to spite me. But he wasn't angry at me. For the love of God, why would he . . ."

Mahaffey clapped me on the shoulder. "Take Mrs. Conway into the other room," he said. "Let her freshen up her face and drink a glass of water, and make sure the kids are all right." I looked at him, and he gave my shoulder a squeeze. "Something I want to check," he said.

I went into the kitchen, where Mrs. Conway wet a dishtowel and dabbed tentatively at her face, then filled a jelly glass with water and drank it down in a series of small sips. Then we went to check on the children, a boy of eight and a girl a couple of years younger. They were just sitting there, hands folded in their laps, as if someone had told them not to move.

Mrs. Conway fussed over them and assured them everything was going to be fine and told them to get ready for bed. We left them as we found them, sitting side by side, their hands still folded in their laps. I suppose they were in shock, and it seemed to me they had the right.

I brought the woman back to the living room, where Mahaffey was bent over the body of her husband. He straightened up as we entered the room. "Mrs. Conway," he said, "I have something important to tell you."

She waited to hear what it was.

"Your husband didn't kill himself," he announced.

Her eyes widened, and she looked at Mahaffey as if he'd gone suddenly mad. "But I saw him do it," she said.

He frowned, nodded. "Forgive me," he said. "I misspoke. What I meant to say was that the poor man did not commit suicide. He did kill himself, of course he killed himself—"

"I saw him do it."

"—and of course you did, and what a terrible thing for you, what a cruel thing. But it was not his intention, ma'am. It was an accident!"

"An accident."

"Yes."

"To put a gun to your head and pull the trigger. An accident?"

Mahaffey had a handkerchief in his hand. He turned his hand palm-up to show what he was holding with it. It was the cartridge clip from the pistol.

"An accident," Mahaffey said. "You said he was joking, and that's what it was, a joke that went bad. Do you know what this is?"

"Something to do with the gun?"

"It's the clip, ma'am. Or the magazine, they call it that as well. It holds the cartridges."

"The bullets?"

"The bullets, yes. And do you know where I found it?"

"In the gun?"

"That's where I would have expected to find it," he said, "and that's where I looked for it, but it wasn't there. And then I patted his pants pockets, and there it was." And, still using the handkerchief to hold it, he tucked the cartridge clip into the man's right-hand pocket.

"You don't understand," he told the woman. "How about you, Matt? You see what happened?"

"I think so."

"He was playing a joke on you, ma'am. He took the clip out of the gun and put it in his pocket. Then he was going to hold the unloaded gun to his head and give you a scare. He'd give the trigger a squeeze, and there'd be that instant before the hammer clicked on an empty chamber, that instant where you'd think he'd really shot himself, and he'd get to see your reaction."

"But he did shoot himself," she said.

"Because the gun still had a round in the chamber. Once you've chambered a round, removing the clip won't unload the gun. He forgot about the round in the chamber, he thought he had an unloaded weapon in his hand, and when he squeezed the trigger he didn't even have time to be surprised."

"Christ have mercy," she said.

"Amen to that," Mahaffey said. "It's a horrible thing, ma'am, but it's not suicide. Your husband never meant to kill himself. It's a tragedy, a terrible tragedy, but it was an accident." He drew a breath. "It might cost him a bit of time in purgatory, playing a joke like that, but he's spared hellfire, and that's something, isn't it? And now I'll want to use your phone, ma'am, and call this in."

• • •

"THAT'S why you wanted to know if it was a revolver or an automatic," Elaine said. "One has a clip and one doesn't."

"An automatic has a clip. A revolver has a cylinder."

"If he'd had a revolver he could have played Russian roulette. That's when you spin the cylinder, isn't it?"

"So I understand."

"How does it work? All but one chamber is empty? Or all but one chamber has a bullet in it?"

"I guess it depends what kind of odds you like."

She thought about it, shrugged. "These poor people in Brooklyn," she said. "What made Mahaffey think of looking for the clip?"

"Something felt off about the whole thing," I said, "and he remembered a case of a man who'd shot a friend with what he was sure was an unloaded gun, because he'd removed the clip. That was the defense at trial, he told me, and it hadn't gotten the guy anywhere, but it stayed in Mahaffey's mind. And as soon as he took a close look at the gun he saw the clip was missing, so it was just a matter of finding it."

"In the dead man's pocket."

"Right."

"Thus saving James Conway from an eternity in hell," she said. "Except he'd be off the hook with or without Mahaffey, wouldn't he? I mean, wouldn't God know where to send him without having some cop hold up a cartridge clip?"

"Don't ask me, honey. I'm not even Catholic."

"Goyim is goyim," she said. "You're supposed to know these things. Never mind, I get the point. It may not make a difference to God or to Conway, but it makes a real difference to Mary Frances. She can bury her husband in holy ground and know he'll be waiting for her when she gets to heaven her own self."

"Right."

"It's a terrible story, isn't it? I mean, it's a good story as a story, but it's terrible, the idea of a man killing himself that way. And his wife and kids witnessing it, and having to live with it."

"Terrible," I agreed.

"But there's more to it. Isn't there?"

"More?"

"Come on," she said. "You left something out."

"You know me too well."

"Damn right I do."

"So what's the part I didn't get to?"

She thought about it. "Drinking a glass of water," she said.

"How's that?"

"He sent you both out of the room," she said, "before he looked to see if the clip was there or not. So it was just Mahaffey, finding the clip all by himself."

"She was beside herself, and he figured it would do her good to splash a little water on her face. And we hadn't heard a peep out of those kids, and it made sense to have her check on them."

"And she had to have you along so she didn't get lost on the way to the bedroom."

I nodded. "It's convenient," I allowed, "making the discovery with no one around. He had plenty of time to pick up the gun, remove the clip, put the gun back in Conway's hand, and slip the clip into the man's pocket. That way he could do his good deed for the day, turning a suicide into an accidental death. It might not fool God, but it would be more than enough to fool the parish priest. Conway's body could be buried in holy ground, regardless of his soul's ultimate destination."

"And you think that's what he did?"

"It's certainly possible. But suppose you're Mahaffey, and you check the gun and the clip's still in it, and you do what we just said. Would you stand there with the clip in your hand waiting to tell the widow and your partner what you learned?"

"Why not?" she said, and then answered her own question. "No, of course not," she said. "If I'm going to make a discovery like that I'm going to do so in the presence of witnesses. What I do, I get the clip, I take it out, I slip it in his pocket, I put the gun back in his hand, and then I wait for the two of you to come back. And *then* I get a bright idea, and we examine the gun and find the clip missing, and one of us finds it in his pocket, where I know it is because that's where I stashed it a minute ago."

"A lot more convincing than his word on what he found when no one was around to see him find it."

"On the other hand," she said, "wouldn't he do that either way? Say I look at the gun and see the clip's missing. Why don't I wait until you come back before I even look for the clip?"

"Your curiosity's too great."

"So I can't wait a minute? But even so, suppose I look

and I find the clip in his pocket. Why take it out?"

"To make sure it's what you think it is."

"And why not put it back?"

"Maybe it never occurs to you that anybody would doubt your word," I suggested. "Or maybe, wherever Mahaffey found the clip, in the gun or in Conway's pocket where he said he found it, maybe he would have put it back if he'd had enough time. But we came back in, and there he was with the clip in his hand."

"In his handkerchief, you said. On account of fingerprints?"

"Sure. You don't want to disturb existing prints or leave prints of your own. Not that the lab would have spent any time on this one. They might nowadays, but back in the early sixties? A man shoots himself in front of witnesses?"

She was silent for a long moment. Then she said, "So what happened?"

"What happened?"

"Yeah, your best guess. What really happened?"

"No reason it couldn't have been just the way he reconstructed it. Accidental death. A dumb accident, but an accident all the same."

"But?"

"But Vince had a soft heart," I said. "Houseful of holy pictures like that, he's got to figure it's important to the woman that her husband's got a shot at heaven. If he could fix that up, he wouldn't care a lot about the objective reality of it all."

"And he wouldn't mind tampering with evidence?"

"He wouldn't lose sleep over it. God knows I never did."

"Anybody you ever framed," she said, "was guilty."

"Of something," I agreed. "You want my best guess, it's that there's no way of telling. As soon as the gimmick occurred to Vince, that the clip might be missing, the whole scenario was set. Either Conway had removed the clip and we were going to find it, or he hadn't and we were going to remove it for him, and *then* find it."

" 'The Lady or the Tiger.' Except not really, because either way it comes out the same. It goes in the books as an accident, whether that's what it was or not."

"That's the idea."

"So it doesn't make any difference one way or the other."

"I suppose not," I said, "but I always hoped it was the way Mahaffey said it was."

"Because you wouldn't want to think ill of him? No, that's not it. You already said he was capable of tampering with evidence, and you wouldn't think ill of him for it, anyway. I give up. Why? Because you don't want Mr. Conway to be in hell?"

"I never met the man," I said, "and it would be presumptuous of me to care where he winds up. But I'd prefer it if the clip was in his pocket where Mahaffey said it was, because of what it would prove."

"That he hadn't meant to kill himself? I thought we just said . . ."

I shook my head. "That she didn't do it."

"Who? The wife?"

"Uh-huh."

"That she didn't do what? Kill him? You think *she* killed him?"

"It's possible."

"But he shot himself," she said. "In front of witnesses. Or did I miss something?"

"That's almost certainly what happened," I said, "but she was one of the witnesses, and the kids were the other witnesses, and who knows what they saw, or if they saw anything at all? Say he's on the couch, and they're all watching TV, and she takes his old war souvenir and puts one in his head, and she starts screaming. 'Ohmigod, look what your father has done! Oh, Jesus Mary and Joseph, Daddy has killed himself!' They were looking at the set, they didn't see dick, but they'll think they did by the time she stops carrying on."

"And they never said what they did or didn't see."

"They never said a word, because we didn't ask them anything. Look, I don't think she did it. The possibility didn't even occur to me until some time later, and by then we'd closed the case, so what was the point? I never even mentioned the idea to Vince."

"And if you had?"

"He'd have said she wasn't the type for it, and he'd have been right. But you never know. If she didn't do it, he gave her peace of mind. If she did do it, she must have wondered how the cartridge clip migrated from the gun butt to her husband's pocket."

"She'd have realized Mahaffey put it there."

"Uh-huh. And she'd have had twenty-five thousand reasons to thank him for it."

"Huh?"

"The insurance," I said.

"But you said they'd have to pay anyway."

"Double indemnity," I said. "They'd have had to pay the face amount of the policy, but if it's an accident they'd have had to pay double. That's if there was a double-indemnity clause in the policy, and I have no way of knowing whether or not there was. But most policies sold around then, especially relatively small policies, had the clause. The companies liked to write them that way, and the policy holders usually went for them. A fraction more in premiums and twice the payoff? Why not go for it?"

We kicked it around a little. Then she asked about the current case, the one that had started the whole thing. I'd wondered about the gun, I explained, purely out of curiosity. If it was in fact an automatic, and if the clip was in fact in his pocket and not in the gun where you'd expect to find it, surely some cop would have determined as much by now, and it would all come out in the wash.

"That's some story," she said. "And it happened when, thirty-five years ago? And you never mentioned it before?"

"I never thought of it," I said, "not as a story worth telling. Because it's unresolved. There's no way to know what really happened."

"That's all right," she said. "It's still a good story."

• • •

THE guy in Inwood, it turned out, had used a .38-caliber revolver, and he'd cleaned it and loaded it earlier that same day. No chance it was an accident.

And if I'd never told the story over the years, that's not to say it hadn't come occasionally to mind. Vince Mahaffey and I never really talked about the incident, and I've sometimes wished we had. It would have been nice to know what really happened.

Assuming that's possible, and I'm not sure it is. He had, after all, sent me out of the room before doing whatever it was he did. That suggested he hadn't wanted me to know, so why should I think he'd be quick to tell me after the fact?

No way of knowing. And, as the years pass, I find I like it better that way. I couldn't tell you why, but I do.

The Funniest Thing Has Been Happening Lately

Mary Higgins Clark

F RED Rand did not need to read the list of the four people
whom he was compelled to kill to know their names.
They had been engraved on his soul for fifteen years. He had
come back to Long Island from Florida hoping to learn that
they had suffered in some way, that their comfortable, self-
centered world had been altered, that life had treated them
harshly.

I would have accepted that, he thought. I could have
made it do. I would have gone back to St. Augustine and
lived out my life.

But to his dismay, they were all functioning very well,
very well indeed.

Genevieve Baxter. Known to her friends as Gen. She was
the first on the list who would be punished, because she
would be the easiest. She had contributed to the chain of
events that ended in the tragedy that had destroyed his life.
Gen was now seventy-five years old and had been a widow
for several years, a sadness but under careful consideration,
nothing he would deem as sufficient punishment. He had
been following her on and off for the past few weeks and
had a very fair idea of her present activities.

From all appearances, Gen was leading a busy, contented life. Two of her children lived in nearby towns. She was active in the affairs at her church, Our Lady of Refuge.

There is no refuge for me, he thought.

Six grandchildren.

Gen lived in the house she had shared with her husband. One of those pleasant imitation Tudors that had been a favorite middle class design in Long Island suburbs in the 1950s.

He knew. He had lived in one of them only a few towns away until fifteen years ago.

This afternoon he had stood at the next checkout counter from Gen Baxter in the supermarket and heard her talking to the clerk. She was planning to go to her granddaughter's ballet recital tonight.

She would never see another one.

• • •

VINNIE D'Angelo. The second person on the list. Vinnie had been reprimanded for dereliction of duty after it happened. That hadn't stopped him from being promoted a year later. He'd retired as head of security at the Long Island Mall, the very place where his goofing off had cost a life. He spent winters in North Carolina now. But in March he came back to Babylon and put his boat in the water. Vinnie was an avid fisherman.

Babylon was only half an hour away. He'd watched Vinnie at the dock, his step jaunty as he cast off the lines and revved up the motor.

He already had the plan in place. He'd take a boat out, get close to where Vinnie was fishing, and pretend to be stalled. Then when Vinnie, helpful Vinnie, offered to tow him in, he would have his chance to even the score.

Lieutenant Stuart Kling of the Manhassat police force might be the hardest one to corner. He'd been a brash young cop anxious to fill his quota of speeding tickets when he could have prevented a murder. He would not get the chance to prevent his own death.

And finally . . . regretfully . . . Lisa Monroe Scanlon. After following her for several weeks he had impulsively decided to speak to her. He'd pretended to be astonished when he passed her in the Island shopping center. Her three children were with her. Seven-year-old twin boys and a baby girl. He still wasn't sure if it had been a good idea to make that contact, but he'd kept the conversation very casual, even to the point of saying he was only up from Florida on business and going back the next day.

Lisa had become an interior decorator, married Tim Scanlon, and now was balancing work and children. "Busy, but lots of fun," she'd said, smiling.

Lots of fun. I bet, he'd thought.

And her parents were fine. Doting grandparents.

Isn't that grand?

The acid in his throat had almost choked him as he'd walked back to his car.

If Lisa hadn't been so happy, so fulfilled—that was the word, *fulfilled*—he might have changed his mind. Smiling, happy Lisa had been the catalyst.

Tonight was Genevieve Baxter's turn.

• • •

GEN Baxter locked the door and turned the alarm on. It was almost ten-thirty and she was tired. She'd attended her nine-year-old granddaughter Laurie's ballet recital. Afterward the family had gone out for pizza.

The last few days had been warm for March, but tonight had turned sharply colder and the arthritis in her hands and ankles was sending throbbing pain throughout her limbs. I feel every day of my age, she thought ruefully as she changed into a warm nightgown, tied the sash of her robe, slid her feet into comfortable old slippers, and went back downstairs.

The hot cup of cocoa was a longtime tradition. Sip it

propped in bed with a book or watching the eleven o'clock news.

At the foot of the stairs Gen hesitated. It had been three years since she'd been alone in the house, but until lately she'd never felt nervous. The house was so familiar that she was sure she could go through it blindfolded and never make a misstep, but for some reason tonight was different.

Oh stop it, she told herself. You're imagining things. Why would anyone want to follow me? Of course it was silly. She knew that. It was just that she'd had an impression of being near the same person a couple of times in the last few weeks.

I never was good at remembering faces unless I see them regularly, she reflected as she measured the cocoa into a cup and filled it with milk, then placed the cup in the microwave oven. That's why today when that man was on line at the next checkout counter I knew that I've seen him at least three or four times lately and that maybe I should recognize him.

Today she'd been so sure that he was following her that she'd sat in the car until she saw him carry out his groceries and walk across the parking lot. She'd watched him load the groceries in the trunk of his car and start to drive toward the exit at the other end of the mall.

I'll follow him, she thought, just until I'm able to make out his license number and jot it down.

The paper with the number was in her pocketbook. She'd almost talked to Mark, her son, about it at the ballet tonight, but it was such a happy night and he was so proud of Laurie being the swan princess in the recital that she hadn't want to throw a shadow on the evening.

Anyway the family would all joke and say that Mom is just trying to pick up a fellow, Gen told herself.

The microwave beeped to indicate that the two minutes were up. With a potholder she took the cup out, put it on a saucer, and started for the stairs. Charlie always used to say he didn't know why I don't blister my tongue the way I like everything so hot, she thought with an affectionate smile.

Charlie. She missed him all the time in the quietly constant way that widows her age miss the husband they'd shared their lives with for so many years. But as Gen turned out the kitchen light and walked down the dimly lit hall to the staircase, she felt a wild primal need for Charlie to be there with her. She needed him.

And then it began. The handle of the front door was turning.

"Who is it?" The involuntary question died on her lips. The lock was clicking. She heard it release. The door opened.

The man at the checkout counter was coming toward her.

He did not bother to close the door but left it open and stood staring at her, his hands at his side. He didn't even seem to notice when the alarm began to shriek. Tall and gaunt with thinning black hair, his face had a dazed expression as though he had wandered in by mistake and was frightened.

But then he said, "You should have tried to help her, you know," and his hands were suddenly claws, snapping around her neck. Gen sank to her knees, gasping for the breath that would no longer be granted her. As the cup of cocoa fell from her hands and through waves of blackness she felt splashes of heat burning her skin, she realized who her assailant was. In the moment before she died, a flash of pure anger permeated her soul that he would dare to blame her for something she could not have foreseen.

• • •

FRED made his escape cutting around the house and through the backyard to the garden apartment development where he had parked his car.

He was driving down the street when a squad car screamed past him, probably called by the security monitoring service that responded to the alarm at Gen Baxter's home. A few minutes later, as he turned onto the highway, he relived the moment Gen Baxter had died. Just before her eyes became fixed and staring, he'd seen an expression in them. What was it? Anger. Yes, and reproach. How dare she reproach him? How dare she be angry at him? She had helped to kill his only child and had now paid the price for that terrible dead.

Back in the motel, he poured a drink from the bottle of scotch that was his bedside companion. He stripped to his shorts and got into bed, but for hours lay sleepless. He had expected Genevieve Baxter's death to give him a measure of release, but he sensed immediately that release would only come when all four were dead.

Tomorrow it would be Vinnie D'Angelo. The weather prediction was good, so he was bound to go out on his boat. Then in the next day or two, Stuart Kling would pay for his role in the tragedy. He would be a little harder, a little more challenging. Fred smiled to himself, a sad, tired smile. Planning Kling's death would keep his mind occupied, keep the demons away. Or at least he hoped so.

• • •

DETECTIVE Joe O'Connor of the Nassau Police Department had known Mrs. Genevieve Baxter since he was a kid. He'd gone to high school with her son Mark and had even dated her daughter Kay when they were teenagers. He asked to be assigned to investigate the Baxter murder.

Now, three days after the funeral, he sat having coffee with Mark in the kitchen of the home that had become the crime scene. "I can't help thinking how much you look like your mother," Joe told him.

A hint of a smile turned up the corners of Mark's lips. "I guess so. I hope so." Forty-three years old, he was a handsome man with blue-gray eyes, a well-shaped nose, sensitive mouth, and firm chin. His sandy hair was streaked with gray. He was clenching and unclenching the coffee cup he was holding.

"Mark, it doesn't make sense." Joe's beefy frame was hunched forward, his dark eyes narrowed, his frustration barely in check. "There was no robbery. This guy broke in, strangled your mother, and got out. Was he some nut who just happened to pick this house, or is there some reason he wanted to kill her?"

"Who in the name of God would want to kill my mother?" Mark asked wearily. "She always kept the front door locked. How could he have forced it open so easily? It's obvious she was just about to start upstairs with the cocoa. She must have heard or seen him trying to get in. She never even had time to push the panic button. It was right there in the vestibule next to the door."

"That lock was probably the one that came with the house forty-some-odd years ago," O'Connor told him. "The guy had to have had a professional tool that jammed and released it in ten seconds. I think your mother was targeted. Maybe the guy who did it is a nut, but I don't believe this is a random murder. Mark, you've got to help me. First, start thinking. Did your mother say anything about anyone bothering her with phone calls or maybe mention that a repair man was at the house lately? You know what I mean. When you go through her clothes and mail, keep an eye out for anything that in any way seems unusual."

Mark nodded. "I understand."

The next day he called O'Connor at headquarters. "Joe, something did occur to me. The last time I saw my mother was at Laurie's ballet recital. You know that. Then we went out for pizza and she started to say—I remember her exact words—'The funniest thing has been happening lately,' and unless I'm imagining it now, Mom looked worried. But then the waitress came and took our order and some people came up to the table to congratulate Laurie on her dancing and that was it. Mom didn't bring it up again."

Something was going on that had her worried, Joe thought. I knew it. "Mark, whatever it might have been, you couldn't have prevented what happened to her a few hours later," he said, "but this is exactly what I meant when I asked you to keep alert for anything that seems unusual. And remember, watch for any repair bills that might come in the mail these next few weeks."

• • •

FRED was at the pier in Babylon waiting for Vinnie D'Angelo to show up, and suddenly decided to call Helen in Atlanta. Even though they had divorced ten years ago, as Jenny had kept them together in life, by her death, she also had created an unbreakable bond between them. It was the one thing they ever really shared, the joy she had given, the grief she had left.

"Where are you, Fred? You didn't sound good when I spoke to you last month."

Last month, February 28, had been the fifteenth anniversary of Jenny's death.

"Oh, thought I'd come back up to the old neighborhood. Sentimental journey, I guess. Hasn't changed much. Visited Jenny's grave. Put some flowers on it."

"Fred, are you taking your medicine?"

"Sure. Love my medicine. Makes me feel happy all the time."

"Fred, go home. See your doctor."

"I'll see him when I get back. Everything okay with you, Helen?"

"It's okay."

"Still like your job?" After Jenny died, they'd moved to Florida and Helen had gone to nursing school. She was now a pediatric nurse in a hospital in Atlanta.

"I love it. Take care of yourself, Fred."

"Yeah. I rented a boat. I'm going fishing today."

"Now, that's good. How's the weather up there?"

"Couldn't be better." Suddenly he was eager to end the conversation. He could see Vinnie D'Angelo, fishing gear in hand, heading for his boat. "Gotta go, Helen. Be well."

He had attempted to pass time in Florida by buying a top-of-the-line thirty-five-foot Chris-Craft and taking up fishing. Now his hands felt sure on the wheel as he followed D'Angelo's boat out from the marina. It was still so early in the season that there were few boats out and, as he had hoped, D'Angelo went a good distance from the others.

An hour later he was drifting past D'Angelo's boat. He was sunning on the deck, his rod fixed in place in a bracket. "Any chance of a tow?" Fred called. "This thing conked out on me."

It was even easier than killing Gen Baxter. In his boat, D'Angelo the retired hotshot head of security was a jovial Good Samaritan. Hail-fellow-well-met; come aboard; have-a-beer: you-should-know-better-than-to-rent-from-that-jerk; all-his-boats-are-worn-out-tubs!

It was when D'Angelo was bending to get a beer out of the cooler that Fred took the hammer out of his windbreaker, and struck the blow. D'Angelo slumped over, blood gushing from the back of his head. He was a thick-bodied man and it was a struggle to drag him up and then shove him over the side of the boat.

Fred sat down and had a beer, then found a towel, mopped up the blood, and threw the towel in the water. He got back into his rented boat and sped away, enjoying the sequence he knew would follow.

On the days he'd observed Vinnie's habits, he'd seen that Vinnie fished until one o'clock and then drove to his house about fifteen minutes away. Probably had lunch with his wife. Nice and cozy for the two of them.

Around two o'clock she'd probably call the boat to see what was keeping him. No answer. Then she'd call the manager's office at the pier. No, Vinnie isn't back. His slip is empty. Probably they'd notify the coast guard or ask someone to go looking for him. Or maybe by then someone in a passing boat would have wondered that there didn't seem to be anyone on board a boat that had been anchored in the same spot for so long. Maybe even one of good old Vinnie's buddies would have pulled alongside and taken a look to see if he was okay.

I know all about the ritual of learning that someone is missing, Fred thought. I know all about the waiting.

He returned the rented boat, got into his car, and drove to the motel to shower and change his clothes. The motel was in Garden City, far enough away from Manhasset where Gen had lived, and Babylon where Vinnie had lived, and Syosset where Stuart Kling lived, to make him confident he wouldn't run into anyone who might know he'd been hanging around observing Baxter or D'Angelo.

Stuart Kling was next. He was a lieutenant in the Nassau County police. No more prowling around in a squad car on the highway for Stu. No more books of traffic tickets to fill. Fred had already figured the best way to get him. Nice and simple. Kling worked out in the gym early mornings three days a week. He wouldn't be armed going in or coming out of there.

Fred tore a page out of his daily reminder notebook, in block letters printed: "traffic ticket to hell," and put it carefully in the pocket of the jacket he would wear in the morning.

He'd throw it on Stu's body after he shot him.

• • •

IN Atlanta, Helen Rand was about to leave for the hospital when she received the phone call from her ex-husband. As always, speaking with him was an unsettling experience. In the fifteen years since Jenny's murder, she had managed to create a new life for herself. The intensive nurses training course had kept her busy and exhausted those first few years, then the job in the hospital in St. Augustine, combined with studying for her master's degree at night.

And finally ten years ago when she knew she could no longer live with Fred, she took the job in Atlanta and filed for divorce.

At first he'd called her constantly, not because he missed her, but because he needed to be sure that she still shared his heartache about losing Jenny. It was typical of him, she thought, to call to tell her he had visited Jenny's grave.

A year ago he had told her he was seeing a psychiatrist and taking medication for depression. But there was something else. About six months ago when he called, he began talking about the trial and cursing the people who testified at it. Jenny's murderer had been a twenty-six-year-old ne'er-do-well who had been hanging around the mall trying to urge young women to get into the van that belonged to the service station where he had a part-time job.

One of them had complained to the security guard who was going off duty. Instead of detaining him, the guard had shoved the guy into his van and told him to get out of the mall. Under cross-examination the guard had admitted that he hadn't wanted to be detained. He was meeting his bowling team.

Another witness had been that nice woman who'd cried when she talked about seeing Jenny pulled off the highway with a flat tire. "I drove onto the breakdown lane to see if I could help her," she'd explained, "but then the van from the gas station pulled in ahead of her car and I thought she had phoned for help, so I didn't stay."

If the guard at the mall had done his job, if the woman had stayed to be sure Jenny was all right, if the cop who actually saw her getting into the van had checked to be sure she was all right instead of going after the speeder, if Lisa had gone shopping with Jenny that day . . . If . . . If . . . If . . .

And the biggest *if* was the one that was never spoken.

Whenever she talked to Fred now, Helen felt as though all the terrible pain and anger she tried so hard to put behind her poured back into her soul. Stop it, stop it, she told herself. But maybe I should call his psychiatrist, she thought as she reached for her jacket. Fred mentioned his name once or twice. What is it? Raleigh? Renwood? Raines?

She lived in an apartment building ten blocks from the hospital in downtown Atlanta, and unless it was pouring rain she walked both ways.

Today was a bit overcast, but early spring was in the air and Helen felt better as soon as she stepped outside. She would be sixty her next birthday, but knew she looked at least five years younger. Her hair was salt and pepper and cut short with the natural wave framing her face. When she was young she'd worn it long. Old friends from her days at St. Mary's Academy always said that at eighteen Jenny had been a mirror image of her.

Jenny. Eighteen, never to see nineteen.

Jenny. Eighteen, going on eternity.

Jenny. Eighteen and accepted at Georgetown, the college she and Lisa had planned to attend together and take by storm.

I didn't think I could ever get up in the morning again after she died, Helen thought, her mind still awash in the remembered pain that Fred's phone call had triggered. But then, Fred's terrible inability to accept or cope had forced her to be strong for his sake. Until she could no longer put up with his . . . say it, she thought . . . his *dishonesty*.

Unconsciously, she walked more quickly as though hoping to outpace her thoughts. Resolutely she made herself think of her life as it was now, Atlanta, the new friends, the pediatrics intensive care unit where she was part of the team that helped keep the flicker of life alive in a dying child. And in the last year, after all this time, Gene, sixty-three years old, a widower, the director of Orthopedic Surgery. They were seeing each other regularly.

Raleigh. Renwood. Raines. What was that psychiatrist's name? Something was shouting at her to get in touch with him. She knew what she'd do. There had to be a list of psychiatrists who practiced in or around St. Augustine. She'd ask Gene to see if any of the doctors in the psychiatric section could check for her. Then if they could identify the right one, she could phone and explain that she was Fred Rand's ex-wife and worried that he might be on the verge of some sort of breakdown.

If she could talk to Fred's doctor, maybe he could call Fred on his cell phone. At least it was worth a try.

Or maybe she should just stay out of it. Fred always calmed down eventually, and she didn't even know where he was staying. He probably wouldn't answer his cell phone anyway. He almost never did.

• • •

EARLY the next morning Stuart Kling did an extra half-hour at the gym. He showered and changed into his sweats. From there he planned to go straight to headquarters. Feeling particularly pleased with himself that he'd finally shed the five pounds he'd been trying to lose since Christmas, his step was light as he walked out the side entrance of the gym to the parking lot.

He heard rather than saw the window being lowered on the van that was parked next to his car. An instinct of nearby danger made him whirl around, his car key in hand. Stuart Kling had a nearly infallible memory for faces, and in the final moment before he died, he identified his murderer. His finger plunged involuntarily on the remote control in his hand and the trunk of the car sprang open as he crumbled to the ground. A sheet of paper fluttered from the car and was anchored by the blood that poured from the wound in his chest.

"Traffic ticket to hell" was what the stunned employee of the gym who ran out at the sound of the gunshot and reached Kling first was able to read before the printed letters on the paper became too stained to distinguish. Frantically the employee rushed to try to get the number on the license plate of the van as it roared out of the parking lot, but the plate was missing.

• • •

THREE days after his meeting with Detective Joe O'Connor, Mark Baxter found the torn edge of a checking account deposit slip with a license plate number jotted on it in the large handbag his mother had regularly carried unless she was dressing up for a particular event.

It was in the zippered section where she always kept her checkbook and wallet, and somewhat crumbled. In the past few days, as well as phoning O'Connor about his mother's ambiguous reference to "something funny happening lately," Mark had called him about a new handyman a neighbor had told him his mother had been using, a new deliveryman from the dry cleaner, and several e-mails he found on her computer from a distant cousin who asked about getting together when he was in town.

He was beginning to feel somewhat foolish because O'Connor had checked out all the leads and they had led exactly nowhere. It's probably been buried there for months, he thought, vaguely remembering that a neighborhood kid had slightly dented his mother's car when he parked too close to her in the church parking lot. But she'd decided to let it go because she was trading the car in anyway and didn't want the kid to get in trouble with his parents.

He crumpled the deposit slip, tossed it in the wastebasket, and went home. The house where he had been raised, the house that had always been warm and welcoming, was now the scene of his mother's murder, and the less time he spent in it, the better. On the way to his law office he listened to the radio and heard the news that Nassau County police lieutenant Stuart Kling had been murdered as he was leaving the gym where he regularly worked out.

Kling, Mark thought. Poor guy. Why does that name sound familiar? The newscaster was saying that the prime suspect was a man Kling had arrested six years earlier who had just been released from a psychiatric hospital. I never used to think it was a lousy world, Mark thought, but I'm beginning to wonder.

His first appointment was at eleven o'clock. Because of his rearranged schedule since his mother's death, he had a busy day, but underlying all the meetings two things kept throbbing from below the level of conscious thinking. He should at least pass the license number he'd found in his mother's pocketbook over to Joe O'Connor, and why did Stuart Kling's name feel as though it should have great importance to him?

• • •

TOMORROW would finish it. Lisa Monroe Scanlon. After to-morrow she wouldn't be alive to go into that handsome house in Locust Valley, that symbol of the early success of two talented young people. Tim Scanlon was a stockbroker, and at thirty-eight a vice president of a prestigious financial giant. Fred had looked in the window of Lisa's interior dec-orating studio. Couches draped with a variety of expensive upholstery samples, chairs and antique tables. A mantel with candlesticks, a delicate painted clock. Floral prints on the walls.

She did all right for herself, Fred thought. A husband, a family, a business. And her parents reveling in their adorable grandchildren, while my grandchildren were never called into existance.

That day Jenny had gone to pick up Lisa. They had planned to go shopping together, but then Lisa changed her mind.

If she had gone with Jenny, if there had been two of them

in the car when the tire went flat, Jenny would be alive today.

That night as Fred listened to the news reports of the shooting death of Lieutenant Stuart Kling, he cleaned and loaded the gun he would use to complete his task. He knew exactly when he would go into the house. Tomorrow morning. Tim Scanlon left at quarter past seven. The twins got on the school bus at 8:05. The bus was at the corner of their street, just a few houses down. The three mornings he'd watched, Lisa had walked with them to the corner and then scurried back home. She always left the door slightly ajar.

If she did that tomorrow, he'd slip inside and be waiting for her. If she didn't, he'd ring the bell and tell her he'd stopped with a gift for her. She'd let him in. After all, he was Mr. Rand, Jenny's father.

Then when the baby-sitter arrived at nine o'clock, she would find Lisa's body.

And I will go home, Fred thought. And visit Dr. Rawlston, my psychiatrist, and tell him that I do feel I am making progress in my struggle to accept my daughter's death. I will tell him that seeing my daughter's grave made a profound sense of peace come over me and I am sure it will stay with me. I will tell him that I no longer hate the people who caused Jenny's death.

I gave him their names, he thought. That wasn't wise. For some reason he was suddenly uneasy. The euphoria that began the moment he squeezed the trigger and watched Stuart Kling crumble on the ground was evaporating. He had a feeling of people waiting in the shadows, approaching him.

His cell phone rang. He did not answer it. He guessed it might be Helen. He knew she suspected that something different was going on inside him. He knew he had talked too much to her about the people who had caused Jenny's death.

She had urged him to call his psyciatrist. Would she have

called Dr. Rawlston? Between them would they decide to call the police and suggest that Fred Rand was a deeply troubled man and perhaps certain people should be warned if he tries to contact them? And then they would learn that three of those certain people were already dead.

Abruptly Fred finished loading the gun, put it in his briefcase, stood up, and began to pack. It was time to get out of here. He'd drive to Locust Valley now. The house next to Lisa's was obviously used only as a summer home. He could park in the back and never be noticed.

Even if it meant that he would be caught, he had to complete the job.

At eight-thirty, Fred Rand checked out of the motel in Garden City, got in his car, and drove forty minutes to Locust Valley. Just after he turned off the highway, he stopped at a small restaurant and had dinner, remembering to slip a few rolls in his pocket in case he felt like nibbling during the night. At ten o'clock he was parked deep in the shadows of the house next to the Scanlon home. Tonight the sleep that had been denied him in the quite comfortable bed in the motel came easily when he leaned his head back and tilted the seat to a reclining position.

He awoke at dawn and waited.

• • •

MARK Baxter slept restlessly. Kling. Stuart Kling. Why should he know that name? He woke up, puzzled over it, and went back to sleep. This time he dreamed that his mother was in the bank and making a deposit. But instead of the amount of the check she was depositing, she had written a license number and was trying to make the clerk accept it.

At seven o'clock when Mark grabbed a cup of coffee and kissed his wife and daughter good-bye, he did not drive to his office. Instead he turned the car in the direction of his late mother's home. He knew that he had to fish the license

number out of the wastebasket, give it to Detective Joe
O'Connor, and tell O'Connor that for some reason he should
be remembering a connection with the murdered Nassau
County police lieutenant.

• • •

HELEN Rand had a sleepless night. She spent it berating
herself that she had not attempted to reach Fred's psychiatrist. At dinner she had talked about her concern to Gene
and he had told her Bruce Stevens, a psychiatrist friend of
his, could undoubtedly track down a psychiatrist with a
name like Rawlings or Raines or Renwood in the St. Augustine area.

When Gene dropped her off, Helen had actually tried
through the telephone information operator to obtain the
psychiatrist's number, but without the exact name, she got
exactly nowhere.

At seven-fifteen she called Gene at the hospital. "Please
call Dr. Stevens, Gene. I don't know why, but I'm suddenly
terribly worried."

At eight o'clock she was speaking to Dr. Richard Rawlston who practiced in Ponte Vedre, some fifteen miles from
St. Augustine.

Quickly she explained her concerns to him, then waited,
hoping against hope that he would, if not dismiss them, at
least tell her that in his opinion there was no serious threat
that Fred would do something rash.

"You say Fred is in Long Island now and you don't believe he is taking medication, Mrs. Rand?"

"That's right."

There was a long pause, then the psychiatrist said, "I had
been quite concened about Fred, but then he told me that
he was going on a cruise with friends and feeling much
better. If that was a lie and he is in Long Island, I think
there are three people who might need protection. I have
their names. They are all people whom he blames for not

preventing your daughter's death. A security guard, an elderly woman, and a police officer."

"Yes, those are the people he blamed."

"Do you know where Fred is staying, Mrs. Rand?"

"No, I don't.

"Then I think I have no recourse but to call the Nassau County police and notify them of our concern. I would like to give them your number in case they want to talk with you."

"Of course. I'm off duty today. I'll be here."

Helen hung up the phone. And waited.

• • •

MARK was in Joe O'Connor's office when the call from Dr. Rawlston came in. They had just traced the license number that Genevieve Baxter had jotted down on the deposit slip. It belonged to a Volvo that had been rented by Fred Rand of St. Augustine, Florida.

"He took my mother's life because . . ." Mark broke into sobs. "He blamed her! He blamed her!"

"And Stuart Kling and Vinnie D'Angelo, whose body washed in yesterday afternoon. They suspected foul play in D'Angelo's case," Joe said grimly.

"If only Mother had told me that night," Mark said.

"You don't know how many 'if only's' we hear in this business." O'Connor picked up the phone. "Put out an all points bulletin . . . armed and dangerous . . ."

• • •

AT seven-fifteen Fred watched as Tim Scanlon left his home. Hidden in the heavy foundation shrubery outside the kitchen windows, he saw Tim drop quick kisses on his family, could even hear him calling from the vestibule, "Remember, I'll be a little late tonight, honey."

No you won't, Fred thought. You'll be back here in a couple of hours. After you get the call about Lisa.

In her bathrobe, her hair twisted up on the back of her head, Lisa looked very young, he thought, almost as young as she'd been in the days when she and Jenny were always together.

You'll be together soon, Fred thought.

• • •

THE news that Fred had killed the three people in Long Island left Helen in absolute shock. For an hour she sat motionless, unable to grasp the awfulness of his crime. But then she realized that through the horror she was also feeling a terrible sense of being warned. Jenny's voice was shouting to her.

At ten of eight, she called Dr. Rawlston back. Her voice frantic with fear she asked, "Doctor, did Fred ever say anything about blaming Jenny's friend Lisa for her death?"

"No. He did tell me Lisa was her friend and was supposed to go shopping with her that day but changed her mind. But that was all he said."

"There's a reason he might have held that back, something he's never been able to face. I've got to call the Nassau police. Who did you speak to there?"

• • •

MARK was just about to leave when Helen Rand phoned. He watched as the furrows on O'Connor's face deepened. "You say her married name is Scanlon and you think she lives in Locust Valley. We'll get right on it." O'Connor hung up and looked at him. "There may be someone else on his list, Mark."

• • •

"OKAY, you two, have a good day." With a final kiss, Lisa watched her twins climb onto the bus and hurried back home. Ever since the morning she'd locked herself out, she not only unlocked the door when she went to the corner with the twins but also left it slightly ajar.

For those two minutes she left fifteen-month-old Kelly in the playpen with plastic blocks she couldn't possibly swallow and a rubber ball. Anything she could put in her mouth was out of reach.

But this morning, it was clear that something had frightened Kelly. She had pulled herself to her feet and was wailing, *"Mammmmaaaaa!"*

Lisa picked her up. "Hey, what's your problem?"

I'm her problem, Fred thought. He was in the vestibule closet, aware that he didn't have to rush. He could wait five or ten minutes and savor his generosity in granting Lisa a few minutes more of life.

And he certainly wouldn't kill her while she was holding the baby. He wanted to see her more clearly and carefully pushed the door open a fraction wider then realized it had made a noise. Had she noticed?

• • •

Lisa heard the familiar faint creaking of the vestibule door opening. There's someone here. That's why the baby is frightened, she thought. What should I do?

Don't let him know you're aware of him. Pick up the baby and walk toward the door. Push the panic button.

Oh, God, please help me.

She *had* noticed. He could tell by the sudden rigidity of her body. "Lisa," he said softly.

Lisa spun around.

"Put the baby back in the playpen and then walk away from it. I don't want anything to happen to her. Sometimes bullets ricochet, you know."

Jenny's father was standing there, a gun in his hand. Why was he here? She knew. Because he hates me. He hates me because I'm alive and Jenny is dead. She had felt strange after she met him that day. She remembered how she had prattled on and on about her life and watched his eyes grow bleak and angry. He was going to kill her.

She tried not to show how afraid she was. "Please, I'll do anything you say. Let me put the baby down and let's walk into the kitchen."

"That's very motherly of you. Too bad you weren't as good a friend."

Lisa held Kelly tightly, kissed her, and started to put her back in the playpen. Kelly wrapped her arms around her neck. "No, No, No."

Gently Lisa tried to disengage them.

"Hurry up, Lisa." Fred heard the wail of a siren. A police car was pulling into the driveway. "Hurry up," he shouted.

Frantically Lisa bent over the playpen, pulled the baby's arms from around her neck and dropped her onto the plastic matting. The rubber ball rolled forward. A sudden incongruous image of Jenny and herself, the stars of the softball team, she pitching, Jenny catching, jumped into her mind and she knew she might have a chance to save herself. In one lightening movement Lisa scooped up the ball, bolted away from the playpen, whirled around, and with a powerful thrust of her arm threw the ball at Fred. The ball hit his hand and the barrel of the gun leaped up as he pulled the trigger.

The bullet passed inches over her head and lodged in the wall. Before he could aim again the police were in the house wrestling him to the ground.

• • •

FIFTEEN minutes later, Detective Joe O'Conner called Helen Rand. "Thanks to you, Lisa is okay, Mrs. Rand," O'Connor said. "Our guys got there in the nick of time. Lisa told us that she didn't think she had a chance but then when she saw the ball in the playpen it reminded her of playing softball with Jenny. She felt as though Jenny was telling her what to do."

"Fred?"

"Under arrest. Violent. Not sorry he killed them. Blamed them for Jenny's death. You know that."

Helen's long-held control snapped. "He's blaming them! Do you know who killed my daughter? Fred did. He has family money but he was always cheap. Jenny was his only child. He bought her a car when she was eighteen. Sure he did. An old car with bald tires. That's why Lisa's father wouldn't let her ride in it that day. I begged Jenny not to set foot in it, but he told her to go ahead. He'd replace the tires when Sears had a sale. Tell him something for me. Tell him he killed his own child."

She choked back a sob. "I should have made him face the truth long ago. He was heartbroken after Jenny died. I felt so sorry for him but I should have made him face it."

"Mrs. Rand, you couldn't have made him believe Jenny's death was his fault. People like your ex-husband always blame everyone except themselves. And always remember that if you hadn't phoned me, Lisa would be dead now. You saved her life."

"No," Helen whispered. "You're wrong. You just told me yourself. Jenny saved Lisa's life." She managed a smile. "Jenny was one terrific kid and it looks as though even now, wherever she is up there, she hasn't changed a bit."

A GIRL NAMED CHARLIE

Stanley Cohen

"WAIT!" Harry Waller said. "Stop! Just stop! Put your clothes back on. I've changed my mind."

"You what?"

"I've changed my mind. So just put your clothes back on. Okay?"

She stopped disrobing, and she didn't say anything, but she was clearly annoyed.

He watched her get back into her things, a bizarre collection of tacky, youthful clothing. His earlier impression of her had been dead wrong. She was no adult! He refused to believe that she could be nineteen. Or even eighteen. She might not yet be seventeen! A kid who might've been coming home from high school, in a plaid miniskirt, a blouse getting a little threadbare, and a worn, rope-knit sweater. But a beautiful kid, with virtually no makeup. Beautiful! She had to be younger than his own two daughters in college, either of whom would have envied her perfect, light auburn hair that fell straight from the crown of her head down around her shoulders.

Now that he looked at them for the first time, her shoes

gave some things away. Street-worn wooden platforms with what looked like six-inch heels, the uppers attached to the blocky platforms by brassy nails, a few of the nails missing here and there. Without the shoes, she was *really* tiny. He glanced at her coat, lying across a chair, that had to keep out the bitter winds of the city's winter, and it was a ratty little thing of nondescript fake fur.

He was glad he'd stopped her before she finished removing everything. And he felt queasy as he shook his head and wondered: How in God's name had he ever allowed himself to come to be in that grubby little room with her? She was definitely not an adult! And even if she were . . . But when she'd first approached him on the street, she was a beautiful young woman with a smile that would easily capture any man's fantasies, and he rationalized that he was away from home, in another part of the country, where no one knew him, and it had been such a long time . . .

"Listen," she said, and she wasn't smiling anymore, "even if we don't do nothing, if that's the way you want it, I still have to have my fifty. If we come up here to this room, I have to get my money."

"I'll give you your money. Don't sweat it. Okay?" Anything to just get himself out of there, and try to forget that he'd ever set foot in the place. But then, on a sudden impulse, he asked her, "Tell me something. How much of that fifty dollars do you get to keep?"

"Who wants to know?" Her facial expression had become rock-hard.

He hated seeing her face change that way. Where was that totally disarming smile he'd seen back on the street when she first approached him? That had been really something. "I do," he answered.

"What do you wanna know for?"

"I don't know. Just curious. I'm not asking for any particular reason."

"You a cop?"

He chuckled. "No," he answered as benignly as he could, "I am *not* a cop."

She studied him. "You older ones always ask the same damn questions."

It served him right. She'd probably heard more than a few reformers' diatribes from her customers. Her "johns." But afterward, most probably. After they'd allow her to ply her chosen trade. He was not about to become one of her johns. But he really did want to know. "Look. I changed my mind because . . . I really just don't feel too hot. Okay?" Then he quickly added, "Listen, I'm sure you'd've been great. Something really special. I'm real sure you'd've made my trip to New York something to remember. Okay?"

This made her smile, and once again he saw the face that had so completely captured his attention when she first approached him on Eighth Avenue, standing in the entryway to an adult books, videos, and specialties shop. "You don't know what you missed," she said with a confident smile as she finished getting back into her clothes. "I'll tell you that. And now, if you don't mind, give me my fifty dollars. I've got to get back down on the street."

"Wait!"

"What for?"

"I really want to know."

"Know what?"

"How much of that money you get to keep."

"You're a cop!"

"Oh, come on. I'm not a cop. I don't even live around here. I'm from Ohio, as a matter of fact. Just another visitor to this big city of yours. But I like knowing about things. How much of this money do you get to keep for yourself?"

"Look, I've got to get back on down there. If I don't make my quota, sometimes it gets a little rough."

He saw a trace of fear in those clear blue eyes of hers and it almost made him flinch. Did this kind of story still exist in the world? Wasn't it ancient history? He took out his money clip and peeled off three twenties. "Here's your fifty and an extra ten. Now you don't have to be in such a hurry. Okay?"

She eagerly reached for the money. "Thanks." A windfall. It brought back her smile.

"Now, I really want to know. How much of this sixty dollars do you get to keep?"

"Why do you older guys always wanna ask a bunch of crazy questions?" Then she said, "Okay, if you wanna know so bad, I'll tell ya. I don't keep any of it."

"Not even the extra ten?"

"I don't keep *any* of it."

"Who gets it?"

"I give it all to my man."

"Your pimp."

"If you don't mind, I'd rather you don't call him by that word. Okay?"

"Just one big happy family? Right?"

"Matter fact, yeah."

"What do *you* call him?"

"I call him Cecil. His name is Cecil."

"Cecil?"

"That's what I said. That's his name."

"And you're telling me you just hand over every nickel you take in? You don't get to keep anything for yourself? No percentage? Absolutely nothing?"

Defiantly she said, "That's right!"

"What's in it for you? What do you do if you need something? A drink. Something to eat. Some clothes or whatever."

"He *gives* me money. Whatever I happen to need, he takes care of."

Well, of course! He could easily tell that by looking at her lovely, stylish clothes. He shook his head. "What about the extra ten I just gave you? Are you maybe going to at least keep that for yourself?"

A trace of a smile and a devilish gleam in her eye. Like she was going to be getting away with some big-time larceny. "Yeah, I might keep that."

"Where do you live, sweetheart?"

She shrugged. "Right here, mostly. Once in a while, Cecil takes me out to his place." Her face brightened. "God, you should see his pad! Really fancy place. He's got this great view of Central Park! . . . And he took me to this really fancy restaurant once. French."

He looked around the grubby room. A bed and not much else. A small three-drawer dresser and a couple of wooden chairs. And a tiny bathroom with fixtures that belonged in a junk heap somewhere. He glanced into the bathroom and saw a filthy shower curtain and a couple of unclean-looking towels hanging from hooks. And the room was one flight up a littered stairwell above an adult books and videos shop. He looked back at her. "Why the hell are you . . . If you were at least a smart little operator, quietly building yourself a small fortune, then *maybe* . . . maybe I could understand . . ."

"I'm doing all right," she snapped with all that defiance.

"I can almost tell." He shook his head. "Look, if this is what you want to do, it's your business, but it seems to me you should at least be getting a little something for yourself out of what you're doing here."

"Mister, if you don't mind, I'd like to go back downstairs. You came up here because you wanted to. Right? Nobody forced ya. You coulda gotten what you paid for. Right? Now, if you don't mind, let's go!"

"Hold it a minute!" he said, almost shouting. "I'm paying for your time. Right? I even gave you more than you asked for. Remember?"

She recoiled from the abrupt change in his raised voice. She was suddenly a child being scolded by her father.

"How many men a day do you, uh, bring up here?" And as he asked the question, he was thinking, for his own amusement, "up here, to this lovely super-palazzo of sensuous pleasure."

She shrugged. "I don't know. Different numbers. Six. Seven. Eight, sometimes. The best I ever did was, I think it was . . . I think it was ten. Boy, was I hustling that day! Cecil doesn't like it if I don't get at least four."

"And you give all the money to him?"

"I already told you that."

"And it's fifty every time?"

"Once or twice I got talked into going for less and Cecil wasn't too happy about it." That little shadow of fear crept back over her eyes.

"Do you ever get more than fifty?"

"Sometimes. Listen, I'm good. You don't know what you're missing."

"And you give all the money, every single bit of it, to Cecil?"

"I already told you that."

"How often does he come and check up on you?"

"Usually once a day. Sometimes twice, but not often. And then at the end of the night."

"I suppose he's got other girls working for him as well. Right?"

"That's right."

"How many, all together? Do you know?"

With a shake of her head, she said, "Matter fact, no. I really don't know."

"You girls ever get together and compare notes?"

"Oh, Cecil don't allow that."

He shook his head. "What's to stop you from keeping some of what you take in? Keeping it for yourself?"

"He *definitely* don't allow that."

"How would he know?"

"He just comes and takes it all."

"Hide some of it, then."

"I can't do that." Once again that little specter of fear moved across her face.

"Now listen to me for a minute," he said. "And listen carefully. Suppose you kept what you got from just one man each day and put it in the bank. Just one. And otherwise went right on, business as usual. Come on. It seems to me that you're certainly entitled to do that. And he'd have no way of knowing you were doing it if he only comes around once a day. Now *think* about this. At fifty dollars a day, do you realize you could put away over a thousand dollars a month?"

"But I already told you, I can't do that."

"The hell you can't! You can!"

"No, I can't!"

"Yes, you can. And I'm going to set it up for you. I'm going to open you a savings account in the closest bank around here. And every day you go and take your little passbook and deposit what you get from just one man. Just one. And give the rest to Cecil like you've been doing. Before you know it, you'll have a lot of money. Do you understand?" He studied her fragile, clear-skinned face as she looked away in deep thought. How in God's name had she gotten to where she was? . . . And how often, during a day's work, had she probably had to endure some kind of terrible abuse at the hands of some who-knows-what kind of john?

"I better not try it," she said, finally. "I don't need it. He takes care of everything."

"The passbook is small. You can keep it someplace." He looked at the cavernous shoulder bag she carried. "You could hide it somewhere down in that. What about in the lining? Or you could hide it here in the room. He won't find it. You said he only comes around once or twice a day. Why is it you don't want some money of your own?"

She looked away again. Her mind was finally dealing with the possible treasure he was setting before her. The wheels were turning. "I don't know . . . You really think over a thousand dollars in a month? That's a lotta money."

"I'll set the whole thing up. You won't have to do a thing. I'll bring you the passbook tomorrow. I'll meet you here in front of the shop downstairs at noon tomorrow. Okay? Tomorrow, twelve noon, sharp. Incidentally, I guess I need to know your name."

She hesitated a moment. "You have to know that?"

This amused him. "How can I open the account in your name if I don't know your name?"

A trace apprehensively, she said, "It's Charlie."

"Charlie?"

"That's what I said."

"Is that short for . . . uh, what . . . Charlene or something like that?"

"It's Charlie. Just plain Charlie."

"How'd you happen to get a name like that?"

"My daddy wanted a boy." A look of severe pain darkened her face.

"Then change it! A name's a name. You can have any name you want. . . . I don't suppose your daddy's anywhere around to object. Am I right?"

"Hell, *I* don't know where he is. I don't even know if he's still alive."

"I might have guessed as much. And your mother, too, probably. Right?"

"I'm not exactly sure where she is, either. And I'm not looking for her. Not with the man she's with now."

"That's too bad." But not all that surprising. "Where do you live, Charlie?"

"Right here. I told you that"

"Oh, right. You did." He looked around the room again and shook his head. "Okay, so we'll stick with Charlie for now. Charlie what? What's your last name?"

"Sweeney."

"And I'll probably need your address. What's your address, Charlie Sweeney?"

She thought a moment and then shook her head. "I don't know what it is. I never looked. We'll have to get it off the door downstairs. If there is a number . . . Hey! Why do you want to go to all this trouble, anyway?"

It was time for *him* to think a minute. He smiled. "Don't worry about it. I really don't think you'd understand. . . . C'mon. Let's go."

As they walked out of the room, he said, "Listen. Why don't you give me back my fifty and I'll use that to open the account for you? And keep the ten, in case something comes to mind that you need for yourself."

She looked sharply at him, her expression tough once again.

He laughed and shook his head. "Forget it, forget it, I'll use another fifty to open the account for you. And don't worry about it. I can afford it."

• • •

HE spotted Charlie in front of the same shop, her hands in the pockets of the ratty coat, her voluminous bag slung over her shoulder. She was walking back and forth, doing her thing, approaching one man after another with her disarming, absolutely unforgettable smile. Her long hair shone in the brilliant winter sun.

As he was about to cross the street, she spotted him. She immediately turned and reversed her direction, quickening her steps as she did.

He had to hustle to catch her, dodging the heavy traffic as he made his way across the street. "Charlie!"

When he finally caught up with her and touched her shoulder, she stopped and spun around, defiant again, her eyes blazing.

"What the hell's the matter with you?" he said. "I'm bringing you the bank passbook just as I said I would."

"I don't want it. I told you I didn't want it, and I *do not* want it."

"Don't be a fool! I want you to have it. Now listen to me. I've gone to a lot of trouble and expense for you to have this. Okay?"

"I said I don't want it!"

"Well, want it or not, you've got it." He took out an envelope, removed the passbook, and showed her the deposit notation. "See right here? Fifty bucks for a start. You're all set up. One deposit a day and you'll have a thousand dollars in less than a month. In fact, in a little over three weeks."

"*You* keep the book," she said.

"It's for you. Don't you understand?" He looked helplessly around. He had a plane to catch. "Here. Take it." He stuffed the envelope into her bag.

She reached into her bag, found it, took it out, and threw it down onto the sidewalk.

He quickly picked it up and grabbed her arm and stuffed the envelope back into her bag. "Charlie, listen to me! You keep this!" He looked around him, wondering if anybody was watching this bizarre little scene.

She shrugged, finally, and then turned and started walking away from him, the passbook still in her bag.

"Wait a minute. I've got to tell you a couple of things. It's the bank right down there on the corner." He pointed at it. "There are two signature cards in there with it. Sign them by the red *X* and take them to the bank. That gets the account started. Okay? Ask for Mrs. Walsh. That's *Walsh*. W-a-l-s-h. I wrote her name on a little slip of paper and it's in there, too. She'll take care of you. Okay? Charlie, you're gonna be rich!"

She studied him for a moment and, finally, the defiance slowly disappeared from her face. She smiled her smile. "Thanks."

He made a mental note to remember that smile. It was a great smile. "Good luck, Charlie."

• • •

THE flight attendant handed him two little miniatures of good scotch and he poured them over ice. He took a sip and shook his head. Charlie Sweeney. A young girl named Charlie Sweeney. Sixty and then fifty more. A hundred and ten dollars! But what the hell! It'll have been well spent if it helps her. Before coming to New York on this trip, he wouldn't have considered himself capable of going anywhere near any part of the Charlie business. But that was only until he got a look at that captivating smile in the dark light of evening.

"Look out for Sin City, Harry. And all those ladies of the night. They'll see you coming and pick you like a Christmas goose! Any you won't have your wife to keep you out of trouble this time."

He'd heard all of the usual, silly locker-room-style banter before leaving for New York, and found it amusing but inconsequential. Yes, he'd often taken Martha with him when possible, on trips of this kind, but, regrettably, they'd been separated for almost a year. But still, he was no candidate for any contact with the ladies of the night. He never had been and, even without Martha, wasn't about to ever start.

He'd worked in New York for a couple of years before his work took him to the Midwest, and during those early years, while still single, he'd had good relationships with a couple of rather nice women, but none of them led to marriage. But even when he wasn't involved in one of those affairs, the thought of going anywhere near one of the play-for-pay ladies, on the stroll, as they were called, had never so much as entered his mind. And on subsequent trips back, his total disinterest had been exactly the same.

His four days in New York had gone well. He'd been tied up with business contacts the first three nights. A lot of good food, and even more satisfying, good business results, and to add to the pleasure of the trip, a chance to enjoy some real theater for a change, by taking clients, something he'd missed since moving to the Midwest. So, finding himself totally uninvolved and bored his last evening, he gave in to the silly urge to just take a walk and behave like a tourist and wander over to have a quick tourist's look at some of the seamy underside of the world's greatest city.

After an early dinner alone in a good restaurant near his hotel, he walked out of the hotel on Lexington, up to Park Avenue, south on Park, through the newly renovated Grand Central (he'd been told *not* to miss that), onto Forty-second Street, and west on Forty-second. When he reached the Times Square area, it wasn't the glitter in the glitter capital of the universe that impressed him (he knew it would still be there), as it was just the quantity of it, the absolute glut. No other place in the world was anything like it.

He continued walking west on Forty-second, and this block had definitely changed for the better since his last visit. Two large, newly renovated and reopened Broadway theaters. In fact, he'd even taken his clients to one of them the previous night, where he thoroughly enjoyed actually getting to see the spectacular, tough-ticket Disney production of *The Lion King*.

He reached Eighth Avenue, looked north, and to his surprise, most of what he remembered seeing there over the years was gone. This particular strip of Sin City, for the most part, had been cleaned out. The marquees of all the porno theaters he vaguely recalled along there, hyping double and triple features in lurid titles, were dark. And since it was not yet eight o'clock, patrons of the many legitimate theaters in the area were scurrying around to make their curtains.

He decided to walk up Eighth and take a closer look. He headed up the street, did notice the bright lights of one place that called itself a sex club, and also saw a couple of shops offering adult books, videos, and other merchandise. He stopped for a moment in front of one of the more provocative shops, and suddenly found himself face-to-face with a girl named Charlie Sweeney.

"Hi." Her smile had been simply beautiful.

"Hello," he'd responded with his own smile. How could he not do so to a person with that face?

"Wanna go out?"

"Want to do what?" He understood perfectly but asked the dumb question anyway.

"Would'ja like some company? . . . You know."

• • •

HE sipped his drink and gazed out the plane window at the horizon. Flying had a pacifying quality about it. Rationalizations came easier, especially with a double scotch in hand. On the first moment he saw her, he considered it virtually impossible that *her* face could exist against the backdrop of those surroundings. But since it had been almost a year, and he was miles away from home, it was easy to convince himself that he had been possessed by the moment.

The hundred and ten dollars helped ease the guilt he felt for that brief moment of lunacy. As things turned out, he didn't let it happen. And besides that, he'd done something *for* her. Something worthwhile. Maybe he'd changed her life, turned it around, helped her go from there to, hopefully, someplace better . . . He'd be back in New York again in a couple of months. He'd have to wander back over to her territory and check up on her. See if she was still around there. See if she was getting rich.

He drained his glass. The liquor helped a lot.

• • •

BACK in the Big Apple with a couple of midday hours to waste before his flight home, and consumed by curiosity, he headed straight for Eighth Avenue. He walked up and down the street looking for her, but didn't see her anywhere. He considered forgetting about the whole business, just leaving well enough alone, but his curiosity got the best of him.

He entered the sex shop uncertainly and looked around the place. The proprietor was the only person there.

Feeling like an idiot but determined to go ahead with it and check up on his one-hundred-and-ten-dollar invest-ment, he said, "Uh, I'm looking for . . . Uh, would you hap-pen to know the whereabouts of a young woman named Charlie Sweeney?"

The man studied him for a couple of seconds. "Just a minute." Then he walked through a door behind a wall of paperbacks. He picked up a phone and dialed a number.

The heat of extreme uneasiness crept over him as he waited for the proprietor to return. He considered just walking out and not risking any further embarrassment. But, what the hell! He was from out of town, so to speak. And he really wanted to know about Charlie. He glanced around him at all the book covers and videocassettes and other items on display. He heard the man's low voice as he talked into the phone, but couldn't make out anything the man said.

When the man reappeared, he asked the man, "Is she around here somewhere, do you know? Will she be very long? I really don't have a lot of time. I, uh, have to catch a plane."

"Just a couple minutes." The man's expression was some-what cryptic.

He suddenly wished he hadn't come back to the shop. It wasn't all that important, all that big a deal. Curiosity. Maybe a chance to see that face and beautiful smile again. Just see how she was doing . . . After all, he'd invested money. Right? . . . He decided that he hoped she *wouldn't* be anywhere around, and he considered just dashing the hell out of there, but the proprietor's reaction to his inquiry had him intrigued. And, as he stood there, feeling like some kind of idiot, fidgeting as the minutes ticked by, he admitted to himself that, yes, he was *really* curious to see her again.

After some ten or fifteen minutes, a man in a rumpled jacket and tie entered the shop. "Are you the man looking for Charlie Sweeney?"

"Uh, not exactly, I, uh . . ."

The man drew a gold detective's shield from his jacket pocket. "I'd like to ask you to come over to precinct headquarters and fill out a statement for us."

"There must be some mistake, I, uh . . ."

"You asked about Charlie Sweeney. Right?"

He felt like an idiot. Why did he ever come back to this place?

"Look," the cop said. "It's just a routine thing. There's no charges involved . . . Hey! Take it easy! I told you there's no charges. We won't do *anything* that would cause you any kind of embarrassment. Okay?"

"Uh, I really don't have any time for that sort of thing. I have to get to the airport to catch a plane."

"We'll give you a ride to the airport." The cop smiled. "In an unmarked car."

"I have to go back to my hotel first and pick up my stuff. I don't want to miss my flight. I really don't have enough time, if you don't mind."

"What time's your flight?"

He hesitated, and then blurted out the truth. "It's at three-ten."

"Where's your hotel?"

"On Lex."

"We've got plenty of time. We'll be glad to take you by your hotel and then give you a lift to the airport. Okay?" The cop smiled again. "And like I said, I'm in an unmarked car. Okay?"

"Then, can you at least give me some idea of what this is all about?"

"You came in here and asked for Charlie Sweeney. Right?"

Reluctantly, he admitted, "Yes."

"Well, she's dead. And we're working on the case."

He gasped. "Dead! Of what?"

"Her pimp beat her to death. But we think we've got a pretty tight case on him, and anything you can add could turn out to be a big help. And, like I said, everything'll be held in strictest confidence. We won't do *anything* to cause you any embarrassment. Okay?"

"I'd still rather not be involved in all this."

"I'm afraid we're not going to give you that option. I'm going to have to insist that you come to the station with me. But the whole thing won't take but a few minutes. And like I said, we'll be more than glad to take you by your hotel and then get you out to the airport in plenty of time for your three-ten flight."

• • •

HE sat in front of a desk, the detective who'd picked him up sat in a chair next to him, and another detective behind the desk sat with his hands on the keyboard of a typewriter, asking the questions and typing in his answers.

"And you did go up to her room with her?"

"Yes, but we didn't do anything. Really. I absolutely did not touch her."

"Something made you change your mind? I assume that when you went up with her, you'd planned to"—a trace of a smile—"avail yourself of her services."

"This is very embarrassing . . ."

"As we've assured you, we'll protect your privacy. We're just trying to get all the stuff we can get our hands on to nail this bastard. Cecil Brown is a lowlife of the first order, and we want him bad. And I think we've got him on this one. Anyway, go on. What happened when you went to her room?"

"Nothing. I suddenly realized how young she was, and felt like a complete idiot, and that was that. I felt really terrible about the whole thing. I still can't believe I'd gone up there with her."

"You give her any money?"

"Oh, she insisted. Whether we *did* anything or not."

"Even though you didn't do anything?"

"That's what she said. And she was, how shall I say it, pretty emphatic about that."

"How much did you give her?"

"She said I had to give her fifty. Which, incidentally, she told me was all going to Cecil, as she referred to him. Well, what I had handy was a bunch of twenties, and I was feeling sorry for her, so I gave her three twenties. Sixty dollars. I figured maybe she'd at least keep the ten."

"And then you both just returned to the street? That's it?"

"That's it. . . . Tell me something. Why'd he kill her? She gave me the impression she was making a lot of money and giving every penny to him."

"Well, it was apparently because she was holding out some of her take. And the Cecil types don't go along with that. But we think we've got a pretty tight case on him. She'd been squirreling some money away in a bank over in the neighborhood she worked, and when we brought the son of a bitch in, we found her passbook in his briefcase." A snicker. "Can you imagine an animal like him with a briefcase? Alligator leather, no less."

He felt a little sick. "Just out of curiosity, do you think I might see the passbook?"

The cop thought a minute. "Sure. I don't see any reason why not." He went to a file cabinet and returned with a large envelope. He reached into it and fished around until he found the little book. "This is it. One thing I can't fathom

is why he kept it. But those guys aren't too smart, fortunately."

Harry recognized the soiled and bent but familiar little
passbook the cop handed him, and opened it. . . . The book
still contained only one entry, a deposit of fifty dollars.

THE LETTER

Dorothy Salisbury Davis

THE letter came after her parents left for the city. Until the last minute, she had expected to be taken along even though her father had said she was not to go. Sometimes he relented, but not this time. So she stood at the door and looked out as they drove off. She wasn't going to give him the satisfaction of tears. It wasn't really a big lie she had told, and she'd said she was sorry as soon as she was found out.

"Sorry's not enough," her father said. "Do you lie to the sisters at school?"

"No."

"Then why can't you tell the truth at home?"

She had not quite suppressed the shrug in time. It was a gesture she had picked up from one of the older girls.

"Stop that!" Her father hadn't struck her, but he looked like he wanted to.

It was the shrug she was being punished for, she thought now. He ought to have said so. Wasn't it a lie for him not to? She went to a window at the front of the house and watched until they disappeared from sight. They were not going to come back for her.

The dog, Jock, nudged her hand with a wet muzzle. She kicked at him, not to hurt him, but she did not want sympathy. She wanted to do something mean, but not to him, not to any dumb animal, only to a human being. She thought of Micky, the hired man. She didn't like him very much. He was polite to her when her father was around, and spitting mean when he wasn't. She was not supposed to go near him when her parents weren't home. That made it tempting. She'd like to see just how mean he could get. She knew how to take care of herself. She was twelve, and big for her age. But the rural mail delivery truck pulled up to the driveway just then, and the mailman put a book-sized package and some letters in the box. It was the promise of a book that made her go out to pick up the mail on that sultry Saturday morning in late September, 1927.

The book was nothing but another volume of a children's encyclopedia that arrived on the monthly installment plan. The one handwritten letter, addressed to Mr. and Mrs. Thomas J. Dixon, looked foreign, although the two-cent stamp was USA. She could not make out the smudged postmark. The writing looked a little like her father's, only not so round. He always rolled his hand three or four times, his arm on the table, before he started to write. Like letters that came from her aunt in England and her mother's cousins in Ireland, this one had no return address on the envelope. She held it to the sun. She could see the writing on lined paper, but the way the paper was folded, the words seemed to cross one another out. Except for the greeting: "Dear Margaret and Tommy." Lainie had never in her whole life heard anyone call her father Tommy. His own sister Eleanor wrote him "Dear Thomas." She wondered if the letter could be from her only living grandparent.

All she knew about him was that he was very sick and had to live in a hospital far up north. She assumed he had consumption. Somebody was always dying of it in the letters from Ireland. Her mother hadn't said that was what ailed

him and Lainie hadn't thought about it. Her father couldn't
remember anything about him. He'd run away from home
when he was twelve. Lainie thought if she ran away—and
she had dreams of doing it—she would certainly remember
her father.

She dawdled returning to the house. To tell the truth,
she liked to be home alone. It was just that she liked to go
to the city better, to ride on the moving stairs in the Boston
Store with her mother, who was always afraid Lainie would
lose her balance and fall when she herself was the one who
almost toppled getting on and off. That summer her father
had taken her to a ball game at Wrigley Field while her
mother went to the beauty parlor. Lainie could name every
player on the Cubs, give his batting average, and tell you
whether or not he chewed tobacco.

The air was muggy and smelled of manure. Micky was
running the spreader in the west field. He was going to
bring the smell with him into the house at supper time. She
unpacked the new volume of the children's encyclopedia,
the letter *S*, and looked up the word *shit*. It wasn't there.
Silly little books: She could have read the whole set of them
when she was seven years old.

She sat at her father's desk and rolled up the top. The
mail went into a wire basket there. She took a last look at
the letter. Tommy . . . if you called him Tommyhawk,
maybe. Tommyhawk Dixon. The idea made her laugh. She
got the magnifying glass from its case, and letter by letter,
made out the postmark: Jamestown ND. North Dakota.
That was up north, all right. If it wasn't for *Dear Margaret
and Tommy*, she'd have guessed it might be from an Indian
mission or somebody selling land. She expected to find out
when her father read the letter aloud to them after supper.
But she'd just bet he wouldn't read Dear Tommy. Lainie
put away the magnifier and closed the roll-top. The desk
took up the whole corner of the dining room. Neither Lainie
nor her mother was allowed more than to look at it, and

dust it once a week. There was one drawer, the top side drawer, they were absolutely forbidden to go near. It was kept locked anyway, the place where her father kept his service revolver and a box of cartridges. The government permitted him to keep his World War army rifle and the revolver. He was a deputy sheriff and he took target practice with the county officers. He drilled with the army veterans, too. He'd be in the Armistice Day parade. Her mother called him Captain Ever-ready, which made him spitting mad.

Lainie did the breakfast dishes and made the egg sandwich that Micky would pick up at the back door at noon. She was tempted to cheat him out of one of the chocolate Marsh-Mello cookies, but she didn't.

She went next to the living room to get her hour of piano practice over with. After the warm-up scales, she made up a connecting story while she played through her whole repertoire. With the marches, she could topple two or three of the family pictures on top of the piano. It did please her that morning to topple Captain Thomas Joseph Dixon, U.S. Army, in dress uniform. He had also served in the Spanish-American war, in the Philippine Islands. There was a wonderful big book with color pictures about the Philippines on the bottom shelf of the bookcase. The natives didn't have many clothes on and if you looked hard enough, you could see their parts.

There used to be a picture of her grandfather up top in a wooden frame, the only picture of him she had ever seen, real perky-looking, wearing a hat with a tassel and holding a violin and bow. She couldn't remember when last she saw it. It could have fallen into the corner back of the piano. Her father said there was enough space back there to pitch a tent, the piano took up too much room. Her mother said his desk took up too much room, too.

• • •

WHEN her parents got home, her mother went upstairs to change her clothes, one slow step at a time. She hated the stairs. Her father went first to his desk to look at the mail. He sat down and opened the letter and unfolded it carefully. His hand was shaking. When he saw Lainie watching him he sent her to bring her homework down. He'd go over it with her after supper. She hurried, but by the time she got back he was already closing the roll-top. He changed and went out to milking without a word to Lainie or her mother. She thought of telling her mother about the letter, but she didn't get to it. Her mother made her spitting mad, telling her about the movie that they had gone to see in the city. With Dolores Costello, Lainie's favorite actress.

"Did you have to go to that one?"

"I'll see it again with you," her mother said.

"You don't have to. I'd rather read than go to a movie anyway."

Lainie didn't expect her father to talk about the letter at supper with Micky at the table. They never did talk much, but that night the only thing was Micky making sure he'd get paid since Sunday was his day off and he was getting a ride right after breakfast. Her father paid him in cash out of his wallet when they got up from the table. He got eight dollars a week plus board and a room over the dairy.

Her father sometimes read aloud to them after supper if he couldn't get anything on the radio, but that night after going over Lainie's homework with her and not making a single correction, he sat at his desk and read *The Hoard's Dairyman* to himself. Lainie and her mother played casino at the dining room table. Lainie kept thinking of "Margaret and Tommy." She wanted to go upstairs and read *Wildfire,* but she didn't want to miss anything. Finally her father took out his watch and wound it. "Bedtime, Lainie," he said.

"I think I'll go up now, too," her mother said.

"I'd like you to wait for me, Margaret."

Well, to hell with them, Lainie thought. Old Tommyhawk didn't want papoose around when he was powwowing with heap big squaw.

Just when she was able to get into her "golden dream"— she was a streetcar conductor in this one—her father's voice brought her wide awake. He was swearing and he shouted, "No, no, no," and began to knock things out of his way as he went outdoors. Lainie raced to the hall railing and heard her mother call after him, "He's your own flesh and blood, Thomas."

Her mother came up the stairs as slow as a cow getting up. Lainie waited for her at the top.

"Go back to your bed," her mother said. "He'll be over it in the morning."

"Is it about my grandfather?"

"Och, Elaine, were you listening at the door?"

"I wasn't. It was what you said—'Your own flesh and blood.' "

"Did I say that? I don't think I said that, Lainie."

"I won't say anything," Lainie said, and went back to her room.

All through Sunday Mass, she thought about the letter and the quarrel. She knew her father had run away from home when he was twelve. It must have been before that when he was called Tommy. She was no longer so delighted with herself for Tommyhawk. Her father was hunched down in the pew, his head on his hands. With him on one side of her and her mother, praying the rosary, on the other, Lainie felt closed in, trapped, like a sausage in a bun.

They met the O'Malleys on the church steps after Mass. They were Irish, but from a different county than Lainie's mother. You'd have thought it was a different country to hear her make fun of their brogue. But it was Ireland, and she enjoyed a visit with them once in a while. When Mrs. O'Malley suggested the Dixons come home to Sunday dinner with them, Lainie's mother put it up to her father. The hired man was off for the day and Lainie had finished her homework.

"The darling girl." Mrs. O'Malley gave her Mary Jo a poke. Mary Jo was the oldest of four and in the same grade as Lainie, but she never got above sixth or seventh in class. They didn't like each other, and Lainie hated the rest of the O'Malley kids for letting their sister boss them around.

"Margaret, you and Lainie go," her father said. "I'd be glad to have the house to myself while I write the letter."

Lainie couldn't think of a worse arrangement: He was going to pick them up before milking. He would answer the letter to her grandfather and that would be the last she'd ever hear of it. "I want to go home with you, Dad. I'm feeling sick, and I've got the pain in my side again."

"Another time," her mother said to Mrs. O'Malley. Her husband was already sitting in their car, ready to blow the horn.

Lainie's father got his way. "You need to get out of the house, Margaret. The girl can go to her bed when her and I get home, and we'll call the doctor in the morning."

"Is it the appendicitis, do you think?" Mrs. O'Malley sounded hopeful.

• • •

As Lainie got into the Chevy, her father looked at her as though he was reading her mind. He didn't say anything until they were outside the village limits. Then he said, "I don't suppose you're feeling well enough to drive the car."

There was nothing she loved to do more. "I'm feeling a little better." But he didn't stop.

"Please, Dad."

She knew she drove well. She'd once overheard her father say she'd soon be as good a driver as he was. But all he ever said to Lainie was, "Don't show off now."

When they got into the house, Lainie said, "I don't have to go to bed, do I?"

"You've had a miraculous recovery, haven't you?"

"I did have a pain," she said.

All he said was, "Make us some sandwiches from last night's ham. Then you can go off on your own."

Lainie wanted to ask him about the letter. After all, she wasn't blindfolded when she brought it into the house. But she didn't dare come right out with it. Then, when they were at the kitchen table, she asked him, as though it had just popped into her head, "Dad, do I take after you?"

"What gave you that notion?"

"Mrs. O'Malley says I look like you."

"Mrs. O'Malley needs new glasses."

"I don't think you look like my grandfather, either." She knew it was a mistake the minute the words were out.

"Where's this grandfather business coming from? I had no idea you knew him that well."

"I make him up. That's all."

"Out of whole cloth?"

"From the picture we used to have on the piano. I pretended he played 'Turkey in the Straw' with me."

Her father took up his sandwich from where he'd set it down on mention of her grandfather. "Your aunt sent that from England. It was taken before we came to America. Eat your sandwich."

He didn't eat. He sat staring at something she couldn't see. Why can't he tell me? Lainie thought. I'm his own flesh and blood, too, aren't I?

"Mother's always telling me stories about how she grew up in Ireland, how her father took the kids to hunt for duck eggs in the river. She talks a lot about my Grandfather Lavery."

"So that should be grandfather enough for you."

"But he's dead."

That amused her father, a bit of a smile that made Lainie hope he'd tell her about her grandfather. She was sure he remembered. He had to. But he only kept looking at her, like he was trying to see through her, like he did when he was sure she was lying to him. He ate part of his sandwich and threw the rest to the dog. Lainie would have liked to have had it. Jock didn't even eat the bread. All her father said was, "You're not changed out of your good clothes."

When she came down he was at his desk in his shirt sleeves. He'd hung his coat on the back of a dining room chair, and he was reading the letter again. Lainie thought that to hang up his coat in the hall would be a good excuse to go into the room.

It put him into a rage. "Will you get out of here, girl, before I do something I'll be sorry for? You're turning into a little sneak, Lainie. You're as sly as a lizard."

Lainie fled outdoors. Jock came as far as the door with her and then went back to her father. She was hurt, ashamed. She walked toward the river. She cut through the fields but kept the road in sight for a while. There were cars and dust, but she did long to drive a car. Her father was going to buy a new one, brand-new, next year. They would drive to Boston, where her mother had friends. But not to North Dakota. She liked the idea of Boston better herself. It was only a dream anyway, something her father and her read and talked about, the Old North Church, Concord, Lexington, a live history book of places.

She cut away from sight of the road and through woods. The leaves kept falling. If she found a perfect one, she'd send it to her aunt in England who'd never been to America. Red, yellow, orange, everybody liked maple trees the best. Her favorite was the oak, tall, rough, dark. At the river's edge, the trees were mostly willow. They reminded her of ghosts, the way they swayed whatever way the wind blew. One of the pieces in the song book she played from sometimes went willow, tit-willow . . . "And I said to him, Dickie Bird, why do you sit, singing willow, tit-willow, tit-willow?"

She was almost home again when she heard her father's whistle. She didn't have hers. She'd got out of the house so fast she forgot to take it from the kitchen hook. She moved a little faster, but not much. She wasn't in a hurry. After he left the house, then she'd hurry.

He didn't even ask where she'd been. All he wanted was to make sure she'd feed the chickens and get the cows in while he went for her mother.

There was nothing more poky than cows going into the barn. The more Lainie tried to push them ahead, the more stubborn they were, going into the wrong stanchions and having to be turned around to get them out. No matter how you tried, you couldn't shift a cow into reverse. All the same, Lainie got into the house well before her parents were due home. She could see from the door to the dining room that her father had left the roll-top up. She shoved Jock outdoors again and went to the desk. No letters. Only the box of Eaton's stationery, his pen and a bottle of ink, and the big blotter. She lit the lamp to see if she could read any words on the blotter. It was a terrible idea. She turned it off. But just from the way he'd left the desk, the top up, his writing things out, she got the feeling he mightn't be finished. He'd have stuck the letter—both of them, maybe, his and her grandfather's—in somewhere, put on his coat, and left. Not with her home alone, Lainie thought, not the way he felt about her now. If there was any letter there at all, it had to be locked in the gun drawer and she could forget it. But she wasn't going to forget it. She tried the drawer. It blasted wide open with a loud crack. Lainie leaped back. It wasn't the gun that went off; there was no smell, no smoke. Then she knew. It was a big ugly rat trap. It wasn't going to hurt her now, but it could have. The gun wasn't there. The trap had been set and put on top of the box of cartridges. Set for her.

She thought of trying to set it again, but she was shaking and they'd be home soon. She closed the drawer and went outdoors. What could she say? Say she hadn't gone near the desk? Pretend she'd been outdoors all the time, that she didn't know what happened? He'd know. She knew he'd know. Even if he didn't say anything, if he waited for her to tell on herself.

The dog sat on his haunches and watched for her next move. Dumb dog. What did he care what happened to her? She didn't care, either. But she did. She was the dumb one, to touch the gun drawer for the first time in her whole life. It was humiliating. "It was a dirty trick," she told Jock. "Dad's a mean son of a bitch."

Lainie watched from behind the garage. The trap had been real handy. He'd brought two of them into the house when her mother saw a rat in the root cellar. He swore he caught it, but she still wouldn't go down there. She'd send Lainie. When the car turned into the drive Jock raced to the welcome. Lainie took her time, but she followed them into the house.

They'd brought home the Sunday paper this time. Her father left it on the kitchen table while he went into the hall to change into work clothes. Her mother shook up the fire and put on the kettle first thing. She always did. Her mother said the O'Malley meat was as tough as bull's beef, and she was glad she'd put away a bit of ham after last night's supper. Lainie didn't tell her what had happened to it. She listened to her father go from the hall into the dining room. She took the paper into the living room and tried to read the "Teenie Weenies." Her heart started to thump when she heard the ratchety sound of the roll-top closing. But her father went outdoors through the kitchen without a word to anyone except the dog.

• • •

THE only talk at the supper table was her mother's about the O'Malleys. She could make you laugh, the way she told things, but nobody laughed. At last her father put his knife and fork crosswise on his plate.

"So, Elaine, you fed the chickens and brought in the cows.

What else did you do, you're always so busy?"

She didn't say anything.

"Lainie, get the pudding from the icebox," her mother said.

"The girl's talking to me, Margaret." He didn't take his eyes off Lainie.

It was no use trying to pretend she didn't know about the trap. "When I came in from the barn," she started, "I was going to set the table and I noticed you hadn't closed your desk like always. Then I noticed the gun drawer didn't look tight, and I was trying to close it when the trap went off inside. It almost scared me to death and the drawer blew open." She stopped. She was saying too much and she hated herself.

"Is that all?"

Lainie nodded.

"Now start over and this time tell the truth."

"I thought you might have hidden the letter there."

"Where you were forbidden ever to touch."

"I know."

"Oh, you always know. You always know everything."

"If the letter was from my grandfather—"

He cut her off. "What made you think that?"

"Tom," her mother said, a plea.

"You stay out of this, Margaret." He turned to confront her mother, where she sat on one side of him, opposite Lainie. "Or have you been telling tales to her?"

"She didn't tell me anything, Dad. I just pretended."

He turned back to Lainie. "Pretended what?"

"Pretended the letter was from my grandfather."

"And what did you pretend it said?"

"That he'd come and live with us. He wasn't sick anymore. He'd bring his violin . . ." More and more ideas popped into Lainie's head. "He'd tell us about bears and moose and Indians . . ."

"All right, Lainie, that's enough. Your grandfather is still sick and he's not going to get better, and he's not going to come to live with us."

He'd won again, Lainie thought. Next he'd say what her punishment was going to be. She didn't care. She'd even like to say thank you.

"Lainie," he started, "I didn't think for a minute you'd open that drawer—"

"That's a lie!" she shouted. "You did!"

It happened so fast, she didn't see it coming, the back of his hand across her face. She was dizzy before she knew she hurt. Her eyes misted but she saw her mother pick up her knife and shake it at him. "Don't ever lay your hand on the girl again." The knife clattered to the plate.

"She will not defy me, Margaret. I'll break her will if it's the last thing I do."

"She's not a horse, Tom."

He pushed away from the table and slammed out of the house. The only sound was Lainie's sniffle.

• • •

LAINIE omitted her father from her prayers that night and included her grandfather. She couldn't imagine him without the violin, so she thought of them playing together the way she'd made it up before. She'd like to be a musician, but she didn't think it would ever happen. It wasn't one of her favorite things till now. Maybe he could teach her. She wasn't going to get very far with Sister Benedict and her metronome, seventy-five cents a week. Seventy-five cents wouldn't mean much to her grandfather. Doctors and hospitals cost a lot of money, unless you were a veteran. She just knew her grandfather wasn't. He'd come over to Canada from England with two sons and their stepmother when Lainie's father was five. She knew these things from her aunt's letters. How she wished she'd listened better! Aunt Eleanor had been raised by an uncle, who made bells and iron fences. Lainie knew she was rich because she'd helped Dad buy the farm. She'd pay the hospital bills for Grandfather. Lainie was beginning to write letters to her aunt. Her father always wanted to read them first. He'd make her write some of them over. To hell with him.

Lainie had closed her bedroom door. Her mother came in and tucked her in with a "God bless" and left the door open. Her father did not like to see it closed. Lainie got up and closed it. To hell with him.

• • •

LAINIE woke in the morning to the sound of her father shaking the grate in the kitchen range. It wasn't even daylight and she'd been dreaming. Her grandfather was in the dream. He had a gun he was showing her and it went off. Then what happened at the table came back to her, so real, she jerked her head out of the way. That part wasn't a dream. Jock bounded into the room and jumped on top of her, all yips and slobber. He raced out as fast as he'd come and Lainie got out of bed feeling as heavy as her mother. In the bathroom she examined her face in the mirror. There wasn't even a bruise mark. Her father called up the stairs to her softly not to waken her mother. Lainie figured it meant that Micky hadn't gotten back and she'd have to help out in the barn. She wasn't in a hurry to get dressed. Her father called up again. "Just come down as you are."

He was standing in front of the stove, the front lid off; he fed more kindling into the flames. Then he took the letter from his breast pocket. He showed her the envelope. "You've seen it before, haven't you?"

She nodded.

He took the letter from the envelope, unfolded it, and put it to the flames. He held it until what dropped last from his fingers was no bigger than a snowflake. He licked his fingers where he'd burned them and held the envelope to the fire in the same way. She could smell the scorched hair on the back of his hand.

"Now let's have some peace in the house," he said. He looked at her as though he wanted her to do something or say something, but she couldn't.

He picked up the coal bucket and stoked the fire, then he went out, sending Jock ahead of him.

When her mother came downstairs, Lainie told her, "He burned Grandfather's letter."

"Who is *he?*" her mother said.

Lainie wanted more than anything that morning to get away from the house as fast as she could. Maybe forever, she told herself. Her father'd run away when he was twelve. He was so proud of it, it was the only thing he ever told about himself growing up. She did her chores, which included getting the laundry started for her mother. She had to go out and take the sheet and pillowcase off Micky's bed. He was supposed to bring them in, but he forgot. Half drunk, she thought, on a Monday morning. The bootleg stuff was going to kill him, her father said. She hoped it would. All the same, she was glad to see him pull up in the truck. He tooted the horn even though she was watching for him from the doorway. Either her father or Micky took the day's milk to the depot at the crossroad every morning. It was where, too, she was picked up for school.

They weren't out the driveway when he forgot the clutch when he tried to shift gears. "You're going to strip the gears," Lainie said.

"Smart alec," Micky said. "Going to tell the boss about it?"

"Maybe." She wouldn't.

"No, you won't. You're scared of what he'd say. He won't believe you against me. He knows you got it in for me. What did I ever do to you, Lainie?"

"Does he tell you everything that goes on in the house?"

"A man talks about some things." He took a rag from his pocket, wiped his nose, and put the rag on the seat between them. Lainie moved away. "I ain't catching," he said. He glanced at her and grinned. He didn't have many teeth, and the ones he had looked awful. After a while, he said, "He likes to tell about you when you were a good little girl. Told me he put you on his horse when he was in the army. You could ride a horse when you were two years old. Do you believe that?"

"Sure, the horse was willing." Lainie had heard the story often enough.

Micky gave a bark of a laugh. It sounded dirty.

"I mean it was a gentle horse—it liked me."

"I know what you mean, little Miss Lainie." He reached over and patted her thigh.

"Watch the road!" Lainie shouted.

They were in a rut and headed for the ditch. He jerked the wheel and got them to the middle of the road.

"I hate you," Lainie said. "I don't know why Dad doesn't fire you."

"Because I do him a day's work, and I know to call him boss."

It wasn't a good school day for Lainie, either. She was caught during catechism reading about North Dakota in her geography book. She put the book away. It wasn't going to tell her anything about her grandfather anyway. But it kept her from thinking about Micky better than the quiz on sacraments and sacramentals did. She could still feel where he'd touched her, and he'd looked at her that way before, like he was half asleep. She wondered if he told her father dirty stories. She'd heard them laughing in the dairy, but she never got close enough to hear what they were saying. She didn't want to hear it, either—but at the same time, she did.

• • •

LAINIE sat on the kitchen stool and watched her mother iron. *Press.* She was pressing Lainie's father's army dress uniform. He wasn't going to wear it till Armistice Day, but he wanted it ready, and as long as she had the ironing board up . . . Lainie ate her pea soup. You could almost taste the ham.

"Don't *shlupp*," her mother said. "You sound like Micky."

Lainie gave a long, noisier *shlupp*. "That's how Micky sounds. He's a pig."

"Don't let your father hear you say that." Her mother softened then, remembering something. Lainie could always tell when her mother was remembering. It seemed she almost always was. There'd be a story, long or short—like the crazy woman in Ireland who prayed out loud all through the Mass, "Haily holy, haily holy, haily holy . . ."

"I taught your father not to *shlupp*. I was giving him his supper. It was on my aunt Mary's farm before we were married. Wasn't I the bold one to mention it even? He went out of the house roaring the same as he does today. But I never heard more than an accidental *shlupp* out of him after that."

Lainie washed her bowl. She waited to take over the ironing when her mother was done with the uniform.

"He wasn't long out of the army," her mother went on. "And not much more than a boy. I swear he hadn't stopped growing. His sleeves were never long enough. The army didn't want him after the war, either. Farming was the only thing he knew. He loved horses. More than people, I used to think. I'd try to get him to go to the church parties with me. Isn't it funny? Now he's the one that's into everything—the American Legion and the Foreign Veterans and Grand Knight of the Knights of Columbus, and him born an English Protestant." Her mother let the iron cool for a minute. "I've almost scorched his trousers. That's talking to you, I did that."

"Mother, do you hate Micky like I do?"

"I don't hate him, but he's lucky to be working for your father. He's what we called a *gobbeen* at home."

"He sounds like one."

"You don't even know what it means, Lainie."

"I'll bet I do. He's stupid and dirty and I'm always afraid he's going to touch me."

"Then don't go near him. You're not supposed to anyway."

"I have to ride in the truck with him, don't I?"

Her mother hung the trousers on the back of a chair. She turned to Lainie, quick as a cat. "Has he ever touched you? You know what I mean."

"No," Lainie said.

• • •

HER father was out that night. It was a week of meetings for him. Running himself to the bone, her mother said. It suited Lainie just fine. She finished her homework and left it for him to go over by himself when he got home. Her mother was listening to the radio in the living room. More static than music. She turned it off when Lainie went in. "I can't stand him," her mother said. It had to be Rudy Vallee.

Lainie took a volume of the children's encyclopedia from the bookcase. "I'm glad to see you using the little books," her mother said.

Lainie settled in the rocker under the lamp and looked up North Dakota.

"Is it something I'd be interested in?" her mother asked. She did love to be read to.

"North Dakota," Lainie said.

"I don't think I'd be interested in that," her mother said.

"That's where my grandfather Dixon is."

"I know that. I'll just sit here with my eyes closed for a few minutes. Don't let me fall asleep."

What did she think about, Lainie wondered, that she never told? Were her stories about Ireland all true, even the crazy ones, or did she make them up? Lainie read the two pages about North Dakota. The Badlands interested her most. But she didn't learn anything about her grandfather. There was no mention of Jamestown.

"Mother, didn't you ever visit Grandfather Dixon?"

"I did not." Nothing more.

"Doesn't anybody visit him?"

"I don't know who they are," her mother said, and began to push herself up from the chair.

"I'm going to someday," Lainie said. "I don't care what Dad says."

"I'll go up now." Her mother stopped and looked down at her. She pulled Lainie's face against her, a smothering of laundry soap and lavender and sweat. "Lainie, Lainie, Lainie," she said, and at the door, "You'd better come up soon if you don't want your father in on you."

The next night the two of them were home by themselves again. The rain was heavy and Lainie thought there'd be a fight about her father going out in it, but her mother let him go with the caution to drive slowly and come home early.

Lainie got out the cards, pencil, and tablet. "You owe me sixty-two cents from last June," she said.

"I'd rather owe it to you than cheat you out of it," her mother said. It was make-believe gambling anyway.

But the game soon lagged. Her mother seemed to have trouble keeping her mind on it. Finally, she gathered her cards without counting the points and set them aside. "I've been thinking all day of the Dolans, a family at home. I'm not sure of the name. I'm not even sure I knew them, or if I had it told me.

"They were a queer family. It was said they washed ashore from Scotland or one of the islands. They might have come down from the Spanish, way back—the pride or arrogance, they didn't fit. None of us owned the land we lived on— we couldn't, all tenant farmers without the nails to scratch ourselves, most of us. The landowners were a greedy lot. Oh, some of them weren't. But I'm getting away from my story.

"They said when Michael Dolan landed he'd bought a horse and a dray at dockside and drove it into town himself with two children—don't ask me how old, I don't know. It was long ago—two children and a long wooden box. It was his dead wife's body, though who in the town knew it at the time, I can't say. . . ."

Lainie knew. She could tell from the little roll of her mother's shoulders that she was speaking of the dead.

"Well, Michael Dolan arrived with a piece of parchment to show he'd inherited, freehold, a parcel of land above the town. It was always thought to belong to the absentee landlord who'd for years been collecting grazing money from us. So nobody begrudged Michael Dolan his inheritance. He buried his wife to the seaward side and settled in well enough for a stranger. But the town never took to him or him to the town, so people knew what they meant when they said Michael Dolan lived above the town.

"I don't know how long after when, lo and behold, the absentee squire showed up and took Michael Dolan to the courts, claiming the Dolan inheritance a fraud. I only know what I heard, mind you, your grandfather Lavery talking, but the squire won and ordered Dolan evicted. The first thing he wanted off the property was the remains of poor Dolan's wife, and cruel devil that he was, he made Dolan the gift of a plot in the town graveyard.

"Well, Dolan laid in wait for the squire one night, and killed him dead. The next day he was digging up the wife's coffin himself when they arrested him. He was tried and found guilty but instead of hanging or prison, he was committed for the rest of his life to the asylum for the insane."

Lainie's mother drew a breath you could have heard in the next room. "It's a sad kind of love story, isn't it?"

"Oh, wow," Lainie said. "What happened to the children?"

"I knew you were going to ask that, and I don't know.

It must have been terrible hard for them, their father put away like that."

Lainie lay awake a long time thinking about Michael Dolan. She heard her father come home and send Jock out to pee in the rain. She hoped the dog wouldn't come up and shake himself in her room.

• • •

LAINIE got permission during study period the next day to spend it in the library—a room divided between books and first aid—the library-infirmary. Except for Sister Alberta working at the sink, she had the place to herself. Alberta was not a busybody, but she reminded Lainie she was not allowed to sign out books during school hours.

"I've read them all anyway," Lainie said.

"I can believe that you've read most of them," the nun said.

"Most of them," Lainie repeated, and lugged the atlas from its shelf to the table. The map of North Dakota had a whole page, and it didn't take long to find Jamestown. It was on the James River and on the Northern Pacific Railway line. Population at last census, 5265.

She closed the book and sat a minute. At least she could be sure now there was a town called Jamestown. It wasn't mentioned in the children's encyclopedia or her geography book. She returned the atlas to its shelf. The library had two large sets of encyclopedias.

Sister Alberta came from the sink, rolling down her sleeves. "Do you need help, Lainie?"

"Which encyclopedia is best, Sister?"

"Better," Alberta said.

"Better," Lainie repeated.

"I'd put it this way," the nun said. "The World Book is easier to read. But if you can't find what you're looking for in the World Book, you may find it in Britannica. But if you don't find it in the Britannica, you're certainly not going to find it in the World Book."

It took Lainie half a second. "I should look in Britannica first."

"That's it," Alberta said.

Lainie liked her. She talked to you like a person, and she knew how to throw a baseball.

There was a Jamestown, North Dakota, USA, in the Encyclopedia Britannica. Lainie didn't read what it said line for line. Her eyes leaped to the word hospital, and she read: "The State Hospital for the Insane is just beyond the city limits." The room turned nearly upside down and then came right again. She pretended to read the book until Sister told her that the bell was about to ring for the next class.

Lainie mixed and sorted things in her mind in the hours and days after that. She didn't feel bad, and she didn't feel good, about knowing something her father didn't want her to know ever, but she couldn't help thinking about it. Why couldn't they've told me, she kept asking herself. Her mother had told her, if you figured it out. Was that supposed to shut her up? She was shut up, all right. She wasn't ever going to tell them what she knew.

At the first chance, she asked her mother to help her move the piano, and had to tell her she wanted to see if her grandfather's picture was back there. "I promise I won't ask any more questions."

"That'll be the day," her mother said. Then, "It's not there, child. I think your father took it away."

"Did he burn it?"

"You weren't going to ask any more questions."

She shouldn't have promised. The more she tried to fit her mother's story to what she knew, the more questions came up. If her grandfather killed a man, was it so terrible if it was a bad man? The coffin in her mother's story was spooky. Her grandmother Dixon—her step-grandmother: Lainie's father couldn't remember about her, either. And

maybe her mother made up that part. She did make up. Her
father couldn't remember and her mother couldn't forget.
She didn't let herself forget. Her father made himself forget.
All those native tribesmen they had to kill in the Philippines, he'd told her once, it wasn't the same in war. It was
you or them. When the police came to arrest his father, was
that when he ran away? Or was it afterward, when they put
Grandfather away? Was Dad ashamed? Scared? Dad scared?
She wasn't scared of Dad, either. Not anymore. She didn't
hate him, but she didn't think they were going to have fun
together like they used to.

• • •

BUT that Friday night they did have fun, all three of them.
They had supper in a Chinese restaurant and went to the
village theater. Micky was left his meal on the kitchen table,
and when Lainie's father insisted, was allowed to stay and
listen to the radio in the living room. Both Lainie and her
mother knew better than to argue over it and spoil their
evening. It came pretty close to that when her mother said
that Micky had to be told to change out of his work shoes
and overalls.

"For God's sake, Margaret, he knows that."

"He didn't do it last time, and I'll not have him traipsing
through the house bringing the barn in with him."

Her father muttered that he wouldn't be traipsing
through the house, and they got off without a quarrel.

The night was just about perfect, Lainie thought by the
time they were headed home. Fred Thomson was her favorite
cowboy, and Silver King her dad's favorite horse in the movies. Her mother, with a robe over her legs, sat in the backseat. She always did. She thought any movie was better than
none, and she did enjoy the beautiful wild country—the
wilds of America.

Lainie asked her father if he would soon let her drive after
dark.

"Sh-sh-sh," he said.

"I heard you," her mother said.

• • •

LAINIE didn't care whether Micky had traipsed or tiptoed, she knew when she got upstairs he'd been in her room. Nothing looked different, but she knew. She could smell him. What good was Jock? The stupid dog probably took him through the house. He'd washed up and put away his dishes, and he'd put the key to the door back in its place on a nail under the step. He'd even remembered to leave the kitchen light on. Saint Micky. The *gobbeen*: She'd bet he didn't even know he was one.

In the morning, Lainie's mother was sick. Something she ate in the restaurant, but Lainie and her father knew from the sounds of her retching, it was a bilious attack, something she got every few months. She vomited green bile. Her father said she was getting Ireland out of her system. Her mother said she'd kill him when she got over the attack.

Lainie made breakfast for the men and took her mother half-cups of tea. She never wanted more than a half-cup, and Lainie and her father always humored her, making the full cup and then throwing half of it out before taking it upstairs. Lainie listened to her father on the hall phone try to change his plans for the day. He was supposed to pick up two of his Foreign War comrades and go to the county seat for a meeting that afternoon. It was an important meeting. They all were, Lainie thought. Two of the girls from down the road were supposed to come to supper. Her mother was going to teach them how to play whist. Lainie already knew, but she'd made up her mind not to show off. She wanted to play. But not that day. She'd call them when her father finished with the phone. When he hung up Lainie said she didn't see why he couldn't go to his meeting.

"I can take care of Mother," she said, "and she can tell me when to put the beans in the oven."

"I'll build up the fire before I go," he said. "It'll last." It seemed a long time ago that he burned her grandfather's letter. "And would you give Micky a hand? He can manage the milking, but you might bring in the cows and feed them, and turn them out afterward."

"Sure," Lainie said.

"I'll make it up to you," her father said.

Lainie did her regular chores first. She fed the chickens and gathered the eggs. The days were getting shorter. The hens were laying better, indoors more. The cows had come home by themselves and waited to be let in. She was sure they were all there, but she called out from the door, "C'boss, c'boss . . ." mostly because she liked to hear her own voice carry into the near dark and send back the hint of an echo. You could hardly hear it for the noisy bunch trying to get into the barn.

When Micky came he stood around waiting for her to finish. He'd brought in two buckets, she noticed, along with the five-gallon can and strainer. "You can start," Lainie said. Dad never waited for the last cow to be fed.

"Ain't you going to help me? Your dad said you would."

"He didn't," Lainie said. She could milk and sometimes did when it was just her and her father. But he didn't think it was the right work for a girl, and her mother was dead certain it wasn't.

"You can weigh up and mark the chart for me," Micky said. Lainie's father kept track of how much milk each cow gave each milking.

"Mother's sick," Lainie said. "I'll come back and let the cows out."

"It gets real lonesome here, nobody to talk to," Micky said.

"You got the cows," Lainie said.

"And one bull," he said, and looked up at her with a silly grin as though he was going to squirt milk at her.

Lainie didn't run, but she didn't hang around, either. The

bull was quiet, in a pen of his own, and he had a yard pen to himself. Lainie knew what went on there, though she was kept in the house when it happened. As though you couldn't see anything from an attic window. Or feel anything.

Lainie put the beans in the oven and waited to see the dairy light go on before she went back. Jock went with her as far as the barn door. She shut him out. Inside was cat country, and Jock was all dog, as her father said. Lainie released the bolt on the cow door and started the cows on their way out.

"They know how to go out," Micky said, close behind her. She didn't hear him come with the clop and the plop the cows made.

"You're not supposed to be here," Lainie said, and moved to go around him.

He backed her toward the wall and dodged to block her every move. "Your dad don't need to know."

Lainie screamed at him. She'd butt him if she could get her head down. She slipped when she tried to kick him, and now she could feel the cold, damp masonry at her back, and she knew she was afraid. She fumbled for the whistle, but she'd not taken it from the kitchen hook.

"Don't make me hurt you. I ain't wanting much."

She spat at him but her mouth was dry and there wasn't much spit. In the misty glare of the barn light, she saw the flash of his pocketknife as he clicked open the blade. She saw then, too, the white naked part waiting to get at her. She didn't care if he killed her, he wasn't going to get to her alive. She tried to scream and tightened all her muscles to go at him. He put a hand to her throat and held her head against the wall.

Jock came leaping, scrabbling over the backs of the cows that clogged their door. He hit the floor and sprang up, teeth bare, at Micky. Micky threw up an arm to ward him off, but Jock tore it away and sank his teeth into Micky's face. Micky howled and begged Lainie to call him off. She hesitated. She didn't want to. Micky brought his knife up and then drove it down with all his strength between Jock's shoulders. The dog still wouldn't let go, not till Lainie cried him off. "Down, Jock, down! Please, down," and caught hold of the scruff of his neck. He let go and dropped himself at Lainie's feet.

Micky ran for the far door, twisting his way through the stanchions. Jock tried to get up but he couldn't. Lainie tried to help him but he growled at her until she stopped trying. He let out a great howl that stampeded the cows, but their rush was outdoors, past Lainie and Jock. She knelt down by him, whimpering herself, swearing, praying—praying for the dog, please God. Her hand and jacket were dark and wet with his blood. She stroked his head and he didn't growl anymore. She brought armfuls of hay from beneath the chute and put it around him. She tried to tuck some underneath him, but she knew from the weight of him and the stillness that he was dead.

• • •

"LET me be the one to tell your father," Lainie's mother said. She'd come down in her robe, a roll of toilet paper in her hand to spit into. She fired up the stove and made tea. Over and over she said, "We should've known—I blame myself as much as your father. What do you know of a man that comes in to you off the road?"

"He's gone," Lainie said. She'd heard the truck, and he'd left the gate open. Her father would know something was wrong.

Lainie watched from the living room window. Several cars went by and she followed the lights of each one until it passed the driveway. Shouldn't the police be called if he'd stolen the truck? Her mother didn't say no, but she said, "Your father'll be home any minute now." She waited for him in the kitchen, and when he came, Lainie didn't go out there right away. She heard their voices, but not what they said. She felt ashamed, and guilty. She'd never felt anything that hurt so much.

And the first thing her father said when he saw her was, "It's not your fault, Lainie."

"But it is, Dad. It is!"

His face crumpled like an old man's. He went through to the dining room and switched on the desk lamp.

"Don't, Tom," her mother said when he unlocked the gun drawer.

"Dad, he's gone," Lainie said. "He stole the truck and he's gone."

Her father took out the gun, broke it, and rolled the empty chambers.

"Think of Lainie and me," her mother said. "You know what they'll bring up, Tom. It'll all come out. . . ."

He sat, the gun in his hand, and looked at it while she railed on.

"All you thought you were hiding won't be hid anymore—and they'll take back your medals and ribbons, and all them foolish things you're so proud of."

"Don't, Mother, please," Lainie said. It was all wrong, what she was saying, turning mean on him.

But he didn't get up and stomp out of the house. He looked at Lainie's mother. "What do you know of my ribbons and medals? What do you know of me, Margaret?"

Her mother put a handful of tissue to her mouth.

"Dad," Lainie said, "I know about my grandfather. I know where he is. I learned it for myself."

He looked at her queerly, and then put the gun back in the drawer.

"Why couldn't you tell me?" Lainie said.

He shook his head a little, confused, maybe.

"Why can't you tell me *why*?"

He didn't say a word.

Her mother was about to say something, to start all over again. Lainie put out her hand to her mother to stop her.

Her father's voice was so low, she could hardly hear, but she did.

"I informed on him when he killed a man. I told the police where they could find him, and then I ran away."

He locked the drawer and got to his feet. "I'm going out to the barn now," and to Lainie, "Take care of your mother."

When he'd lit the lantern and gone, her mother said, "He'll be crying his eyes out over that dog. You'd better go to him, Lainie."

TANGO IS MY LIFE

Mickey Friedman

Salida

THE music pulsed, its insistent throb speaking of desire and loss, the torment of remembrance, the despair that follows ecstasy. Its rhythm was the rhythm of the surging heart, of the blood in the veins. This was the music of passion in all its guises, of abandonment in every sense of the word.

The music stopped. Rafael said, "Ladies and gentlemen! All of you have taken the Beginning Argentine Tango class, no? It is required. Is there anyone here who has not had the first class?"

The two dozen students eyed one another. Could any of them have been foolish enough to sign up for pre-intermediate Argentine tango without the proper foundation? If so, nobody was owning up to it.

"Very well," said Rafael after a long and skeptical pause. "I have asked you to show me the *salida* to the *cruzada*. Please try once more."

Flushed with embarrassment for her fellow students, teetering in the new shoes she couldn't really afford, Nona

Wells turned to her partner. In the shuffle to pair up, she'd gotten a rotund, sweaty-palmed fellow whose eyes barely reached her chin. He had already proven himself clueless about the *salida cruzada*. As the music swelled, Nona left him to stumble in her wake while she executed the opening steps smartly, ending with her ankles neatly crossed in the prescribed position. The music stopped.

"Gentlemen, on count two you step outside partner," Rafael said. He surveyed the group. "Gentlemen, do you know what we mean by 'outside partner'?"

Embarrassed silence. Nona knew, of course, but since he had specified "gentlemen" she didn't speak up.

Rafael sighed. "Gentlemen, join me please on this side of the room. Ladies, opposite."

As Rafael and the men struggled through the *salida cruzada*, Nona used the time to practice her *ochos*, studying her form in the mirrored wall of the studio and, incidentally, admiring her feet in the new shoes. The shoes were black suede, with dangerously high heels, open toes, and crossed straps at the ankles. Beyond that they were naughty-looking, expensive, and designed especially for dancing tango. Nona would have to give up something, maybe even something as significant as lunch for a while, to pay for them, but she would do it gladly.

Trying to keep her balance while pivoting back and forth in the figure eights of the forward *ocho*, Nona raised her eyes to watch Rafael's reflection. The instructor looked tired tonight, with dun-colored circles under his eyes. His chinos were rumpled, his blue crew-neck sweater frayed, his black practice shoes battered from long use. Yet how beautiful he was, as he showed the lumpish men how to lead the *salida cruzada*. His long neck was straight, his dark, close-cropped head regal, his slim body upright, his stride commanding. His every move was a picture of grace and self-containment. Nona sighed and shifted her attention back to her own feet.

"Now! Ladies?" Nona's heart was pumping fiercely as she

joined the other women. Maybe Rafael would choose her to demonstrate the *salida cruzada* with him. He knew she could do it, as this was the sixth time she had taken one of his tango classes. In a few past instances, he had selected her to step through a figure with him. These moments blazed in her memory. She could summon at will the sensation of his dry, warm palm against her own, the firm pressure of his hand on her back, the aroma of cigarettes that rose from his clothes, the whiff of peppermint on his breath.

She steeled herself against disappointment, and indeed it came. Rafael turned to a pretty Asian woman in a tight blue velvet turtleneck to demonstrate with him. The woman, despite her beauty, was not particularly adept, and Nona looked away rather than watch a subpar performance. When it was over, Rafael told them to change partners and try again.

As usual, Nona had a couple of questions after class, but before she could reach him Rafael had taken his tapes and vanished. She didn't see him in the hubbub around the registration desk, so she assumed he'd gone downstairs for a smoke. When she emerged onto the freezing Manhattan sidewalk, however, he was not huddled in his usual corner of the doorway.

Nona wilted. Shivering as the cold wind cut through her coat and chilled her perspiring body, she settled her new vinyl shoe bag on her shoulder and shoved her hands deeper in her pockets. The evening was over. There was nothing to do but go home.

From time to time Nona, marveling at the vicissitudes of life, reminded herself that six months previous she had known nothing of tango. As she approached the age of twenty-five, how drab her existence had been! Her job as assistant office manager for an Upper East Side dentist; her home, a dark little maid's room sublet with kitchen privileges; her mousy looks and clerk's wardrobe; her chronic lack of funds—all were the attributes of a pathetic loser, which Nona had been before she discovered tango.

When Nona thought back on it, the entry of tango into her life was haloed with a mystic glow. It was a sweltering July afternoon. Kevin, the man Nona had come to think of as her fiancé, had invited her out for coffee after work and informed her that his company was transferring him to Chicago. He thought it best, given the circumstances, that he and Nona suspend their relationship.

The coffee shop had been a regular, crummy New York coffee shop, not even as nice as a Starbucks. The coffee was the usual New York coffee. Even on the occasion of breaking up with her, Kevin was too cheap to pay for a cappuccino or a latte. Nona gazed into her thick white cup of pale brown swill and half-listened as Kevin spoke of being very busy getting settled in a new environment, and not wanting her to hope for more than he was able to offer. When he stopped for breath she glanced at him. His eyes were small and shifty behind the lenses of his glasses. His haircut was ragged, and his tie was polyester. Had she actually considered marrying this creep? I've always compromised, Nona thought. Why have I always settled for less?

"I hope you'll still think of me as a friend, Nona," Kevin said.

Nona gathered herself. "I don't know why I should ever think of you at all," she retorted. Buoyed by this perfect parting shot, she rose and floated out the door, leaving Kevin agape behind her. She made it almost as far as the subway station before her eyes started to well up. Stopping to dig a tissue from her bag, she blotted her tears and found herself staring at a flyer taped to a lamppost: ADD ROMANCE TO YOUR LIFE! LEARN ARGENTINE TANGO! it said. Beneath the heading was a picture, a silhouette of a man and woman locked in intimate terpsichorean embrace. *All levels, beginner to advanced!*, the flyer offered, followed by the name and address of the Do You Wanna Dance Studio.

Studying the flyer, Nona blew her nose. As if hypnotized, she detached the sheet of paper from the lamppost, folded it, and put it away in her bag. She deposited the used tissue in the nearest garbage receptacle and, in no further danger of crying, proceeded to the subway. The defining moment had come and gone.

Cruzada

THE Do You Wanna Dance Studio was a fourth-floor walk-up in Greenwich Village, a warren of mirrored rooms off dusty corridors with a registration lobby near the stairs. By dumb luck, Nona signed up for a Beginning Argentine Tango section taught by Rafael. Five minutes after the first class began, she had already begun to feel momentous changes blooming inside her. She, Nona Wells, assistant dental office manager, could learn tango. And if Nona Wells learned tango, she would no longer be the Nona Wells of old. Rafael was explaining the *salida*, the entrance to the dance. He played a pulsing instrumental and asked them to clap to the surging beat. Clapping energetically, Nona let the music speak to her. It told of circumstances that were dark, enticing, and foreign to the previous experience of Nona Wells.

"To dance tango, you must free your mind and your body," said Rafael in his intriguing Argentine accent. "Nothing is regimented. You must find yourself in the music. I will simply suggest, point the way. The discovery belongs to you." Nona was breathless with excitement.

Never having been much of a dancer, Nona admitted freely that she did not have a natural aptitude for Argentine tango. As she saw it, this was besides the point. Because she lacked talent, Rafael would be all the more impressed with her diligence. Nona imagined attending, at sometime in the future, a tango night at one of the clubs around town. Rafael would be there. Recognizing her as a student, he would invite her to dance out of politeness. They would enter the requisite close embrace. The music would swell. And then . . . And then . . .

The problem, as always, was money. With some difficulty Nona had gotten together the seventy-five-dollar tuition for the beginners class, but classes lasted only four sessions per month. She would need another seventy-five the next month, and the month after that, and the month after that, and onward until the faraway day when she could be a worthy partner for Rafael. In the short term, how could she possibly afford seventy-five dollars for the next class?

The answer came as the end of the first month approached. Nona had developed the habit of showing up early for class and hanging around, hoping to catch a glimpse of Rafael. Often, he arrived only minutes before class began, but on one or two red-letter occasions she found him downstairs smoking and was able to overcome her shyness and pepper him with questions on the finer points of tango. He answered courteously, if languidly, drawing deeply on his cigarette and emitting small puffs of smoke, glancing occasionally at his watch.

One evening before class, having failed to find Rafael downstairs, Nona was dawdling near the unmanned registration desk when the phone began to ring. No one showed up to answer it after five peals, so Nona reached over the counter, picked up the receiver, and in her best office-manager manner, said, "Do You Wanna Dance Studio. This is Nona. How may I help you?"

The caller had a question about the schedule, which Nona handled easily. By the time she hung up, the woman in charge had returned from the ladies' room and had heard enough to be convinced of Nona's competence. On the spot, a deal was struck: Nona would help out at the desk three nights a week in return for a deep discount on class tuition.

This was a perfect arrangement. Nona now had an excuse

to hang out at the studio. She also had clandestine access to
the Do You Wanna Dance personnel files. During quiet
moments she perused Rafael's. Rafael Estrada, she learned,
had arrived in the United States only a few months before.
His previous work experience had been in Buenos Aires,
where he danced in tango shows presented to the tourist
trade. He was thirty-five years old and divorced. He had an
East Village address.

Nona copied Rafael's address into her book. Within a
day or so, she had decided to take a trip downtown to see
where he lived.

On a Saturday afternoon, Nona got off the subway at
Astor Place and wandered off through the East Village
streets. Despite the continuing gentrification of the neighborhood, Rafael's block, when she found it, was unimpres-
sive. The street was strewn with garbage, and Rafael's
building was a decrepit-looking tenement structure with a
couple of basement windows boarded up. Next door was a
weed-choked vacant lot surrounded by a chain-link fence.
Nona stood across the street for a while, surveying the de-
pressing scene. A man of Rafael's talent should not have to
live in such a place. She wondered if any of the windows
overlooking the street belonged to his apartment. She imagined him glancing out, and catching sight of her here on
the sidewalk. He would smile and hold up a slim finger to
tell her to wait and he'd be down in a minute, and he would
bound gracefully out the shabby front door and down the
dirty steps, and when he reached her side he would say,
"Why, it's Nona from my class! What are you doing here,
Nona?" And Nona would say she was just passing by, and
he would invite her to have a coffee at the grubby-looking
cafe on the corner. They would drink lattes and Rafael would
smoke and they would talk about tango. Nona smiled to
herself, cozy in the warmth of her thoughts.

After that day, Nona often found the time to visit Rafael's
street. As the weather grew colder, she began to frequent

the grubby-looking cafe on the corner. The Java Time Coffee Bar, she discovered, had window tables with a perfect view of Rafael's building. Treated with total indifference by the ever-changing staff, Nona spent hours there, sipping a decaf latte, dreaming of Rafael and wishing he would appear.

The day after Rafael chose the Asian woman to demonstrate the *salida cruzada* with him, Nona felt low. She knew the *salida cruzada*. She even had new shoes. Why hadn't Rafael picked her? Perhaps she would feel better about the situation if she took a trip down to his neighborhood after work.

Icy wind swept the street, rattling bottles in the gutter and flattening runaway plastic bags against the chain-link fence. Nona's coat, adequate for brisk fall weather, was overmatched by the winter blast, and she was glad to step into the dim fug of the Java Time. She was making her way to a table when she saw, tucked in a back corner, a familiar face. She couldn't believe it at first. After all the time she'd spent thinking of Rafael, had she actually caused him to materialize? Wasn't that Rafael, sitting at a table near the rest rooms? Nona's heart contorted with painful, inexpressible joy for a split second before she was plunged into the depths. It was Rafael, it truly was. And he was not alone.

Rafael had not seen Nona. How could he have seen Nona, when he was focused so intently on his woman companion?

Rafael's companion was speaking in an animated way. In the half-light in the back of the room, she seemed to glisten. Her frosted hair, long enough to sweep her shoulders, gave off the gleam of expensive treatment in a carpeted and aromatic salon. Her simple and exquisite suit clung to a slim body that surely had been toned by the most chic personal trainers. Her crossed legs shimmered all the way down to feet clad in shoes whose value was roughly equivalent to several months' rent. And tossed over the back of her chair, its sleeves resting on the dusty floor, was a sable coat capa-

cious and luxurious enough to drive animal rights activists
to despair.

Nona stopped gaping and stumbled to her accustomed
window table. She sank down in a chair, her head and shoulders drooping. If she looked out the window to her right,
she could see Rafael's building. If she looked across the room
to her left, she could see Rafael himself, deep in oblivious
conversation with the rich bitch. Both of them were smoking, although they were undoubtedly seated in a no-
smoking area. Their words were inaudible, but their every
movement, the attitudes of their bodies, bespoke intimacy.

There was a sour taste in Nona's mouth that her decaf
latte did nothing to dispel. Wretchedly, she watched as,
some fifteen minutes later, Rafael and his companion prepared to leave. After the woman put down money for the
coffee, she allowed Rafael to help her into the sable. Taking
no notice of Nona, nor of the other patrons, they swept out
the door. With a better view, Nona saw that the woman,
for all that she was trim and toned, was not as young as
she'd appeared from a distance. This was small consolation
when Nona's perfectly situated table allowed her to watch
the two of them crossing the street and entering Rafael's
building together.

Nona spent the next day in a hell of desolation. It was
an effort to get out of bed in the morning, much less hassle
with nervous patients and wrangle with insurance companies. Still, she managed, just barely, to get through it. That
evening at the studio, as Nona brooded at the desk, the
phone rang and she answered. A woman with a Spanish
accent said, in a husky voice, "I'm calling for Rafael Estrada."

It was the same woman. There was simply no doubt about
it. Swallowing her agitation, Nona said, "I'll see if he's in.
May I tell him who's calling?"

"It's Carolina."

Rafael was not at the studio, as Nona already knew. She

gave herself a minute to calm down and got back on the line. "I'm afraid he isn't here. May I give him a message?"

"Ask him to call Carolina," the woman said, and added a number that, Nona could tell from the prefix, was for a cell phone.

Nona repeated the number and added, "Carolina, you said? Is there a last name?"

"He knows," Carolina said, and hung up.

Nona put the message on the instructors' bulletin board after copying the cell phone number in her book. She gave it fifteen minutes before dialing back. Carolina picked up on the first ring and said, breathlessly, "Rafi?"

Her gorge rising, Nona broke the connection. Rafi, for God's sake.

When she tried again later, Nona was more successful. A recording of the now-familiar accented voice said that Nona had reached the voice mail messaging system of Carolina O'Toole, who asked that she leave a name and number after the beep. Nona hung up. Next to the cell phone number in her book, she wrote: "Carolina O'Toole."

The next step had to wait until Nona got home that night. Sitting in her pajamas at the folding card table she used for a desk, a cup of tea at her elbow, Nona flipped open her laptop and logged on. She called up a search engine, entered "Carolina O'Toole," and sat back to see if she'd get any hits.

The results exceeded, by quite a bit, her most extravagant expectations. Within half an hour, Nona had learned many salient facts about Carolina O'Toole, starting with the most striking: Carolina was married, the third wife of one Lucius O'Toole, a billionaire philanthropist and financier. On the web site devoted to The Lucius Companies, the umbrella organization for the varied interests of Lucius O'Toole, Nona clicked the "Our Leader" option and discovered a profile of Lucius and Carolina, complete with a photo of the happy couple. Lucius, squatty and ferocious-looking, with a formidable nose and shaggy eyebrows, sat on a sofa while Carolina, perched on the arm, draped herself above him. The woman in the picture was indeed the same shimmering woman Nona had seen with Rafael in the Java Time Coffee Bar.

Surfing around, Nona found out that Lucius and Carolina had apartments in Manhattan and Paris, a seaside estate in the Hamptons, and a villa in the South of France. For relaxation, they shot skeet and took friends for cruises on their yacht.

Lucius, Nona learned, had given away millions of dollars to worthy causes. He was widely quoted as saying honesty and integrity were the qualities he valued above all else. Nona gathered from some of the less laudatory sources that Lucius was also known for his volcanic temper and intolerance of disloyalty. He had summarily divorced the previous Mrs. O'Toole after discovering that she had given clandestine support to a charity of which he disapproved. Lucius and Carolina, by contrast, were divinely happy after three years of marriage. "Carolina keeps me young," Lucius was quoted as saying.

There was a great deal more. Charity balls and foundation boards; skiing vacations and fashion shows; opera galas and museum openings.

Nona sat back and rubbed her weary eyes, then squinted at her watch. It was after one in the morning. She'd have to be sure she didn't oversleep and come in late to the office. Unlike some people, Nona had to work for a living.

Nona dragged herself through the following day, constantly tormented by thoughts of Carolina O'Toole and Rafael together. At the studio that evening, she was so exhausted she almost didn't notice the stack of brochures on the counter next to the class schedules. Advertising materials were often put out for students to take, and at first glance this brochure seemed much like many others. It was an announcement of a dance tour: *Tango in Buenos Aires* in large black letters on a bright red background. In smaller letters, underneath—

Nona blinked. In smaller letters underneath, it said, *with Rafael Estrada*. Tango in Buenos Aires with Rafael Estrada. Rafael was leading a tango tour to Argentina.

Trembling, Nona devoured the brochure. Yes, there was a photo of Rafael, smiling as she had never seen him smile. Rafael, "renowned in the *milongas* for his refined technique," would share his secrets with tour participants on the sites where tango was born. For ten full days in April the group would study and practice with Rafael and other masters of tango, dance at the most up-to-the-minute clubs and salons, experience the dazzling city of Buenos Aires by day and by night. They would be accommodated at a four-star hotel in the vibrant city center, with breakfast, but no other meals, included.

Yes. Breakfast, but no other meals, included in the price of the package. Nona swallowed rapidly as her eyes skimmed down the page. There at the bottom, she found it. The price of the package was: three thousand five hundred dollars.

Oh, God. Nona put down the brochure and stared at it dully. There was no way.

But she had to go. Nona had to go on that tour. It was her chance to make an impression on Rafael, let him get to know her, show him how much more Nona had to offer than an older married woman, wealthy though the woman was. For three thousand five hundred dollars, Nona could be with Rafael in Buenos Aires for ten days. She had to go. She had to.

There was no way. No way. No way.

Nona rested her face in her hands. She gave herself up to despair.

Ocho

THE next day, Nona was calm. Sometime during the night, clarity had emerged. Nona was going to Buenos Aires. She would do whatever it took to get herself on that tour. Once she had accepted that proposition, the struggle ceased and a plan evolved.

That afternoon after work, Nona took a crosstown bus and disembarked in a West Side neighborhood she rarely frequented. The sky was overcast, a few fat snowflakes swirling in the wind. No one on the sidewalk was likely to notice unremarkable Nona, in her inadequate coat and her knitted cap. She was just one more person among the cold multitudes.

She spent a while looking around, and found a working telephone booth on a busy corner. She closed herself inside, dropped her quarter in the slot, and dialed the number. This could be the first of many attempts, but Nona had accepted that possibility. She would do what had to be done, if it meant phoning every hour on the hour for a week.

In the event, that wasn't necessary. After three short rings, Carolina O'Toole said, "Hello?"

Nona gazed out over the windswept street. "I know about you and Rafael Estrada," she said in a chilly, uninflected voice.

"What? Who is this?" Carolina, Nona was pleased to note, sounded apprehensive rather than outraged.

Nona went on, "How would your husband feel if he knew about Rafi? That's what you call him, isn't it? Rafi?"

"I don't know what you think you're playing at, but—"

"I hear Mr. O'Toole has a temper. He might not be too happy with you."

"You're insane!"

Her tone more steely, Nona said, "You'll regret it if you don't take me seriously, Carolina. I suggest you stop pretending."

There was a long pause. Nona watched the sluggish traffic moving through the thickening snow. Her feet were cold.

"What do you want?" Carolina said.

Capitulation! Now that she'd won, Nona started to shake. Trying to keep the tremors out of her voice she said, "I want five thousand dollars in twenties. Put it in a plastic bag and drop it in the trash can in the ladies' room at the Java Time Coffee Bar." Having visited the ladies' room often, Nona knew that the trash can was the metal swing-top variety, so no one could see what was in it. She also knew that the rest room door could be locked from the inside while she took the money out.

"Where?" Carolina sounded confused.

"The Java Time Coffee Bar." Nona named the street and said, "You were there with Rafi, remember?"

"Ah. Yes."

"Do it tomorrow night at eight-thirty."

Carolina hesitated. "Tomorrow night? Tomorrow night I have a commitment already."

Intense fury rocketed through Nona's body. "Do you want me to call Lucius?" she snarled. "I can call him right now, if that's what you want!"

"No! I was just—"

"Then shut up about your commitments and do as I tell you!"

"All right! Yes! Tomorrow night!"

Nona lowered her voice to an ominous whisper. "Don't say a word to anyone about this. If you let me down you'll be very sorry, Carolina." She hung up and pushed the door of the phone booth open. Cold air and snowflakes came gusting in.

That night, in Rafael's class, they worked on the back *ocho*. Nona wore her new shoes. She had practiced the back *ocho* to exhaustion, steadying herself against the wall of her bedroom. Step back, shift weight, pivot to face the opposite direction. It was difficult to keep her balance, especially in the shoes.

Rafael stopped the music. He said, "Ladies, you must shift the weight before you turn. Do not fling your leg out. Come."

He was holding his hand out toward Nona. Rafael was inviting Nona to join him in the middle of the floor.

Nona stepped forward into Rafael's arms. She felt the rough wool of his sweater under her left hand, the dry warmth of his palm in her right. She smelled the cigarettes on his clothes and the peppermint on his breath. She saw a pulse beating in his neck, and black stubble on his chin, and a patch of chapped skin on his bottom lip. She responded to the pressure of his hand on her back as he led her into the steps that would culminate in a back *ocho*.

A fleeting burst of enchantment, and it was over. "Very good," Rafael muttered, and patted Nona briefly on the shoulder in dismissal. Addressing the class he said, "Did you see how economically she moved? How balanced she was? Keep your knees soft, and then . . ." Nona bent her head. She blotted the sweat from her hairline with her sleeve.

The next night, Nona treated herself to a taxi downtown to the Java Time. She had planned to arrive at eight-forty-five, but the traffic was heavy and it was nearly nine when she walked in the door. The coffee bar looked much as usual—dim lights, scattered patrons, lackadaisical staff. There was no sign of Carolina.

Although she was anxious to have the episode finished, Nona would not allow herself to rush directly to the ladies' room. To avert suspicion, she forced herself to sit down and have a decaf latte. When she had taken her last milky sip and paid the check, she gathered her things, including her largest shoulder bag, and went to the ladies' room.

Someone was in the stall, so Nona busied herself combing her hair and applying lipstick until the woman emerged, washed her hands, and left. After the door closed, Nona punched the lock and turned to the trash can. Pushing back the swinging metal lid and peering inside, she saw a layer of wadded paper towels, with the odd tissue mixed in. She lifted the top of the can in order to dig deeper. Delicately moving aside the waste paper, she caught a glimpse of white plastic. Was that it? She tugged on a corner and lifted it out. It was a Gristede's bag with the handles knotted together. From the heft of it, it definitely could be holding something like two hundred fifty twenty-dollar bills.

Nona untied the handles and looked inside. There was indeed a fair-sized packet of money, neatly bundled in plastic cling wrap. Nona pulled off the cling wrap and riffled through the bills. It looked as if Carolina had followed instructions exactly. Shaking with relief, Nona tied the cash in the plastic bag again, shoved it in her shoulder bag, put on her coat, and opened the bathroom door. She was suddenly desperate to get out of the Java Time Coffee Bar. She hurried across the room toward the front door.

Nona smelled Carolina before she saw her. A whiff of tuberoses wafted by, and then a husky, accented voice behind her said, "Now we will get to the bottom of things." A strong grip closed on Nona's elbow. "I have a gun in my pocket, my dear little friend," Carolina said. "Be quiet and calm, and continue out the door."

Nona was numb. Although she could see that the wind was howling down the street, she did not feel the cold. She said, "Where were you?"

"I gave the manager fifty dollars to let me hide in the kitchen and watch for you through the door," Carolina said. "I told him you were my estranged daughter, and I was seeking you out to make amends for our differences. I said I was afraid if you saw me you'd run away before I could apologize."

"But—" Nona turned to look over her shoulder as Carolina frog-marched her down the deserted sidewalk. "How did you know it was me?"

"I didn't, until I saw you walk in."

"But you'd never seen me before!"

"Of course I had. I saw you goggling at us the day I was there with Rafi. When people stare at me, I always notice."

"I'll give you the money back," Nona said. "It's in my bag. Go ahead and take it."

Carolina laughed. "Darling, what is five thousand dollars to me? No, no. I think we must sort this out, all of us together." She gave Nona a push. "We're going to cross the street now."

Looming across the street was the tenement building where Rafael lived, the building Nona had spent so many hours watching. "No!" Nona struggled and tried to pull away. "I won't!"

Carolina's gloved hand slipped from the pocket of her sable coat. In it was a small, snub-nosed gun. "Don't be stupid," she said. "Let's cross the street, shall we?"

They crossed the street and climbed the dirty stone steps. At the top, Carolina pressed a buzzer and after a moment or two a voice said, "Yes?"

"Carolina," she said, and the door clicked to let them into a dingy lobby.

"Upstairs," Carolina said, gesturing with the gun toward a dark staircase. They climbed two flights, Nona first and Carolina right behind. Then Carolina directed Nona down a faintly-lit hallway toward the back of the building. Rafael had no front window after all, Nona thought. There was no chance he'd look out and see me. No chance, ever.

They stopped in front of a scarred metal door. Carolina rapped, the door opened, and Rafael stepped back to let them in.

Rafael was in sock feet, wearing a white sleeveless undershirt and his chinos. His sinewy shoulders were pale in contrast to his tanned face. The room was small and smoky, the furniture dilapidated and sparse. A cigarette burned in an ashtray on the coffee table next to a bottle of red wine, a half-full glass, and a crumpled McDonald's carton. Rafael gave Nona a blank look as he closed the door, then turned to Carolina and said, "*¿Que pasa?*"

Carolina chuckled. Glancing at Nona she said, in English, "I've brought your friend for a visit, Rafi. I'm afraid she screwed up your plan."

"My plan? My friend?" Rafael looked more closely at Nona. Frowning, he said to her, "Haven't you taken one of my tango classes?"

Rafael barely recognized her. The bitter irony was not lost on Nona, even in her present circumstances. She tried to say "Six," but choked on the word. She cleared her throat. "I took six of your classes."

"I'm disappointed in you, Rafi," Carolina said. "What a stupid, small-time scheme. And to use this poor girl to do the dirty work! I thought you had more panache."

"Look. Let me say something," Nona put in. "Rafael had nothing to do with—"

"I'll tell you what I'll do," Carolina said. "Keep my five thousand dollars, all right? Keep it with my compliments. Take it, go away somewhere, and leave me alone."

Rafael's eyes narrowed. "Five thousand dollars? Don't be absurd. You spend more than that on manicures every year. You and I have only begun to discuss what I want from you, Carolina."

Beneath her flawless makeup, Carolina's face flushed. "You greedy bastard! How much do you think you and your friends are going to bleed out of me? I see now what a mistake I made, trying to treat you with courtesy."

"Courtesy! You mean you condescended to me," Rafael said. "But whatever airs you put on, you're as much a whore today as you were when you walked the streets of Buenos Aires!"

Carolina took a step forward and spat vigorously at Rafael, a cloud of saliva exploding from her lips.

Rafael turned to Nona and said, mockingly, "Do you see how refined she is?"

Carolina, her nostrils flaring, also spoke to Nona. "He enjoys insulting me, but he's nothing more than a blackmailer, a leech who can't make his own way without preying on others."

Rafael's mouth contorted. "Carolina never preys on others," he said. "She wouldn't dream of preying on anyone, especially a billionaire who believes she's forty-five years old when she's nearly sixty! Especially an old man who thinks she was bred in a convent instead of in the gutter!"

"Keep quiet, Rafi," Carolina said in a soft voice.

Rafael ignored the warning. To Nona, he said, "Do you want to know what kind of woman she is? A woman who abandoned her son, her own little son, in the streets! She left him to fend for himself while she went away to create a new life. I suppose she thought he'd forget her after all those years, but he didn't!" Rafael's voice was hoarse, his eyes red. "He didn't forget, not for a day. And when he saw her photograph in the newspaper with the rich man she married, he knew he had to find her again. He would find her, and he would get what she owed him!"

"I said keep quiet!" The gun was trembling in Carolina's hand.

"Five thousand dollars!" Rafael sneered. "You think I would take five thousand dollars and go away? Well, I refuse your generous offer, Mama! I'm staying here, Mama! You'd better get used to it, Mama! You won't get rid of me again!"

"I told you never to call me Mama," Carolina said. She set her feet, took aim, and pulled the trigger.

Nona shuddered and jumped away as Rafael crumpled to the floor, a red stain spreading on his undershirt. She saw his eyes lose focus, and heard him whisper *"Mama!"* as his head dropped to one side.

"Rafi!" Carolina dropped the gun and fell to her knees

beside Rafael. "Rafi," she sobbed, cradling his head. "Rafi! My baby! My son!"

Nona ran for the stairs.

Resolución

NONA lay on the bed in her room, watching the curtains blow in the warm February breeze. Sounds of the city drifted in, the bustle of traffic, and, somewhere nearby, the pulsing beat of a tango coming from somebody's radio. She had a lesson later this afternoon. She had practiced hard. She hoped Diego would be impressed with her progress.

After a couple of days in a youth hostel, Nona had found a small room for rent not far from the San Telmo district, the center of tango in Buenos Aires. A fellow boarder at the hostel had told her about Diego's classes. After a few more weeks of study, Nona might work up the courage to go out to the *milongas* that lined the San Telmo streets. She would wear her shoes, now well broken-in. Although her budget was tight, perhaps it would allow her to buy a black skirt and a red satin top. She would ask Diego where to go, and perhaps, just perhaps, he would offer to accompany her.

Diego was gorgeous, with tousled brown curls, dimples, and full lips that curved upward in a charming way. He wore loose black trousers, black silk shirts, and shoes with a slightly built-up heel. His dancing was fluid and graceful, natural as the swirls and eddies of a river.

Nona had decided it was wise, under the circumstances, to get out of New York. Luckily, she had had in her bag the means to do it, and do it quickly. Not that she expected Carolina to pursue her. Nona thought Carolina would leave Nona alone if Nona returned the favor. As for Rafael . . . Nona chewed her lip. She didn't like to think of Rafael. Even in her rush to get out of town she had taken time to skim the newspapers, and she had come across a small paragraph dealing with the discovery of his body in his East Village apartment. The police were searching for leads. They suspected that the killer was a desperate drug addict.

Nona sat up. She had to get ready for class. She wanted to arrive early, because she had thought of a couple of questions to ask Diego. His English was quite good, although sometimes he made adorable mistakes. Nona's Spanish was improving every day, too. It should be adequate when the time came to look for a job.

Nona fished her tango shoes from under the bed, slipped her feet into them, and started to fasten the straps. She had a few extra minutes to practice her *ochos*. Then it would be time to go.

IN THE MERRY MONTH OF MAYHEM

Joyce Harrington

A MELIA Potter sat at her parlor window watching the street. There was plenty to be seen, and she saw it all. And she wrote it all down in the small leather-bound diary given to her by the strange young man who had knocked at her door one day several weeks ago when she didn't know how she would pay the grocer's bill without taking in boarders. Red-haired he was, and bespectacled, and very polite. And he instructed her in her duties with a grave reverence befitting her age. Amelia was as pleased by his manners as she was by the generous wage he offered for her trouble.

It wasn't a room he wanted but her help in locating a missing person. He was a private detective, he told her, and a young woman was thought to be hiding from her parents in one of the houses on this street. It was a delicate question of the girl refusing to marry the man her parents had selected for her. He could not tell her the girl's name; her family was well-known in the city. Nor could the police be called in, for the same reason. All Amelia would be required to do was to write down in the diary everything she saw: visitors to the houses across the street, deliveries of goods, removal of luggage or furniture, and so on. And of course the presence of young ladies of any description going into or coming out of any of the houses.

Hour by hour, night after night, and all her waking hours during the day, Amelia watched and wrote. The young man had told her that night-watching was more important to his purposes than was the day, so Amelia slept for a few hours after the sun rose. At her age, she didn't seem to need much sleep, and it didn't matter to her when she slept.

Whenever she had to leave her post, she called her simple, but much beloved, son to sit there in her stead, and then quizzed him thoroughly upon her return. It was a peculiar kind of job, but it suited her well. She liked sitting at the window, watching the passing parade. She'd been doing it for years. The only thing that was new was writing it all down.

For instance, at that very moment, in the gathering twilight, before the electrified street lamps came on, a group of four young men came hurrying along, two abreast, on the narrow sidewalk. Definitely not laboring men. Too dandified for that. Nor were they prosperous businessmen on their way home to hearth and family. Their peacock clothing and stiffly waxed mustaches spoke loudly of the racetrack or the theatrical trade. They might even be traveling salesmen or newspaper reporters.

Through her open window, Amelia caught snatches of their banter.

". . . so I gave it to her right back. 'You're no lily-white blossom yourself,' says I. 'If it's wedding bells you're after, you'll have to find another damned patsy. Nobody forced you to team up with me.' The hell with her."

"That's givin' it to her straight. But do you think she'd really get the shysters on you?"

"Don't be such a noodle. What lawyer would touch it? She can't prove the kid is mine. That's if there really is a bundle on the way."

"Ah, Frankie, you've crowed plenty about all the by-blows you've got scattered around town. Don't start denying them now."

As the group passed out of sight and hearing, Amelia shook her head as she jotted down their description and as much of their conversation as she could remember, leaving out only the profanity.

It was terrible the way the city had changed since she was a girl growing up in this house and the lamplighter came around every evening at dusk to light the gas. And the shame of it was that no one seemed to care. The city swarmed with rough immigrants from every country on earth. There was noise and filth and danger everywhere. Women had grown bold, and men, well, she'd never understood them anyway, but they seemed louder, coarser, less respectful than the godlike beings of her girlhood.

Her handsome father had been distant and preoccupied with his shipping business, but when he found time for her, he always spoke gently and praised her small accomplishments. She had married late, partly out of reluctance to be separated from him, and then, when she finally agreed to a wedding date, the Civil War intervened. Her betrothed, who was tall, attentive, endearingly clumsy, and not at all handsome, had been killed at Antietam. Some years later, after her father had died, she had married Mr. Eldridge Potter, his bachelor business partner, out of no great love but a simple need for even so tenuous a link with the idol of her childhood. Mr. Potter had treated her with great civility but, like her father, was distant and preoccupied with business. When he succumbed to the cholera, she scarcely noticed his absence. Their son, Amos, was then four years old and claimed all her time and affection.

And so they had lived together, mother and son, for thirty years, in the house where Amelia had lived her entire life. Her own mother, once a fashionable beauty, had grown bitter and solitary after the death of her husband, refusing to see her grandson and keeping to her rooms at the top of the house. "Amelia," she would mutter when her dinner tray was placed before her, "you should have him put away. I'm ashamed to show my face. All my friends know there's an idiot in the family."

"He's not an idiot," Amelia would murmur softly. "Why, he can button his own shoes, and he speaks quite nicely sometimes. He understands more than you think. And I love him."

"Love!" the recluse would snort. "What do you know of love? I loved your father and look what it's done to me. Left me alone and ill, with no one to look after me."

"But, Mother," Amelia would protest. "How can you say that? I'm here."

"You! Well, thank you very much for the few minutes you can spare from watching over your simpleton. I don't know how this could have happened to me. There's never been any insanity in my family. Here. Take this food away. The mere thought of that beastly child destroys what little appetite I have."

Amelia felt nothing but relief when her mother finally complained her last. By that time, her son was twelve years old, tall for his age and amazingly strong. She had tried to teach him his letters and simple arithmetic, but he grew violently angry when he failed to master them, and so she gave it up. The doctor had suggested placing him in an institution for the feeble-minded, but Amelia had fainted dead away at the suggestion and it was never mentioned again. There was no question of sending him to school. No school would have him. And after catering to her mother's every whim, there wasn't enough money left for hiring private tutors. The boy was happiest when given chores to do that taxed his strength. He carried coal for the kitchen stove and rolled up the carpets for the annual spring-cleaning. He learned to whistle, and could imitate the chirp of the birds that visited the small rear garden. And he adored his mother.

Peering into the deepening darkness beyond her window, Amelia noticed a ragged child picking over a pile of refuse in the gutter. Her heart ached at the sight, but there were so many of these urchins swarming through the streets at all hours of the night and day. Where did they all come from? This one had the thick, curly black hair and swarthy complexion that stamped him one of the recent hordes of Italian peasants that flowed into the city from Ellis Island. The child picked something up, wiped it on his grimy shirt, crammed it into his mouth, and ran off. Amelia noted the event in her diary.

Then, her own stomach advising her that it was supper time, she went to the parlor door and called, "Amos. Amos, dear. Come here, please."

She closed the window and waited, listening for the heavy footsteps of her thirty-year-old son. What would become of him when she died or became too feeble to care for him? Would he be reduced to scraping in the gutters for food? Shuddering, she called for him again.

Amos came, his slow steps resounding from the stairs leading to the cellar, where he had made for himself a sort of nest behind the gigantic furnace that heated the entire house during the winters. There he kept his collection of feathers dropped from the birds captured by the fierce cats that prowled freely through the back gardens. There he kept his quilt and his pillow and a candle to light the ever-present gloom.

When his enormous round head rose from the stairwell, Amelia bustled forward to greet him. "Are you hungry, Amos, dear?"

His head bobbed enthusiastically, causing the fine, thin hairs to bounce about his ears. "Mmm," he droned. "Hungry." And a huge grin enlivened his moon face.

"That's a good boy," his mother said. "Come sit by the window and I'll bring our supper presently."

She guided him to the window seat, grasping his arm

firmly and steering him away from the fragile ornaments that decked most of the flat surfaces in the room. The giant towered above her, but meekly allowed himself to be led.

"Now, you remember what you must do, Amos. Watch the street every minute and then tell me what you see. Tell me you remember."

"Remember," the giant assured her, with much head-bobbing. "Amos good. Amos watch. Tell Ma."

"That's right. And you'll have a fine dessert. But you must eat your supper first."

"Supper first," he echoed, licking his wide lips extravagantly while a happy rumble emanated from deep in his throat. Then he turned his face to the window and froze into an attentive, forward-leaning position.

Amelia stood looking at him for a moment, her lined face a battleground of pity and despair. Then she hurried away to the kitchen, where the daily scullery maid, the only help she could afford to hire, had left a supper of cold chicken, pickled beets, and rice pudding.

When she returned ten minutes later bearing their modest supper on a tray, she found Amos standing with his nose pressed against the window, his entire body quivering with excitement.

"What is it?" she asked, setting the tray down on the marble-topped table in the window bay. "What have you seen?" She joined her son at the window, but saw nothing out of the ordinary.

Amos babbled and pointed, unable to make clear to her what had transpired in the street that had so unnerved him.

"It's all right, my dear." She petted him and stroked his wildly rolling head, urging him with little pushes toward his chair. "Be calm, Amos. Be very calm, and then try to tell me. Take a sip of this nice lemonade. It's sweetened just the way you like it. Just a little sip, and then another little sip. That's right, my dear. Now, isn't that better?"

Little by little, the giant child-man ceased his trembling.

His head steadied itself upon his massive neck, although his eyes remained fixed on the window as if in hypnotic dread of the scene he had witnessed. He breathed deeply and uttered a dismal wail.

Amelia berated herself for being the cause of his distress. If she had waited only a few minutes, she would have seen the disturbing event herself. It was probably nothing worse than a passing cabman mistreating his horse. Amos could not abide any kind of cruelty to animals. Nonetheless, she would have to encourage him to speak of it, although it might upset him even more.

"Take some food now, Amos," she instructed. She placed a fork in his hand and curled his thick fingers around it. Still he sat staring out the window. "G-g-gone," he mumbled.

"Yes," said Amelia. "We'll talk about that later. Now you must eat. You'll feel much better then." There was some risk that he might forget what he had seen, but you could never tell with Amos. He was good with colors and smells, less good with size and numbers.

But Amos could not be deflected from his purpose. "Box!" he announced loudly. "Big, big box!"

"How big?" his mother asked.

Amos stood up and touched his head, then bent and touched his feet.

"As big as you are?"

"That big."

"How wide?"

Amos grinned and looked puzzled. "Big box fall," he offered tentatively. He sat down before his heaping plate and with both hands crammed his mouth full of chicken.

"That's right, Amos. Eat your supper." Amelia let his absence of table manners pass unremarked. To chide him now would only upset him further. She took a bite of her tiny portion and chewed it meditatively. What kind of box, she wondered, and whose box was it? And where had it gone? There was certainly no box in the street now.

Amos reclaimed her attention with a disjointed string of words that poured out of his mouth along with shreds of food and drops of spittle. From the torrent, Amelia could distinguish the word *box* repeated many times, and thought she heard the words *man* and *blood,* although she couldn't be sure. Attempting to divert the flow, she asked, "Did you see any horses?"

Amos stiffened. His jaws champed slowly at his food and presently he swallowed. His head bobbed once and he said quite clearly, "Hundred horse." Then he smiled.

"Very good, Amos," said his mother. "A hundred horses. That's very important. That's a fine thing to remember. Was there a carriage?" Amelia knew that Amos's hundred horses could mean any number greater than one.

"Black," Amos answered and resumed his attack upon his food. He seemed much calmer now, and Amelia decided to pursue the discussion before he forgot what he had seen.

"Was the carriage black?"

"Black."

"And the horses?"

"Black," came the impatient response.

"And the box?"

"Box fall. Man fall."

"Did the man fall out of the box?" Amelia was beginning to think that her son had witnessed the inept removal of a corpse from one of the houses opposite. The undertakers, no doubt drunk, had dropped the coffin, discharging its contents upon the sidewalk. A heartbreaking event for the family of the deceased, if true. The only thing wrong with such a theory was that, in all her hours of watching, she had not seen a medical man visit any of the houses, nor had she overheard, through her open window, any passing news of illness. Such news spread quickly through the streets; people became inflamed by the fear of epidemics. Amelia ceased her speculation. Amos was attempting to answer her question.

"Man," he said and paused, frowning over the memory. "Man," he tried again, ". . . jump. Have blood here." He struck his own forehead and wailed loudly.

"That's all right, Amos," his mother said. "We won't talk about it anymore." Quickly, she jotted a few notes into her diary. "Eat your rice pudding now."

She had not eaten more than a few mouthfuls of her own supper, but the food had lost its appeal. What on earth could he have seen, she wondered. A bloody corpse that leaped out of its coffin? Hardly likely, on this quiet street. But was it, in fact, the event that she'd been watching and waiting for all these weeks? She had never questioned the young man as to what exactly she should look for, and he had not volunteered any further information. "Write down everything you see," he had instructed her. And so she had done, and collected her five dollars every week. And so she did now, trying to make sense out of the strange tale Amos related.

But what would she tell young Mr. Crane when he called tomorrow? He would undoubtedly be disappointed that she had not more details. Perhaps he would decide to dispense with her services. Oh, if only she had waited a few more minutes before fetching their supper. Not only would she have spared Amos any distress, but she would have seen for herself this strange box and the man with blood on his head.

As she brooded over her failings and Amos lapped up his rice pudding, there came a sharp rapping at the front door, as if the bronze knocker had come alive and was beating out a tattoo to lead a charge into battle.

Amos dropped his pudding dish and scuttled for the stairs down to his nest in the cellar. Amelia rose and went to the door.

She peered through the lace-curtained glass pane in the center of the heavy door, but in the gathering gloom could not distinguish who was there. The rapping continued.

"Who's there?" she called out.

"Police!" came the muffled response. "There's been a murder."

"Oh, dear," Amelia murmured. "So that's what Amos saw." And she flung wide the door.

The man who stood there was no policeman. He was shabbily dressed and reeked of whiskey. He pushed her aside and entered the hall, slamming the door behind him. In his hand there suddenly appeared a dagger.

Amelia stood her ground. She was aware of Amos lurking on the back stairs, keeping well out of sight. "What do you want?" she demanded. "Get out of my house instantly."

"I'll get out," the man growled, "after I take care of you, ye old busybody. I seen ye watchin' at the window."

Amelia snatched up her umbrella from the coat rack and leveled its point at him. "Yes, I was watching, and I've already called the police on the telephone. They'll be here presently." Silently she prayed that Amos would stay where he was and not come rushing to her rescue.

"Then I'd best be quick," said the ruffian. He knocked the umbrella aside and lunged at Amelia with his dagger. Amelia, with an agility and strength she did not know she possessed, sidestepped his thrust, picked up a marble bust of Cicero from the hall table, and hurled it at her attacker. It struck him on the shoulder, but only enraged him further. He forced her to her knees and his dagger rose and fell, rose and fell, until she lay still and bleeding upon the hall runner. He stood for a moment, panting and viewing his handiwork with some satisfaction. Then he wiped his hands and the dagger on her skirts and fled, leaving the door behind him wide open.

After a time of silence, Amos crept out of his hiding place and along the hall to where his mother lay. "Ma?" he queried in a child's voice. He touched her face and her dress and examined his bloodied hands. He stroked her disheveled gray hair. "Talk, Ma," he begged, and when she did not, he tried to make her lips move, poking at them clumsily with his thick fingers. When no sound issued, when nothing he did evoked the usual loving response, the child-man rose to his feet and howled his longing. Then, attracted by the open front door that had never been left wide open in his experience, he went out and stood gazing into the night. A while later, he descended the stoop and shambled away westward along the street.

. . .

THE next morning, the neighbors gathered around the stoop and whispered among themselves as the police trooped in and out of the house. They all blamed Amos for the dreadful murder of his mother. The boldest among them, a stout gentleman with a remarkable set of handlebar mustaches, strode up to an official-looking person to offer his opinion.

"Find the idiot and you'll find the killer. The city's not safe with him abroad in it. He'll come back. This is the only place he knows. And he'll murder us all in our beds. I trust you'll be setting a guard on this house."

The official, who was, in fact, a captain of police, nodded sagely and said, "Thank you for your advice, sir. We'll certainly keep it in mind."

The crowd grew as passers-by joined it. Children who should have been on their way to school stopped to peer in the windows if they could. Businessmen and servants alike looked grave and troubled. Sedate matrons and silly shopgirls twittered to one another of what they would have done in Amelia's predicament. "I have no doubt that the poor creature would have been happier locked away with his own kind," a stately dame announced, "and his mother would be alive today." The plumed hats surrounding her bobbed in agreement. "I suppose he won't be coming to church anymore," murmured a wispy purse-mouthed creature swathed in voluminous folds of mauve bengaline and ivory lace. "It was always so distressing to see him there, sitting beside her, nodding as if he understood the sermon. She should have known better."

No one took any notice of the bespectacled young man in the nondescript brown suit and bowler hat who mingled with the throng. He spoke to no one, advanced no opinions, and avoided any encounter with the officiating policemen. But he never took his gaze away from the open doorway through which, eventually, the shrouded corpse of Mrs. Amelia Potter was carried to a waiting horse-drawn ambulance, past the thrusting photographers and the importunate reporters. For them the day's ration of news had got off to a fine start. The young man stationed himself near the news-gatherers and listened carefully to the answers they received from the men in charge.

As he was about to leave, he felt a heavy hand on his shoulder. "It's young Timothy Crane if I'm not mistaken," said a silky tenor voice.

The young man whirled around. "Captain Schmitt!" he exclaimed. "Haven't seen you in a while."

"Not since you left the force, what is it, three years ago by now?"

"Something like that," said Crane. "Well, I'll be getting along now. Just stopped to see what all the commotion was about."

But Captain Schmitt took him by the arm in a grip that was firm, verging on painful. "Seems I heard somewhere that you'd set up in the private detective business."

"True enough, sir," Crane replied. "I was just on my way to my office and saw this crowd as I was passing."

"It wouldn't be that you're working on something that brings you to this part of the world? I heard you have an office down by Printing House Square."

Crane snorted with laughter. "True enough, sir, if you want to call a two-by-four cubbyhole in the attic an office. T. Crane Investigations and Security Company. At the moment I have no case at all. That's why I'm walking to Printing House Square. To save on the carfare, although it's murder on the shoe leather. Would you be needing a body-guard, sir? I just finished a job of body-guarding a boxer."

"Gentleman Jim Corbett, I suppose," said Schmitt with a sneer.

"How did you ever guess?" said Tim soberly. "It was tough keeping the women away from him. Especially when he kept inviting them out to the training camp. Would you care for a ticket to the match tonight? I happen to have some in my pocket."

"No, thank you. But if it's a job you're wanting, I'm sure we could accommodate you down at headquarters." Captain Schmitt wore the mocking look that Tim Crane remembered from the times when he was a fresh-faced recruit and the captain had roundly rebuked him for thinking for himself. "I heard that the commissioners are looking for a new spittoon polisher and errand boy."

"Thank you, Captain," Crane said politely, "but I was well enough paid by Corbett, and before that I did some undercover work for Governor Roosevelt. And more is on the way. It seems that former Police Commissioner Roosevelt remembered my enterprising ways from his old reforming days on the force. And perhaps you didn't know that I rode along to Cuba with Colonel Roosevelt." Crane suppressed a smile at the expression on Captain Schmitt's face, best described as a blend of chagrin and outrage. "But what seems to be the trouble here in this quiet street?" Crane went on. "Has there been a suicide?"

"There has not," Schmitt replied. "We'll have this one wrapped up as soon as we find the poor old woman's idiot son. There's no question he stabbed her and ran off. But we'll find him before this day is out."

"I'm sure you will, Captain," said Crane. "But tell me, have you any idea why this woman's son would kill her?"

"I just told you, didn't I." Schmitt frowned in irritation. "He's a murderous idiot. A regular Jack the Ripper. All the neighbors say so. They're afraid of him and that's good enough for me. You'd best be on your way, Tim Crane. And don't you go thinking you can find him and claim a reward. There isn't one."

As Timothy Crane walked away from East Eleventh Street, he tormented himself with guilt over Mrs. Potter's death. If only he had found someone else to keep an eye on the houses directly across from her own. All the sharp kiddies who hung out at his brother Jimmy's saloon were members of the Gophers, the ruling gang of Hell's Kitchen, and of no use to him in a delicate affair such as this one. But they did odd jobs for him and kept him informed of the news of the Tenderloin and of points east, south, north, and west. One of them had spotted his quarry going into one of those posh houses and told him of it. But couldn't tell him exactly which one it was.

No, there had been no one to help him find Miss Dandy Dover, no innocent damsel she, hiding from a proposed husband she did not love. That was a romantic fancy intended to allay the old woman's misgivings. The Dandy Dover he knew was a gambling woman and former lush-roller. She had recently returned from the Klondike with a satchel full of gold she had mined with her own hands, or so the story told on the street went. More than likely she had mined it from the pockets of drunken miners who didn't realize what a trickster she was. Every ganef in town was itching to find her and relieve her of her famous satchel. Maybe even of her life.

And now there was Amos Potter to worry about. Where could he have gone? Who would take him in? And how would he survive in a city that delighted in destroying the weak and innocent?

But find Amos he must, before Captain Schmitt and his men did. The poor lad must be frightened out of what few wits he had about him, not to mention that he had probably witnessed his mother's murder and just might be able to enlighten him on that score. Crane was positive that Amelia Potter had been killed because she had seen something she shouldn't have. Something connected with Miss Dandy Dover or those who were hunting for her.

She was a kind old lady and had treated her son with a gentle firmness that commanded his respect and devotion. He had seen the young man's regard for his mother in the short time he had spent with the two of them when he first broached the idea of employing Mrs. Potter to keep an eye on the events that passed before her parlor window. It had been obvious that they received but few visitors. Amos had been painfully shy, hiding his face behind his enormous hands and peeking out between his fingers. And Mrs. Potter herself was not given to much conversation, although in thanking him for the assignment she mentioned that she was a widow and lived alone on a small annuity with her son in the brownstone house and the remuneration would afford them a few luxuries.

At first, she protested that she could not possibly do anything that might be considered unladylike. "I would feel like a spy," she said. But after Tim had assured her that all she would be doing was keeping a journal of events on the street, she became more amenable. "After all," she said, "Fanny Kemble published her journal about her life on a slave plantation in Georgia. And got paid handsomely for it, I trust. I was sorry to see that she died just a few years ago." She blushed as if comparing herself with Kemble, a very public woman, was not quite respectable.

Tim had no idea who Fanny Kemble was or what her journal was about. But he was canny enough to guess from the threadbare carpets and the carefully mended draperies that a small stipend would not be frowned upon. And so he had handed Mrs. Potter the leather-bound diary he had purchased for this very mission after he had seen her several times sitting quietly in the window of her home, her knitting neglected in her lap, watching the passing scene before her. No one would think anything of it, he reasoned. She was almost always there. He hadn't known about Amos until he had rung the doorbell and introduced himself.

And now Mrs. Potter was dead, killed by a slasher, and Amos was wandering the streets of New York with no idea that he was wanted for the murder of his mother.

Yet another one to chalk up to the reckless, selfish ways of Miss Dandy Dover. Or could she herself have murdered the watcher in the window? No! Crane shook his head almost in despair. Dandy was as bent as any hoister or dip in the Tenderloin, but she wasn't a killer. Of that he was certain. Else how could he have kept the sight of her dark eyes and shining black ringlets in his mind's eye all these years since she had conked him on the bean with a broken chair leg and laid him flat out while she made her escape. He'd been on the Metropolitan Police Force then, on night patrol on the West Side streets, and she'd made a fool of him easily enough when he'd tried to arrest her for robbing a young swell on a tear in the Tenderloin.

And now he was foolish enough to think that he could keep her from the harm that seemed to threaten her from her erstwhile companions in crime. He could think of five or six of them who had good reason to plot evil against her. He knew he shouldn't be wasting his time or his money on a fool's errand, but he couldn't help it.

He walked down Fifth Avenue, berating himself for a dunce and a billy noodle to even think that Miss Dandy Dover would welcome his protection.

• • •

BY daybreak, Amos had gone no further than Washington Square Park, where he had often walked with his mother on fine days and sat patiently with her on a bench facing the fountain while she read to him from books she thought he might understand and even enjoy. He didn't care much for *Oliver Twist*. "Too many people," he would say and then fall asleep. But he could listen forever to the tale of Rikki-tikki-tavi, the brave little mongoose who ate the big, bad snake. Best of all, he liked *Black Beauty*, the life story of a horse from newborn colt to bedraggled hauler of wagons.

He had slept on the very bench they were accustomed to use for their sojourns in the park and woke up ready for his usual breakfast of oatmeal and toast. But even his hunger could not drive him back to the house where he had seen his mother lying bloodied on the hall carpet. Tears sprang to his eyes and he wiped them away with his sleeve.

"Now, what's a great lump like you blubbering about?"

Amos looked up. He saw the young man who had given his mother the smooth brown book in which she wrote down so many things. Amos stared at him, openmouthed.

"Man jump," he mumbled. "Run away."

"Ah, yes," said Tim Crane, sitting on the bench beside Amos. "Well, sometimes running away, is the only thing to do. You ran away, too, didn't you, Amos? You did the right thing."

The tears rolled down Amos's smooth round face and dripped onto his wrinkled yellow-and-brown checked shirt. His brown canvas trousers were torn at the knees and he had lost a shoe. His companion offered him a handkerchief, but he seemed not to know what to do with it.

"Ah, you're just a big baby, aren't you? Here. Let me help you." He wiped Amos's face and insisted that he blow his nose. When the tears finally stopped, Amos crumpled the handkerchief and stuffed it into his pocket. He wiggled the toes on the foot without a shoe and smiled at them. "Ma be mad," he said. "Shoes cost money."

"Indeed they do," said Crane. "So let's go see if we can find you some new shoes. And some breakfast. How about steak and eggs?"

"Oatmeal," said Amos. "Every day oatmeal. Amos likes oatmeal."

"Fine. We'll find you some shoes and some oatmeal.

Come on, kid. I got a lady would like to meet you." Crane stood up and pulled Amos to his feet. He waved toward a hansom that had just passed under the Washington Square Arch and was heading toward the turnaround at the other side of the fountain. The cab stopped and Crane helped Amos up the step and into the leather seat below the driver's perch. "Ninth Avenue and Forty-seventh Street, and make it speedy, if you please," he directed that worthy gentleman as he mounted into the cab beside Amos. The driver grunted and flicked his whip over the rump of his dappled horse and the hansom quickly rattled its way around the fountain and out of the park, heading north on Fifth Avenue.

His mother wouldn't relish taking in another of his strays, Tim Crane mused, but she'd never turned him down yet. Still, he wasn't sure exactly how she would feel about Amos Potter, who was obviously not right in the head. But Amos needed a safe hiding place, at least for a few days, and maybe he could fit into some of his brother Jimmy's old clothes. One good thing, his mother usually had a morning pot of oatmeal on the back of the stove and surely she wouldn't refuse a hungry and homeless refugee, escaping from the unjust clutches of the coppers. She had some definite and colorful views about the Metropolitan Police, especially since he'd been turfed off the force.

They trundled on northward, contributing to the midmorning thunder of hooves and iron wheels on cobblestones. There were private carriages, omnibuses, trolley cars, other hansom cabs, delivery wagons, and nondescript vehicles of all sorts that made New York the busiest and noisiest city in the world.

"Ah," Crane sighed, "we'll be all right, won't we, Amos?"

"All right, yes, we be all right," Amos echoed. "Get some oatmeal? Be all right." Then he turned his head from side to side to admire the passing scenery as the cab sped northward as fast as the dappled horse could take it.

"Ma write in book," he murmured as he examined the

elegant brownstone housefronts as they passed. "Man fall
down. Got blood on head. Amos tell Ma. Ma write in book."

"You don't say," Crane remarked. "And then what?" He
kept his voice soft and displayed not a flicker of excitement.
But his heart leaped. If only he could get his hands on Mrs.
Potter's diary. There might be something in it that would
point toward the killer.

"Eat supper then," Amos moaned. "Eat breakfast now?
Amos want oatmeal."

"Soon, Amos. Soon. What happened then?"

"Man come. Hit Ma with knife. Got blood all over."
Amos stared at his hands. There were still traces of dried
blood on them. He seemed about to cry, but then he shook
his head wildly and blurted, "No! Ma dead. No more talking."

Tim Crane leaned back against the leather cushion, scarce
believing what he had heard. Amos had seen something in
the street that Mrs. Potter had written about in her diary.
Then someone had come to the house and killed her. And
Amos had seen it all.

The only problem was that no one would ever believe
him. Especially not Captain Schmitt if he ever got his hands
on him. Schmitt would be only too happy to lock Amos up
in the Tombs until he could be strung up by the neck or
fried in the new electric chair up at Sing Sing.

"Amos, where do you think your mother's book is now?"
Tim kept his voice low and casual.

"Book?" Amos looked bewildered.

"The one she wrote in, Amos. After you told her what
happened."

Amos grinned as if everyone in the world would know
where that book was. "On that table," he said. "By that
chair. Next to click-clack."

"Click-clack?"

Amos made clumsy writhing motions with his huge
hands.

"Ah, I get it. She kept it by her knitting." Tim would give anything to get his hands on that leather-bound diary, but there was no possibility of getting into the house with Captain Schmitt's fearless guardians of the city's peace and tranquility posted at the front and probably the back doors. Maybe he could get in through the roof, but first he'd have to get into another house on the block, cross a few rooftops, and hope to find a skylight he could open or break through. A bit risky if anyone was at home to resent his intrusion.

The cab was nearing Forty-first Street, where demolition work was just beginning on the Croton Reservoir. The city had outgrown its water supply and the old reservoir was to be replaced by a grand new public library. Tim Crane jerked on the cord that communicated with the driver. The little flap in the roof of the cab opened and the driver peered down at them.

"Would you take us over to Ninth Avenue now?" Tim requested.

"My intention indeed," said the driver. "You wouldn't be related to Mr. James Crane, publican, by any chance, would you? You look a good bit like him. Only he's a bruiser, he is. Taller and a lot wider than you."

"He's my brother," Tim replied.

"And would you be going to his place of business?"

"That I would," said Tim.

"Well, that's remarkable, since I was just thinking that it's time for me mid-morning bracer. Since we're going that way, I'll just stop by and pay a visit to your brother."

The flap closed and the driver, eager for his dram of spirits, maneuvered swiftly through the oncoming traffic at great risk to himself, his horse, and his passengers. As they rounded the corner onto Forty-second Street, he spewed forth a stream of invective directed at a slow-moving wagonload of hog carcasses that obstructed his passage. When they finally had negotiated the turn, the cab resumed its journey at a breakneck clip toward the restful premises of Jimmy Crane's Saloon.

Amos Potter had left off peering at the scenery and was morosely rocking back and forth as if in time with the motion of the carriage. He said nothing, but a low humming sound accompanied his rocking.

Crane patted him on the shoulder and said, "Don't worry, kid. We'll find the hacker who slashed your ma. But first we've got to get you a place to stay and some food."

Amos looked up brightly. "Shoes, too?" he asked, wiggling the toes of his unshod foot.

"Shoes, too," Crane assured him.

• • •

ALTHOUGH it would not open officially until Decoration Day, Coney Island was abuzz with excitement by noon of May 11, 1900. Despite the chilly sea breeze and the threat of rain, every hotel, restaurant, and saloon along Surf Avenue was thronged with a growing mob of sharp customers, betting fools, rogues, dips, grifters, and working girls from the city. Policemen could be seen actively looking the other way. The Police Board had done its best to put an end to the "brutal sport of prizefighting" in New York City, but they were overruled just a few days before by a magistrate of the court.

The center of all the excitement was the Seaside Athletic Club, where the match of the new century was to take place in just a few hours. Located on Surf Avenue within sniffing distance of Feltman's restaurant, where the aroma of frankfurters and sauerkraut competed with those of steamed clams and hot corn, the club had been freshly painted and fitted out with new seating for the momentous occasion. Still, it was nothing more than a huge windowless and airless amphitheater in which pugilists battled each other in the acrid fug of cigar smoke and stale beer. And where that evening Gentleman Jim Corbett would try to regain his heavyweight title from Jim Jeffries, almost ten years younger and thirty pounds heavier.

On the veranda of the Albemarle Hotel, directly across Surf Avenue from the club, a foppish young man contemplated the festive crowd with satisfaction. He was tastefully dressed in a dark gray morning coat and slender black-and-gray striped trousers. His shirtfront was blindingly white and his necktie was one of the floppy kind, of red silk with a tiny purple pattern. He wore pearl-gray gloves and shining black patent-leather boots. On his head, a broad-brimmed black slouch hat tilted rakishly over his brow. If anyone were to peer closely into his face he would see just the trace of a small white bandage on his brow, almost entirely covered by the unruly black locks that tumbled from under his hat.

But no one looked closely at him. Despite the elegance of his attire and his careless attitude of superiority, to the crowd assembled, he was just another rich gambler come to try his luck. Would it be Corbett? Or would it be Jeffries?

And indeed, the young swell had placed a few early bets and would likely place a few more when he saw which way the odds were laying. But even if he lost every cent he had bet, there was always more where that came from. For the moment, he was simply enjoying the day and the prospect of winning through the application of logic.

He had studied both fighters and visited their training camps in New Jersey. He knew that even Corbett's supporters were reluctant to put money on their man no matter that he had rigorously trained himself into fighting trim. His dissolute life of the past few years was bound to tell. The Tenderloin dollies and Corbett's old drinking buddies might bet on him out of admiration or friendship, but Jeffries was sure to hang on to the title. Jeffries was not handsome as Corbett was, nor elegant in his style, but in his plodding, determined way, the California boilermaker turned boxer was invincible.

The young man removed his gloves and drew forth a

golden cigarette case from his inner breast pocket, plucked out a Sweet Caporal, and lit it with a lucifer that he struck against the side of a golden matchbox. His hands belied his elegant attire; they were rough and weatherworn. His face, too, had the bronzed texture of someone exposed to the elements, a sailor or a rancher. He drifted off the veranda and down into the swirling crowd. The fight was scheduled to start at nine o'clock and go for twenty-three rounds. It would be a long day and an even longer night. Might as well see what was happening over at the Manhattan Beach Hotel, where the respectable crowd congregated. Even refined gents or their ladies might like to try their luck on the fight of the new century.

• • •

TIM could hear his mother warbling before he even opened the downstairs door. She was much happier now that she was back in Hell's Kitchen among her old friends. His brother, Jimmy, since he became prosperous, had persuaded her to leave their old cold-water flat and move to a fine cottage with a garden deep in Brooklyn, but she missed the city where she had lived all her life, became morose, and took to drinking a bit too much of her Lydia Pinkham's. Now she lived just above Jimmy's saloon on Ninth Avenue and never touched anything stronger than over-brewed tea. Her voice floated down the staircase, off-key and mournful as befitting a "bird in a gilded cage," but as long as she was singing, she was in a good humor.

"Hey, Ma," Tim shouted, "the concert's over. Company's coming up."

He turned back to the doorway and motioned Amos to follow him up the stairs. But Amos hung back. He seemed frightened of the strange surroundings.

"Come on, Amos," Tim coaxed him. "I think I can smell that oatmeal. And that's my own mother making all that racket."

Slowly Amos climbed the steep stairs behind Tim Crane. The stairway was lighted only by a skylight six floors above, although there were gas jets on each floor. Mrs. Crane had the habit of thrift from her long years of raising two sons alone by cleaning other people's houses and taking in laundry. Now she still scrimped and saved, and even took in the occasional bundle of washing from one or two favored old customers. "Just to give me something to do with my time," she said. Both Tim and Jimmy had given up trying to change her ways.

"Is that you, Tim?" she called down the stairs. "And who have you brought me this time? Sounds like an elephant climbing the stairs."

"Are we in time for breakfast?" Tim shouted back. "This one is mighty hungry for some of your good old Irish oatmeal."

"Welcome to you both then. And when has there not been something to eat in the house, I'd like to know?"

As Tim neared the top of the stairs, followed by Amos straggling a few steps behind, his mother emerged from her open doorway and peered down at them. "Saints above!" she exclaimed. "You've brought me one of them Mongolians. And a big one at that. Is he housebroken?"

"Sure he is, Ma. He comes from a fine family, but he's got a bit of trouble for the moment." Tim took Amos by the hand and pulled him along to the kitchen that overlooked the backyards. "Is there any tea for us?"

"Next thing you'll be wanting ham and eggs, I suppose." She tapped him smartly on the head and then chucked him under the chin. "Just let me get the stove nice and hot."

As she reached for the coal scuttle, Amos hurried to her side. "Amos do. Amos know how."

"Is that right? Well, help yourself, me lad. It's a fine thing to be useful on this earth." Mrs. Crane stood aside and watched as Amos carefully lifted the iron stove lid with its removable handle and scooped the chunks of coal into the

burner, spreading them over the embers that smoldered at
the bottom. Then she turned to Tim and said, "At least
you've brought me someone who knows what he's doing
this time."

"We'll be finding out what he can and cannot do, Ma,"
said Tim. "I only just found him in need of some help this
morning. The police are after him for killing his mother.
His name is Amos Potter and you'll be reading about him
in all the newspapers this afternoon. And his poor mother,
too."

Mrs. Crane shrieked. "Timothy Crane, you dare to bring
a killer into my house! Out with him, this instant!" She had
picked up a broom as if to sweep Amos out the door.

"Calm down, Ma. He didn't do it. But I aim to find out
who did, since I happen to be partly responsible for what
happened. Now how about that oatmeal for Amos? And I
won't say no to your ham and eggs."

Mrs. Crane muttered to herself but headed to her pride
and joy, a brand-new iron cookstove with compartments for
everything and a hot water heater on the side. Amos stood
beside the stove grinning from ear to ear. "Look, Ma," he
said as he lifted the stove lid to show her the cooking fire
he had stoked up for her. "You cook now. Amos hungry."

Mrs. Crane eyed him up and down. "Well, my boy. If
Tim says you're okay, I'll believe him. But don't let me catch
you pulling any funny business. Understand?"

Amos nodded vigorously, his hair waving wildly with
each motion of his huge round head. "Amos good. No business. Eat now?"

After breakfast, Tim went through the wardrobe in the
side bedroom where he and Jimmy sometimes slept when
it was too late to get to their own places before the sun came
up. He had fitted up his office with a cot and a cupboard,
while his brother had a grand new apartment right on
Broadway at Fifty-ninth Street, near Central Park. The saloon business had been very good to him.

There were two beds, a wardrobe, and a small sofa in the room, as well as a washstand and a chifforobe that held a plaster statuette of the Virgin Mary on a pedestal under a glass dome with a votive candle at her feet. The candle was unlit and a bit on the dusty side. Mrs. Crane wasn't much for devotions or dusting. She just liked to stay on the good side of the Lady in the blue bathrobe.

Amos sat on the sofa and watched as Tim rummaged through the cast-off clothing in the wardrobe. At last he came up with a huge pair of hobnail boots that might have belonged to Sandow the Strongman, a pair of tweed trousers, and a thick wool coat. "Here, kiddo," he said to Amos, "try these on. You'll need a coat. And here's an umbrella for you. It looks like rain today."

"Get book now?" Amos asked.

"What?"

"Ma's book. I get for you."

"Oh, thanks. But I think there'd be a couple of coppers who might not let you just walk in the door and get it."

Amos snickered. It was a strange sound, but undeniably a laugh. "Not door," he whispered. "Go by tunnel."

Tim stared at the hulking young man. "What are you talking about, Amos? What tunnel?"

"Sssh! You see. I take you there." Amos grinned. "Secret place. Mine."

"Well, I'll be damned!" Tim whispered. "Ain't you the cagey one! I'd like to know what other secrets you're harboring."

"Go now?" Amos persisted.

"All right. Go now. But first, button those trousers and lace up your boots. And would you be kind enough to just give me a hint about this famous tunnel of yours?"

"Better I show you." And with that, Amos fell silent and marched out of the bedroom toward the door to the hallway. Tim followed, wondering where they were going and what they would find when they got there.

After they left, Mrs. Crane went into her bedroom and took an old velvet-covered photograph album from its hiding place in the bottom of a shabby trunk. For a while, she sat in her rocking chair clasping the album to her breast and rocking slowly back and forth, back and forth. After perhaps twenty minutes, she opened the album and gazed at the photo on the first page. It showed a young man with curly hair, long sideburns, and a full beard and mustache, looking intently into the camera. He was dressed in the style of thirty years past and seemed impatient to be on his way. Mrs. Crane touched his face with her worn fingers and then touched her own. Then she quickly flipped through the photos on the remaining pages. They were all of a pretty young woman wearing only tights and a short diaphanous tunic. Slipped in among the photos, there was an assortment of yellowing theatrical programs. She sighed heavily and then closed the album and put it back into the trunk, making sure it was buried under all the other contents.

• • •

THIS time, it was Amos who led the way. He refused Tim's offer of a cab or at least a trolley ride. Instead, he loped along, back the way they had come: down Ninth Avenue, across Forty-second Street, and back down Fifth Avenue.

Tim stopped him once and cautioned, "You know you can't go to your house, don't you?"

Amos said nothing, but continued on his way, with Tim trailing along behind, until they reached Fourteenth Street, where he turned abruptly and raced along the crowded sidewalk, past the oyster houses and beer saloons, the dry goods shops and piano showrooms, the fire insurance and theatrical agents' offices. At last he came to a breathless stop before a four-story house that seemed to be a private residence. When Tim caught up with him, Amos grinned and said, "We go in now."

"In?" Tim exclaimed. "Amos, are you loco? Do you know what this place is?"

Amos smiled and descended the stairs to the basement entrance. "Nice ladies," he said.

"Oh, very nice. Amos, you don't want to go in there." Tim grabbed his arm and tried to haul him back up the stairs. But Amos shook him off with hardly more than a shrug and rang the basement doorbell.

"Amos! Come away from there. This is Mrs. McCready's fancy house. She'll throw you out in a flash." But the door opened before Tim could do more than pluck at the immovable Amos's sleeve.

And there she was. The infamous Ida McCready, splendid in a lilac satin dressing gown with her masses of bright orange hair piled up in a rat's nest of terrifying proportions, was the proprietress of one of the many brothels that dotted the Union Square neighborhood. She smiled up at Amos and stood on tiptoe to kiss him on the cheek. "Well, look who's here," she chortled. "Our wandering boy, the tunneling mole, the splendid dummy who makes us all laugh. How are you, sweetheart?"

Amos uttered a low hum that seemed to mean he was happy to see her.

"And who's that lurking behind you, eh?" Mrs. McCready eyed Tim thoughtfully and said, "I know you. Ain't you some kind of a Pinkerton, maybe? What do you want here?"

"Could we come inside?" Tim said. "The coppers are after your wandering boy and I'd like to get him out of sight."

Mrs. McCready glanced quickly up and down and across the street. Then she drew them into the house and closed and locked the door behind them. Amos knew exactly where he wanted to go. He headed into the kitchen at the rear of the basement and opened a low door beside the fireplace.

"Hold on a minute, Amos." Mrs. McCready took his arm and led him to a chair at the round oak table in the center of the room. "Sit down a spell, and tell me what this is all about." She turned to Tim. "You keep quiet for a minute. I want to hear what he has to say for himself."

Amos slumped into a chair and gazed down at his hands, folded in his lap. "Ma got dead," he whispered. "No more talking."

"Ah, now, that's a crying shame," said Mrs. McCready. "I knew your pa, but that was long ago."

Amos stared at her. "Pa?" He shrugged and shook his head. "No Pa. Just Ma. Ma and Amos."

Mrs. McCready turned to Tim. "All right now. Suppose you enlighten me about what's going on. I can't have the police barging in here, you know."

"Someone killed his mother last night," said Tim. "Amos ran off. The police think he did it. I'm sure he didn't. So I'm trying to help him. That's it."

"Oh, is it? Would you mind very much telling me how you know he didn't do it and why you're so eager to help him?"

"Why should I tell you? How do I know you won't go running off to the police with the information?"

Mrs. McCready roared with laughter. "Tim Crane! Now I remember who you are. You're the one that used to be a cop until you went soft over Dandy Dover. And you obviously know who I am. So let's stop dillydallying. You know I won't peach to the coppers. They mind their business and I mind mine. I might even be able to help you. For a price, of course."

"Oh, of course," said Tim. "But first, would you mind telling me why you're so glad to see Amos Potter. He's not exactly your usual type of client."

Mrs. McCready set a pitcher of cold tea on the table and fetched three tumblers from the sideboard. She poured glasses for the three of them and sighed. "This could be thirsty work," she said. "How's your mother, Tim? And your brother, Jimmy?"

"My mother?" He gaped at her. "How do you know my mother?"

Mrs. McCready smiled. "Would it surprise you to know I rocked you to sleep once or twice when you were a wee lad?"

"It would," said Tim. "I suppose you were a midwife or some such in another life?"

"No," she said. "Your mother and I were the closest of friends at one time. That was before I went into business for myself. But maybe you'd better ask her about it. Tell her Ida says to remember the old vaudeville days at Tony Pastor's. I guess she's never told you about that."

Amos had gulped down his cold tea and was fidgeting in his chair. "Go now," he said. "Get book."

Mrs. McCready patted his shoulder and soothed him. "Just you wait a bit, Amos. I want to talk to your friend." She got up and placed a cookie jar in front of him.

"Now then, Tim Crane. You want to go through the tunnel to the Potter house. That's okay with me. But I want to know what you want to do when you get there. I doubt very much you intend to rob a deceased widow of all her worldly goods and leave poor Amos an orphan and a pauper in the streets. And what's all this about a book?" She stood before him, arms akimbo, in an attitude of determination that she had often used when she was playing the ingenue in vaudeville skits.

"My mother . . . she didn't . . . she wasn't . . ." Tim began, but seemed unable to finish his sentence.

"Oh, faith and all the angels!" exclaimed Mrs. McCready, dropping her attitude and plopping herself into a chair. "No, laddie. Your mother was never a minute in this business. No, sir. We were just in the same vaudeville shows that Mr. Pastor put on at his Opera House years ago. We even went on tour with him. Ah, she was a true beauty then. And all the gentlemen were wild about her. But she stayed simple and pure. A bit too simple and pure, if you ask me.

But now, let's get back to the book. What exactly is in this book that Amos is so keen to get?"

While Amos gobbled up many more cookies than he had ever had at one sitting, Tim told Ida McCready the story of the journal that Amelia Potter had been keeping for him and why he needed to get hold of it before the coppers did. That's if they hadn't already taken it out of the house. But since most of them couldn't read beyond the baseball scores or the racing tip sheets, he had no fear of that.

"So Dandy is back and you're all moon-faced over her. I might have known," said Mrs. McCready, shaking her head in despair at the foolishness of men in general and Timothy Crane in particular. "I heard she was back flush with Klondike gold, and now she's got you in the middle of a pickle without even trying. I also heard that Bert the Barber had sworn to get even with her for cheating him out of his share of a dodge they were working together before she left town. Where is she?"

"That's what I'd like to know," said Tim. "I haven't even seen her. But I got information that she was hiding out in one of them swank houses on Eleventh Street. So I hired Mrs. Potter to watch all the houses across the street from her and write down everything she saw. I think she wrote something in her journal that was the death of her. Amos says we can get into the house through the tunnel."

"That you can," said Mrs. McCready. "That's how Amos found his way here when he was still just a boy. Not to mention his father before him, God rot his soul. They say that this place and the house on Eleventh Street were way stations on the Underground Railroad and the tunnel was used to hide the runaway slaves until they could get across the river to Mr. Beecher's church in Brooklyn. Where they went from there is anyone's guess. But the tunnel is there all right, and it goes on past this house, probably down to the East River. You'll have to ask Amos about that. He's quite a tunneler, he is. I tried it once, but it was dirty and damp, so I never went very far."

Tim was entranced with his hostess. She had given him some intriguing hints about his mother's past and now she had cursed Amos's father. But the story of Amos's father was ancient history and had nothing to do with finding out who killed his mother. Maybe another day he could come back and ask her some questions, but right now he wanted to get to the other end of the tunnel and find Mrs. Potter's journal if the killer or the police hadn't taken it.

"Well, Mrs. McCready, that's all very interesting and I thank you, but Amos and I had best be on our way." Tim swallowed the rest of his tea and got to his feet. "Amos, it's time for us to go. You lead the way, my friend."

Amos lumbered to his feet, almost knocking his chair over. "Yes. Your friend. I am. We go now." He pulled open the low door beside the fireplace and bent double to make his way through it. In a moment, Tim could see the dim light of a candle bobbing in the dark.

"Thanks, Mrs. McCready. Is it all right if we come back this way?"

"Yes, but don't be too long about it. This place starts getting busy around mid-afternoon and I don't want you or Amos around when there's business to be done." She smiled at him and added, "Unless, of course, you'd like a private visit with one of the ladies? They treat Amos like a mascot, you know, or a little brother. They think he brings good luck."

"Maybe he does," said Tim, following Amos into the tunnel.

Mrs. McCready closed the small door behind them and the tunnel went dark except for the flickering light of the candle in Amos's hand.

• • •

A fine, cold drizzle sifted down onto the crowd churning along Surf Avenue but few sought shelter while there were bets to be made and plans to be laid for mischief before, after, or during the fight. Bert the Barber sidled among the merrymakers, keeping a weather eye out for the object of his wrath. He had yet to lay eyes on her since her return to the city with her rumored satchel of gold, but he knew her ways. Dandy Dover would no more miss an opportunity to wager mightily on the fight of the century, picking a few pockets along the way, than she would grow wings and fly over the moon. For reasons of self-preservation, Bert thought it best to make himself scarce for a time from his usual haunts on the Manhattan side of the East River. Coney, with its crowds and its fleabag hotels in the alleys off Surf Avenue, suited him just fine. He could lay a few bets on the fight, and there was nothing wrong with killing two birds with one stone, if one of the birds was Dandy Dover. He had learned the hard way that when it came to Dandy, it was better to take care of business himself and not trust the job to one of his boyos. She could twist her way out of any pickle; talk her way into anyone's confidence. He didn't really want to stop her clock, but he'd been waiting a long time to get some of his own back for the fifty dollars she'd cheated him out of before she made tracks for the goldfields. Fifty dollars, plus three years interest. Some might call him a shylock, but he suspected she had enough gold in her kit to pay him off royally and still have some left over for frolicking. He wasn't greedy and Dandy was an old friend. She could easily afford to eradicate her debt with a neat bundle of three hundred spondulicks. Otherwise . . . Well, he'd have to find her first.

As he oozed along the edges of the crowd, Bert kept a watchful eye on the women. It was a pleasant chore. Dandy would be a stand-out in any crowd, but there were scores of stunners strolling by, some half hidden by their umbrellas, others skittering for shelter from awning to awning. Bert was enjoying his day at the shore.

• • •

THE tunnel twisted and turned under the sidewalks of Manhattan. Tim Crane imagined he could hear the muffled clop, clop of horses and the distant trundling of iron wheels above his head. He had lost all sense of direction, although he assumed they were headed on a generally southwesterly course. He envisioned himself trapped in a cave-in. He felt as though they had been underground for hours. He dreaded an attack by unseen many-legged creatures that dwelt in darkness. But the light in Amos's candlestick kept moving steadily forward as he followed a well-worn path through the gloom and the dank effluvia of the tunnel. It was curious, Tim thought, that Mrs. McCready had cursed Amos's father. He wondered what that was all about. But the thought melted away as Amos beckoned him on and pointed up a sloping offshoot of the tunnel floor.

"Home!" he shouted. "We go in now."

"Hush, hush, kiddo. We don't make a sound from here on."

Amos turned and trudged up the slope. At the top he pressed a lever and a slab of board in the brick wall swung away letting in a faint smear of daylight. As Tim followed Amos out of the tunnel, he saw a stairway rising to one side of a vaulted cellar, a monstrous furnace toward the front of the house with a sizeable coalbin adjacent, and a pair of small windows set high up in the wall and looking out directly into the areaway. Amos went immediately around behind the furnace to his hiding place. He inspected all his possessions carefully, giving special attention to his collection of bird feathers, stored in a number of gaudy cigar boxes. He selected a sleek white feather with a black tip and handed it to Tim.

"Very nice feather," he said. "For you."

"Thank you, Amos," said Tim. "It really is nice. And large, too. Must have come from a migrating goose on her way down south for the winter." He carefully deposited the feather in the inside pocket of his coat.

"Yes?" said Amos, dubiously. "Where is south?"

"Ah, you don't know, do you? I keep forgetting." Tim thought a moment, then smiled. "Suppose I take you south this afternoon. We'll go to Coney Island and eat wieners. We'll go on the train and have a good time. Would you like that?"

"Is that south?"

"Yes, it's kind of south and we have to cross the river on the train. I'll bet you've never done that, either. But you'll like it, I promise."

"Amos like it. Yes. Now get book." He headed for the stairway, still holding his candlestick to light the way.

"Hold it," said Tim. "I think you'd better blow the candle out. Don't want anyone lurking outside to see any lights moving around inside. Okay?"

"Okay. Here. You blow. But I light it later. Okay?"

"You bet," said Tim, chuffing the candle out. "We'll need it to get back to Mrs. McCready's. And from there we can go to Brooklyn."

Amos shook his head doubtfully. "Too much," he said. "Makes head hurt."

"Ah, get along with you. Up the stairs and show me where the book is. If all goes well, we'll be out of here in two shakes of a lamb's tail. But keep it quiet, Amos. We don't want to rouse the bluebottles."

Amos tried to walk up the stairs on tiptoe but soon reverted to his normal plodding gait, sending echoes of his heavy tread throughout the cellar. Tim hoped the sound couldn't be heard by any patrolmen who might be stationed outdoors. At the top of the stairs, there was a sturdy wooden door with a bronze doorknob, which Amos twisted. The door opened into an alcove off the kitchen of the house. Tim motioned to Amos to wait in the alcove while he took a look into the kitchen. There were two tall windows, curtained with faded blue-and-white gingham, that looked out into the garden, where a glum-faced patrolman sheltered himself from the drizzle under an ancient grape arbor that leaned against the back fence. Tim was satisfied that they could not be seen from the yard so long as they didn't go directly into the kitchen. He took Amos's arm and guided him out of the alcove and into the passage that led up another flight of stairs to the parlor floor.

Once in the hallway that led to the front door, Tim could see stains on the carpet in the foyer. They were undoubtedly bloodstains, and he hoped that Amos wouldn't notice them. He took the lead and walked slowly and quietly toward the front of the house where the entrance to the parlor was framed by a pair of ornate sliding doors of polished walnut. As he moved closer to the front door, he saw that there was a dark shape standing on the stoop. A twin of the patrolman in the backyard. He turned to warn Amos to be very quiet and saw that his companion had frozen in place and wore a look of sheer terror.

"Amos," he whispered. "What's the matter?"

Amos stood still, his eyes fixed on the front door. "Man," he muttered. "Man come in. Hit Ma down. Run away." He seemed on the verge of letting out a howl of woe.

Tim clutched his arm and dragged him toward the front parlor, where they would be hidden from the eyes of the copper on the stoop. Captain Schmitt had posted the troops on the outside of the house to intercept Amos, should he come home. They would never dream that he might have gotten in via a secret tunnel from Ida McCready's bordello. They considered Amos an idiot. Tim thought he was pretty damned cagey, if maybe a bit unpredictable. And far too sheltered for his own good. He deposited Amos in a wing chair facing the stone-cold fireplace and crept along the floor toward the bay window. He had spotted what he hoped was

Mrs. Potter's knitting basket on the floor near the marble-topped table that was still set with the remains of her and Amos's supper of the night before. But there was no sign of the diary on the table. He picked up the knitting basket and thrust his hand into it, being careful not to impale a finger on a pointed needle. But the diary was not buried in the skeins of wool.

"Amos," he whispered, "where did your mother put the book while you were eating?"

"Not hungry," Amos moaned. "Ma dead. Not talking."

"Hush now, Amos. Not so loud." Tim tiptoed around the wing chair and knelt in front of the sad-faced child-man. "Think back, Amos. When your mother put the food on the table, where was the book?"

Amos squinted his eyes and stared into the fireplace. Tim picked up the poker and shifted the logs and kindling that were set waiting for the touch of a match.

"Not there, silly," said Amos, snickering. "I get." He rose from the chair and lumbered over to the chair by the window. It was the chair his mother had been sitting in when the knock had come at the door. He reached down beneath the cushion and retrieved the diary. "Ma put it there," he said triumphantly, handing it to Tim.

Tim took the book and opened it, swiftly leafing through to the last page that bore handwriting. There, neatly scripted in pencil, were the words he had hoped to see. "To-night Amos saw a strange occurrence from the window." There was more, but he quickly closed and pocketed the book and guided Amos toward the passageway to the basement stairs. But Amos stopped and gazed upward toward the floor above.

"Maybe Ma in bed?" he asked, his eyes bright with hope.

"No, Amos. Your ma isn't in bed. I saw the coppers put her body in the ambulance wagon and take her away. She's not here. Hush! What's that?" Tim clutched Amos's arm and drew him into the shadows of the narrow hall. Turning back to glance at the front door, he spied the police guard twisting a key in the lock.

"Come on, Amos! Be quick! Down the rabbit hole and away!" Amos moved as quickly as he could, with Tim urging him on from behind. Down to the kitchen area and then down again to the cellar. The policeman had opened the front door and Tim could hear his footsteps patrolling the parlor floor. No doubt he would soon be patrolling the kitchen and dining room areas. Then he might check the backyard and maybe even stop for a smoke with his partner lazing in the grape arbor. Or he might head straight for the basement.

Instead of going to the small door in the brick wall, Amos disappeared behind the massive furnace. "Step on it, Amos," Tim whispered in the gloom. "What are you doing back there?"

Amos reappeared carrying one of his cigar boxes and a new candle for the return journey.

"Good for you," said Tim. "Now let's get moving."

As Amos unlatched the door to the tunnel, they heard heavy footsteps on the cellar stairs. The light from a lantern crept into the gloom, widening its circle of illumination as it descended. They lost no time in crowding together into the tunnel, quietly shutting the door behind them. Not daring to show a light or make a noise, they huddled together in the darkness, scarcely breathing, waiting for the sound of the guard's departure.

But what they heard was the sound of the guard urinating and then the familiar gurgling flush of an overhead water closet tank. The guard sighed with relief, struggled briefly with his buttons, and whistled his way back up the stairs. The two lurkers in the tunnel waited until they heard him go out the front door to resume his post on the stoop. Then they lit both of their candles and hurried off through the tunnel to return to Mrs. McCready's kitchen.

• • •

As more and more elevated trains unloaded their passengers and every steamboat that moored at the Iron Pier discharged crowds of merrymakers, Coney Island seemed to be absorbing the entire population of the city. The young man in the slouch hat had returned to the Albemarle Hotel and enjoyed a fine and solitary late lunch in the dining room. Now, over coffee in the hotel's pleasant lounge, he leafed through the afternoon editions of all the New York newspapers he could find. In addition to the endless speculation on the fitness of both Corbett and Jeffries and which one would claim the world heavyweight title that evening, there were reports of children having been killed in elevator accidents, articles on plans for the opening of the yachting season, and the usual dreadful fires and ghastly murders, among which was noted the unfortunate demise of a Mrs. Amelia Potter of East Eleventh Street, apparently stabbed to death by her idiot son, who had disappeared.

The young gentleman grew thoughtful and lit another cigarette from his gold case. It was exceedingly unlikely that there could have been so much activity last night on such a quiet residential street just off Fifth Avenue. There was no mention of his own adventure on East Eleventh Street, but that was only because he had escaped his tormentors and made his way to the Albemarle in his spanking new Clement-Panhard automobile. He had taken a suite of rooms there a few days earlier so that he would be assured of accommodations for the night of the fight. There was no denying that a couple of rowdies had tried to abduct him last night in a shipping crate. But he had kicked the lid loose and given their horses a few sharp boots to the rear, sending them careening off to the other side of the island. He thought he knew who was behind the attempt. But that was a personal matter and could have nothing to do with the murder of an old woman by her son.

He folded up his newspapers and left them for the next searcher for enlightenment.

• • •

WHEN Tim and Amos tumbled through the secret door in Mrs. McCready's kitchen, they found a welcoming committee. His mother was there and so was his brother, Jimmy. They were sitting at the round kitchen table looking at some old photograph albums and didn't seem a bit surprised to see him, although they did give a great deal of attention to Amos. Mrs. McCready was ready with tea and a bottle of good Irish whiskey.

"We have something to celebrate!" she shouted, as they emerged from the tunnel covered in dust and cobwebs. "Come, sit you down, boys, and get ready to learn of a miracle!"

"Ah, Ida, you're making a mountain out of a molehill," said Mrs. Crane. "There's not much to celebrate, if you ask me."

"Rosalie, you may have been prettier than I was back in the old days, but you sure weren't smarter. And that hasn't changed a bit. Now let's tell these boys what they've needed to know ever since they were born." Mrs. McCready pulled out chairs and forcibly sat Amos and Tim side by side at the table. Jimmy was already sitting beside his mother, idly paging through the photograph albums that contained many pictures of Ida McCready as a young woman and a few yellowing newspaper clippings. "Hey!" he exclaimed. "Here's a program with your name in it, Ma. See? Look at it. Right here, Miss Rosalie Crane, the Loveliest Rose of Broadway. That's swell, Ma. Really swell."

"I know, I know, Jimmy," his mother sighed. "That was a long time ago. Before you were born. And it's best forgotten."

"But that's what we're all gathered together for," said Mrs. McCready. "At least one part of it. James, Timothy," she said. "Did you know that your mother was the youngest and prettiest darling girl of Mr. Tony Pastor's Variety Show? All the gentlemen were in love with her. Why, she could have become a star, bigger even than Lillian Russell."

Mrs. Crane shook her head. "Ida, you always did exaggerate. But you're right about one thing. It's time my sons knew something about their father. So let's get on with it."

Jimmy Crane took his mother's hand and said, "I already know some of it, Ma. I guessed that he was already married and I remember when I was little, there was a tall man with sideburns and a mustache who used to come to see us and bring toys and candy. But I don't know who he was or why he stopped coming, and I don't think Tim knows anything at all about it. Right, Timmy?"

Tim jumped up and shouted, "What's going on here? What don't I know? And why don't I know it? Am I the only dumbbell in the family?"

"Are you going to speak up, Rosalie?" asked Mrs. Mc-Cready. "Or do I have to do what you should have done years ago? Here, have a tot of whiskey. It'll help oil your memory." She handed her old friend a brimming shot glass.

Rosalie sipped daintily at the glass, then set it down. "I don't need my memory oiled," she said. "I've never forgotten a moment of those days. And I'd do it all over again." She took a deep breath as if to steel herself, then motioned to Tim to sit down by her side. "Boys," she said. "I've never told you anything about your father because I wasn't married to him. So you guessed that much, Jimmy. It didn't matter so much when I met him, because he always held out the notion that we would soon be wed. As Ida has told you, we were both working for Tony Pastor at the time and all the girls had dozens of admirers. But as far as I was concerned, your father was the only one for me.

"Today, when the telephone call came in to Jimmy's saloon and I heard Ida's voice on the other end, I knew the time had come. You see, she was the one who told me when your father died years ago, and I realized that I would never in my life be a respectable married woman. Until that moment, I had hoped he might find a way to be a real father to his sons."

It was Jimmy's turn to jump up from the table. He wrapped his arms around his mother's shoulders and shouted, "Hey, old girl, you're respectable enough for all of us. Nobody I know can beat you at that game. Least of all anyone here." And he stared around the room belligerently, ready to do battle with anyone who disagreed with him. No one did.

His mother said, "Sit down and shut up, James." She took another sip of her whiskey and continued with her story. "And I knew I had to tell you because of Amos here."

It was Tim's turn to be surprised. "What's Amos got to do with our family troubles?"

Mrs. Crane smiled wanly. "In a way, son, he's got everything to do with them. You see, Tim and Jimmy, your father's name was Eldridge Potter." Giving up all pretense at refinement, Mrs. Crane lifted her glass to her lips and swallowed every drop. She sighed. "That feels better," she said. "You're right, Ida. I should have told them long ago. But what good would it have done? He died when Tim was just a baby."

"And so was Amos," Ida prompted.

"Yes, so was Amos. And now Amos has no family at all."

There was silence in the room. No one knew what to say. Neither Jimmy nor Tim could fully comprehend what had been said, but they both stared at Amos as if he could make everything clear.

Amos smiled and said, "We go to Coney now? We eat wieners?"

Everyone, except Amos, roared with laughter. Tears were rolling down Mrs. Crane's cheeks even as she tried to stifle her guffaws. Mrs. McCready began dancing around the table, clapping her hands and singing "Sweet Rosie O'Grady" at the top of her lungs, with special emphasis on the words "when we are married, how happy we'll be."

"Stop that now, Ida. I don't appreciate you laughing at me like that." Mrs. Crane rose from the table and went around it to where Amos sat in complete ignorance of why everyone was laughing and singing. She bent to put her arms around him and kissed him gently on the cheek. "I'll be your ma now, Amos. And my boys will be your brothers. And we'll all look after you. Maybe not as well as your own mother, God rest her soul, but we'll do our best. Right, boys?" She straightened up and looked sternly at her sons.

"Yeah, sure, Ma," they both answered. "Anything you like."

Jimmy added, "I think we'd better see a lawyer about this. If it's true that Amos now owns a fancy house on Eleventh Street, we'd better make sure that no one cheats him out of it."

And Tim said, "Before we do that, I think we'd better find out who killed his mother. The police think Amos did it. But I know he didn't." He pulled Mrs. Potter's diary from his pocket and flipped to the last page of her notes. "See. Here's what she wrote last night." And he read aloud the scanty notes that Mrs. Potter had jotted down describing what Amos had seen from the window.

Amos listened intently, nodding his huge head. When Tim finished reading, he turned to Amos and said, "Can you tell us anything else? Did the man who fell out of the box run away? Did someone drive the team of horses and the wagon away? Was he the same man who came into the house?"

Amos covered his ears and shouted, "Too much!"

"All right, Amos. I'm sorry," said Tim. "But we have to find out who stabbed your mother. You want to help us do that, don't you?"

"No, no, no!" Amos wailed, wagging his head rapidly

back and forth. "Don't want Ma dead like that. Want Ma talking to me."

"I wish she could talk to you, Amos. But she can't. It's up to you to speak for her."

Amos opened the cigar box, which he had been holding on his lap. He picked up handfuls of bird feathers and tossed them up into the air, sobbing and laughing all the while. When the box was empty, he threw it at Tim. "All gone!" he shouted. "Man come. Say police. Say murder. Hit Ma down. That's all." He put his great head down on the table and wept uncontrollably.

"There now, there now," crooned Mrs. Crane, taking him in her arms. "Don't fash yourself. You'll be with us now and you'll be our boy. We'll take care of you and you'll be happy." She tipped his head up and made him look at her. "Do you believe me?" she asked.

"Believe," said Amos, wiping his tear-stained face on his sleeve.

Mrs. McCready handed him a dish towel in lieu of a handkerchief. "Here, kiddo. Mop up and listen to Rosalie. She'll be your ma now. And lucky you are to have her. Although I don't know why she wants to add you to her burdens."

"Hush, Ida. Amos won't be a burden. Amos is Eldridge's boy. Just a little older than Tim. Now he'll be one of mine."

Amos laid his head on Rosalie's shoulder and beamed up at her. "Now we all go to Coney?"

• • •

As it turned out, only Tim and Amos boarded the crowded train headed for Coney Island. Jimmy said he had work to do back at his saloon, but he would be along later with some of the Gophers to see the fight and would meet them at the Observation Tower. Mrs. Crane wanted to go home and recover from all the excitement and said she didn't care much for prizefights anyway. And Mrs. McCready had no intention of going to Coney Island when there was money to be made right here at home. It was Friday, and by nightfall the revelers would be out in force.

It took the elevated steam train almost an hour to get to the Culver Line terminal just off Surf Avenue. Amos, who had the amazing ability to sleep through any kind of din, had dozed through the entire trip and woke up cranky and famished. Tim herded him out of the terminal and bought him a box of Cracker Jack to quiet him down. "Bet you've never had anything like that before, have you?" he said. "It's some new kind of candy."

But Amos had torn the box open and stuffed his mouth with the sweet popcorn and peanuts, and was happily munching away.

"Let's get over to the Athletic Club," said Tim. "I might want to place a bet or two."

Amos followed along, taking in the garish sights and the surging crowd of people. He had never been so happy in his life. No one stared at him. No one made fun of him. Everyone was having a good time, despite the spring drizzle that came and went. He finished off his Cracker Jack and licked his fingers clean. When they came to Feltman's restaurant, he tugged at Tim's arm.

"Oh, yeah," said Tim, "I know. Amos hungry. Right?"

But Amos was staring at Feltman's merry-go-round that stood just before the entrance to the restaurant. "Horses?" he said. "Hundred horses all go around? Amos ride hundred horse?"

Tim could barely hear his questions over the blaring music of the calliope, but gathered from his yearning gaze that he wanted to ride on the merry-go-round. "Sure. Why not, kid? I guess you've never done that, either."

He bought tickets for both of them and when the merry-go-round stopped, he guided Amos on board and asked him which horse he wanted.

"Black Beauty," said Amos, heading straight for a coal-black steed that seemed larger than all the others. Tim helped him climb aboard and stood beside him as the merry-go-round began to turn. Amos hummed along with the thumping music and bounced in his saddle.

"He's like a little kid in a grown-up body," Tim brooded. And then reminded himself that this was his half brother as well as someone to whom he owed an enormous debt. Not only had he been the cause of Mrs. Potter's death, but he was abetting Amos's escape from the police. He had to prove Amos's innocence, but he hadn't a single idea how to go about it. The best he could offer was to act as the huge child's nanny while he had a bit of fun for himself and hope for a miracle.

As the merry-go-round speeded up, Amos clung to the pole with both hands and shouted with glee. His words were unintelligible. It didn't matter. The look on his face said it all. His grin was as wide as that on the clownish face hanging over the entrance to Steeplechase Park. But suddenly his face clouded and he tried to clamber down from his horse.

"Hold on, Amos," Tim cautioned. "You'll hurt yourself."

"Over there!" Amos pointed excitedly across Surf Avenue, but Tim couldn't figure out what was upsetting him. "Man!" Amos shouted. "Man box jump! Blood on head! There! There! There!" He wriggled off the horse, jumped from the spinning platform, and dashed through the crowd as fast as he could go, knocking people out of his way and attracting the attention of a gang of toughs that was marching six abreast along Surf Avenue.

"Amos! Amos! Slow down!" Tim panted as he raced after the lumbering fool. He feared his charge would foment a mob riot and bring the police with their billy clubs. There were plenty of elbow-benders in the crowd who would be ripe for a fight.

But Amos stopped suddenly in front of the Albemarle Hotel just as the doors swung closed behind a lithe figure in a black slouch hat. When Tim caught up with him, he was almost weeping with disappointment. "Man go in here," he sobbed. "Not see Amos."

"That's okay, kiddo. I don't know what set you off like that, but you sure put a scare into me. Want to sit down and tell me about it?" Tim motioned toward an unoccupied porch glider at the end of the veranda. Amos allowed himself to be drawn toward it, mumbling all the way. "Man fall. Box fall. Man get blood on head."

"Sure, Amos, we'll find out all about that. Just as soon as we can sit down and rest ourselves. Right? Right. Here you go." They sat side by side in the glider and Tim started a slow gentle motion, rocking Amos into a quieter mood just as if he were a baby in a cradle. Amos's head began to nod.

"Hey! Wait a minute," Tim protested. "Don't fall asleep on me. We need to talk."

Amos smiled his most foolish Steeplechase kind of smile. "Talking is nice. Train is nice. Man go in that door. We go in, too?"

"Why, Amos? Why do you want to go into the hotel?"

"Talk to man," he replied. "Maybe man . . ." he paused and frowned over his thought. "Maybe man see who hit Ma down."

"Good thinking," said Tim. "Wait a minute." Tim began searching his pockets for Mrs. Potter's diary. He quickly leafed through the pages until he came to her last entry and read it aloud. "Amos saw a man with blood on his head fall out of a box. He also saw a black carriage drawn by at least two black horses. If I didn't know better, I would think he had witnessed the removal of a corpse from one of the houses opposite. The box that he described could have been a coffin, and the black carriage a hearse. But of course, I didn't see this scene myself and poor Amos can't really describe it with any degree of accuracy. It could have been something completely ordinary, and I am imagining a disaster where there is none. By the time I got to the window there was nothing to be seen in the street."

Tim watched Amos's face. He was learning to read the signs of understanding and confusion in the young man's expressions. So far, so good. "Is that what you saw?" he asked.

"Oh, yes," said Amos. "And some more. Man get up and kick horses. He run. Horses run. Other man run but then come back. Pick up box." Amos closed his eyes and sighed.

"But you didn't tell that to your mother?"

"Amos hungry. Ma brought food. We go in that door now?"

"Might as well," said Tim. "Let's see if we can find your man with the sore head."

• • •

BERT the Barber had found a bookmaker of his acquaintance and laid a tidy sum on Ironman Jeffries. Now he could spend the rest of the day—and the night, if necessary—on enjoying the feminine scenery and keeping an eye out for Dandy Dover. His bookie hadn't seen her at all, at all, but Bert was sure she would turn up before the night was over. As he strolled away from the Seaside Athletic Club, he spied young Tim Crane leading a hulking brute into the Albemarle Hotel. Getting to be a regular reunion of old enemies, he mused.

As much as he resented Dandy Dover for her chicanery, he despised Tim Crane more for having gotten him into so much eternal trouble with Captain Johannes Schmitt of the Metropolitan Police Force three years before. It was only by dint of innumerable "loans" and favors extended to the voracious captain that he had been able to stay out of the Tombs himself. Schmitt's latest demand was for the services of a couple of Bert's tribe of thieves and brigands to do harm to a person unnamed who owed the captain for some real or imagined slight. The captain wouldn't tell him who it was that deserved punishment or what the infraction was. But from the glint in the policeman's close-set eyes, Bert would hate to be in those unlucky shoes.

Bert sidled up onto the porch of the hotel and peered into one of the windows. He saw Crane and the other fellow scanning the lobby as if in search of someone. Then the big clown made a beeline for the tobacco stand with Tim following in his wake. Bert moved quickly to another window where he could get a better view. He saw Tim and his companion in deep conversation with a slender gent in a black slouch hat. The conversation didn't last long. The three of them headed for the broad staircase. Once the three had gone out of sight, Bert entered the lobby and walked up to the desk. "Who was that who just went upstairs?" he asked the hotel official on duty.

"Sorry," said that worthy, eyeing Bert up and down and obviously not thinking highly of what he saw. "I can't tell you that."

"Then I guess I can't give you a finniff," whispered Bert, flashing a five-dollar gold eagle that appeared between two fingers of his left hand.

"But I can write it down. I trust you can read."

"Just so long as you can spell."

The official dipped a penpoint into an inkwell and took his time about writing on a slip of paper, making decorative curlicues and finally caressing his creation with a blotter featuring a photograph of the hotel on the back. He handed the paper to Bert and left his hand lying open on the counter.

Bert, who was not noted for his good manners, hawked and spat a juicy gob into the outstretched palm and plunked the gold eagle, which was bogus, on top of the gobbet. He walked quickly out of the hotel and across Surf Avenue, continuing until he reached the back alley known as The Bowery. There he pulled the slip of paper out of his pocket and tried to decipher the elegant script. But try as he might,

he couldn't decipher the two words written on the paper.
Bert had never learned to read at all. His bookie could read,
though, and Bert headed for the beer stall where his friend
maintained a temporary office.

• • •

TIM and Amos followed the black slouch hat along the
fourth-floor corridor to a corner suite. The young man unlocked the door and ushered them inside. As soon as the
door was closed and locked, he swept off his hat and let his
jet black curls tumble down around his shoulders.

Amos gaped. Tim burst out laughing. And Dandy Dover
grinned and clapped her hands in glee. "Had you fooled,
didn't I, Tim Crane?" she shouted. "I've had everybody
fooled for almost a month. But it's over now. Especially after
what happened last night."

"Exactly what did happen last night, Dandy? I've been
trying to find you for weeks. I had you pegged for one of
those houses across from Mrs. Potter."

"You were right, Tim. I bought a house in that street.
But somebody else knew that, too. I barely got away last
night. I've been lying low, but that's no way to live. I think
the best thing I can do is to use myself as bait, dress as
myself, go about openly, and see what happens. Will you
help me? I'll pay you."

Tim hesitated. He didn't want to accept money from
Dandy. It didn't seem right somehow. But he wanted to
find out who killed Mrs. Potter.

Dandy misunderstood his hesitation. "I'll pay whatever
you ask, Tim. I heard you were working as a bodyguard.
Are you already engaged? I'll pay double whatever anyone
else is paying. I know I can trust you."

"I'll help you, Dandy, but I don't want your money. I
want to find the slasher who killed Amos's mother. If that
helps you, fine. No money, though. I would be doing it
anyway." Tim found it difficult to look Dandy square in the

face. He was embarrassed that he didn't cotton onto her as
soon as he saw her. But dressed as a man and with her un-
painted face roughened and bronzed from the weather, she
really did look like a man. A small and wiry man, but a
man nonetheless.

"Do you know who attacked you?" he asked.

Dandy shook her head. "A pair of roughnecks. Plenty of
those around. No one I ever saw before. But there's a whole
new crop of young hooligans grown up since I left town."

Amos never left off staring at her. Now he approached
her and whispered, "Head hurt?" He reached out to touch
the bandage on her brow. His touch was feather light.

"Not any more, chum," she said. "There was a lot of
blood, but the cut is pretty small. Would you like to see?"

Amos nodded eagerly.

Dandy unwound the bandage and threw it aside. There
was a small lump on her left temple and the skin was slightly
abraded. "I think I can do without that now. Will you fellows excuse me for a few minutes? I'm going to change into
a more ladylike rig, and then we'll go out and see the sights.
I'll only be a few minutes." She went into one of the suite's
bedrooms and closed the door behind her.

"Nice lady," said Amos.

Tim threw himself into an armchair and said, "You think
all the ladies are nice, Amos. This one is nice when it suits
her." He pulled out Mrs. Potter's diary and began reading
some of the earlier pages, pages that he had already seen, in
the hope of finding something he had overlooked that would
help him find a clue to Dandy's dilemma and Mrs. Potter's
tragedy. There had to be a connection, but no matter how
closely he pored over the pages of the diary, he came no
closer to discovering what it was.

East Eleventh Street was not a busy thoroughfare, but it
got its share of transient traffic. Mrs. Potter had dutifully
recorded all the activity that she had witnessed and that
Amos had seen and told her about. Tim had gone over all

of it with her several times during the weeks she had been watching for him. There had been nothing in it that he could interpret as a sighting of Dandy Dover. But if Dandy had gone about in men's clothing, Mrs. Potter would have noted the comings and goings of a young gentleman. He berated himself for not having thought of such a ruse. It was like Dandy to be so bold.

"Amos," he said. "Did you ever see that man before?"

"Man?" Amos looked bewildered.

"The one that had blood on the head."

Amos tittered nervously. "Lady now. Right?"

"Yes, lady now. Did you ever see her dressed in men's clothing before last night?"

"Mmmmm . . ." Amos tried to remember, but was having a hard time of it.

"Well, is she the one who hit your mother?"

"Oh, no! Not him. Other man. Man with box."

"You mean the man with the wagon and horses? He hit your mother?"

"Yes. Him. Come up to door. Bang, bang! 'Police! Murder!' Ma open door. Man hit her down. Say he seen her watching. Amos hide. Man run away. Amos want . . ." Tears were rolling down his cheeks, but he kept on trying to tell Tim everything that had happened. "Amos want Ma to talk. Ma no more talking." He slumped onto the sofa and buried his face in a cushion.

"So all we have to do is find out who that was. And hope that Captain Schmitt will believe us. Maybe Dandy can help us. She says there were two young roughnecks, no one she knew. So they must have been hired by someone who's out to hurt her." Tim paced the room, eager for Dandy to reappear so he could quiz her again. She could have any number of enemies here in the city, and even some who had followed her from the Yukon.

Amos pulled out the handkerchief that Tim had given

him that morning. He wiped his face, blew his nose, and beamed at Tim. "Amos do good?" he asked.

"Amos, you did very, very good. Do you think you would recognize this fellow if you ever saw him?"

"Recognize?"

"Would you remember his face?"

"Yes. Yes, sirree. Amos remember that face. Ugly face. Bad face. Remember that face okay."

The door to the bedroom opened and a rouged and painted Dandy appeared in a pale yellow spring frock with a tight-fitting black velvet jacket and a broad-brimmed straw hat trimmed with yellow tulle and black egret feathers. "It's a nuisance getting into all this paraphernalia," she said. "All the time I was up in the north country, I wore men's clothing and it's a lot easier than struggling with the sheer waste of cloth that goes into dressing a fashionable woman. However, I'll make the sacrifice in a good cause. How do I look?" She posed for them with one hand on her hip, the other toying flirtatiously with the ruffle at her throat.

"You look like the Dandy Dover I used to know when I patrolled the Tenderloin," said Tim. "A little toned down, but it suits you. Red satin might be a bit gaudy at Coney Island."

Dandy laughed. "You didn't forget, did you? I always wore red satin when I was on the job. I'm sorry I beaned you that time, but I had no choice. It was you or me. You looked so adorable out cold. Just like a little baby asleep in the nursery."

Tim blushed and glanced at Amos, who seemed not to understand what they were talking about. He offered Dandy his arm and said, "Well, if we're going to pretend to be lambs to the slaughter, let's go out for a stroll. How about a couple of wieners at Feltman's? I promised Amos."

"It's a deal," said Dandy.

• • •

WHEN the bookmaker read aloud the two words on the slip of paper, Bert the Barber fell into a rage. "Harry Houdini!" he shouted. "That was no Harry Houdini! I've seen Harry Houdini and that wasn't him! I'll go back there and strangle the lying snob and then I'll slit his scrawny throat! I'll pulverize him. I'll chew his ears off and spit them back in his face! And I gave him one of my best sham eagles for the privilege of being conned by a professional."

But on his way back to the hotel, Bert calmed down a bit. He still wanted to know what Tim Crane was up to and mangling the hotel registrar wasn't going to help. But as he was about to cross Surf Avenue he spotted Crane and the big bozo heading toward Feltman's with a fine-figured woman in a yellow gown. He followed as close as he dared, even though he was willing to bet that Crane wouldn't remember him. He watched from across the street as they bought wieners on rolls for the big galoot and then went on their way further along the avenue. As he passed the train terminal, another crowd of merrymakers disgorged from the station almost swamping Bert in their haste to lay down their bets on the fight that was now only a few hours away. When he fought his way free of the horde, he saw that the trio was approaching the Iron Tower.

At the ticket booth, the woman in the yellow gown turned back to look at the crowd moving like a tidal wave toward the Athletic Club. Bert grinned and set off in her direction. He could hardly believe his good fortune. Dandy Dover and Tim Crane, his most hated enemies, together and within his reach. Too bad for the big lunk with them, whoever he was.

So intent was Bert upon the chase, he failed to notice that he himself was being trailed.

• • •

"DON'T look now," said Dandy to Tim, "but I believe Bert the Barber is heading our way. Not only that, but he's being followed by our old friend Captain Johannes Schmitt." Hand in hand, they boarded the steam elevator that would take them 300 feet up to the observation deck at the top of the Iron Tower. Amos followed behind them, still munching on the last of his wieners with sauerkraut and mustard.

"Do you suppose they'd both like to see Coney from the observatory above?" Tim asked.

"That would be an excellent diversion for both of them," said Dandy. "I think we should invite them to join us."

Tim turned to Amos. "Do you see the weasely-looking gentleman just now stepping up to the ticket booth?"

Amos peered nearsightedly at the booth. "I see him."

"Would you kindly give the ticket-seller this ten-cent piece, buy two tickets, and escort the weasel over here? Don't let him get away. Hold his arm as tight as you can."

As Amos set out on his errand, Dandy handed the elevator operator a twenty-dollar bank note and said, "We are expecting a couple of friends to join us. They'll be here in a moment. I'd be obliged if you would hold the elevator until they get here. There's more for you if you disregard any conversation you might overhear."

The operator, a lad of no more than sixteen, was happy to pocket the note and vowed silently to do anything the beautiful lady desired.

While Amos escorted Bert to the elevator cabin, Dandy sashayed down the sidewalk to meet Captain Schmitt. The policeman's eyes narrowed when he saw who was approaching. "I've been looking for you," he said.

"You and half the underworld population of New York," said Dandy. "Two of them almost found me last night. But come with me. There's a business meeting about to commence, and your presence is required."

"I've got some old business to discuss with you," said the captain. "And I don't think you'll like it." He looked past her shoulder and spotted Tim Crane, Amos Potter, and Bert the Barber in the elevator. "Who's that big fellow with Crane?" he asked.

"Oh, just someone else you've been looking for. His name is Amos Potter."

"The idiot who killed his mother? Well, thank you very much. And if that's the business you want to discuss with me, forget it. There's nothing to discuss. I'll just take him into custody right now." The policeman hastened toward the elevator without further prompting. But before he got there, he turned and gave Dandy an oily smile. "If I get a conviction on this one, maybe I can forget that you cost me a promotion three years ago. You and that Crane fellow. I could have been superintendent by now if it hadn't been for you."

As soon as he entered the cabin, Dandy, who was close on his heels, gave the operator the nod to start the elevator moving. He closed the gate and moved the lever to the up position. The elevator started to move, slowly at first and then as fast as it could go. As the cabin rose into the sky, Bert sat down on one of the benches rather suddenly and held on with both hands. Amos sat next to him, still holding on to his arm.

Schmitt frowned at Bert. "What are you doing here?"

"I might ask you the same thing," said Bert. "But instead I'll ask you what happened to the two boyos I loaned out to you last night? They never showed up at headquarters." Bert's headquarters was a ramshackle hotel in the Tenderloin, frequented by thieves, pickpockets, prostitutes, and lush-rollers.

"Ah, Bert, I'm sorry to have to tell you this, but they were incapable of the urgent mission I had for them. They got drunk and failed miserably. The horses bolted and the wagon was smashed. Your boyos are presently in the Tombs sleeping it off." Schmitt affected an attitude of deepest sorrow. "I'll have to add their failure and the cost of the ruined wagon and two crippled horses to the outstanding debt you owe me. You'll have to do better next time."

"Wait a minute." Tim Crane faced the policeman at the center of the elevator cabin. "What's all this about a wagon and a team of horses? And a pair of Bert's roughnecks? Does it have anything to do with a certain event on East Eleventh Street last night?"

"If you're referring to the murder of Mrs. Potter, you're dreaming. You and I both know who killed that poor old woman, and the slobbering idiot is sitting right over there." Captain Schmitt's normally florid face had turned ashen and his breathing was labored. "You, sir," he shouted to the elevator operator. "Take this thing down immediately."

But the lad kept the mechanism on the rise and they soon reached the top. "Now what?" he asked Dandy.

"Oh, I think we'll just get out and take a look around," she said. The operator obligingly opened the gate for her. She told him, "You can take the elevator down, but come up for us when I whistle like this." She placed two fingers between her scarlet lips and emitted a shrill signal that would have outdone Gabriel's trumpet on the day of judgment. "Would you like some fresh air, Captain? You look a little peaked."

Taking him by the arm, Dandy led the quivering policeman out onto the observation platform, where he gripped the iron railing between his massive fists, causing his knuckles to turn an ugly yellowish white. "Isn't it lovely up here, Captain? It sure beats climbing the Chilkoot Pass to the goldfields. Thirty-five hundred feet up and most of the time nothing but snow and ice to put your foot on. But up here, on a really fine day, I could imagine seeing all the way across the ocean to Europe. Have you ever been abroad, Captain?" Dandy chatted on, while the captain leaned ever so carefully over the railing and retched into the wind.

When the other three came out onto the platform, they

found Captain Schmitt sprawled on the floor while Dandy held a vial of smelling salts to his nose.

"Dandy, you certainly have an odd effect on policemen," said Tim. "Here's another one laid out at your feet, just as I was three years ago. Did you bean him, too? Or is it just the overwhelming power of your beauty?"

"I had nothing to do with it. It was the view from the top that did it. But I think the captain is just about ready to see reason. Aren't you, Captain?"

Schmitt raised himself to his knees and groaned. "What? What do you want?"

Tim hauled him up to his feet and stood him against the railing. "I want three things from you. First, I want you to stop the search for Amos Potter. We both know he didn't kill his mother. Am I right?"

"I don't know what you're talking about," the policeman growled.

Tim beckoned to Amos. "Come over here, kid. Pick him up by his ankles and dangle him over the side."

Amos looked startled. "Throw him over?" he asked.

"Only if absolutely necessary. No. Just hold him over the side. But don't let go."

"Now?" Amos was confused. He had never done anything like that before in his life. But there were many things he hadn't done before, and it seemed he was doing them all in one day.

"Now," said Tim.

Amos bent and grasped Schmitt's ankles. He was about to turn him head over heels when Schmitt cried out, "Stop! Stop! You're right! The idiot didn't do it. I'll give you that much."

"Fine," said Tim. "Now, we both know that you are responsible for those two roughnecks attacking Dandy." He turned to Bert the Barber. "Does that sound right to you, Bert? Those are your boyos he hired?"

Bert stared at the groveling policeman. Schmitt would

never forgive him for having witnessed his shame. So he might as well plunge ahead, in for a penny, in for a pound you might say. With any luck, he'd be free of the black-mailing crusher at least for a while. "Yes, they are. And I'll be down to the Tombs to pay their fine as soon as I get back to town. But I swear, Tim Crane, I never knew he was set-ting them on Miss Dover."

"Well, Schmitt, what do you say to that? Or should I let Amos dangle you?"

Amos renewed his grip on the policeman's ankles. "Now?" he asked Tim.

"No!" Schmitt cried. "I'll have you all arrested for this! But for what it's worth, I did engage the services of some of Bert's fellows. They were to bring Dandy Dover to me at my own home. I wanted to have a private talk with her. Just to be sure she remains an honest, law-abiding citizen while she's here. And suggest that she might consider mov-ing on. That's all."

"Is that a fact?" Dandy exclaimed. "Then I must have been mistaken when I heard them talking about the best place on the East River to dump a shipping crate. You wouldn't have any ideas about the contents of that crate, would you, Captain?"

"You can't prove anything," the captain howled.

"It doesn't matter," said Tim. "I believe that when we get down from the tower, the captain will telephone the Tombs and arrange for us to interview Bert's pals. We'll just ask them what they were up to and let Amos identify the one who killed his mother."

"Like hell I will!" The captain clung to the railing and tried to kick Amos away from his ankles. Amos lost his grip on one ankle and the captain found himself lurching out into space. His scream could have been heard for miles had there not been a noisy crowd milling below. A few people looked up and soon most of them were witness to the strug-gle as Amos and Tim hauled him back to safety by one foot.

"My goodness," said Dandy. "You really shouldn't try to fly, Captain. It's best, don't you think, if you keep your flat feet on terra firma? Amos won't always be around to rescue you."

"I wish to God I'd never seen the big lummox." Schmitt did his best to restore his equanimity, but his hands trembled and his breathing was shallow.

"You should be grateful, Captain," said Dandy. "I believe I see some reporters down there, eager to interview you and the hero who saved your life. Your picture will be all over *The Journal* and *The World*. The whole city will know that Captain Schmitt of the Metropolitan Police is afraid of heights. I can hear your colleagues now. They won't let you forget this one so easy. You may even want to retire from the force. I think it's time we descended." And she placed two fingers between her lips.

As the elevator ground its way back up to the top of the tower, the blare of a marching band sounded closer and closer. The brass and drums played heartily but not very well. Mr. Sousa's "Washington Post March" was barely recognizable, but some in the crowd below began to dance a lively two-step.

"Well, I'll be damned!" Tim exclaimed. "Jimmy said he would bring some of the Gophers, but he didn't say it would be their Chowder and Marching Society. Look, Dandy! There must be at least twenty of them, with my brother leading the way."

While his captors were distracted by the scene below, Captain Schmitt climbed over the railing and began clambering down the iron framework of the tower. When the elevator reached the top, all four of them entered and the cage began its descent. By then, Schmitt had shinnied down to the midpoint of the tower where there was a platform that bore advertising signs for Steeplechase Park on all four sides.

Here he was stalled. In the upper section of the tower,

the iron struts and crossbars were close together much like a ladder, but below the middle platform they were farther apart, well beyond the reach of even the longest legs of the tallest freak in the sideshow. Schmitt could go back up, but he couldn't get down without help.

As the elevator passed him by, Dandy waved to him. "Planning to spend the night, Captain?" she called out. She handed another twenty-dollar bill to the elevator operator. "I know you can get him down from there, but I would appreciate it if you would wait until the rest of us have gotten away. Don't pay any attention to anything he says. He thinks he's a policeman but he's really just a harmless lunatic. And if you want to double your money, just put it on Jeffries. He's bound to win."

My Cousin Rachel's Uncle Murray

Susan Isaacs

F AMILY.
My mother. Phyllis Lincoln. In 1971, shortly before
my first birthday, she ran off with a Mr. Maumoon Fathulla
Hussain, bodyguard for the Consul of the Permanent Mission of the Republic of Maldives to the United Nations
whom she had met at a hot dog stand outside a B. B. King
concert at the Fillmore East. That was about five blocks from
home, two rooms on the Lower East Side. My father had
declared it an apartment; my mother, a slum. From what I
have heard, we shared the premises with a heavyset rodent.
My father said, Oh, a cute little mouse, and called it Mickey;
my mother called it a rat. In any case, my mother took off
and I never saw her again.

My father. Eugene Lincoln. Back then, my father was
employed as a part-time driver by Frank ("Clockwork")
Lombardini, a *caporegima* in the Gambino family who had
originally retained him in the mistaken belief that all Jews
are smart.

Our surname, Lincoln. Maybe the family legend is actually true and in the penultimate year of the nineteenth
century, some Protestant clerk on Ellis Island with an antic

sense of humor wrote down "Samuel Lincoln" when my great-grandfather—full of beard, dark of eye, and great of nose—stepped before him. More likely, Great-grandpa Schmuel Golumbek heard the names "Washington" and "Lincoln" while hanging out around the pickle barrel in downtown Minsk listening to stories about the Golden Land. Flipping a kopek, he got tails. Could he truly have believed that by being a Lincoln, no one in New York would notice his six extant teeth and ten words of English? Very likely. By and large, my relatives have never been prone to analytical thought.

Anyhow, my father. When I was four, he was dispatched to the Downstate Correctional Facility for five to seven. On one of my semiannual visits, when I was nine, Dad raised his right hand: "I swear on my mother's grave, Amy baby, I'm innocent."

"Grandma's still alive," I pointed out.

"That's okay. Listen." He explained he'd merely been the driver of the Fleetwood Brougham that had transported Clockwork, Sick Vinny DeCicco, and some poor schnook of a restaurateur to a remote section of Van Cortlandt Park in the Bronx. "It was Clockwork and Sick Vinny that roughed up the guy. I was, you know, sitting behind the wheel. Listening to a Doobie Brothers tape. I was minding my own business."

" 'Roughed up?' " I repeated. "Dad, the guy was in a coma for three weeks."

"Yeah. And what did he prove in the end? He could've gotten his tablecloths and aprons and crap from Lombardini's Linen Service and not wasted all that time in the hospital."

After my father went up the river to Downstate, I was sent to live with his mother. Grandma Milly looked a little like Mrs. Potato Head, with giant ruby lips, over-wide eyes, and stick-out ears. She was one of those unctuous individuals whom other people, who can't stand them, feel obliged to call "well-meaning." Grandma worked a day or two or three a week as a substitute waxer, ripping the hair off the lips, legs, and the random chins of the famous and the merely rich at Beauté, an uptown, upscale salon.

From the jet-set and celebrity clientele, Grandma learned about the finer things of life, which she felt obliged to pass on to me, mainly because no one else she knew would listen. "Always be nice to the help," she told me when I was ten. She held up her finger in a hold-on-a-second gesture. Then, with a hop-step that looked like the opening of an obscure Slavic folk dance, she clunked her foot down on a bloated cockroach; it made a barely audible crunching sound. "I heard about how this guy James who owns a catering business—I told you what catering is?"

"Yeah," I said.

"Don't say 'yeah.' Say 'yes.' "

"Yes."

"Anyways, this James guy is such a shit to his waiters that one of them actually spit on the cheese straws and, like, half the guests at a hemophilia benefit saw him do it!"

"What's a cheese straw?" I asked. I already knew what hemophilia was and could figure out benefit.

"Who the hell knows? Something rich goyim eat. So, Amy, the motto of the story is, treat your help good and they'll be good to you."

So I learned what to do from Grandma. As well as what not to do: I sensed that saying *"Ciao, bella"* in a breathy voice, as she did, while flapping fingers rearward as one dashes toward Delancey Street to get to the subway, was not the way to endear oneself to one's neighbors in one's low-income housing project.

And so I grew. By age fourteen, I sensed a change of scenery might be salutary. My father, who'd been out of jail for a year and a half, was back in. This time, it was for stealing a black Lincoln Town Car in order to become a self-employed limo driver. Within months of Dad's second trip to the Big House, two of my good friends from school dropped out to have their babies. Another left to support her family; she earned fifty bucks a head performing fellatio on homebound New Jersey commuters who would have otherwise gotten irritable during the usual half-hour wait to get into the Holland Tunnel. Another girl, a year ahead of me, died from a crack overdose.

Though my guidance counselor at Intermediate School 495 said "I don't know if you'd be comfortable at a place like that, sweetie," I applied for a full scholarship at Ivey-Rush Academy, a boarding school for young ladies in the Connecticut Valley that Grandma had reported was the "best of the best of the best." I signed her name to the application and request-for-scholarship form in a round, shaky hand to simulate old age (Grandma was fifty-three) and semi-literacy (a promotion). I sensed she might not want me to go, as that would mean not only losing my company, but the eighty-seven bucks a week from the City of New York's Human Resources Administration.

I also submitted a heart-wrenching essay about visiting Dad in prison; "Father's Day" was full of shocking language (in quotation marks) as well as graphic descriptions of nauseating smells, oozing sores, and piercing wails from junkie girlfriends pleading for money. Ivey-Rush was mad for such a well-phrased account of degradation. Graciously, they offered me a more-than-full scholarship. And they were so genteel that when they discovered that Amy Lincoln, the year's Fahnstock Scholarship winner—the traditional black face in the class photograph—was white, they did a reasonably good job of hiding their dismay.

At Ivey, I quickly decided trying to fit in would be a waste of my efforts. I could get far more mileage out of my New Yorkese "tamayta" rather than mimicking the "tamahto" crowd. My accent—"*sooo* refreshing"—to say nothing of my biography featuring runaway mother and imprisoned father, took me places where the F train didn't go. Like Capri and Chamonix. I learned to mesmerize a dinner party in Palm Beach with now-appalling, now-amusing vignettes of the mean streets. By the time I got to Brown University and then to Harvard Law School, I was an accomplished guest. During most vacations, my friends' families—rich, poor, in between—took me in. I'd go from Thanksgiving in Aspen to Christmas in Bedford-Stuyvesant to spring break in Circleville, Ohio.

As for my own *mishpochah*, Grandma Milly began exhibiting symptoms of vascular dementia in my junior year at Brown. She decided I was my mother and would screech "Fucking Phyllis" and try to shove me out the door whenever I came to see her. She died during my second year at law school. The few times I couldn't sponge a free Presidents' Day weekend in Hobe Sound, I stayed in Canarsie with my father's long-estranged sister.

To make a long story shorter, I grew fond of my aunt Linda and her husband, Uncle Patrick. They were a pleasant, ordinary couple (except for a curious predilection for Velveeta cheese) who had a daughter a year older than I. My cousin Rachel.

Rachel looked like a better me. Her hair was a glossier black, her eyes a more chocolatey brown, her body more supermodel than lacrosse defense. Instead of my coloring, which tends toward cirrhotic without great brushfuls of blush, she had inherited her father's O'Toole strawberries and cream complexion. If I was passably pretty, she was a knockout. She had a beautiful face, an inferior intellect, a glorious figure, the kindest heart. And what a live-wire! At least half her sentences ended in exclamation points, so even her most banal utterance had an air of excitement. Excitement!

Rachel taught me the secrets of applying multiple layers of mascara and informed me I looked exactly like Salma Hayek—if Salma had been Jewish and a tiny bit big-boned. Better than Salma Hayek, as a matter of fact, because "you look younger and between me and you, Amy, Salma probably couldn't have gotten into Harvard Law. Next time you see a picture of her, look close. There's no Harvard in those eyes."

I loved my cousin Rachel in that elemental way one ought to love one's family: without reason, simply because of that mysterious blood tie. The two of us had nothing in common except our mindless admiration for each other. When I went off to college, Rachel went off to a job at the men's fragrances counter at Saks Fifth Avenue. She didn't stay there long. Just before her nineteenth birthday, she sold a bottle of *Boucheron Pour Homme* to Danny Glickstein, the thirty-year-old executive vice president of Gladstone Motor Cars, a Mercedes dealership on the Upper East Side. Within two months Rachel O'T. Glickstein was living in a ten-room co-op twenty blocks due north of Saks.

After law school, I moved back to New York, first to clerk for a United States district judge and then to become a federal prosecutor. Rachel and I would meet for lunch every few months. She also insisted I attend her dinner parties. Clearly, she had hopes of matching me up with one of Danny's chums, men with deep golf tans who comported themselves as if intent on refuting Freud's assertion that sometimes a cigar is just a cigar. So when she called me at the office one April morning I was not at all surprised to hear from her. But instead of Rachel's usual spirited "Hi!" (which actually was a prolonged honk of "Hoy!"), she murmured: "Amy, it's me, Rach," in a funereal voice.

"What's wrong?" I demanded. I often worried that Aunt Linda and Uncle Patrick would suffer myocardial infarctions from Velveeta-clogged aortas.

"It's Danny's uncle Murray. Remember him from the wedding?" Rachel asked. "Uncle Murray Glickstein?" As Rachel's maid of honor, I had been mamboed and fox-trotted around the floor by a gaggle of Glicksteins, a clan who resembled ambulatory mailboxes. Most of them sang along as they danced. However, I could not recall if any of the gents crooning moistly into my ear had been a Murray. "He's the big jeweler," she added.

I decided not to say all the Glicksteins seemed big to me, including her husband, Danny, and their two sweet, cube-ish children, Brianna and Ryan. "I'm not sure which one Uncle Murray was," I replied. "Has anything happened to him?"

"He's being questioned."

"By whom?"

"You always know when to say 'whom,' Amy! Prep school, right?"

"Who's questioning him, Rachel?"

"Questioning him? I don't know. The cops, I guess. But he's a very, very important jeweler! Uncle Murray's the G of B and G Gems."

"Right," I said respectfully, while I doodled a diamond ring in the margin of a motion to suppress, not that I felt any pressure to find a husband, even though as Aunt Linda so diplomatically pointed out: You're twenty-eight, Amy, and in two more years you won't be no spring chicken anymore. Look, me and Uncle Pat love it that you're a lawyer—we're so proud—but what can I tell you? I worry about you being too smart for your own good, guy-wise. "What are the cops questioning Uncle Murray about?" I inquired.

"About his partner," Rachel said. "Barry Bleiberman."

"The B of B and G," I observed.

"He's one dead B!"

I took a deep breath and slowly let it out. "Let me get this right. Barry Bleiberman is dead and they're questioning Uncle Murray. . . . Why? Do they think Barry might have been the victim of foul play?"

"He was! He was stabbed!"

"Where?"

"In the heart. With his own letter opener! It had his initials!"

"I mean, where was Barry when he was stabbed?"

"In his office at B and G. The safe was open and some really, really fine jewels were G-O-N-E. Gone!"

"Well, Rachel, I'd say Uncle Murray definitely needs to get a lawyer before he even says 'Good morning' to the cops and—"

"He *has* a lawyer. A very classy criminal lawyer that came with the highest recommendations from B and G's accountant. Nick Schwartzman. He's also Danny's accountant. I trust his judgment totally!"

"Excellent."

"But Danny and I would like you personally to look into this. I mean, Amy, you're not just a Harvard lawyer. You're *family*!"

Once again, as I had done the five or six times Rachel had asked me to fix a parking ticket as well as the once she'd pleaded with me to sue her dry cleaner, I explained I was not in private practice. And not with the District Attorney's office. "I'm an assistant United States attorney in the Southern District of New York. That means I prosecute *federal* crimes: securities fraud, narcotics cases, taking potshots at a bald eagle." I didn't bother mentioning that what with the contretemps between my father and the criminal justice system (to say nothing of Dad's organized crime associations), all that had gotten me an FBI clearance was the unstinting support of the judge for whom I had clerked, an incandescent letter from a senator on the Judiciary Committee whose wife had been an Ivey-Rush girl, stellar grades since kindergarten, having been an editor of *The Harvard Law Review*—plus God smiling down on me. Gem though he might be, I was not going to risk all for Uncle Murray. "The Bleiberman homicide is a state crime, Rachel. I cannot represent Murray Glickstein. I wish I could help you, but—"

"Sweetie, I'm not asking you to do anything illegal—or that other thing."

"Immoral? Unethical?"

"Whatever. Please, please, Amy, please. Just look into it!"

"What if I conclude that it was Uncle Murray who did the dastardly deed?" I asked. Rachel's answer was a peal of girlish laughter: Oh, you're being silly!

At first all I did was check out the reputation of the lawyer representing Uncle Murray. A former assistant DA, he was said to be tough and smart. Splendid. I went back to my two-buy junk case. However, by seven that night, recognizing a major Uncle Murray distraction, I gave up and called my cousin Rachel.

One hour later, as I found myself sitting on a settee in her living room, Aunt Vivian, Murray's missus, was informing me: "We've heard *so* much about you, dear." Obviously, my gray suit, which even I thought was tacky, was causing Aunt Viv to try and suppress a shudder. So I suspected her cordial "dear" was evoked less by the fact of me than by the Ivey-Rush-and-her-roommate-was-a-Collier-of-*the*-Colliers briefing she'd clearly gotten from Rachel. As for appearance, Vivian Glickstein of Park Avenue pretty much resembled a just-budding eleven-year-old. Well, an eleven-year-old got up in a sleek brown-and-black Carolina Herrera ensemble. Except what was going on above her neck, while unlined, was not youthful: Aunt Vivian had the fish face wealthy women in their late fifties wind up with by the time they are on a first-name basis with their plastic surgeons. "You're . . ." She paused for an instant. "What can I say, Amy? You're family."

With a hasty smile, I acknowledged what I assumed was a compliment. Uncle Murray, a multi-chinned man who seemed to have been born with a paisley ascot rather than a neck, separating his head and chest, smiled also. The Glicksteins and I sipped Montrechet and nibbled on shiitake frittata squares and seared foie gras on brioche toast in the Vivian and Murray Glickstein Eclectic Living Room With a Heavy Emphasis on Louis Quatorze. Judging from the

amount of ormolu, to say nothing of the elaborately-framed
Dutch still lifes on the glazed vermilion walls, business at
B and G Gems had been thriving.

The third Glickstein, Ken, son of Vivian and Murray, a
man about my age, sat to my left in a gilt chair upholstered
in deep blue brocade that looked royal enough for the Sun
King himself. Not that anyone would call Ken Glickstein
regal. He had inherited his mother's dainty frame and Uncle
Murray's oversized head, so he resembled a lollipop, albeit
a lollipop dressed in a snazzy black silk shirt. Lost in the
vast luxury of the chair, Ken peeped: "Uh, can I get . . . is
there, uh, anything else you want?"

Out. But I said: "No. I'm fine, thanks." I held up my
three-quarters full wineglass as proof. I wasn't sure if Viv
and Mur had trotted Ken out for me to interview or marry,
and it seemed either prospect was making him dreadfully
anxious. He kept crossing and uncrossing his legs, as if seeking the best position for protecting his privates. So I turned
to Uncle Murray. "Your partner, Barry Bleiberman, was
stabbed?" Uncle Murray nodded once, twice, and then,
seized by some head-bowing frenzy, could not seem to stop.
Ken, clearly perturbed, turned toward his mother. She responded to her son's discomfort by ignoring him and fin-
gering her pearls—each one of which looked large enough
to have come from a fowl rather than an oyster.

"Stabbed three times in the chest," Murray finally said,
slapping his own hand against his chest, Pledge of Allegiance–style.

"Tell me a bit about B and G, Mr. Glickstein."

"Murray, please." At last his head stopped its manic bobbing. "I mean, we're family."

"Murray," I said.

"Well, first and foremost, so to speak, we're jewelry *manufacturers*. Let's say Harry Winston or Tiffany, and of course
some smaller"—he stopped to chortle—"but equally elegant vendors will hand us a design and say, 'Here, B and

G. Make it!' We employ two master gem-cutters from Bel-
gium, and of course we've trained some of our own boys.
And we have a fine, fine staff who can take a model of a
design and bring it to—how shall I put it?—fruition. A
piece of jewelry *any* woman in the world would be proud—
Might I even say honored?—to wear." I was praying he
would go back to mere nodding, but no, he kept spouting:
"And of course we have our own private customers, some of
the most discriminating people worldwide. If I named
names, you'd say 'Oh my God!' Anyhow, they'll give us a
description of what they want and say 'B and G, make my
wildest dream come true.' Or some others will say 'B and
G, do something magical with this eight-carat sapphire.' "

I tried to get a "Riveting!" expression on my face, but
I'd been working fifteen hours a day for the past two weeks
preparing for trial, so I probably looked somewhere between
merely blinky and stupefied. However, the sight of Uncle
Murray's pale peach Egyptian cotton shirt clinging and
turning orange from Rorschach-like patches of perspiration
suggested he might be getting so enthused he would keep
pontificating, from sapphires down through rubies to all
that glittered between amethysts and zircons. So I inquired:
"Were all your company's gemstones and jewelry in that
open safe in Barry's office?"

Uncle Murray's moon-face flushed darkly, as though he
was being strangled by his own ascot. "No, no." He glanced
toward his wife and son, but Aunt Viv was still diddling a
pearl and Ken was engrossed in exploring the weave of his
herringbone slacks just above his knee. "We have the main
safe in the back, behind the cutters' workroom. But both
Barry, may he rest in peace, and I have smaller safes in our
own offices, which are on the floor above. This way, if one
of our clients is looking for, let's say, a diamond necklace,
we can keep certain pieces in our own safe and also some
loose stones to show them. It's much more . . . civilized. I
mean, sitting in a more, shall we say, comfortable environ-

ment with a cup of perfect coffee. Or a glass of lovely wine."

I was curious to learn what constituted perfect and/or lovely, but on the other hand, I was afraid he might actually tell me. "The safe was open?" I asked instead.

Vivian and Ken peered up. Uncle Murray didn't notice because he was gazing directly into my eyes, the way people do when they are trying to appear honest. "Yes."

"Was anything missing?"

"Stones," he said sadly. Sadly as in no big deal, like when the travel section is missing from the Sunday paper, not like when hundreds of thousands of dollars of gems have been heisted.

"Stones? Like diamonds? Those kinds of stones?"

"In this case, a few diamonds and—How shall I put it?— more emeralds than I care to think about."

"Rings? Bracelets?"

"No, no. Loose stones."

"There was no actual jewelry in the safe?" I asked.

"The jewelry wasn't taken," Ken interjected. Both Uncle Murray and I turned in time to see Ken's lollipop of a face turn cherry. His lips looked as though they were sorry for parting and were dying to stick together, but he pried them apart because he knew he had to offer something more. "I mean, the pieces that were in the safe . . . they weren't . . . stolen. But the stones are gone."

"Do you work at B and G?" I asked.

"Yes," Ken said, "I'm—"

"He's a senior vice president," Uncle Murray declared. Since Ken did not turn red this time, I could not tell if his father's speaking for him was business as usual or if Uncle Mur had been trying to shut up his son before he spilled some B and G beans.

"Who found Barry Bleiberman's body?" I asked Ken, just to see who would answer.

Murray obliged. "His daughter." I waited. Long before I became a prosecutor, in the school yard of P.S. 97, I understood that the most efficient way to get the facts was to offer a potential informant nothing. And then more nothing. Few people can bear silence. "Her name's Gabrielle. She's a twin." I waited some more. "Gabrielle and Garrett," Murray went on. "Boy-girl. So they're not identical. I mean, not just counting the boy-girl differences. They're both . . . They're both at B and G." Murray's upper body was wriggling either with unease or the desire to separate skin from the sweaty cling of his shirt. "They're a year younger than Ken. Garrett's a vice president. So is Gabrielle."

"Senior vice presidents?" I inquired.

"In their case, 'senior vice president' is an honorary title," Aunt Vivian murmured. "Not like with Ken."

As far as I can recall, I have never been the sort of person who gets surprised. Thus, let me simply say I was mildly unsettled to discover how unlikeable this particular branch of the Tree of Glickstein was. Rachel's husband, Danny G, while a tad too extroverted for my own taste—given as he was to huggy greetings and uproarious laughter at his own jokes—was a friendly and generous soul. His mother and his father (brother to Uncle Murray), too, were a benevolent couple. They sent me birthday cards with watercolors of pups or kitties or rosebuds on the front, I think in part because they viewed me first as a motherless child and only second as Rachel's adult cousin.

"So until Barry's death, the company was technically BBB and GG," I remarked. No response, though Viv did lay her hand over her sternum; most likely her gesture for "I'm aggrieved." However, she could have been protecting her pearls. Or preparing to burp. In any case I ignored her and concentrated on her (slightly) better half. "Why do the police want to question you, Murray?" I tried.

"I guess . . . I was in my office at the time, but like I told them"—He cleared his throat—"through my attorney: Our offices are soundproofed. Our clients, and us . . . We don't need noise from the workrooms. Like the grinding." A brief chuckle. "You'd think you were at the dentist, which is *not* how you get someone about to spend a couple of hundred thou to relax."

"So in other words, you didn't hear anything? No arguments? No cries for help?"

Uncle Murray's head began bobbing again, saying, That's right, That's right, That's right, until Aunt Vivian commented sharply: "And he didn't see anything, either."

I glanced away. Ken's head was hanging, his jaw drooping. He looked utterly dispirited. For an instant, he peered up toward the hall outside the living room. I sensed he wanted to scurry off, back to his room, where he could get consolation from some ancient teddy bear, probably the only source of comfort in that house. But he turned back to me. "We *all* didn't see anything. My mother, my father . . ."

"Vivian," I said in honeyed tones, "do you work at B and G?"

Startled, she pulled back her head. "No, of course not. I just happened to be there that morning."

"Really?"

"I wanted to pick up a lapis and diamond brooch to wear with my suit to a luncheon." Auntie Viv's voice was harder than diamonds. She then became busy clearing her throat, making much ado about mucous. When that business was taken care of, her nostrils dilated. I surmised all this was an overture to a withering remark directed to me. I silenced her with the disdainful *grande dame* gaze Ivey girls learn in Mademoiselle Charpantier's French class long before the *passé antérieur*.

Ken, realizing his mother was less than overjoyed at his reporting her presence at B and G, added: "Nadine Bleiberman was there that morning, too. We're all on the videotape. See, we have a security camera at the door."

I turned back to Murray. "If the police seem eager to keep in touch with you, may I assume they heard rumors that you and the late Mr. Bleiberman were on the outs?"

"The usual stuff two partners have," Murray remarked before nervously inserting a couple of seared foie gras canapés into his mouth.

"I see," I said, trying to sound pleasant. "In this case, what particular kind of 'stuff?'"

"Lines of responsibility," he declared through a fair amount of goose liver.

"Yours and his?"

"More . . ." He held up his index finger in a Wait-while-I-swallow gesture. "More the kids."

"Ken here and Garrett and Gabrielle Bleiberman?" I asked. This time he offered just a single nod. "What seems to be the problem?"

"Garrett's a bully," Vivian snapped. I focused on her shiny, pulled-tight cheeks so I would not humiliate the bully's inevitable target, poor Ken, by looking at him. "And Gabrielle's a tramp," she went on. "Always was, always will be."

"Are the Bleiberman twins productive?" I asked.

"Work-wise?" Murray inquired. "To be perfectly honest, they're not bad."

"That is not the point!" Vivian said, spitting her T's. "The point is, Murray, legally B and G is and was a fifty-fifty operation." She paused, possibly weary from expectorating so many T's. "All of a sudden when Ken came into the business—mainly so clients wouldn't start thinking, 'Oh, B and G has been taken over by a fraternity moron and a slut who never wears a bra'—Barry Bleiberman started supposedly kidding around: 'Well, there's three of us now, so we can outvote you.' I mean, is that unmitigated gall?" She inhaled and exhaled one of those deep relaxation breaths women learn at thousand-dollar-a-day spas. "Not that I'm not mourning Barry's loss. And murder, no less! Although I don't know why the authorities haven't considered suicide."

"Perhaps because he was stabbed three times in the heart

and was very likely dead before the last two thrusts occurred," I suggested.

Vivian Glickstein, still on a roll, crossed her ankles to give me a better view of her brown alligator pumps and kept talking: "I call the twins 'The Untalented Twain.' Of course you know twain means two. Between the two of them, they don't have half of Ken's intellect—if that. It's not just the future of the business Barry was going to sabotage. It was—"

I stood. "I know how important all of you are to my cousin Rachel, and I'd love to help you. I cannot in any way represent you, of course. I am sure Rachel has explained my position. But I'll be more than happy to look into the matter informally and let you know if I find anything." Now all three were nodding in what I optimistically assumed was appreciation. I grabbed my handbag and restrained myself from hurling my body at the door. Out! Liberated, I would gambol down Park Avenue, shout "Hosanna!" as I flagged down a taxi. I was nearly free of the Glickstein Three!

And then Uncle Murray muttered: "Whatever you can do." His shoulders slumped. And his voice tightened. "The cops . . ." He sounded on the verge of tears. "They said something to my attorney about maybe, you know, having to arrest me."

Because I had a stack of discovery material to read the following morning, when Rachel called I agreed that: 1) Uncle Murray was a doll, 2) Aunt Vivian's taste was quietly elegant, and 3) Ken was a teeny-weeny on the shy side. When I asked her how bitter the dispute between Bleiberman and Glickstein was, she told me: "Don't ask!"

"Rachel, I'm asking."

"Very, very, *very* bitter." As usual, I waited. "See, Ken isn't what you'd call a firecracker. He probably should have some calmer job. Like some science thing with a clipboard. He could do that. No pressure, no people. I hate to say this, but he's a major dork, personality and looks-wise. Unfortunately. I mean, put him in total Armani and he's still a schlepper. Speaking of looks like: Gabrielle Bleiberman looks like a ho—That means, you know, like a hooker."

"Right."

"Except for her jewelry. Huge gold cuff on her right wrist. Gorgeous. Man's gold Rolex on her left, which looks stunning with the cuff! Diamond studs so big, her earlobes'll be hanging down to her shoulders in a few years. But a mind? Amy, like a steel trap! Anyhow, Garrett's nicer but he never got as far as nice, if you know what I mean. He's okay. Good-looking in a sort of Keanu Reeves way if Keanu didn't come from Hawaii and have that permanent tan. Except he's got a schnozz big enough for two. Garrett, not Keanu. He's engaged. And he's smart. They both are."

"Garrett and the fiancée?"

"No, Garrett and Gabrielle. They went to one of those smart little colleges. You know, Ivy League, but not Ivy League. Like whatever that place is . . . Amherst! Except if they're so smart, why aren't they?"

"Why aren't they in the Ivy League?" I asked.

"Yeah."

Best not to begin, I concluded. With Rachel, any well-reasoned response more complex than a single, simple declarative sentence would induce glazed eyes or, occasionally, a remark like: God, you really *are* an intellectual!

"So essentially," I said, "Gabrielle and Garrett have it in them to be successful in business and Cousin Ken does not."

"Right!" However dismissive my cousin might have been of actual thought, she did have the gift of sounding enraptured at the most elementary deduction. The miracle of it was she wasn't just exercising a talent for being effusive; she was genuinely thrilled with me. "That's the problem!"

"Was Barry Bleiberman putting any pressure on Uncle Murray to get rid of Ken?"

"Yes. But it was like this awful double whammy because while he was putting the pressure on Murray, Gabrielle and

Garrett were making Ken's life a living hell!"

"In what way?"

"To tell you the God's honest truth," Rachel conceded, "I don't know."

"Oh."

"But it's what Uncle Murray told my father-in-law."

"When?"

"I guess a month or two ago. And Dad—Dad Glickstein, not Daddy O'Toole—told Danny about it and naturally Danny told me. That the twins were making poor Ken's life a living hell!"

After I got off the phone with Rachel, my first thought was that if I were in the DA's homicide unit, I, too, would be inviting Murray Glickstein for a chat, and, later in the day, perhaps requesting the pleasure of Ken's company as well. Then I banished all contemplation of Glicksteins and reached for the top document on the mountain of discovery material for my upcoming trial, the report of the defense psychiatric expert whose conclusion would inevitably be that Bernard Charles Lee could not be held responsible for selling five hundred grams of cocaine because inefficacious parenting had resulted in a lacuna of his superego.

Less than a minute later, I tossed it to the far side of my desk and meandered out into the hallway. Unfortunately, out of approximately two hundred assistant United States attorneys in the Southern District of New York, I was forced to poke my head into the office of the one I liked least.

Larissa Corrigan had come in second in Louisiana's 1986 Junior Miss Contest. Now, at age thirty-one, she remained the same ponytailed moppet she had been when she'd almost succeeded in capturing the crown by doing gymnastics on a vaulting horse while lip-synching Anne Murray's "You Are My Sunshine."

Periodically Larissa would come into my office and inquire where she could go to get the "true flaaa-va," which I assumed meant flavor, of the Lower East Side or assorted other impoverished neighborhoods. Every so often she seemed to get the urge to visit areas filled with Americans darker than she whom she so genuinely admired fo' desirin' to make a bettah life fo they-ah chil'ren. (Quite in the same way, she'd let me know that when she had first heard about me she was truly, truly touched by larnin' how Ah'd pulled myself up bah mah bootstraps.)

"Why, Amy!" As usual, Larissa sounded close to ecstacy, her usual greeting for someone she did not particularly like.

Before she could drawl Come on in and set a spell! and give me yet another reason to rejoice that the Confederacy had lost, I sauntered in and sat in the chair in front of her desk. It was the standard government issue, with uneven metal legs and a leatherette seat that had retained a vague scent of some forgotten lawyer's lower intestinal turmoil that had occurred a decade earlier. "Didn't you recently have a possession of stolen diamonds case?" I inquired.

"Oh my, did I! Their defense was they had a secret process to quote cook unquote the diamonds, which would add to their value, so if they'd stolen them, they'd have cooked them and—" Enraptured by her skill as a raconteur, Larissa gave a tinkly Junior Miss laugh. "So the defense gave this demonstration. The jury sat fo' five hours watching the diamonds cook and in the end you know what? My chemist said 'My gosh, those diamonds are worthless now!' "

I managed to emit a relatively convivial har-har. Then, before she could resume, I inquired: "Besides the chemist, did you have any other expert witnesses? I need someone who knows the players and the ways of the jewelry business."

"They've given you a case involving the jewelry business?" If one's Pearly Dawn-glossed lips are going to offer a falsely congenial smile, I was tempted to advise her, one should not display all thirty-two teeth and adjacent gums at once. Larissa clearly considered Jewelryland, the area that stretched from Forty-seventh Street uptown to Van Cleef &

Arpels, hers alone. In truth, she was a fairly good lawyer and she ought to have been more confident.

"No!" I assured her, flicking my hand to dismiss utterly the idea of my putting even a toe onto her turf. "A friend of a cousin needs some kind of a jewelry expert."

My smile, also, far more false than hers, was so credible that she quickly typed *diamond* on her keyboard, read from her database: "Jonah Bergman. And Amy, tell him Larissa Corrigan sends her warmest, warmest regards!" She jotted down a phone number for me. From her ardent "warmest, warmest" I sensed old Jonah must be, in Larissa-ese, totally, totally adorable.

He was. And not old. So I was pleased I had accepted his offer of a drink after work. (His work, not mine: From the cut of his suit to the deliberately dulled gleam of his shoes to his first-name ease with the waiter, Jonah Bergman looked to be one of the scions of wealthy families who toiled for toil's sake, because not to work would be a prescription for personal anarchy.) In any case, at about five-thirty in the afternoon, there we were in the yellow damask lounge of the University Club sitting on English furniture a couple of centuries older than we. At first glimpse, Jonah was not much more than ordinary, with standard issue nose and chin, dark brown hair and a generic early thirties urban male body. However, his eyes were the dazzling blue of exam books. They were fringed with such thick black lashes that he came across as handsome, or at least wildly dashing.

He raised his martini glass to me in an affable toasting gesture. Clearly, Jonah came from a world in which actually to say Skäl, L'Chaim, or Banzai was to risk being deemed gauche, a fate not merely worse than death but also as irreversible. "Cheers!" I proclaimed, just to see if he would flinch or cast sideways glances to check if anyone he knew had heard me. He did neither. After elevating a glass of vodka capacious enough to do laps in, I told him: "I appreciate your taking the time to talk to me." Then I took a too-large sip to choke back the Ivey-Rush accent that kept trying to take possession of my tongue; and thereby wow Jonah with my refinement. So, as usual, I wound up being me, sounding like a herring peddler. "I appreciate your meeting with me."

"Glad to help you." He had one of those deep, pleasing voices that called for violins and candlelight. "You're a federal prosecutor?"

I nodded. "But this is thoroughly unofficial. I need some background information on the jewelry business—a favor for a relative."

"So you couldn't say no."

"Not without a process comparable to excommunication by the Grand Inquisitor followed by auto-da-fé." Like most native New Yorkers I talk fast, perhaps in the hope that the next sentence will be more spellbinding than the last. Jonah blinked his glorious lashes at my fusillade of words. Nonetheless, I kept going. (Sadly, while excelling academically, shining at sports and occasionally sparkling in court, I had never mastered flirtation, never even learned to turn on the charm when face-to-face with a man I found attractive. Indeed, in that situation I would become so apprehensive that when quiet sensuality was the ticket, I'd babble, less coquette than locker room buddy.) "Larissa Corrigan said your knowledge of the jewelry business and the people in it is vast and that your family has been in the industry so long your DNA is more diamond-shape than double helix. Well, in truth, what she said, very southernly, was that you knew a lot."

"What are you interested in?"

Ah, I reflected, gazing into his luminous eyes. I told him: "I need some background on B and G Gems. The company which Barry Bleiberman—" He nodded. "Within your world, what was the general opinion of the operation?"

"Good. As manufacturers, first rate. They do quality

work, on time. They bargain hard but don't try to pull any
funny stuff." Jonah fell silent.

"I hear an unspoken 'except.' "

"Except," he said slowly, "this has to be strictly off the
record. I mean, to testify about the art of diamond cutting
or where the highest quality emeralds come from is one
thing, but to sit here and discuss personalities is another."
His accent was New York private school, where vowels are
round and elongated enough to sound clearly sophisticated
and vaguely upper-class, but not draaaawn ooout enouuuugh
to communicate the supercilious cool of a student from a
New England boarding school. "Can I assume you're not
going to subpoena me and ask—"

"Of course not." I transferred my vodka to my left hand
and raised my right. "You have my word."

"It's like this," Jonah began. "There are some very
worldly types in this industry, but there are also a lot of
provincial people, from the guys with the pinky rings . . ."
Perhaps thinking I could be the child of a pinky ring wearer,
he hesitated. I was tempted to tell him to relax, that my
father's taste in jewelry ran more to handcuffs, but he continued: ". . . to the Hasidic Jews. You get used to dealing
with an enormous range of people. So you get to be able to
judge them pretty well. Not on the superficial level, like
whether they wear a gold chain and have their shirts open
to show their chest hair or whether they dress very Savile
Row—custom-tailored and all that. Character counts. Like
honesty. The industry is built on trust. You let a guy show
a few ten-carat diamonds to his customer and you trust he'll
return the same stones to you—all of them."

"Was Barry Bleiberman trustworthy?" I asked.

"Absolutely."

I set down the vodka on a small mahogany table that no
doubt cost quadruple my monthly salary. "What was the
problem with him, then?"

Jonah leaned back his head to think. I noticed he had a

beautifully sculpted jaw. "He was respected as a business-man. He was a fund-raiser for a couple of big charities. He made all the right moves. But he wasn't . . . I know this must sound stupid, but the fact is, Barry wasn't nice. Not likeable. It wasn't just a matter of him having a big ego. Plenty of guys in the industry think they're hotshots, so that's no big deal. It's that Barry had nothing else: no hu-mor, no generosity, no kindness." He sipped his martini in the perfunctory manner of a man who drinks not because he enjoys it, but to be sociable. "I never articulated this before," he went on, "so I'm kind of thinking while I'm talking. I guess what was wrong with Barry Bleiberman was that . . . If you looked into his window, no one was home."

"What about his family? His twins were in the business."

"Well, I guess he was home for them. I mean, I heard talk of some tension at B and G over kids."

"On whose part?"

"Both. Barry brought his two in and Murray Glickstein brought in his son. But in this industry, where companies are largely family-held, there's often tension. Fathers and sons at each other's throats, uncles and nephews plotting against each other, that kind of thing."

"Tension? That seems a pretty mild word."

"Well, call it loathing then, or maybe just acrimony."

"How about plain old hatred?" I inquired, picking up my vodka again. We alumnae of Ivey-Rush, I had noticed, wind up with fingers perpetually curved, trained as we were to being ever ready to grasp either tennis racquet or glass, depending on whether it was before or after five P.M.

"Okay." He smiled agreeably. "Hatred." Nice teeth. They would have looked even more dazzling except for being eclipsed by the brilliance of his blue eyes. "Murray was about as likeable as Barry, except in his case it was because he's never been shy about letting everyone know he's smarter than they are. Plus he's . . ."

It looked as if Jonah was looking for a nice was to say "A pretentious jerk," so I said it for him.

"You've met Murray?" Jonah asked.

"Briefly. Do you know his son?"

"Ken? Yes, we went to school together."

"And?"

"I never knew him that well. He's on the shy side."

"Since this meeting is off the record, is he bright enough to take over the business?"

Jonah shrugged. I waited. "I don't know, at least IQ-wise. Maybe he is. But even years ago, when we were nine, ten, he struck me as kind of . . . Well, now I would call it emotionally fragile. I don't think he's up to it."

"And the twins?"

"Tough and Tougher. Sure, they seem like they could run the business, providing they stick around a few more years, learn more, stay on the up-and-up. They look a little slick, but I've never really dealt with them."

"What's their mother like?"

"I have no idea. If I ever met her, she didn't make any impression."

"If Barry hadn't been killed, do you think he and Murray could have worked out their differences?"

"If he hadn't been murdered, I would have said 'Not without blood being spilled.' But now I'll say probably not. Not unless Murray was willing to abandon all hope for Ken, and I hear that even if he finally came to that, his wife—"

"The lovely Vivian," I said.

Jonah would have won the Talleyrand Diplomatic Trophy for his circumspect nod. "The lovely Vivian would have forced him to back Ken to the death—and beyond."

"If you had to bet, well . . . perhaps the family jewels is an infelicitous expression, but let us say ten dollars. Who would you say stabbed Barry Bleiberman to death?"

"An intruder?"

"His safe was open. Would he have opened it if someone was threatening him?"

"He probably had a discreet silent alarm button on a small section of carpeting under his desk. And maybe a remote panic button on a key chain. My guess? If no one heard an alarm, then the safe was open because Barry felt it was probably all right to open it."

While I waited for Jonah to ask me to join him for dinner—the sort of flagrant female passivity one picks up along with one's teacup at a New England school for young ladies—I mused that an intruder would probably not stab Barry Bleiberman three times. Once. Maybe twice for certainty. Thrice seemed rather mean-spirited.

Alas, Jonah did not ask me to dinner. I wound up buying a hot dog and a Coke from the first street vendor who didn't look as if he were incubating bubonic plague, then took the subway back to the office. I attacked my cocaine case with fervor in order to boot Young Blue Eyes from my consciousness and also because I deemed it advisable to have at least one other sentence to follow "Ladies and gentlemen of the jury." So it wasn't until the next afternoon that I realized I still hadn't done my family duty in the matter of my cousin Rachel's uncle Murray.

"I beg your pardon?" my friend Tatiana Hayes Damaris Collier inquired. (Before her twenty-fifth birthday she had been Tatiana Hayes Damaris Collier Patterson as well as Tatiana Hayes Damaris Collier Martinez, but she had dropped those surnames as hurriedly as she dropped those husbands.) Although my age, born and raised on Beekman Place, she sounded as if she were auditioning for Lady Bracknell. Her voice was cured by expensive tobacco, then filtered through her aristocratic nose.

"I'd like you to pay a condolence call," I told her. "I will go with you."

"Might I ask . . . ?"

"I'm doing a favor for a relative."

"Oh," she murmured, which came out more like *Eewwww.* "How considerate of you. Am I to dribble the milk of human kindness on behalf of one of your little people in obscure boroughs, all of whom speak like Groucho Marx?"

"No. All you have to do is go in and be yourself—upper-class and contemptuous."

"I should be delighted." Tatty had been my roommate at Ivey. We had been best friends from the second day, about twenty hours after she'd called me "rude, crude and unattractive" in front of a group of girls on our floor and I'd punched her in the mouth, knocking out her left lateral incisor and splitting her lip.

"We'll be going to the shiva of the late Mr. B. of B and G Gems. B and G, by the way, is Bleiberman and Glickstein."

"What fun!" Tatty enthused. "Virtually a walk on the wild side." The very next day, we went to offer our condolences to the Bleibermans of Central Park West.

"So nice of you to drop by," Gabrielle said to us. She was in mourning clothes, which in her case meant a low-slung black leather miniskirt, black fishnet stockings, and a black sweater small enough so that a moment later when she raised her arm in order to dab at her tearless eyes, you caught a glimpse of navel. Should this description suggest some hot little number, it should be noted that her figure, while fine, was full, rather like those inflatable female sex toys from whom misguided men seek solace.

Gabrielle seemed a bit tense in her sun-bronzed skin, though to be fair she was probably merely overstimulated, being suddenly in the company of an unknown WASP her own age who kept murmuring "My dear," as in "My dear, shocking. Your loss. Not just shocking. *Profoundly* shocking, my dear." In all the years I had known Tatty, the words "my dear" had never escaped her lips; she was high-toned, not condescending. Clearly though, she was reveling in her role as stereotypical post-debutante.

Meanwhile, Gabrielle was torn between her functions of hostess and jewelry maven, trying to look Tatty directly in the eye while simultaneously estimating the price of the aquamarine and pearl rope twirled several times around Tatty's neck. Personally, I thought the rope with its matching earrings, bequeathed by some Jazz Age Collier, was a bit over the top for a one P.M. shiva call. But my friend had called me an ignoramus for not knowing that aquamarines were semiprecious stones and therefore *only suitable for daytime wear.*

The aquamarines and pearls must have dinged Gabrielle's mental cash register, because in two seconds not only did she ask if we wanted something to eat or drink, she immediately led us over to meet her brother and mother. "Mommy, Garrett, this is one of Daddy's oldest customers' daughters, uh, Tatiana, uh . . ."

"Collier." She elongated her vowels and muttered her consonants until the name was almost unintelligible—in case either of the twins decided to look it up in B and G's records. "And my dear friend Amy." We'd also agreed to drop my Lincoln just in case, in more felicitous times, the Bleibermans had heard of my rags-to-slightly-better-rags saga from the Glicksteins. "Mother's tied up in Paris, but she asked that I drop by and offer our family's deepest sympathy." Tatty's mother, actually, was in the mental institution in Connecticut where she had been for the past fifteen years after having suffered irreversible brain damage from too many of what she had called her happy pills. "Mother said—and these were her exact words—'Who in the *world* would want to lay a finger on my Mr. Bleiberman?' "

Could she have shoveled the shit higher and faster? Truly, no. Yet not a single Bleiberman looked askance. Watching her, I could understand why. Though built along the dainty lines of a wood nymph, Tatty had masses of blond-on-blond-on blonder hair that looked as if it came from years of riding to the hounds or sunning at Cap Ferrat, which of course it did not. Her hollowed cheeks, her pale eyes that appeared blue or gray or white depending on the light, her high-bridged nose, her indecently expensive clothes, her I've-seen-it-*all*-my-dear drone of a voice announced blue blood and silk stockings, a woman not merely not to be trifled with, but to be accommodated.

"I appreciate . . ." Nadine Bleiberman, wife of the late Barry and mother of the twins, was so moved or intimidated by Tatty that the rest of the sentence disappeared as she swallowed hard, making the sort of noise that in comic books is rendered *Gulp!!* Unlike her daughter, her black skirt covered not only her thighs, but her knees as well. Her black silk blouse, while tissue-thin, revealed not even a hint of cleavage. Everything that should be covered was, indeed, modestly hidden beneath a simple black camisole. After Vivian Glickstein's designer clothes and alligator shoes, I had expected a widow fabulously clad in black. However, Nadine's outfit actually looked like something I could afford. The black emphasized her milk-white skin. Her hair was the color of strawberry Jell-O, the sort of tone the maladroit wind up with when they try to become glamorous at home.

Garrett, beside his mother on an endless modular sofa, had her pallor, but not her frame. Like his twin, he came in XL. Like her, too, he had dark hair as well as a thick-lipped mouth kind people would describe as generous. Unlike her, he obviously had no personal trainer; Gabrielle's triceps were in a realm beyond buff while Garrett's biceps would probably dimple like a stale marshmallow. With his black curls hanging over his pale forehead and the tops of his ears, he resembled the bust of some degenerate Roman emperor.

To the Bleibermans' amazement (to say nothing of mine) Tatty somehow fit herself on the three inches of couch that lay between Garrett and Nadine. She took Nadine's blue-veined hand in hers. "He was a splendid man, my dear," she said softly to the air directly in front of her. Both mother and son nodded their thanks. Gabrielle, not to be left out, hastened across the room for two small folding chairs with dark orange seats that could have been the work of some superchic designer as an homage to the fifties. Nevertheless, I suspected they had been left over from someone's grandmother's canasta game. She and I sat, completing a tight little circle that effectively excluded the five or six other callers in the room. For a moment none of us spoke. I glanced around. Unlike the Louis XIV–loving Glicksteins, the Bleibermans' taste was modern—and surprisingly modest: a reproduction of a Mies Van der Rohe Barcelona chair done in pale blue leather instead of the usual brown; a vast royal blue modular sofa that was slightly overstuffed, like the twins.

"Why," Tatty asked, "was his safe open?" Naturally, I wanted to take her swanlike neck and wring it; this had been the final question she was supposed to ask, not the first.

However, instead of gasping, Garrett gave a manly shrug—as in, Beats the hell out of me. And Gabrielle declared: "We keep asking ourselves that." Their mother seemed to have found not only her words, but her saliva, as she turned toward Tatty and sprayed: "He didn't have any appointments that afternoon."

"His secretary said he was alone the whole time!" Gabrielle added, fussing with something at her waist. I glanced over and saw she was adjusting a navel ring to hang over the waist band of her skirt. Tatty, of course, was by nature and breeding too stiff-upper-lip to act appalled, though it could be that she thought the ring was some Jewish mourning apparatus I had failed to mention.

"I'm trying to recall his office," Tatty mused. "I'd been there a couple of times—perhaps more—with Mother." She glanced at me. "The time she bought that glorious diamond spaniel with the ruby collar." She closed her eyes, then opened them an instant later. "Did the room have a window?"

"No," Garrett finally spoke, albeit slowly, as if he wished he didn't have to part with the words. "For security. Inner office. Cuts insurance rates."

"How interesting."

"Well-lighted," Garrett mumbled.

"Of course. One wants to see the cut and color of the gem one is envisioning on one's finger."

Gabrielle was nodding eagerly. "About ten years ago, Dad hired a famous lighting designer. A guy who does Broadway plays."

"Murray Glickstein," Garrett added. "Against it."

"Murray Glickstein was his partner," Nadine explained.

"Murray was, is, the G," Gabrielle explained. "In B and G. He didn't want it. See, Dad believed heart and soul in plowing profits back into the business. Like fertilizer. But instead of bigger, whatever, like roses, you come out with bigger sales. But he had to fight Murray tooth and nail on every capital investment."

"This Murray wanted to take all the profits out?" Tatty sounded scandalized.

Did it not occur to any of the Bleibermans that this was a bizarre conversation to be having with a total stranger just a few days after their father's/husband's murder? Obviously not, which is why I had enlisted Tatty. I could have borrowed her aquamarine and pearl gewgaws, put on the upper-class accent, even, if necessary, the hauteur. Over the years I had discovered I could go anywhere—from a longshoremen's bar to a yacht in the Mediterranean—and be accepted. What I could not fake, however, was Tatiana's assumption of privilege, that inborn assurance that puts the rest of the world on notice: You must please me. So as I had predicted, questions that would have seemed presumptuous coming from me were taken as a kindness coming from Tatty. She *cares*.

"The wife," Garrett mumbled.

"This Murray's wife pushed him to take the profits out

of the business?" Tatty's nostrils dilated, her I-am-appalled expression.

Gabrielle leaned forward so far, her head almost knocked Tatty's. "You should see how they live. Sumptuous is putting it mildly. Palatial."

"Gabrielle, it's really not palatial," her mother suggested, trying to cut off the conversation. Her voice was soft, hesitant. She was not a woman who enjoyed or even tolerated confrontation.

"It is too." Gabrielle dismissed her mother the way someone would brush a fly off his arm, not so much with contempt as mere annoyance; her mother, apparently, was a familiar nuisance. "Even if Murray *wanted* to plow back some more of the profits, he couldn't because he had to finance their lifestyle."

Tatty cocked her head. "I remember your father telling Mother and me that the two of you had joined him in the business. He was so proud." All three Bleibermans nodded at once. "Was it frustrating, to see the future of your business . . . ?"

When a second and a half passed and no answer was forthcoming, Tatty offered Garrett a small smile of encouragement. "Very, very," he answered immediately. What struck me was that, to look at them, the twins seemed tough customers. Overtanned Gabrielle in her leather tourniquet of a miniskirt. Pale, puffed up Garrett doling out each word as if every syllable was a year deducted from his life. Yet both of them were so easily wowed by Tatty that it was hard to imagine them as the bullies making misery for Ken Glickstein.

"It was beyond the valley of upsetting," Gabrielle confided to Tatty. "Daddy and us . . ." She seemed to be hesitating over the *us,* thinking perhaps it might be a *we,* but then she went on. "We wanted to grow the business." The twins sighed in unison. Their mother was busy twisting her wedding band and its matching engagement ring.

"Must you now be partners with this spendthrift?" Tatty inquired. Her inquiries were posing the philosophical question: Can there be any end to chutzpah? The answer was: Obviously not.

"B and G," Garrett said. "Fifty-fifty." Tatty offered a consoling sigh. "Not the end of the world," he added.

"For now," his sister added. "I mean, we know the business as a business, a financial entity. But because Daddy was . . . well, Daddy, we don't know the regular customers all that well. They always asked for him. I mean, Daddy's middle name was Reliable."

"Richard," Nadine said softly, to no one in particular.

After the visit to the Bleibermans', late lunch or tea was called for. But being the new generation of Ivey alumnae, we both went back to work—me to my cocaine case, Tatty to her second doctoral dissertation. She already had a PhD in botany, with particular expertise in bryology, the study of mosses and liverworts. However, she had awakened one morning cosmically bored. Somehow her mind, always peculiar, made the leap that the cure for ennui was the study of medieval Italian politics. Now, as far as I could comprehend, she was writing about the traumatic effects of Savonarola's execution on Niccolò Machiavelli.

Sunday morning's cloudless sky was merely a cover for a cold, windy day. Nevertheless, I put on earmuffs and my old, stiff ski mittens and walked from my apartment in Little Italy uptown to Tatty's grand limestone townhouse on East Sixty-seventh Street. Technically it was her father's townhouse, but as he was usually traveling in foreign climes looking for new varieties of birds to shoot, she had all five floors to herself.

We sat at a giant butcher-block table in the kitchen, a room easily large enough to accommodate a staff of four, which it did on weekdays. "Well, shall we solve this murder?" Tatty demanded. "Or shall we go to the Pietro da Cortona exhibit at the Met?"

I mimed a large yawn, then wound up actually yawning. "Why do I sense Pietro will be a snore and a half? All right, if we can figure out who killed Barry Richard Bleiberman, then I will keep you company." I put a dab of plum jam on my last piece of croissant and popped it into my mouth.

"What shall we talk of first?" Tatty asked.

"Chez Bleiberman," I suggested. "Didn't it strike you as being a little spare?"

"It did. Not simply spare. Bauhaus is not my period, but that yacht of a sofa and the blue leather chairs . . . they did not cry out 'Less is more' to me. They were sadly unattractive. Unless a space is designed by someone with an exquisitely-trained eye, less is invariably less." She stood and poured another cup of coffee from the pot the housekeeper had set up the night before. "But perhaps they are the sort of people who are oblivious to their surroundings."

"I don't know about that. They were all dressed fashionably—"

"*What?* Did you see the ring in that Gabrielle's navel?" Tatty demanded. "I thought I would retch. The mere notion of it! What if she had a large meal? Can you imagine it rubbing against the waistband of her skirt? And picture some poor man gagging in the midst of what might otherwise be a sensual liaison after spying that tawdry little hoop of metal that is probably gummed up with abhorrent navel secretions! How can you call that fashionable?"

"You know I don't mean fashionable à la Mainbocher of Givenchy. And if you would have let me finish my sentence you'd have heard me add, fashionable but not very expensive."

"Cheap." She reached for my cup, poured some more coffee for me, then joined me back at the table. The old white porcelain cups with their dainty traceries of aqua and gold looked even more fragile atop the sturdy wood table.

"Now, the night I went to visit Uncle Murray. If you

sold off all the Louis Quatorze in their living room it could retire the national debt."

"The real thing?" Tatty inquired.

"It would have been discourteous to ask for the provenance of the settee," I explained. "Though the stuff looked pretty good to me. Real or not, I bet they paid a bundle. And Missus Murray—the lovely Vivian—was wearing Carolina Herrera and what looked like Manolo alligator shoes. Plus a really nice Upper East Side duplex. The Bleibermans' place may have been on Central Park West, but it wasn't facing the park."

"And it was a thoroughly undistinguished apartment. Someone had ripped down all the old moldings. And to have wall-to-wall carpet covering what must be beautiful old parquet floors. A desecration." She shook her head. "But all right. They lived modestly."

"Still," I said, "the two men were fifty-fifty partners, Tatty. Clearly Murray had the most power because he was able to pull out most of the profits from the business to keep his wife in Herrera and ormolu. Now, if he's doing this, would it be sound business practice for Barry Bleiberman to have plowed back *his* cut?"

"No." She reached for a brioche, yanked off the top rather viciously, and popped it into her mouth. "Go on."

"So what was Barry doing with hundreds of thousands or, for all I know, millions of dollars *he* was taking out of B and G?"

"Not buying furniture," Tatty mused. "Although it is possible he was buying furniture for *someone*. Perhaps he was keeping a dominatrix with a taste for Chippendale."

"Perhaps. Or perhaps he had an offshore account in the Cayman Islands. Maybe he had a five thousand dollar a day drug habit. The point is"—I sipped my coffee—"all that money was not being conspicuously consumed by his family."

"Nadine's wedding and engagement rings are what I

imagine a working-class man would buy," Tatty mused. "Nice. Tasteful enough. But ordinary."

"They are not what you would expect from a jeweler who dealt in big-ticket items," I agreed. "Even if Barry did not have much money when they got married, what would a conventional man of his current occupation and economic class do?"

Tatty shook her head at my asking a question with such an obvious answer. "Replace them with bigger and better, of course," she replied.

"Of course."

"Unless he was, as my mother so delicately referred to my father, a cheap fuck," Tatty pointed out.

"Hold that thought. Now, let us consider who would profit by Barry Bleiberman's death."

"Murray," she responded. "He still owns fifty percent of B and G. But the twins would be dependent on him, so he'd get to run things."

"Everything I heard from my cousin indicated that Gabrielle and Garrett would own their father's half."

"So then they would benefit from Mr. Bleiberman's death."

"Maybe ultimately, but if they were plotting, why would they kill their father now? They were pretty up front about not knowing the customers. That's why they were so accepting when you whirled in, Tatiana."

"I do not whirl. I glide. I have been called a sylph."

"You have been called many things. Now, does Ken Glickstein benefit if Barry B. checks out?"

"No," she said, "because that would leave him at the mercy of the twins."

"Vivian? Would killing Barry advance her cause of making her son more secure?"

"Only if she's a nincompoop."

"Well, I wouldn't swear she isn't, but she's a shrewd nincompoop. She understood it would be the Twain versus

Murray—with her beloved little boy on the sidelines." I stood. "I am off to Rachel's."

"But you are going to the da Cortona exhibit with me."

"I might meet you there."

"You won't," Tatty sighed.

"I won't," I agreed.

Since I was already in the high rent district, I popped in on my cousin Rachel. She was otherwise engaged at the children's Sunday school, apparently helping first graders dip wicks for Hanukkah candles. But her husband, Danny, who resembled a Range Rover in a red V-neck sweater, was home trying to conquer all the sections of the Sunday *Times*. "Aaa-meee! Hey, great to see ya!" He gave me such an enthusiastic bear hug that I wound up getting red cashmere fibers embedded in my lip gloss.

When he let me go I breathed. Then I asked: "Dear Aunt Vivian: Before this little disagreement over the twins and Ken, was she friendly with Nadine Bleiberman?"

Danny laughed his hearty ho-ho football fan laugh and replied: "You've got to be kidding."

"They do seem an unlikely pair."

"Apples and oranges are at least fruit. Aunt Viv and Nadine . . . jeez, apples and lamb chops."

"Was there any competition between them?"

"How could there be? Aunt Viv has Uncle Murray wound around her little finger and gets whatever she wants. As far as I know, Nadine is one of those old-fashioned wives who, you know, is willing to wind herself around her husband's finger."

"So she didn't want elegant clothes and snazzy jewelry?"

Danny shrugged his bearish shoulders. "I really don't know her well enough to know what she wanted," he said. "But if it cost more than a buck and a quarter, she wouldn't have gotten it. Barry Bleiberman may have been one smart businessman, but he was a cheap, mean you-know-what."

I established that my cousin Rachel would be home late

morning and accepted an invitation to dine *en famille* at six o'clock. Then I called my favorite FBI agent, a Mormon who alternately kept trying to convert me and bewitch me. I told him he could buy me lunch in Chinatown . . . and do me a small favor.

Although I had too many steamed vegetable dumplings and wound up in the agent's apartment listening to a Waylon Thibodeaux recording of Cajun music and profusely admiring the "Choupique Two Step," he was happy to make a few phone calls. By the time I left to go back to the office to work on the opening in my cocaine case, I knew what I needed to know. Several hours later, I hied myself uptown to dinner, unfortunately not yet having digested lunch.

"This is the big question. Who benefits from Barry Bleiberman being . . ." I glanced over at Rachel's progeny, Brianna and Ryan, two thoroughly likeable children who, fortunately, had inherited their mother's dark, liquid eyes and their father's intelligence. Somehow, in the way of children, they sensed this was one adult conversation that had the potential to be interesting. So I began again: "The important question is this: Who benefits from Barry Bleiberman being nullified by three strikes with a desk implement?"

"What?" my cousin Rachel inquired, looking up from the single slice of turkey and mountain of salad she had allowed herself for dinner. She seemed perplexed, but then, the only three-syllable word in my question she probably recognized was Bleiberman.

"Kids," Danny decreed, "out. Grown-up talk. Doubles on Mallomars later if you make yourself scarce."

As they dashed from the dining room, Rachel sighed: "The pediatrician says food should never be used as a bribe."

As this looked as if it could be the opening of a lengthy philosophical discourse between husband and wife, I turned to my cousin: "Zip it, Rach." I took a sip of expensive Italian water, and went on. "Before we talk about who benefits, a couple of off-the-record facts. A law enforcement friend of mine . . ."

Danny leaned forward to listen. Rachel leaned back. "Male friend?" she asked.

"Male friend," I replied. "Anyhow, he spoke with a colleague in the NYPD. The autopsy report indicated that any of the three stab wounds was sufficient to kill Barry Bleiberman."

"So why three?" Danny inquired.

"Certainty, perhaps. The killer wanted to feel sure Barry was done for. Either he or she wanted Barry dead very badly or was afraid of being identified if Barry lived."

Rachel stopped performing surgery on her slice of turkey and asked: "So it was someone he knew?"

"Not necessarily. It could have been a stranger worried about being recognized from a mug shot if Barry lived, or picked out of a lineup or caught from an artist's sketch." I took a wedge of lemon from the lemons and limes arranged starlike on a plate and squeezed it into my water. "But if I were a betting woman, I would say it was someone he knew. There was one entrance into B and G, which is on the fourteenth floor of a building on Fifth between Forty-seventh and Forty-eighth. There is a video camera that allows the receptionist to see who is outside the door. If it is someone who should be let in, she buzzes him or her into an anteroom. If the person has a legitimate reason for being at B and G, the receptionist—who is behind a bullet-proof window—buzzes the person in to the office proper when the B and G employee whom the person is there to see physically comes down to receive him or her."

"Anybody suspicious come in that day?" Danny asked.

"No," I said. "And no one the day before . . . on the theory someone might have hidden there for the night, although that's highly unlikely: The alarm system has pretty sophisticated motion detectors."

"So *who*?" Rachel said. She was able to pause with her

fork a tenth of an inch from her mouth. "Are we doing deduction or logic or something?"

"Rachel," I said, "why wouldn't Murray have killed Barry?"

"Because he's not a killer type."

"Why else?" I pressed.

"Bleiberman was a damned good rainmaker," Danny offered. "With him gone, all that business won't necessarily transfer to Murray."

"What about the other Glicksteins?" I asked. "Ken or Vivian."

"I give up," Rachel said.

"I can't see Ken doing it," Danny said. "He's such a nebbish." He paused and brushed a bread crumb off the Mercedes logo on his golf shirt. "Although it is true that you always hear about these crazy killers: 'He was such a quiet young man.' "

"As far as Ken goes, many of the employees saw him after the body was discovered, which was around one o'clock, when a gold dealer who'd made a working lunch appointment with Barry called to find out where he was. Anyway, neither the other employees nor the cops on the scene noticed any blood on him. Or blood on anyone, for that matter."

"He could have changed," Rachel said.

"You're right. He could have. But let's move on. No one really liked Barry Bleiberman. On the other hand, after all the interviews, there does not seem to be anyone who disliked him in any serious way." At almost the same instant, Rachel's and Danny's brows furrowed. "Okay, so the jewels are gone. Loose stones, not pieces of jewelry. Or at least no pieces of jewelry anyone knows about yet. So what does that tell you about the killer?"

"That he wasn't a rank amateur or a wandering junkie," Danny suggested. "He was someone who knew that when stones are in settings they can be easily identified."

"So what about the twins?" Rachel demanded. "Can you believe that Gabrielle? Wearing a tube top to her father's funeral and then taking off her jacket at the cemetery like it was ninety degrees? And not crying. And the brother not crying, either. Not one tear the whole time. That's what Uncle Murray told Danny." She glanced at her husband fondly. Danny nodded.

"What do the twins have to gain by getting rid of their father now? They are not seasoned enough to take over the business. And they are smart enough to know it."

"So who, Amy?"

I suppressed an urge for a Mallomar and took another sip of bubbly water. "What about Nadine?" I asked.

"The wife?" Danny appeared incredulous.

"She's like . . . so boring, she's not there," Rachel said. "I mean, I hate to be catty, but she's like the Invisible Woman." Her mouth dropped. "Oh."

"In fact, she was in the office that morning. About ten-thirty. Gabrielle was going out for dinner and the theater with a new man. She decided she wanted to wear flats because she was afraid of being too tall in heels. She asked her mother to bring over the shoes. Her mother did."

"Is there a video of Nadine leaving?" Danny asked.

"About fifteen minutes later, time enough to hand over shoes, drop in on husband, kill husband, then snatch jewels from the open safe. But why would she kill Barry?"

"Yeah. Why?" my cousin inquired.

And so I left. And made a phone call. And an hour later, met my father in an all-night coffee shop in Queens. "Amy, sweetheart! You're looking good."

"I am not. I am preparing for trial and I am sallow and dopey with fatigue. But thank you for lying, Dad."

"Would I lie?"

I smiled at him. He, at least, looked good, having successfully stayed out of the hoosegow for more than four years while maintaining a prisoner's weight-lifting regimen. Currently, he was living with a woman he referred to as Mary-the-rich-divorcey. By rich, I believe he meant his lady friend could afford to keep him in the style to which he was accustomed; as he had spent so many years incarcerated, his demands were not much more than a toilet with a door, cable TV, and access to barbells. I had never met Mary. She believed my father was an unmarried stud of thirty-six. It would have been awkward for him to have to explain the existence of a twenty-eight-year-old daughter. "You like your ice cream?" he asked.

"Thank you. It's lovely. Dad, I called because it has been months since I've seen you. But also, I need your professional expertise."

"You gotta be kidding." He laughed. His Adam's apple bounced around in his pumped-up neck.

"No. I am serious. I need some help."

"Tell me, sweetheart." So for the next half-hour, I told him all I knew about the murder of Barry Bleiberman. He asked a few questions, and said "Yeah" and "I get it" several times. While I cannot say he nodded sagely, at least he nodded.

"This is what I need from you, Dad: insight."

"Insect?"

"No. Insight. It is rather like wisdom. Why would a man like Murray kill Barry Bleiberman? Or why would he not kill him?"

My father pushed up the sleeves of his sweater, squeezed his fists, and watched his forearm muscles inflate. I assumed this was a prelude to deep thought, for he fell silent, staring into his vanilla malted. "Not," he said at last.

"Murray would not kill Barry Bleiberman?"

"You got it, Amy baby."

"Why not?"

"You gotta be shittin' me. Oh, sorry, sweetheart. You gotta be kiddin' me. You don't know?"

"That's why I came to you."

He smiled. It saddened me: Dentistry, as practiced in America's penal institutions, left much to be desired. "See, he wouldn't kill Barry because then what would he have?"

"Fifty percent of the business and two young partners who would be dependent on him."

"No, no, no. He'd have two pain in the ass kids who didn't know a pile of shit from a hot rock business-wise. Pardon my French. He could deal with a cheapo like Barry. Do you think he was so stupid he'd want to have to control that girl with the leather mini and that boy who's so constipated, he can't talk? So unless Murray was one big-time dumb schmuck, trust me, baby. He didn't stick no letter opener into the late Barry."

I was sickeningly behind in my preparations for my trial, but I was so tired, I dragged myself to my apartment rather than to the office. Before I fell into a near-lifeless sleep, I called my cousin Rachel. "Remember we were talking about Nadine?"

"Right. About how it wouldn't make sense for her to kill her husband."

"How about this, Rach? That although Barry dealt with wealthy people and was pretty well-to-do himself, the Bleibermans lived a life that was amazingly free of luxury. No fine furniture or rugs. No art. No designer clothes. No glorious jewelry." I regretted not having gone into Rachel's kitchen to get the Mallomar I had been lusting after. "The Bleibermans had no nothing, as it were. Well, Barry had money, but none of it was going to Nadine. What do you think it was like for her, seeing Aunt Vivian all decked out in furs and jewels? Going to the Glicksteins and seeing a small painting that cost more than everything in her own apartment?"

Two days later, after some prompting and threats from Uncle Murray's lawyer, Nadine Bleiberman was again read her rights and questioned, ostensibly to clear up what time she left B and G's offices. Then and there, she confessed to a kindly woman—who happened to be a sergeant in the NYPD's homicide unit.

"She said it was an accident," I told Tatty the following night. She was home reading Machiavelli and drinking Vernaccia. I, of course, was at the office with all my discovery material and an empty can of Diet Coke.

"An accident? Did she trip, grab the letter opener for support, and somehow in regaining her balance stab the man in the heart three times?"

"He had refused to give her money for a new outfit for some ladies luncheon she was going to."

"A cheap fuck indeed," Tatty murmured.

"She went into his office to plead with him again. Vivian and all the other women she knew would be there. Alas, he refused. A magnificent strand of pearls happened to be on his desk just then, a box lined in ivory silk. She told the cop the sight of it made her momentarily lose her mind."

"I see."

"So although he knows nothing about you, Tatiana, Uncle Murray thanks you. My cousin Rachel, whom you met on the occasion of my swearing in, thanks you, as does her husband, Danny, Uncle Murray's nephew. And of course I am infinitely grateful to you."

"Does infinite gratitude include your buying me dinner tomorrow night?" Tatty inquired.

"Not tomorrow night."

"Have you a hot date?"

"With Uncle Murray and Aunt Vivian."

"No!"

"Yes. They sent over a Piaget watch completely covered with pavé set diamonds. Naturally I sent it back."

"Might I ask why?"

"I am your public servant. You would want me to be above reproach."

"I would. But I'll bet you also found it tasteless."

"I did. In any case, they asked to take me out for dinner."

"And you said yes?" Tatty gasped. "Are you an utter ass? Haven't you done enough for them?"

"What can I tell you?" I replied. "They invited my cousin Rachel and her husband. Auntie Viv said: 'Oh Amy, it will just be the six of us. Murray and I. Rachel and Danny. Ken. And you. Family.' So I asked her, 'Family?' And in jewel-like tones, she said 'Yes, family.' So I inquired: 'How about my father?' "

"To which she replied . . . ?" Tatty demanded.

"Well, at first there was utter silence: the universe just before the Big Bang. Then I heard her swallow. And finally she managed to say: 'Of course. Family.' "

THE GRAPES OF ROTH

Judith Kelman

FLIGHT 553 from JFK to Las Vegas smacked the tarmac, lurched to a screaming stop, and then limped toward the terminal, belching smoke. The stench of burned rubber rose from the wheelbase and a gritty dust cloud choked the sun-baked air.

Betsy Mostel peeled her fingers from the armrest. As she stood, the ferret-faced man seated beside her seized her wrist. "You okay, babe? That was some hell of a landing. Reminded me of that crash last year in Illinois that killed all 237 onboard plus 24 on the ground. They're still finding pieces of the victims: fingers, teeth, bits of bone. Almost as good as that one a couple of years back in Cambodia. How about I buy you a cup of coffee and tell you all about it?"

Betsy wrenched free of his sweaty grip. After six hours of his nonstop talking, she was more than ready to be rid of the annoying creep. "I can't, I'm meeting someone."

"So you'll be a little late. I'm a good guy to know, babe. Believe me."

"Look, mister, I'm here on very important business and I simply have no time for anything else."

He stuffed a folded piece of paper into her tote. "Those are my numbers: home, cell, beeper. My name may be Johnny D., but I want you to think of me as Mr. Las Vegas. Anything you need in this town, I can get it for you. Anything you need done, I can do it. And I do mean *anything*."

Betsy nodded curtly and made her way off the plane. Johnny D. followed her, chattering nonstop. "I mean, suppose that very important business of yours goes wrong. You never know. I could turn things around for you, whatever it took."

"Thanks anyway. I'll be fine."

"You want insurance, call Johnny D. Remember that. I'm the ticket."

Off the jet way, Betsy ducked into the nearest rest room and splashed her clammy face with cool water. Fishing through her overstuffed tote, she extracted a mesh bag filled with cosmetics. She masked the dusky troughs beneath her eyes with concealer and relieved her sickly pallor with generous sweeps of rose-toned blush. She slicked on her favorite red lipstick, and then tamed her electrified brown hair with a hard-bristled brush. Satisfied, she extracted a new linen blazer and mock crocodile pumps from her imitation Louis Vuitton carry-on bag. Finally, she wound a bright Hermès style scarf around her neck and knotted it expertly.

Betsy had learned the crucial impact of appearance during her five-year stint as assistant to the personal assistant to the executive assistant to Claris Breen, the most powerful woman in advertising.

Whenever Betsy delivered Ms. Breen's decaf, low-fat cappuccinos or left notes regarding her manicure and waxing appointments or slipped into the executive office to walk Mr. Breen (Claris Breen's Portugese water dog,) she had surreptitiously studied the great woman, seeking to absorb every detail of her elegance, arrogance, and force.

At home, Betsy practiced for at least an hour every night. Slowly, she conquered the signature Claris Breen walk, the imperious head toss and the wilting glare of disapproval, even the melting, enigmatic grin. Using a tape recorder, she learned how to speak with Ms. Breen's fearsome authority. With her rapier tongue alone, Claris could mesmerize a potential client or dice an adversary into impotent bits. Betsy worked until she was confident that she could do the same when the time came.

And the time had come with a vengeance.

Betsy had hit bottom like Flight 553, in a sudden, terrifying plunge. First came the notice early last week from nasty old Mr. Rasweiler, her landlord. The building had been approved for conversion into a condominium. Residents could buy their units for an unthinkable price or vacate in thirty days. To make matters worse, Rasweiler had the audacity to suggest that Betsy would not qualify as a purchaser, given her history of chronic arrears.

Determined to fix the problem, Betsy had asked for her parents' help. All they needed to do was to lend her the back rent, interest, penalties, and down payment, and sign as guarantors, and Rasweiler would allow her to buy. Inexplicably, Betsy's clear, businesslike proposal left them both doubled over with uncontrollable laughter.

Seeing no alternative, Betsy decided to ask for a long-overdue raise. She was still reeling from Ms. Breen's astonishing response. Now she banished the ugly incident from her mind. Soon, very soon, none of that would matter.

For as long as she could remember, Betsy's mother had regaled her with tales of her reclusive, weird, fabulously wealthy uncle Lawrence Mostel. As Sophie told it, her long-lost brother was a self-made man, a business genius who had amassed stunningly valuable holdings. He had never married nor fathered any children. Someday, if Betsy played her cards right, Uncle Lawrence's fortune might fall to her.

Betsy did everything in her power to see that happen. Not once had she missed Uncle Lawrence's birthday or failed to send him a lovely, thoughtful gift at Christmastime.

Whenever she had a special occasion or achievement, she notified her uncle with a charming handwritten note. She included copies of her best report cards and certificates of merit. At least once a month, she wrote to inquire about his health and wish him well. She invited him to her birthday parties and graduations, though he never replied and she knew he would never attend. No one in the family had seen nor heard from the man in more than forty years. Still, Betsy was determined to plant her existence in her rich uncle's mind and demonstrate her suitability to be his heiress. She had even gone so far as to adopt Mostel as her surname as soon as she reached legal age. Her father had been furious, but Betsy could see no particular percentage in remaining a Himmelman.

She starched her spine and strode like Claris Breen through the dizzying chaos of McCarran airport. People with stupefied expressions sat force-feeding quarters into the twirling, flashing, screeching slot machines. The tide of travelers carried a striking number of women with billboard-sized breasts, Elvis impersonators, and men sporting gold chains suitable for restraining attack dogs.

Approaching baggage claim, Betsy spotted her cousin Glenn. When last she'd seen him during a disastrous family reunion two decades ago, he was a portly fifteen-year-old with a crew cut, braces, and a lazy eye. Multiple trips to Dr. Hiram Reynaldo, plastic surgeon to the stars and other vain people with money, had converted him into the lanky, origami-boned creature that slouched against a billboard, talking on a tiny silver phone. His jet hair was slicked back and hooked behind tightly pinned ears. Slim leather pants and a stretch black turtleneck left nothing of his reconstructed body to the imagination. Betsy could envision the liposuction wand, transferring massive mounds of unsightly fat to sunken donor sites. Plus, Glenn must have enough plastic under his skin to stock a Tupperware party. If not for the photo that accompanied his annual Christmas letter,

Betsy wouldn't have recognized the geek in wolf's clothing at all.

Glenn had no such trouble with her. Snapping his cell shut, he smirked. "Well, if it isn't little Miss Thunder Britches."

Betsy's cheeks flamed. "I see that all the abracadabra with the magic fat extractor did nothing for your personality, Glenn."

"Don't be so sensitive, Cuz. It was hilarious. There we were, the warring factions of the Mostel clan gathered for the first time in years. After dinner, my dad makes the speech he's been working on for weeks. He talks about forgiveness and how blood is thicker than water and how we all need to love and care about each other. By the time he's done, there isn't a dry eye in the house. Everyone is forgetting the anger, letting the grudges go.

"And then, at the climactic moment, when everyone waits silent with a raised glass, you cut the cheese. And it's not some dainty girl toot. No, ma'am. This is a long, loud, rolling blast, like a trucker who's chowed down a bowl of beans and a six-pack."

A crowd had gathered, drawn by Glenn's dramatic recital and sweeping gestures. Betsy's cousin, an ardent performer, would do anything to attract an audience. The strangers laughed and applauded, egging him on.

"Your mother tried to blame the whole thing on sweet old Granny Irene. I mean, they are you are, blushing to beat the band, and Sophie has the nerve to point the finger at Irene, of all people. I can't think of anyone more proper and refined. Poor thing all but keeled over from the shock and embarrassment."

A buzzer sounded, and the luggage conveyor began to spin. As she'd hoped, Betsy's matched mock Vuitton cases tumbled out first, waving their red priority tags. "Those are mine, Glenn. If it wouldn't be too much strain on your implants, perhaps you can get them off the belt for me."

The surprise on Glenn's face was enough to justify the cost of the luggage. Betsy had opened four new charge accounts to outfit herself for this trip, bringing the total to a record thirty-six. But as Ms. Breen often said, nothing paid off like a good investment. The effect was furthered when a uniformed chauffeur hurried toward her.

"Ms. Mostel?"

"Yes."

"I'm Crawshaw, here to take you to see Mr. Roth. So sorry I'm late. Are these yours?"

"The matched set of Louis Vuitton pieces? Yes. That's one of the things I love about flying up front. One does not need to wait for one's luggage."

"True, Ms. Mostel. Most convenient."

Glenn cleared his throat. "You're here for me, too, driver. I'm the nephew."

"Oh yes, sir. Of course. Has your baggage not yet arrived?"

Glenn looped the strap of his ratty green knapsack over his shoulder. "I believe in traveling light."

"Certainly, sir. If you'll follow me, the car is right outside."

Betsy affected Claris Breen's imperious strut, leaving Glenn to scurry behind like a lap dog. She waited for Crawshaw to install her regally in the rear of the Mercedes limousine, while her cousin struggled with the lock, bumped his head on the door frame, and landed hard on the leather seat, making a sound like a whoopee cushion.

Betsy chuckled. "Little Mr. Thunder Britches."

On the ride, Crawshaw pointed out some of the town's more jaw-dropping features. Nine of the world's ten largest hotels were located here. They passed the massive pyramidal structure that housed the Luxor. New York, New York spanned several city blocks and boasted a giant roller coaster, which traversed the casino and rattled the guestroom windows. The Venetian contained a canal system complete with singing gondoliers. Lions frolicked in the lobby of the MGM Grand, Pirates battled hourly at the Treasure Island and water displays to rival Old Faithful shot off every fifteen minutes in front of the Bellagio.

Betsy stared out through the dark tinted window, trying to absorb the incomprehensible scale of the place, rising from the arid Mojave like a neon-draped Behemoth. It was impossible and terrible and frightening and fabulous and exciting beyond words, a creation of Claris Breen proportions. And soon, very soon, she would be one of its reigning monarchs.

Glenn wriggled in his seat like a full-bladdered child. "What's your poison, Cuz? Craps? Blackjack? Dollar slots? Roulette? Me, I love it all. Hand me a stack of chips, I'm a happy man."

"I don't gamble, Glenn. I only like to win."

"You got to be in it to win it. Isn't that so, Crawshaw? I come here from L.A. every chance I get. Nothing beats a hot time at the tables. Best fun you can have standing up."

"Personally, I do not indulge, sir," the driver said.

"You live in Vegas and you don't play? You're kidding me."

"There are nearly one and a half million citizens in the greater Las Vegas area. This community is far more than a tourist or gaming establishment," Betsy said smugly. Knowledge was power, as Ms. Breen so often observed.

Crawshaw smiled in the rearview mirror. "That's absolutely right, Ms. Mostel. Our fair city proudly numbers among the fastest growing and most prosperous in the nation. We have excellent schools and medical services, extensive cultural opportunities and recreational facilities. This is a perfect place to raise the family as well as an ideal location for young singles and retirees."

At Tropicana, he turned off the Strip and followed a confusing weave of streets into a mixed residential and commercial area. Soon, he angled into a parking lot fronting a nondescript, two-story office building. Too late, Betsy remembered her intention to pump the chauffeur for any useful information she could glean about her uncle Lawrence's attorney.

She knew nothing of J. Mortimer Roth beyond the certified letter she received from him late last week. She could envision it now: dense ivory paper with an embossed law firm letterhead.

Dear Ms. Mostel:

I regret to inform you of the untimely passing of your uncle, Lawrence Anson Mostel, on Tuesday, December the tenth.

Along with Mr. Glenn Mostel, you have been named a conditional legatee in Mr. Mostel's Last Will and Testament. As Executor of the Estate, it is my duty to define for you the complex terms of these bequests and to afford you every opportunity to fulfill them successfully.

To that end, I request that you meet with me at my Las Vegas office on Friday afternoon of next week and plan to remain through Sunday morning.

As soon as I receive your affirmative response, I shall arrange for your transportation and lodgings.

Sincerely yours,
J. Mortimer, Roth, Esq.

Betsy had searched the Internet for further information about Mr. Roth, but discovered nothing. As a seasoned on-line snoop, she found this very strange, indeed. She had drawn a similar blank when she attempted to gather information on her uncle Lawrence. Somehow, both men had eluded the incalculable reach of the Web. A search on Claris Breen, for example, turned up 17,362 citations. Betsy's own name drew four references to Ms. Breen's international fan club, which she had founded and for which she had served as president for three wonderful years.

Crawshaw led them into the building and up the elevator to the second floor. Mr. Roth's office occupied a large corner suite. When they entered, he was tipped back in his tan leather chair, lithe fingers laced behind his neck. Roth was a dapper man in his late fifties with a gray handlebar mustache and wavy pewter hair. He had pale weary eyes, a truculent mouth, and a long, jutting challenge of a chin.

Betsy approached him with a firm stride and unwavering gaze. "Pleasure to meet you, Mr. Roth. I'm Betsy Mostel."

The lawyer nodded crisply. "I suggest we dispense with unnecessary formalities and get down to business."

"Good by me," said Glenn. "Cut right to the chase, Roth. What did the old man leave, and how soon do I get it?"

"Unfortunately, I can't give you a simple answer. The enterprise your uncle built was complex and demanding, and he devoted himself to it fully. If you worked with Mr. M., it was full time, full bore, all out."

"That's exactly the way I approach my business dealings, Mr. Roth," Betsy said. "I've been working with Claris Breen for most of my career. She's president of Quantum Advertising. Perhaps you've heard of her."

"Yes. Of course," Roth said. "Who hasn't?"

"Then you can imagine how fully devoted I am to what I do. I'm Ms. Breen's right hand, at her service twenty-four hours a day, seven days a week. No exceptions."

"Except that you happen to be here," said Glenn.

"The fact is I haven't taken a vacation in nearly five years. Of course, we'll be in constant touch during my absence. As Claris so often says, she simply cannot get along without me."

Roth's head swung in a rueful arc. "I'm afraid that would eliminate you from contention, Ms. Mostel. What about you, Mr. Mostel? Have you any consuming entanglements like your cousin? Are you committed to anyone who finds you indispensable?"

"Hell no. Responsibility makes me itch. I did have this

cat once, but thank God he got run over by a pizza truck."

"Wait a minute, Mr. Roth. You misunderstand," Betsy sputtered. "Despite our deep mutual admiration and Ms. Breen's utter dependence on me, she understands that I put family first. If dear Uncle Lawrence's final wish was to pass his precious business and hard-earned fortune to the loving care of his only niece, it would be my solemn duty to see that wish fulfilled."

Roth fiddled with a folder on his desk. "I'm relieved to hear that, because obviously, Mr. Mostel is not up to dealing with the level of responsibility this business requires. It takes the kind of twenty-four/seven commitment you seem willing to make, Ms. Mostel."

"Whoa. Wait a minute," Glenn said. "I was talking pets, plants, girlfriends, kids, stupid crap like that. Show me the right gig, and I'll work my butt off."

"Dr. Reynaldo already worked your butt off, Glenn," Betsy said sweetly.

"She'll do twenty-four/seven. I'll go thirty-four/ten," Glenn shot back.

Roth plucked a page from the folder and made two broad checkmarks. "Okay. I'll give you both a passing grade on willingness to take the business on."

Betsy's heart sank as she saw the long list of further qualifications. Roth shadowed the page with his cupped hand, making it impossible for her to read, but clearly this was not going to be simple. "Can you please describe Uncle Lawrence's business? My mother has always been a little hazy about the details."

"I can only offer limited information at this time. Mr. M. prescribed a careful process by which I am to determine whether one of you is suited to take the reins. If the answer is yes, the person I select will have all the information he or she needs to take over the operations."

Glenn frowned. "And what happens if the answer is no?"

"If neither of you proves to be a suitable successor, the

operations will be dispersed and the assets divided according to a formula spelled out in the will."

Betsy sat straighter. "I'm sure I can prove myself equal to the task, Mr. Roth. Exactly what information do you need to make your decision?"

A sly grin lit the lawyer's face. "Telling you that would be tantamount to giving you answers to a test, Ms. Mostel. Suffice it to say that the next several days will tell the story. Now, I'm sure you must be anxious to get to your hotel and freshen up."

Betsy rose to make a controlled, dignified exit. She needed time to digest this new information and formulate a revised plan of attack.

Glenn stayed rooted in his chair. "Just a darned minute. What about the old man's millions? My pop always told me Lawrence was swimming in green. How soon do I get my hands on some of that?"

Roth's smile fell away. "Your uncle's wealth is tied up in complex holdings that are inextricably linked to his business endeavors. Those holdings will pass to whoever assumes control of the operations or failing that, they will be apportioned according to the same formula that Mr. M. devised for disposing of the enterprises. Now, if that's all, I'll have Crawshaw drive you to your hotel. I've arranged for dinner in a private suite at eight-thirty. See you there."

Glenn smacked the desk and sent papers flying. "That's not close to all, Roth. I know my rights. I'm entitled to at least half of the old man's megabucks. In fact, I can make a damned good case for claiming the whole enchilada. My pop was the oldest. Plus, he happened to be really close to Uncle Larry as a kid. They used to horse around and try to kill each other, all that brotherly stuff. Meanwhile, Betsy's mother was nothing but the pain-in-the-ass baby sister neither of them could stand. Larry would never want his money to go to her kid."

"That's ridiculous. Lawrence adored my mother. He

thought your father was a lazy slob and a horrible bully. In fact getting away from your pop and his endless freeloading was one of his biggest reasons for moving out here in the first place."

"Why you lying, little—"

"That's high praise coming from a veteran phony like you, Glenn."

"That will do," Roth marked a bold X for each of them halfway down the page of qualifying questions.

"What was that?" Betsy asked.

"Mr. M. felt very strongly that impeccable emotional control was essential to his business dealings. He would never tolerate displays of temper or acrimony."

"We were just kidding around." Glenn put his arm around Betsy. "We're really crazy about each other. Aren't we, Cuz?"

Betsy squirmed in his gym-toned grasp. "Let me reassure you, Mr. Roth. I am prepared to dedicate myself one hundred percent to carrying on my uncle's legacy. I shall be the picture of self-control. Whatever it takes, you can count on me."

Glenn squeezed her shoulder with excruciating force. "Me too, Roth. I'm a regular rock. Ask anyone."

"The next two days will tell."

Crawshaw drove them to the five-star Four Seasons. The parking attendant welcomed them by name. A smiling bell-man swooped by to retrieve their bags. Roth had arranged for an expedited check-in, so a towering blond desk agent named Yanush escorted them directly to their adjoining thirty-ninth-floor rooms.

Betsy's was a sumptuous junior suite with a sparkling view of the Strip. While Yanush, the Russian Adonis, demonstrated the use of the air-conditioning, sound system, and elaborate remote controls, she observed his thick wavy hair and the sexy curl of his well-defined lips. Mammoth shoulders tapered to a slim waist and abs flat as a landing strip.

He had powerful legs, a perfect butt, and extra-large hands, which as everyone knew, meant other things were extra large as well. Betsy imagined strolling into Quantum Advertising with Yanush on her arm. Dreamily, she pictured all the girls, Claris Breen included, turned inside out with envy. Then the sound of Glenn talking on the phone next door broke her delicious reverie.

"Will there be anything else, Ms. Mostel?"

Reluctantly, she tipped Yanush and showed him out. First things first. Once she had caged Uncle Lawrence's fortune, she would see to a complete overhaul of her pitiful love life.

Safely alone, Betsy pressed her ear to the wall. Glenn's voice seeped through, dripping with venom and spite. "Don't worry, Pop. I've got the perfect plan. I'm going to butter up the little bitch and get her to trust me. Bet you anything she gives me more than enough rope to hang her with."

Glenn went silent for a while, listening. Then his slimy voice sounded again. "Sure I can pull it off, but only because I'm a damned good actor. You should see her, Pop. She's this frizzy-haired, no-class twig with clown makeup. She walks like she has a broomstick up her ass and puts on this stupid accent that sounds like a cross between Dracula and the Queen Mother. My biggest problem is going to be keeping a straight face. Sure, Pop. Great idea. I'll call tomorrow and let you know how it's going."

Glenn's door slammed, and Betsy heard his approaching footsteps. He rapped lightly on her door.

"Are you decent, Cuz? I thought you might enjoy kicking back with a couple of drinks before dinner."

Betsy forced the strangled rage from her tone. "I'll be ready in a few moments, Glenn. Why don't I meet you down at the bar?"

"Sure. Take your time. I'll be waiting."

Betsy sat on the bed and breathed deeply and tried to

devise a constructive response to Glenn's duplicity, but she was too furious to think clearly. Rifling through her tote, she pulled out the small imitation crocodile album she always carried. Inside were several pictures of Claris Breen, clipped from *The Wall Street Journal* and *The New York Times*. There was a handwritten note from Ms. Breen, thanking Betsy for the gourmet doggie treats she had given Mr. Breen for his fifth birthday last March. Other plastic sleeves held a cocktail napkin used by Claris at last year's agency Christmas party and a Season's Greetings card signed by a computer trained to reproduce Ms. Breen's signature. Betsy had even collected toenail clippings from one of Claris's office pedicures and an empty lipstick tube from the executive office wastebasket. She had worn the identical color ever since: Femme Fatale.

Even now, she found comfort in these special souvenirs. She smiled at Claris Breen's image, and Claris smiled back. Suddenly, Betsy realized that their little falling out had meant nothing. Dear Claris could be so hotheaded at times, saying things she didn't mean. Of course, that's all it had been.

Betsy applied some fresh lipstick and replenished the rest of her makeup. She brushed the lint from her linen blazer and rearranged her faux Hermès scarf. She would not allow a jerk like Glenn to get to her. Now that she thought about it clearly, she realized he had given her a strategic edge. Gathering the necessary props, Betsy resolved to take full advantage.

Stepping off the elevator at the lobby level, Betsy spotted a slim, lurking figure down the hall. Closer, she recognized the irritating man who had talked her nearly to death on the plane from New York. She averted her gaze and kept walking, hoping he wouldn't notice her, but no such luck.

"Look who's here. Small world, huh? How's it going?"

"Fine. But I'm very busy. If you'll excuse me."

"Sure, babe. If you need me, you got my numbers. Don't forget."

She found Glenn sprawled in an armchair in the lobby lounge. He smiled up at her. "I must say, you look fabulous."

"Why, thank you, Glenn. Aren't you kind."

"I call them like I see them. What are you drinking?"

She ordered Claris Breen's favorite cocktail. "A Bombay Sapphire martini. Extra dry with olives. Perhaps you'd care to join me."

"I probably shouldn't. Martinis put me on my ass."

"Not to worry, dear. You're safe in the bosom of your family."

The waiter delivered a pair of enormous drinks. Betsy sipped at hers demurely.

Glenn took a hefty slug. "You must be quite something to work for a heavy hitter like Claris Breen."

"Yes. I suppose that's true."

"What did you say your title is, exactly?"

Masking a smirk, Betsy fished the wallet from her tote. She had printed special business cards for the occasion, which read: *Betsy Mostel, executive vice president, Quantum Advertising, Inc.*

As Glenn examined the card, Betsy's cell phone sounded. She squinted at the caller ID. "Excuse me. That's Ms. Breen now." Betsy spoke calmly over her mother's frantic questions. "Yes, Claris. I understand. Not to worry. I took care of everything before I left. You'll find the storyboard for the Reynolds presentation on my desk. The budget for the Barons project is filed with the proposal. I've arranged to outsource the Davison computer graphic work as you suggested and lined up the supermodels for the Lightworks shoot. Anything else? Yes, of course, Claris, dear. If you hit a snag, just call."

Glenn fished an olive from the massive glass. "Must be

tough working for that Breen woman. I hear she's a bitch on wheels."

"You mustn't believe all those silly things they say in the media. Ms. Breen is a perfect manager. She only demands of others the same high standards she sets for herself."

"But she works you to death, doesn't she? Leans on you like crazy? You said so yourself."

"Quite honestly, I thrive on it. I suppose I'm a bit of a workaholic, like Uncle Lawrence."

"Yeah? Where do you figure that's going to get you?"

"I see myself on a steady course of personal growth, well on the way to self-actualization, which is, of course, my goal. What about you, Glenn? Acting seems so tough."

"Tell me about it. L.A. is crawling with no-talents, begging for a part. You go on auditions, and there's a line halfway to Carmel. If you're not the kid or the arm piece of a major star, forget about it."

"Still, I gather from your Christmas letter that you've had considerable success: a daytime Emmy nomination. What show was that for exactly? I don't believe you mentioned the name."

Glenn took another strong pull at his martini. "Nothing I hate more than name-dropping. Like my good pal Stallone always says, it's the mark of a real nobody."

"I understand. But still, I'd love to see some of your work. You also mentioned featured roles in major motion pictures. What are some of the titles? I could rent the videos."

He downed the last of his drink and motioned for another. "I'd rather you wait for this really terrific thing I just did with Penn and DeNiro. We're in post production now, but soon as it's out, I'll get you a screening copy."

"All those stars. How exciting. I can't imagine how you could give that up to go into some mundane business."

"Been there, done that. You know how it goes."

Betsy observed the thickening tongue and the hot flush rising in his cheeks. "Yes, I do, Glenn. Absolutely."

Betsy approached dinner in a victorious mood, but the evening took a swift, disastrous turn. A stranger sat across from Roth at an oval table in the dazzling presidential suite. He was a thick, pugnacious-looking man, whom the lawyer introduced as "my associate."

Betsy turned to him brightly. "Sorry, I didn't catch your name."

"I didn't throw it," he growled.

"As I mentioned earlier, you will have all the information you need when the time comes," Roth added.

Betsy placed a hand over her glass as Roth wrenched the cork from a dusty bottle of Cabernet. "None for me, thanks. I'm allergic to any wine that's not really, really fresh."

Roth's face darkened. "I see. Some for you, Mr. Mostel?"

"Is that really Lagrange '89? Sign me up! Stuff is supposed to be nectar of the gods. Rarer than black swans. Can't believe I actually get to taste it. I have to tell you, Roth. I'm blown away."

The lawyer beamed. "Then I'm sure you'll be glad to hear that we hold a controlling interest in the winery. It's been a pet project of mine for some time."

"In that case, I'll be delighted to try some. Honored, in fact," Betsy said.

"I wouldn't hear of it. Allergic reactions can be nasty."

Betsy sank in her seat while the men sipped and savored. "It smells wonderful," she ventured. "Like flowers."

Glenn rolled his eyes. "Flowers. Sure. And butterflies, too. Don't you think, guys?"

The thug stuck his nose in the glass. "Nah. I'd have to say moonbeams, maybe with a touch of clouds."

While the men enjoyed a raucous laugh at her expense, a waiter appeared with four enormous blood-rare steaks. Betsy, who had embraced Claris Breen's vegetarianism years ago, prodded the repulsive oozing flesh around her plate. She was helpless to join the men, who gobbled in frenzied unison. They bonded further over dessert, a chocolate and whipped cream concoction that caused Betsy's stomach, shrunken from years of near starvation dieting, to roil. After dinner, they lit fat Cuban cigars, whose stench left her queasy and lightheaded.

Roth chose that moment to assault them with loaded questions. "Tell me, where do you picture yourself in five years?"

Glenn answered first, holding forth about personal growth and self-actualization, a blatant theft of Betsy's words that left her speechless.

Roth nodded approval. "And you, Ms. Mostel? Where do you picture yourself?"

In desperation Betsy tossed out the first thought she had. "Here, Mr. Roth. I picture right myself here in Vegas, running things."

"Real profound," Glenn said.

"And how would you describe your management style, Mr. Mostel?" Roth asked.

Glenn spoke through an acrid smoky haze. "I'd expect my people to meet the same high standards I set for myself."

"You, Ms. Mostel?"

"I would be hands on." Then, noting a tiny downturn in the lawyer's expression, she added, "But laissez-faire. In other words, I would surround myself with the best people and allow them to flourish independently." At that, Roth's left brow edged up a notch. "But of course, I'd keep them on a tight lead."

"I see." Roth marked two checks in Glenn's column and two bold X's in hers.

That night, Betsy paced her suite in a restless rage. Far below, the neon lights on the Strip winked like cruel, taunting eyes. Near midnight, she heard Glenn slip out of his room. It was after two when his door creaked open and then shut with a resonant smack. Moments later, he was on the phone to his father.

"Couldn't have gone better, Pop. You should have seen

that scrawny twit, twisting in the wind after I strung her up. It was priceless. I've got Roth in my hip pocket. You were a hundred percent right about getting his driver to open up. All I had to do was promise him an introduction to my good friend Jennifer Lopez. He told me everything I needed to know to impress the hell out of Roth. Sure I'm brilliant. I've been telling you that for years, Pop. One more day, and it's all ours."

Too enraged to sleep, Betsy spent the rest of the rest of the night plotting ways to get the better of her wretched cousin. Near dawn, she had a brilliant idea of her own.

Roth's driver was at their disposal twenty-four hours a day. Betsy dialed his number and asked him to come for her at once. She dressed quickly and met him in front of the hotel.

"Sorry to get you out this early, Crawshaw. But I needed to see you alone to discuss a proposition I believe you'll find interesting. Perhaps we can go somewhere and have a cup of coffee."

At a strip mall Starbucks, Betsy matched Glenn's offer and raised him one. Claris Breen had used Jennifer Lopez in several major ad campaigns, she explained. If Jen, as Betsy referred to her, was the object of Crawshaw's fancy, she could do far better than an introduction. She promised to arrange a romantic evening, just Crawshaw and the sex kitten starlet. She would have Jen wear one of her more daring outfits, the kind that would allow a dermatologist to perform a thorough and complete examination.

Soon the driver was spewing information like the Bellagio fountains. To be named as Uncle Lawrence's successor, she would have to convince Roth that she was an unfailingly ethical person. Religious devotion would help. So would a hard-line stand on law and order.

Crawshaw sipped the last of his double espresso. "Roth is big on gun control and a huge supporter of the death penalty. Take his side, and you can't miss."

Betsy's heart sounded drumbeats of victory. "That's great, Crawshaw. Now all I need to know is what he has planned for us today. I want to be completely ready."

The driver shrugged. "I can't say for sure, but my guess is he'll take you shopping and out for a nice lunch. He's big into clothes and all that. You can probably tell that from the way he puts himself together."

"A man after my own heart."

Betsy donned her desert beige Armani-style pantsuit and the Gucci pumps she had picked up on sale. She stuffed all three dozen of her credit cards in the matching purse, even though they were all at or slightly past their allowable limits. In the lobby, she bit her lip to keep from smirking at the sight of Glenn looking pitifully inappropriate in plaid Bermuda shorts and a garish yellow shirt.

Then in walked Roth clad in khaki walking shorts and a floppy hat. "Your cousin tells me you're quite the golfer. It so happens golf is my passion, too, so I've arranged for us to spend the day at the country club, Ms. Mostel. We tee off at nine. Why don't you go change and we'll meet you down the hall for breakfast?"

Frantic, Betsy raced to the gift shop, where she hastily purchased a golf shirt and placket-front shirt. Thankfully, she was able to charge them to the room.

She forced down a half slice of wheat toast and two sips of juice. Glenn had put her in a dreadful position. If she admitted she hated golf, she lost yet another point with Roth.

The lawyer signed the check. "Ready to hit the links?"

"I'm afraid I'll have to watch. I was in a tournament with Ms. Breen last fall, and I developed this dreadful case of golfer's knee."

"Really? Never heard of that," Roth said.

"It's rare, but quite painful. I'm better now, but the doctor says I mustn't even hit a ball for at least another month."

"In that case, why don't you meet us back here later? It's

shaping up to be a scorcher. I'm sure you'd be more comfortable in air-conditioning."

"Not at all, Mr. Roth. I thrive on the desert climate."

Betsy drove the cart, bumping over rocky footpaths in the searing sun while Glenn and Roth played eighteen leisurely holes under the broad shade of a golf umbrella held by a smiling caddy. By the end of the round, every inch of her exposed skin was sun-scorched, and a searing headache thumped behind her eyes. Her throat was parched, and she was convinced that she could smell her hair burning.

At the clubhouse, Roth clapped Glenn on the back. "I could use a couple of cold ones, buddy. How about you?"

"You bet. Meanwhile, you look like you could use a shower and a nap, little cousin. Why don't we catch up with you later?"

"No way. Couple of cold ones are just what the doctor ordered," Betsy croaked.

She gulped down half a glass of beer, which went straight to her head. For the rest of the afternoon, while Roth and Glenn ate lunch, played poker, and watched a brutal boxing match on TV, Betsy struggled to sit upright. She fought against the ponderous weight of her eyelids. Her limbs hung like lead.

At six, Roth drove them back to the hotel. "See you for dinner at eight. I've booked a private room at Chez Montand, so you may wish to dress up. Afterward we'll have another little Q and A session. If all goes as I expect it will, I should have my decision for you at breakfast tomorrow morning."

Betsy requested a wake-up call and fell hard asleep. An hour later, she woke up refreshed. She showered quickly and donned her new black sequined dress, a genuine Bill Blass copy that had cost a fortune. Faux pearl and diamond earrings, silk pumps and an organza stole completed the outfit.

The maître d' showed her to the restaurant wine cellar, where a table had been set with opulent silver, china, and crystal. Roth and his nameless associate, clad in tuxedos, were seated when she arrived. "Good evening, gentlemen."

Glenn loped in moments later, looking hopelessly out of place in his leather pants and stretch turtleneck. "Okay, Roth. Let's rock and roll."

Another bottle of Lagrange '89 stood open on the service bar beside a screw-top liter of Beaujolais Nouveau, Vintage March. "That is about as fresh is it gets, Ms. Mostel," Roth said.

Betsy accepted a glass with dignity and cheer. "How very kind of you." Dinner was venison, Bambi on a plate, but she forced herself to eat. She even choked down half of her cheesecake and sipped gamely at the after-dinner cognac.

Roth dabbed his lips with a large linen napkin. "Now, Ms. Mostel. Tell me. What two words would best describe you as a person?"

"That's easy. Ethical and religious."

Glenn frowned when Roth turned to him. "I guess I have to say adventurous and fearless. Nothing I like better than living on the edge, pushing the envelope."

Roth sipped his Lagrange. "And what if your adventurous behavior put you at odds with the law?"

"Simple. Everyone knows the criminal justice system is a joke. It's all about money and who you know. I'd find a way to beat the rap, or go down trying."

"I'm shocked at you, Glenn," Betsy said. "My parents brought me up to believe in strict law and order. I firmly believe that we need strong gun control and swift, iron-fisted criminal prosecution. If you ask me, the best thing that's happened in this country in years is the reinstatement of the death penalty. Murderers deserve to die, pure and simple."

Glenn sniffed. "Pure and simple, my butt. You put a guy to death, you're the murderer. Plus, the courts make mistakes all the time, put the wrong guy on death row. It's a lot of bunk, if you ask me."

Roth raised his brandy glass and tapped it against Glenn's. "I'm with you one hundred percent, young man. Your uncle would have been as well." His look soured as he turned to Betsy. "I'll give you my decision in the morning, Ms. Mostel. Then Crawshaw can drive you to your plane."

"Great guy, Crawshaw," said Glenn.

"Yes. I especially admire his loyalty. Once you win his allegiance, he'll never betray you," Roth said.

Back in her room, Betsy flopped on the bed in despair. Even her album of Claris Breen memorabilia brought no solace. In fact, the silly souvenirs only darkened her mood. Claris was a rotten viper like her cousin. Betsy's devotion had gotten her nothing but a pink slip and a monstrous lecture. Claris had accused her of being a stalker. She'd said that Betsy gave everyone the creeps, including Mr. Breen, the Portugese water dog, who only agreed to walk with her out of necessity. Betsy tossed the album across the room. The hell with Claris. Two-faced monsters like that deserved cellulite, cystic acne, and a lifetime of really bad hair days.

Next door, she heard Glenn exulting on the phone. "You should have been there, Pop. It was priceless. She repeated all the crap the driver fed her. Roth wouldn't have her now if she was the only one left on earth. So pack your bags. This town is ours."

Betsy's mind filled with murderous images. She pictured Glenn falling from the thirty-ninth-floor window, landing on the pavement like a smashed tomato. She conjured her cousin sucking down a martini spiked with lye. No, she decided, rat poison would be far more appropriate. The image of him keeling over, foaming through his cold, blue lips made her feel a bit better.

And it gave her an idea. She rummaged through her tote until she found the folded slip of paper. He picked up on the second ring.

"I'm the woman who sat next to you on the plane, Mr.

D. You said to call if I needed anything, *anything* at all. Remember?"

"Absolutely, babe. What can I do you for?"

"I don't think I should say on the phone."

They met at a bar in The Mandalay Bay Hotel. Though she was frightened at first, Betsy found it surprisingly easy to explain what she needed done. Glenn had stolen her rightful place, crushed the remains of her piteous existence. If anyone deserved the death penalty, he did.

"Consider it done," said Johnny D.

"How much will it cost? I'm afraid I'm a little strapped at the moment."

"No problem. You can take care of it after you inherit your uncle's fortune."

"What if that doesn't happen?"

"Oh, it'll happen, babe. Wait and see."

All night, Betsy waited. Over her thunderous heartbeats, she listened hard for the sound of trouble next door: the pop of a silenced gun, a struggle, muffled screams. There was nothing.

Roth had requested that they meet for breakfast in a private suite at eight. At eight-fifteen, Glenn had yet to arrive. The lawyer was clearly annoyed.

"Maybe he overslept," Betsy suggested. "Why don't you have someone from the hotel go up and check on him?"

"Good idea."

As Roth picked up the house phone, Glenn walked in. "Sorry I'm late. I had a few loose ends to tie up."

"Everything is all right now?" Roth said.

"Couldn't be better. All I need now is your answer, Mr. Roth. Which one of us gets to carry on dear Uncle Lawrence's business?"

A table near the window was set for three. Warm morning light bathed a bottle of sparkling Lagrange that sat cooling in a crystal bucket. At Roth's direction, Betsy sat facing out beside Glenn.

The lawyer took his place. "Quite to my surprise, both of you have proven yourselves capable of taking over your uncle Lawrence's core enterprise. But as I explained, Mr. Mostel's will called for a single successor."

"Come on, Roth. You know I'm the one for the job. Look at her. Listen to her. She's a joke."

"You're the joke, Glenn. Playing games, bribing Mr. Roth's driver. You'll stop at nothing to get what you want.

"And neither will you, Ms. Mostel, which is precisely how I know you are capable of taking over your uncle's business. Come in, gentlemen," he called.

The door opened, and in walked Johnny D. Beside him was Roth's unnamed associate.

"What the hell is this?" Glenn shrieked.

"I don't understand. How did you . . . ?" Betsy sputtered.

Johnny D. pulled a pistol from under his jacket and pointed it at Glenn's head. "Au revoir, ass wipe."

Betsy shrieked. "No, don't. Look, I was only kidding. I couldn't really k-kill anyone."

Roth's associate leveled his 9-mm semiautomatic at Betsy. "Night, night, Cuz. Don't let the bed bugs bite."

Glenn leaped to his feet and blocked the killer's aim. "Me neither. I didn't really mean to shoot her. It was just talk."

Roth sighed. "I suspected as much. If you'll excuse us, gentlemen."

After the men filed out, Roth extracted a thick document from his briefcase. "This is your uncle Lawrence's last will and testament. In it, he clearly states that his first preference was for one of you to take charge of the operations if that proved appropriate. Unfortunately, it has not."

"Why not?" Glenn demanded. "I said I'd do anything."

"So did I," Betsy said.

"Except murder. And it so happens that murder is our stock in trade. Your uncle ran the largest contract killing operation in the world. We can proudly claim credit for major political assassinations, alleged terrorist attacks, and

of course, the fulfillment of thousands of more ordinary con-
tracts. Our client list is most impressive, though I see no
point in boring you with the details, especially given how
little time you have left."

Betsy trembled with fear. "What are you going to do to
us?"

"Nothing, Ms. Mostel. You have no incriminating evidence. I've seen to that. I was simply referring to your
flights. We have time for a quick bite, and then I'm afraid
Crawshaw will have to take you to the airport."

"Don't we get anything?" Glenn whined.

"Of course you do. Your uncle was very specific. He demanded that you both get your due, whether or not things
work out with the business. As soon as the estate goes
through probate, I'll be able to distribute those funds."

"That's great. Perfect. Don't you think, Glenn?"

"You bet, Cuz. All I really wanted was some green in the
first place."

"Let's toast to that. I believe you'll find this wine to your
liking, Ms. Mostel."

"It's a little early for me," Betsy said.

"Yes, but please don't say no. I shall remember this special moment when I calculate the precise sum of your inheritance."

"I'll drink to that," Betsy said.

"To all that green," said Glenn.

Roth popped the cork on the sparkling wine and poured.
After Glenn and Betsy had drained the glasses, he pushed
his aside.

Betsy felt the effects right away. The walls began to waver
and her throat tightened. "Gee, I feel strange. I must be
allergic."

"Me too." Glenn was sinking in his chair, oozing lower.

"Most people do have a nasty reaction to lethal poison,"
Roth observed mildly. "Fighting it will only make this more

difficult, so I suggest that you both relax while I tell you a nice bedtime story."

Roth folded his lithe fingers and spoke in a lilting tone. "Once upon a time there was a bad, bad man named Lawrence Mostel, who always talked about undying loyalty but turned out to have none at all. When this bad man found out that he was dying, he decided to leave everything to a niece or nephew that he'd never even met.

"Fortunately, he had his trusted attorney draft the will, and this attorney was a clever, clever man. He wrote in a tiny little clause that bad old Lawrence never noticed, which stated that if neither the niece nor nephew proved suitable, everything would be distributed according to the lawyer's discretion. And so it shall. My discretion says that J. Mortimer Roth shall have it all. And, as they say in storyland, he lives happily ever after."

Glenn fell to the floor in a boneless heap.

Betsy felt herself letting go as well, riding a tumultuous tide of terror and regret. As she slipped off the chair, she wondered what Claris Breen would do in such a situation. Of course, Claris would make a proper, dignified exit. She would exude sheer perfection to the end.

And naturally, Betsy would do likewise. Actually, this was easier than she ever imagined. All she needed to do was relax, as Roth had suggested, surrender to the inevitable.

A tiny smile bloomed on her face as she imagined her funeral. Naturally, Ms. Breen would be there. Clearly, Betsy pictured Claris dressed in designer black, weeping softly. Betsy imagined Claris stroking Mr. Breen, the Portugese water dog, as he sat regally beside her, brimming with doggie empathy, fully aware of the monstrous depth of her loss.

Motherly Love

Warren Murphy

"Do *you hate your mother?*" The voice sounds faraway.

I don't hate my mother. Of course I don't hate my mother. What kind of person do you think I am?

But she is not easy to deal with.

Like, you remember Karl Malden, the actor? Yeah, "Don't leave home without it"? That's him, that's the one.

So get this. I am sitting at her kitchen table and she says, "Karl Malden's got a fake nose, you know."

"Excuse me?"

"Malden, that actor guy, the one—"

"I know who he is."

"He's got a fake nose."

"Where did you hear that?"

"I heard it on television."

"From who?"

"Television. Some guy. He said Malden's got a fake nose 'cause that's where he hides his card thing, you know, his card."

"His American Express card?"

"That's right, the card thing."

I sigh and I try not to lose my temper and I say, in very measured and reasonable terms, "You were watching a comedian. That was what is called a joke."

"Yeah? Don't kid yourself. A lot of people have fake noses."

A lot of people have fake noses? The only one I could think of is Tycho Brahe, and I don't think my mother is up to date on sixteenth-century Danish astronomers with silver noses.

So I explain gently: "Yeah? A lot of people have fake noses? Then real stupid people ought to get them made. That way, they could take it off when they stick their heads up their ass. It'll make for a better fit."

And my mother just smiles and says, "I made potato salad for you."

This is another thing she does. She makes potato salad out of those sliced canned potatoes that the supermarket periodically tries to get rid of by selling them six cans for a dollar. She uses one can of potatoes and four gallons of cheap generic mayonnaise, flavored with a pound and a half of salt. I have two spoonfuls of her potato salad and my blood pressure has jumped six hundred points and I can feel the cholesterol congealing inside my left carotid artery.

My mother is eighty-five years old. She is the single most unconscious human being I have ever met. I once told her that she was the dumbest creature ever to walk erect on earth. She didn't have anything to say to that because I think she thought erect was a dirty word.

Not that she's got anything against dirty words.

"What's new?" That is her regular greeting.

"Nothing." That is my regular response.

"Same old shit, huh?" That is what she says next. She has said that to me every day for the last five years that I have taken to visiting her house. Jesus, I'm tired.

"So you get mad at her, huh?" Who is asking all these questions?

Well, of course I get mad at her. Sometimes I want to strangle her. So why, you ask, do I keep visiting her? Because I live right next door. She is camped out in a small house that I own next to my house. My wife used to go over every day to visit just so she wouldn't be too lonely. Now my wife isn't around to do that anymore. So I go over every day to make sure she hasn't died.

Not that I really need to worry about that. I told you she's eighty-five? Did I tell you that she smokes four packs of cigarettes a day and washes them down with a half a dozen highballs? Seagrams's Seven, club soda, and slice of lemon, tall glass.

And the last time she was in the hospital was when she had me, back in the middle of the last century. She is as eternal as the Pyramids. She will always be here, always ready with a growl, a grimace, a snarl, and a ready: "What's new? . . . Same old shit, huh?"

She likes to be called Gran. I guess that she thinks this is like real down-home American, something right out of Norman Rockwell, if she knew who Norman Rockwell was, which of course she doesn't. So everybody calls her Gran, at least to her face.

Everybody who really knows her—myself included—call her, when she's not around to hear, "Fart Blossom." This is because my mother, among her other charms, is as deaf as a post. She cannot hear herself break wind, so she thinks she has invented a new form of silent flatulence and she walks around, tooting constantly like a cross between a carnival calliope and the Energizer Bunny, utterly convinced that no one knows because she is absolutely silent while doing it.

Not that she'd care much anyway. That's the way it is with old people, you know. They only think about themselves. Forget about a tree falling in the forest, not making a sound with no one around to hear. If some old nitwit is involved, if the tree doesn't fall right on top of their damned empty heads, they don't even believe there was ever a tree.

If they can't hear it, it's not making a sound. And just try telling some old slug sometime about an illness of yours.

"Hello, Gran, I've got stomach cancer and I'm going to die."

"I had a bad stomach myself for the last couple of days, but you know what I did, I took a couple of the Alka Seltzer and it's a little better now but I keep taking them, you know, 'cause you gotta keep taking them."

"Yeah, but I'm going to die."

"I says to myself, I says, I'll really feel bad if the Alka Seltzer don't work, but it did, so I'm feeling better."

"I'm so glad for you, Gran. I'm going now to go pick out a coffin for myself."

It would sound like that, you know?

Also, my mother knows that Preparation H cures cancer and that the common cold is trumped by Comtrex. "I gets a cold and I takes the Comtrex and it knocks it right out."

"Nothing cures a cold, Gran."

"Don't kid yourself. Try the Comtrex."

It's enough to make you crazy.

"Are you saying she made you crazy, like in a legal sense?"

Well, of course she made me crazy. She makes everybody crazy. You know, I teach at a college, which doesn't mean much maybe in this day and age where all kinds of truth are considered relative, but my subject is math, which deals in eternal verities, right and wrong and no maybes, and so I can honestly say I think I have my wits about me and I'm at least no dumber than the next person, and if the next person happens to be my mother, well, hell, I'm a lot smarter than that. And yeah, real dumbness makes me crazy, I guess. Legal or illegal sense.

My wife, Glenda, she spent a lot of time watching Gran in action, and she said to me once, "You're like a rare tropical bird that was raised by a flock of chickens."

Did I tell you what my mother dresses like? She wears sweatsuits, disgusting old sweatsuits that have been washed so many times, they all have the color of chicken bones that have been dug up in the yard. Not quite white, not quite tan, not quite clean looking, not quite dirty. They're sort of dust-colored.

That is, unless of course, she's going out, if we take her to dinner or something or to cash "the Social Security," or to buy groceries (you don't want to know what kind of groceries she buys). Anyway, when she goes out, she dresses up. Usually in a pink sweatsuit. Or, it used to be pink.

Oh, yeah, talking about my wife. My poor wife. It was her idea to bring my mother out here. We had this little second house next to us and the people in it moved away and my softhearted wife, said, "Your mother's seventy-five. She shouldn't be alone; bring her out here."

"You don't want to do this," I said. "The woman is awful."

"She's seventy-five. How awful can she be?" my wife asked.

Well, we brought her out to live next door and my wife found out just how awful she could be.

For five years, my wife went over to have coffee with my mother. Every single day. And every single day she would come back home, quivering with annoyance, irritated beyond measure.

She told me once, "Gran is giving me heart palpitations."

"Why?"

"She sits there with the television blasting and the house filled with cigarette smoke and she stares at that stupid television and I try every day to have a conversation with her and she is so dense that there is nothing she can talk about. I even try to talk to her about the old days, when she was young and growing up and what it was like then, but you know what?"

"What?"

"She didn't notice the old days. She never notices anything. Life just passes by and she sees nothing, notices nothing, understands nothing. She sits there every morning watching the Phyllis Reejbin show and I might just as well be talking to the wall."

"What the hell is the Phyllis Reejbin show?"

"That's Regis Philbin. She's been watching it for five years and still doesn't know his name."

My wife was drumming her fingers on the table top. "Phyllis Reejbin," she said. Over and over. "Phyllis Reejbin. Are you sure insanity doesn't run in your family?"

"It moves along at a fairly good trot," I said.

"She's getting worse. She thinks infomercials are news shows. Do you know that in the last month, she has bought two separate electric paint sprayers and four sets of wrenches? She forgets she buys them and orders more."

"Maybe they're gifts. Maybe she's getting her Christmas shopping done early."

"No. That would be sane. She buys things because they're shiny. She can't resist junk. And when I ask her why, she always says the same thing: 'Hey, only nineteen-ninety-five. How can you go wrong?' Of course that doesn't include tax and the shipping charges, which are like ten dollars each. She spends a hundred dollars a week buying junk. She spends another hundred on lottery tickets. I asked her, don't you ever try to save any money? And she says, 'For what? I got the Social Security.'

"Suppose you get sick, I say, and she says, 'They'll take care of it.' But if you ask her who are these 'they' who are going to take care of it, she doesn't know. Just not her. Somebody else."

"Take some Maalox," I said.

"Prozac. I need Prozac. Lots of it. The woman is a retard."

I had to go to my morning lecture and I left my wife sitting at the kitchen table, drumming her fingers, grumbling into her cup of green tea.

My wife was an artist, you know, so her emotions were always kind of close to the surface. And she was one of those over-dramatic people. You know, every word that's not in 100 percent lockstep agreement is considered a terrible violent argument and every upset stomach is a near-death experience. You know the kind. Sweet but an exposed nerve nevertheless. And my mother plucked on that exposed nerve all the time.

One day, I remember I came home and just as I pull into the driveway between the two houses, I could tell it had been another bad day.

Have you ever heard of the Pink Flamingo Protective Association? No? Well, that's this mysterious group of people who wander around neighborhoods where I live and steal pink flamingos off people's lawns because, they say, they're too ugly to leave out in the yards. "Protective" means to protect us from the ugliness of pink flamingos, got it?

To Gran, the pink flamingos clearly would have been the height of elegance, an adventure in taste clearly beyond her reach and her grasp, because when I came home I see she has implanted on the little piece of land in front of her property two plywood cutouts. The cutouts are painted; they are supposed to be the back view of a man and woman, both wearing jeans, bent over as if they're gardening. So all you could see was their asses, which were tremendous, and of course their jeans had slipped down because they're bent over and so you could see their buttcrack.

This, I knew, to my mother must be a real grand slam. Not only was it wildly decorative for an otherwise dull piece of property but it was knee-slapping funny. After all, two fat people with their asses hanging out. Can it get any better than that?

I went inside my house and found my wife sitting on the kitchen floor with her back against the cabinets, her legs spread out before her. She had a butcher knife in her hand and she was pounding it point first into the floor—thump, thump, thump, thump . . .

Without looking up, she asked, "You saw it?"

"Yes."

Her voice was small and pained. "Why?" she said.

"Because she has no taste," I tried. "She really does think those things are funny."

"She can't," my wife said. "She really can't think those things are funny."

"But she does."

She looked up and shook her head at me, vigorously from side to side. For a moment, I wished she weren't holding that butcher knife. "No, she doesn't," my wife insisted. "No one can think those things are funny. She is evil and she is trying to destroy us. She is trying to make people in the neighborhood think we are stupid and crass, like hillbillies. She thinks she's Mammy Yokum. You're Li'l Abner and I'm supposed to be Daisy Mae. We're doomed, you know. We're all doomed. That woman is nuts and will make us all nuts before she's finished."

I took the knife away from her—actually, I think she didn't even remember that she had it—and I sat on the floor next to her and put my arm around her.

"Don't take it so hard," I said. "I'll remove them and it's nothing personal. It's not that she hates you. She just doesn't even know that she's a pain in the ass."

"You think not?"

"I absolutely know it. She's got no standard of comparison. Everybody in her family had two heads and seven fingers on each hand. How's she supposed to know how normal people think?"

My wife looked at me. "She really doesn't know she's a pain in the ass."

"No," I said.

"I wish I could believe that." My wife sat there for a moment, my arm across her shoulder, and then she winced and buckled forward. "Oh, the stomach," she said.

"I think you're getting an ulcer," I said.

"Doctor can't find one," she said. "Says to just take it

easy. Stop worrying and take some stuff for my stomach."

My wife laughed and did an eerily perfect impersonation of my mother's voice. "I takes the Pepto-Bismol. It knocks the stomachache right out. You know whatcha need to do is take the Pepto-Bismol."

Another day, I came home and parked out in the street in front of my house. As I walked toward the house, I saw something glinting in an upstairs window. When I went up there, I found my wife, hiding in a corner of the window behind a pair of curtains, holding binoculars, staring into my mother's house.

"She's been there all day, just watching television," she hissed to me, softly, as if she was afraid of being overheard from a hundred feet away by a woman as deaf as a foam pillow.

"What did you expect her to be doing?" I whispered back. "Hosting a Mensa meeting?"

"I don't know what she does," my wife said, glancing quickly again toward the other house. "But she sneaks around. I know she's always sneaking around when you're gone. Every time I turn around, I expect to see her behind me."

"But you never do, right?"

"Not yet. She's clever, that one."

"Come on," I said, affecting the voice of sweet reason that usually worked. "Listen to yourself. You called her clever. She's as clever as a rhinoceros. And she couldn't be sneaking around. She's too noisy to sneak, passing gas and then whistling, always with that damned whistling."

I didn't tell you that, I guess. My mother whistles. Over and over again. "Lady of Spain."

"She doesn't whistle when she sneaks around. That's how sneaky she is."

There was no point in arguing about something like that, was there? So I just let it go.

But my wife couldn't let it go. Wouldn't let it go. She

seemed to be getting this idea that my mother was responsible for everything that ever went wrong in anything. In her mind, my mother had changed from being a pest into being a saboteur. If we got a leak in a water pipe, somehow it was my mother's fault. There was a kind of crazy paranoia about the whole thing. Now, listen. I think I made it clear, my mother's not easy to put up with but she wasn't like this crazy demon from hell. She's just a dumb old lady, not some kind of wild scheming plotter.

"*I guess your wife was getting on your nerves then, too.*"

You bet. Take the mail. We had side-by-side mailboxes out on the street. My wife used to go get the mail from our box and from my mother's and then drop her mail off on her way back to our house. How simple is that? You know, just normal courtesy, saving the old lady a trip to the mailbox. Then one day my wife goes to the mailbox and what does she see? She sees my mother there. Not at my mother's mailbox but at ours.

"What are you doing?" Glenda asks.

"I was getting your mail. I was gonna bring it up to your house."

"I always get our mail," my wife said. She told me about all this later.

"I just thought I'd save you a trip," my mother said.

"I don't want you to save me a trip. Give me that mail."

So my wife grabs the mail and stomps back to our house.

All right, that sounds like a garden variety misunderstanding, right? No harm, no foul.

Except now Glenda has a new worry . . . that my mother is sneaking down to the mailbox when she's not looking and taking out some of our mail.

"I haven't gotten a catalog from my art supply house in months," she told me.

"Do you ever buy anything from them?"

"Not lately."

"They probably took you off their mailing list."

"Nobody ever takes anybody off a mailing list. Not ever. Not for death or plague or flood or natural disaster. Oh, they're sending me my catalogs, all right. They're just be-ing"—She leaned close again although there wasn't anyone within shouting distance—". . . intercepted. By her."

You've got to understand how weird this all is. Here's my mother, eighty years old then, and my pretty, intelligent wife is convinced that this old toot is scheming and plotting her destruction. Yeah, so sometimes, I started to think my wife was losing it, too.

I began to wonder if maybe my wife was having early menopause or something. Or maybe she was having troubles I just didn't know about. Whatever. I just hoped it would go away, this crazed suspicion of my mother for all kinds of things. Christ, next my wife would be blaming her for global warming. You know, she's walking around sneaking out all these farts, maybe the methane gas is blowing away the ozone layer. God, who knew what these two were able to blame on each other.

This wasn't just one-sided either, you know. My mother couldn't stand my wife but she didn't dare criticize her around me. What she did instead was she started referring to my wife as *she*. As in, "You know what she did?" or "You know what she said." And that annoyed the hell out of me and I had to keep reminding her, "My wife has a name, don't call her *she*."

But my heart wasn't in it because my wife was referring to my mother all the time as *she*. Not Gran, not Fart Blossom, not even "your mother." But as *she*.

"She was at the mailbox again today."

"She was sneaking around the house again today."

"She was talking on the phone. I heard her." That last one really got me. I asked my wife, "Why shouldn't she talk on the phone? It's her phone."

"Who would she be talking to?" my wife demanded. "Who'd want to talk to her? It's not like she can carry on a conversation. What's she going to talk about? Phyllis Reej-bin? The years of winning lottery numbers she's got taped on her refrigerator? She has, you know. The last five years of winning lottery numbers. She keeps them in a notebook and uses a magnet to hold it on the refrigerator."

"What for?" I asked.

"That's exactly the point. There is no what-for. She just writes them down. Every time I go in there for coffee in the morning, she is writing down last night's winning lottery numbers. I asked her why. She says so they don't make mistakes. I said, for Christ's sakes. You watch them call out the numbers live on television. They don't make mistakes. And she said, 'Don't kid yourself.' The woman is trying to drive me crazy. It's part of her plan, you know. Drive me crazy and then she's got you to herself."

What could I do except sigh? I was beginning to think they were both nuts and I was doomed to spend my life in some kind of snake pit, with nut-women to the left of me, nut-women to the right of me, everywhere I turned . . . here a nut, there a nut, everywhere a nut-nut, old MacDonald had a farm, E-I-E-I-O.

"Sounds like enough to push anybody over the edge."

Finally, my wife struck. We were sitting at the dining table early one Sunday afternoon, drinking coffee, talking about getting our records together to do our income taxes, when she said, out of the blue, "She's got to go to Happy-dale."

"Huh?"

"Happydale. We've got to send her."

Happydale was always a family joke. You know, from *Arsenic and Old Lace*, it's the name of the haha-house where Cary Grant is going to send his homicidal aunts. We used it as a joking kind of synonym for the old folks' home.

"Oh, come on, it's not that bad."

"It is," Glenda said. "She's getting crazier and crazier. I think maybe it's Alzheimer's. She used to not talk to me.

Now she does. Every day, she tells me the same story she told me the day before."

"She's old; her memory's slipping."

"It's not that. She's trying to make me insane with these stories. How many times do I have to hear how she saved money by buying Christmas present ties at Tie City because it's cheaper at Tie City than in a regular men's shop where 'you're just paying for the name, you know. Don't kid yourself. Tie City has the same ties but they're a lot cheaper.' "

"It was one of the great triumphs of her life, buying a tie for three dollars that some other store wanted to charge her six dollars for."

"I know, I know, but must I hear about it every day? And how many times must I be told that 'Whatcha gotta do is make a pot of coffee and then turn it off and then if you want a cup of coffee, you just heat in the microwave.' I don't want coffee out of the microwave; I want it steaming hot out of the pot. So I tell her that and the next day she says to me, 'Whatcha gotta do is make a pot of coffee and then turn it off and then if you want a cup, you just heat it in the microwave.' She is driving me mad and I want you to send her to Happydale. Before you have to send *me* to Happydale."

What do you say to things like that? I don't know. I just got up and walked over to the window to look out the open window into the yard and I see my mother kind of hurrying up the steps of her house. So I sort of wonder where she had been but I didn't say anything because Glenda would no doubt have some kind of weird explanation about the whole thing. I didn't think I could take it.

So I didn't say anything. Meanwhile, Glenda was talking, talking, talking.

"That house of hers, do you ever smell it?"

"What do you mean?"

"It smells like a freaking ashtray. She sits in there smoking four packs of cigarettes a day. The walls are brown.

Everything reeks of cigarette smoke. What the hell must her lungs look like? They must have an inch of crud coating them. How is she still alive? People get lung cancer from secondhand smoke and this woman's been chain-smoking for sixty years and she doesn't even have morning cough. She's immortal, you know. She's never going to die. I'm going to die and you're going to die and she's going to come and visit our graves and empty her ashtrays on them. Some people leave flowers at the graveside. She's going to leave cigarette butts. And then she's going to dance. She'll do a little mazurka, wearing her best ratty pink sweatsuit, and she's going to stomp all over our earthly remains. And then go find somebody else to make crazy."

So that was how it all started. You know, I never believed before that people's attitudes would make them sick. I thought that was just some new-age bullshit, you know, think happy thoughts and happiness will follow, blah, blah, blah. But from that day on, my wife really started to fade. I told you she had a bad stomach, you know, nervous, ulcerous, that kind of thing. A lot of artists I guess are like that. But once my mother got into her craw, my wife went downhill.

Every day I'd come home from the school and my wife'd be in bed, not feeling well, stomach pains, feeling sick. She went to the doctor, who basically said, more Pepto-Bismol, and sent her home. I told her she had to stop obsessing about my mother. In fact, we had a big argument about it. We never argued in our marriage and now suddenly we had this screaming match so loud that the neighbor on the other side of our house called to make sure everything was all right. Boy, talk about being embarrassed.

Then the next day, I came home from the college and my mother is in my kitchen, putzing around the stove, cooking some kind of slop.

"What's going on? Where's Glenda?"

"I was just making you some dinner."

"Where's Glenda?"

She finally turned around from the stove. "She got sick," my mother said, "and they took her to the hospital."

"When? Who? Did you hear from them? What happened?"

"She got sick and the doctor wanted like tests or something. I didn't call you because I didn't want to worry you."

I was astonished, and plopped in a chair. "Didn't want to worry me?"

"No, so I came over to cook you dinner 'cause I know you like to eat early."

"Screw dinner," I said.

"Well, you've got to eat."

I got it together enough and called the doctor, who said he just wanted some tests done in case Glenda had a perforated ulcer, and she'd be out in the morning. When I went over to the hospital to visit her, Gran insisted on coming along.

I shouldn't have taken her. I knew it was just going to make Glenda feel worse, but I was tired of fighting and my mother said she would bring her some chicken soup because chicken soup is good for everything. God, her chicken soup is like this mess of yellow congealed grease and noodles that have somehow amalgamated into one big slab of noodle.

But I couldn't figure out a way to tell her no, and so we went over and visited and Glenda felt lousy and hated seeing my mother there, but she ate the goddam chicken soup that my mother had in one of those bigmouthed thermoses and then we came home.

And the next day Glenda was dead. It must have happened during the night and she was found dead in her hospital bed in the morning. The doctor gave me some mumbo jumbo about her ulcer exploding or some goddam thing, but it didn't change the fact that she was dead. And so I buried her.

"Did you give her anything to eat or drink?" I bet he's a cop. He sounds like a cop.

What are you talking about?

"When your wife was in the hospital?"

No. Why the hell would I do that? She's in the hospital with a freaking ulcer, I figure the hospital knows what she ought to eat. Except for that stupid chicken glop my mother makes. Oh, God, I loved that woman, and I was just so sorry that her last couple of years were lousy, that she was so consumed by her craziness about my mother. I wished her last years could have been the happy kind we had early in our marriage but I wish, I wish, I wish doesn't change anything, does it?

So then it was just me and my mother. I never realized how much Glenda had taken on herself in dealing with her every day. Because she always went over there for coffee and dealt with her every day, I hadn't had to. But now I did. I couldn't just ignore her, so I started visiting every day and chatting her up and Christ, she made me as nuts as she made my wife.

She started making noises like she was going to come over and share my house, but I put the squash on that right away. I like to read. I like solitude. What I didn't want was a TV blasting all the time with Phyllis Reejbin and game shows from 1915 and the house cloudy with cigarette smoke.

Still she was around more than I'd like. She came over most days either to cook dinner or to bring me a package of something supposed to resemble food. She is the most god-awful cook I have ever seen. Her idea of cooking is to put stuff in a pot, boil it for days until it is a uniformly mush-colored glob of gelatinous puke, and then give it a name. It was pepper steak or goulash or one-pot meal, and they all looked and tasted the same, namely like shit. Can I rest now?

"A couple more minutes. You didn't have any new romances in your life?"

What's that? No, I didn't have any girlfriends, and tell the truth, I wasn't interested. Not anymore. I had Glenda. She was all I wanted and then she went and died on me and I just didn't have any interest in finding someone new and getting left behind all over again.

Hell, I could see the personal ad anyway.

> LONER COLLEGE PROF seeks love chickie. No money, no prospects, no ambition, clinically depressed. Lives with mother, crazed Mammy Yokum look-alike.

And so one rotten day became another rotten day and one crappy year became another crappy year. And I was getting old and Fart Blossom was getting to be more and more of a dependent pest, needing more and more attention. She was afraid to ride a bus to go shopping. Too timid to call a cab. Too afraid to get on a plane and go visit a relative somewhere. All she had was her son living next door and apparently that was all she wanted.

I finally got to understand how it was that grown-ups could beat on their aged parents, because she made me absolutely insane. She learned nothing; she understood nothing. Day after day, night after night, the same stupid stories, the same lack of anything resembling human thought, total absolute world-class ignorance. I took to yelling at her. I told her not to smoke in my house. I told her I didn't want her passing gas anymore in my kitchen. I told her her cooking sucked and shouldn't be fed to pigs. I didn't want to hurt her feelings, but the truth is, I was just tired of her.

Very, very tired.

And the fact is, nothing I said many any difference. She smoked and farted and cooked up her usual rations of gruel as if she hadn't heard one word I said. And probably she hadn't. As I said, old people just listen to themselves and an unanticipated belch is far more important in their lives than an announcement from the White House that World War III has just started and we'll all be incinerated in ten more minutes.

I started seeing, too, the things Glenda used to see. My mother was getting older, more feeble, even more forgetful. She had had no contact with the world besides us and now, if possible, she was having even less.

And a couple of years had gone by. I was starting to feel staled up. The thought came to me that I might take early retirement from the college. I had enough time in to draw a good pension. I had money in my retirement account. Maybe, for the first time in my life, I'd go travel. If I didn't see the world, I might at least go see America. Who knows? Maybe I could still find some kind of a piece of a life out there.

But what about Fart Blossom?

She couldn't stay by herself. She couldn't live by herself. She routinely forgot now about bills that were due to be paid. On the telephone, she was prey for any solicitor with the price of a phone call. Sometimes she even gave these fly-by-night outfits her checking account and savings account numbers and they would draw on her account for junk that she ordered and maybe for anything else they wanted to charge to her. In a world of sharks, she was chum.

It became obvious that now it really *was* time for Happydale.

So a couple of nights ago, when I came home from school, I went over to her house for a cup of coffee.

"What's new?" she asked me. I grunted and she said, as always, "Same old shit, huh?"

I didn't waste any time. I told her that it was time for her to go to the old folks' home. I painted the picture as pretty as I could. There would be people around, people her own age. She wouldn't be lonely anymore. There were games and shopping expeditions and they had a medical staff on duty all the time. She would have friends again and a life.

She could take the bus rides to the Indian casino and gamble away her whole Social Security check if she wanted.

All the while I was telling her this, she stood with her back to me, doing dishes.

When she turned around, she was doing her deaf act, pretending she had not heard one word I said. So I sat her down with a cup of coffee and went through the whole routine again.

She started shaking her head after my first sentence and kept doing it all the while I was talking.

When I finally stopped, she said, "No."

"Why no?"

"Because I want to be with you," she said.

"That's not possible. I'm going to retire and I'm going to travel."

"I'll go with you," she said.

"No, you won't," I said. "I'm going to become a mountain climber and a deep sea diver. So you can't come with me and you can't stay here alone."

"Then I'll take the gas pipe."

"No, you won't. You'll go to the new senior apartments."

"Never. I said before I would never go and I never will."

I didn't know what the hell she was talking about. When did she say before she would never go? I'd never brought it up before. But I just didn't have the stomach to argue about it.

I admit I probably could've handled the whole thing better. Maybe brought it up slowly over a perod of time, but I was just tired of fooling around. Sometimes, some things, it's just better to get them over with. I went home and figured I'd let her stew on it for a while. Maybe, just maybe, for once, she would see the sense of what I was saying and just do it and stop arguing.

So last Saturday, I drove her to the grocery store. We didn't talk about it and then I went home to wait for her to call me to pick her up with her usual six-year supply of sliced potatoes.

When I walked by her house, though, I thought I heard a sound in the cellar, so I went downstairs in case there was something wrong with the plumbing or furnace, but I didn't see anything. And then, I don't know, I just started pooching around and in a small cabinet over the utility sink, I saw a can with a skull and crossbones on it. The label read ARSENIC.

Now what in the hell was that doing there? I had never seen it before. What did my mother need arsenic for? Maybe it had been there forever and I had just missed it. Ah, who cares? She never threw anything away; why shouldn't she have arsenic?

Sunday, I went over there to talk to her again. I sat in the living room watching a baseball game on television. That's another thing. All summer long she watches baseball games on television. She's been doing that for thirty years and still doesn't know one damned thing about the game. She doesn't how many outs there are in an inning. She doesn't know a double play from a home run. I try to talk to her sometimes about the game and she doesn't know what I'm talking about. She doesn't know the name of one player. She doesn't even know what teams she's watching.

So I'm sitting there, but before I could say one word about Happydale, she said, "I'm not going."

And, again, even though I told myself I wouldn't lose my temper and I would be the voice of sweet reason, I snapped back.

"Yes, you are. The only question is how soon."

So she turns and walks out of the living room, trailing cigarette smoke in her wake. Man, it would take Bette Davis to tell you what a dump this place was.

I sat there for a while, figuring she'd calm down and eventually we could talk. Or at least try to. And a few minutes later, she came back in with two cups of coffee for us and put them on the table, one in front of me. One on the other end where she was going to sit. Then she went back out in the kitchen for milk.

"You both had coffee?"

Yeah. I noticed that she gave me a cup with a dark green inside. All these years, I've told her I don't like coffee in cups that don't have white insides. How can you tell if coffee is strong or weak if the inside of the cup is colored? But she never listens to anything anyone says. I remember I switched the cups.

And then she came in and put milk in her coffee and drank it and while she was drinking it, she said, "I'm not going there. Ever. You can't make me. All I ever wanted was for us to be together. That's what I told her a long time ago."

"Everything was a long time ago, Gran. Times change. Time for you to change, too."

"Never." And then she finished her coffee and later she got sick and I called the ambulance.

And then I woke up here.

"Is this a hospital?"

"You've been out for a day. The doctors say you had a stroke."

"Oh, Jesus. What about my mother?"

"She's okay now. They pumped her stomach out. She'd been poisoned. With arsenic."

"How? How'd that happen?"

"You don't know?"

"Of course I don't know."

"I have to tell you that we're applying for a court order to exhume your wife's remains. We want to look at the cause of death again."

"That's ghoulish. You've got no right to do that."

"We'll see what the judge says. Remember, your wife died right after you visited her in the hospital. The neighbors had heard you fighting. Don't worry, we'll sort it all out."

"I don't want to talk to you anymore."

"We've talked enough. For now, at any rate. But I'll be back."

So here I am, stroked out, lying in a hospital bed and I

can't think straight. So this cop thinks I killed my wife? And my mother gets poisoned? What the hell is going on? I have to rest. My brain's not working anymore.

Pieces of dreams. Bits of memory. How I won't drink coffee from a cup that's dark green inside. How quick my wife died. How my mother says, "I said I'll never go and I never will." Then a noise. My eyes are open.

● ● ●

"HELLO, *son. Are you awake?*"

"Gran, what are you doing here?"

"*Where else would I be? My son gets sick, I'm going to be there. I'm always going to be with my son. Now, don't worry. I'm all right. They said I'll be fine.*"

"Why? Why did you. . . . ?"

"*Shhhh. No time for questions now. We should just enjoy being with each other.*"

"Fat chance."

She smiled at me. The hospital people must have taken away her dentures because all I saw was a mouthful of gums, twisted in some parody of a smile. She stood next to the bed.

"*I brought you coffee. Just like you like it, in a white cup. Whatcha gotta do is drink it all down. Just drink it all down.*"

CAT IN LOVE

Justin Scott

WHEN the cat got done killing the possum, he sat down to count its teeth.

This took all his concentration, so he relied upon the outer edges of his brain to keep track of threats and annoyances while he labored. The prime threats of the moment were the Jack Russell terrier racing angry circles in the front yard of the new house that city people had built across the road, and the truculent mink stirring inside the sugar maple at the edge of cornfield.

The Jack Russell was a dangerous dog even by terrier standards. It had already killed a kitten. Now it was contained inside an invisible fence that was supposed to zap it with an electric shock if it tried to get out. So far it hadn't figured a way to escape, but the cat had noticed it was working at it.

The mink in the maple cavity was an odd one, living closer to the barnyard than most would dare. The cat made a practice of staying out of its way. All minks were fierce fighters, cousins to weasels, only bigger, stronger, and meaner. But this one actually went looking for trouble.

Current annoyances were represented by the human father carrying a pitchfork and the squirrel that was yelling down at him from the barn roof. Believing that no surprises lurked on his perimeter, the cat kept counting.

But at forty-nine teeth, a stealthy flicker in the corner of his eye set him back on his haunches. Around the barn, where a heartbeat earlier there had been nothing but empty air and silence, stole a long white cat he had never seen before. She was a beautiful sight, sleek as snake skin, snowy as a cloud, graceful as a deer—as pleasing to the eye as his own reflection in the pond.

She was also as big as he was, which made her one enormous cat. And a dangerous one at that, if she had speed to go with her shapely muscles. He stood transfixed. It was a pleasure just to watch her walk.

Ten feet above her, the squirrel found an acorn in the gutter and shut up long enough to open it and sprinkle her back with hull chewings. The cat—whose own lightning reflexes were the subject of awed whispers in every burrow in the county—barely saw the blur of what happened next. In a single bound, she clawed up the side of the barn and came down with the squirrel dead in her jaws.

The cat stared in frank and open admiration.

She fixed him with fierce green eyes. "My squirrel."

"It's okay. I've got my possum."

"You're going to eat a possum?" she asked, but did not wait for an answer as she dragged her squirrel behind the barn.

The cat went back to counting possum teeth. Which he did whenever he killed a possum, because he had an unreliable memory. What brain power he had served his keen eyes and ears, his strong, agile body, his pleasure senses and his instincts, and there was precious little left over to ruminate upon the past. Most days dawned new to him, blue skies mysterious, food an unprecedented delight.

Matters that pertained to survival, however, he remembered always. He remembered the vicious Jack Russell across the road. He remembered the mink in the maple. He remembered speeding cars and trucks, giant owls, hungry coyotes, and the human father with a pitchfork.

The possum was a wonderment. He had never encountered so many teeth on a single foe. Fifty teeth. More teeth than anyone. He wondered if all possums had so many teeth and he vowed to compare next time he killed one.

Around the corner of the barn came a long white cat. She was a beautiful sight, sleek as snake skin, snowy as a cloud, graceful as a deer—as pleasing to the eye as his own reflection in the pond.

Big cat, he thought. Big as he was. Tough customer if she had the speed to go with that build. Great walk.

"I left a haunch and the tail," she said firmly. "I expect to see both there when I get back."

Oh, now he remembered: the beautiful white cat that snatched the squirrel off the barn roof like she had wings.

"I'm still working on my possum."

She breezed past.

"Where you going?"

"Meet the humans."

"My humans."

"We'll see."

"Hey, where did you come from?"

A long look up at the darkly wooded hill that loomed across the cornfield was all she revealed of her past. But she did say, "I just hope to settle down, somewhere, one day." She gave him a sidelong glance and sauntered to the house. The cat felt confused. The arrival of a strange cat on his territory was usually followed by its immediate departure minus an ear or an eye. But he was still transfixed by her beauty. Although this "We'll see" stuff would grow old fast.

"What's your name?" he called after her.

"Same as yours," she answered, rocking him back on his haunches again.

She was one of the tribe.

He should have known. There were cats, a very few cats, whose names were known only to themselves and possibly, though rarely, one special friend. In the cat's case, the human mother—whose scent made his knees go weak with pleasure—knew his name. The rest just guessed.

"Careful of that Jack Russell across the road," he called after her.

"Look out for the mink," she called back.

The cat looked over his shoulder and felt his liver freeze. Addled by the beautiful newcomer, instinct dulled, memory scrambled, he hadn't heard the mink creeping up behind him. The killer exploded into full motion, pouring over the ground, halving the space between them in a dash that brought it close enough to smell its breath, a not soon to be forgotten potpourri of fish and rodent flesh rotting on its fangs.

The cat jumped twelve feet and hit the ground running. Where to was the problem. He could climb a tree, but so could the mink. He could dive into a hole in the wall, but so could the mink. He could jump onto the front wheel of the pickup truck. So could the mink, but it probably wouldn't.

Squeezed between the rubber tire and the steel fender, he looked out. The mink was dragging his possum back to the maple tree.

The cat went to sleep.

The pickup truck engine started like thunder sometime later. He jumped up, banged his head on the fender, and scrambled off as the wheel started rolling. The human father, predictable as the seasons, yelled, "Damn fool cat," and roared away. Hungry, the cat walked to the house, a place he enjoyed most when the human father wasn't there.

"There you are!" called the human mother when he emerged from his cat door into the kitchen. "Look what I found."

The white cat was sitting on the human mother's lap.

"Say hello to our new friend." said the human mother. "Her name is Vanilla."

The cat said nothing. If anything, Vanilla was even more beautiful indoors. But she was in *his* indoors.

"Go on. Say hello."

The cat went out his cat door and sat down on the porch to think. Inside, he could hear the human mother cooing. "Don't you worry about that grumpy cat. He's just in a bad mood. You are so beautiful. You are the most beautiful cat there ever was. Beautiful. Vanilla, you are beautiful."

It was impossible to think.

He walked down the driveway. The Jack Russell terrier, which was occupying a disconcerting amount of his mind lately, started barking and galloping the perimeter of its invisible fence. The cat watched it wearing a rut in the grass, a rut that marked the boundary of the buried cable that would set off the shocker it wore on a snug collar around its miserable throat. In fact, the cat observed, it wouldn't shock the dog straight off. First it beeped a warning, a beep that got louder as the dog got closer to the wire, a beep that said, One more step, you misery, and you'll get it in the neck. You had to get the dog really close to the wire to make the shocker work.

The cat checked for trucks and cars and sauntered across the road.

"Hey, Jack," he called. "How you doing?"

The Jack Russell's barks grew shrill. It galloped faster. The cat could hear the beeper getting louder.

"Want to come out and play?"

The Jack Russell begin whirling circles, like it was going to drill a hole in the ground.

"Come on," said the cat. "You can't be that busy. Let's go get a bite."

"I'll kill you, I'll kill you, I'll kill you," screamed the Jack Russell.

The cat lay in the dust, ten feet from the raging dog. "Well, Jack, you'll have to come over here to try that. Now, if you'll excuse me a moment, I'd like to get some dust on my fleas."

"One of these days," the Jack Russell raged, "the batteries will die in this thing and I will get out of here and find you."

The cat stretched out full length and rolled on his back, staring at the sky, while watching very carefully from the corner of his eye. The dog lunged.

"*Yaaaaaaaaaaaa!*"

Jack ran howling back to his house on three legs, scratching madly at his neck with the fourth. The cat walked home, feeling a lot better.

But as he neared the porch he could hear the human mother still cooing in the kitchen, "Vanilla, Vanilla, Vanilla, it is not possible that there could be a more beautiful animal on the planet than you."

The cat fell asleep on the bottom step.

A while later he heard the pickup truck. Then the human father stomping up the stairs, muttering "Damn fool cat," and banging through the screen door. "What the heck— Wow, what a cat! Hey, beautiful what's your name?"

"Her name's Vanilla."

"Boy, you're pretty. Welcome, Vanilla. Stay as long as you like. Just don't bother old Roger—poor old poodle's got no teeth left. And look out for that damned fool cat on the porch. I warn all my friends, don't try patting him less you've got on a welding glove." The human father bellowed laughter at this inanity. A pop and a hiss announced a beer had been opened; thunder, that he was stomping downstairs to the cellar workshop.

The cat went back in for another look. Vanilla was hunkered comfortably on the kitchen floor—her tail stretched flat behind her—eating daintily from his soft-food dish. She was so beautiful. The human mother refilled the dish with his absolute favorite Grand Union mackerel—from the last can of the stockpile she had bought for him when the grocery store went out of business.

The cat ventured closer and crunched a nugget from his dry-food dish.

Vanilla gave a low growl and the cat gave her one back.

"Be nice," warned the human mother. "Both of you."

Vanilla stopped growling instantly and said to the cat, "I'm so happy to be here. I hope you don't mind."

The cat went back out and sat on the steps to try again to think.

A strange sound woke him. A loud, grating *eee-YOOOWWrrr* noise that made his unusually sensitive ears hurt. When he opened his eyes and saw the source, he recoiled. Standing, swaying, on the path below the steps was a misshapen, bent-backed, rack-ribbed, scraggily-haired, toothless, rheumy-eyed, seven-toed cat.

"eeeYOOOWWrrr," it said again.

It looked to be at least twenty human years old, which made it a hundred and forty, though on close inspection, the cat pegged it as considerably older. Its thin gray-and-white coat was splotched in a pattern vaguely reminiscent of a skunk.

"eeeYOOOWWrrr," it said, an ear-splitting racket as annoying as it was pathetic.

"What?" said the cat.

"I'm hungry."

"I've got my own problems."

"eeeYOOOWWrrr."

"I'm going to give you a choice," said the cat. Like most powerful hunters, he was not unkind. "If you make that noise again, I'm going to kill you. But if you go through that door"—He indicated his cat door—"you'll find my dry-food dish still has some food in it. Which do you choose?"

"eeeYOOOWWrrr!"

The cat stood up. He routinely slaughtered creatures

ranging from beetle size to slightly larger than himself. But even as he unsheathed a foreclaw, he knew that this misery had called his bluff. It was too pathetic. "What?" he said.

"I can't chew dry food."

It had a point. It had one yellow tooth left and that looked wobbly. "Okay. Just—let me think. *Don't make that noise*. Okay, here's what you do. Go inside, sit by the human mother. She'll take care of you."

"Thank you," said the old beast with immense dignity. It tottered across the porch. Then it stood swaying before his cat door, planning the six-inch jump like a leap from the barn roof to the pig house. Finally, it gathered its bones and lurched through the flap like a mudslide. The cat, who named things to keep track of them, dubbed her Skunk Cat, on account of her skunk markings, and sat down to think some more.

From inside the kitchen came a sharp "No."

The cat froze. No one said *No* like the human mother. She rarely spoke the word. But when she did, her *No* was cold as a blizzard, dark as the back of the deepest cave, sharp as a chainsaw. Her *No* thundered.

Vanilla flew through the cat door, skidded across the porch, hit the stairs running, and raced down the path and under the pickup truck.

The cat sauntered over and peeked under the truck where she cowered. "What did you do to my human?"

"I didn't do anything to your human. All I did was— Get out here!" she spat. "Leave me alone."

The cat trotted back to the house and poked his head through the door just as the human father pounded up the stairs yelling, "What happened?"

"Look at this poor cat."

"Auuughgh. That is horrible. Get that out of here."

"Stop frightening her, she's trying to eat."

In fact, the cat saw, Skunk Cat was so busy licking her dinner that she didn't notice the human father, who now bellowed, "Hey, don't feed it. It'll stick around."

The human mother glanced at him. That glance, the cat knew, was as rare as her *No* and just as sharp. The human father quieted abruptly. *"It'll stick around,"* ended in a meek, "won't it?"

"Look at the poor thing. She's so old. She has nowhere to go."

Skunk Cat finished obliviously gumming her meal, looked up from the dish, and let loose another ear-aching "eeeYOOOWWrrr."

"What's the matter, honey? More food? Here you go. . . . Poor old cat."

The human father watched her fork some salmon from the can. "What happened to the white one?"

"Vanilla tried to claw this poor thing. I told her *No*."

"Yeah, well . . ."

The cat could almost feel the human father's sympathy for Vanilla.

"What are you going to call this one?" he asked resignedly.

Skunk Cat, thought the cat. Its name is Skunk Cat.

The human mother looked at him sitting quietly by the door. He held her gaze until she said, "I think its name is Skunk Cat."

"Looks like one," the human father agreed and stomped back down to the cellar grumbling, "Another mouth on the payroll."

"Poor old Skunk Cat," said the human mother, crouching to pat its bony back. "Was that horrible Vanilla mean to you?"

"eeeYOOOWWrrr."

The cat went out, found Vanilla still under the pickup truck, and asked, "Why'd you claw that old bag of bones?"

"None of your damned business."

"Do you know that cat?"

"None of your damned business."

"I was just curious why a magnificent hunter like you

would bother some poor old bag of bones. Unless you know her and have something against her."

"She's ugly."

"I wouldn't argue with that. On the other hand, the human father is ugly, but I don't claw him for it."

"You're not big enough to claw him."

"But if I were, I still wouldn't claw him just because he's ugly."

"I'd claw him if I were big enough."

You probably would, the cat thought, not without admiration. But for some unfathomable reason he felt compelled to show her the error of her ways. Or at least help her understand that making an enemy of the human mother was foolish beyond description. Why not just walk down to the interstate and sit in the passing lane for a while?

"Well," he said to the stiff white ball under the truck. "The thing is, if you look closely at that old bag of bones you can see she wasn't always like this. Look at those huge paws. And how long she is. She's a long cat, like you. And you realize that in her day, that was one fine, big, strong cat. Big as you. And a jumper like you, I'll bet. An excellent cat. In her day."

It was like talking to a boulder. Vanilla just stared into the middle distance and exuded misery.

"Why are you so unhappy?" asked the cat.

Vanilla crawled out from under the pickup truck. "Get out of my way," she said, and when the cat didn't move fast enough she knocked him flat with a swift hard jab of her forepaw and stalked toward the barn.

The cat saw blood. He surged to his feet in a powerful liquid motion and started after Vanilla, ears flattening, claws spreading. One-eyed cats and one-eared cats and three-legged cats limping about the county were proof that no one ever messed with him. It was time to put Miss Magnificence in her place. But even as he caught up with her swishing tail, he realized that he wasn't bleeding. She had sheathed her razor sharp, barn-climbing claws when she hit him, which, considering her general demeanor could be interpreted as an act of friendship if not downright camaraderie.

"Hey, where you going?"

"I just need some time alone."

"Anything I can do for you?"

"No. I'll be all right." She looked back, her eyes suddenly warm as a sun-drenched lawn. "Will I see you later?"

"Count on it," said the cat. He climbed happily onto the front wheel of the pickup truck and went to sleep. When he awoke sometime later, he went into the house and crunched a couple of bites of dry food. Then, thinking it was time for a nap on his favorite couch, he walked into the living room—a cool, dark place shaded from the sun by the front porch. He found Skunk Cat sprawled on his couch, still as stone. While he was staring at her, his ancient housemate, Roger the huge black standard poodle, stumbled into the living room.

"Awwwgggh! What is that?"

"*Her* new friend," said the cat, loudly, because Roger was quite deaf.

There was only one *Her* in the house and old Roger said, "If that's what she wants."

"She felt sorry for it."

Roger blinked and peered myopically at Skunk Cat through his cataract-blued eyes. "Quiet sleeper, isn't she?"

"That's because she's dead," said the cat.

• • •

"Poor old cat. . . . Well, that's the way I'd like to go if I ever get old. Just climb up on the couch and go to sleep."

"You didn't happen to hear anything, did you?"

"Like what?"

"Like whoever snuck in here and killed her?"

"*Killed* her?"

"Is your nose gone, too, Roger? Can't you smell the blood?"

"My nose is as good as it ever was. Yeah, now that you mention it, I can smell blood. And I'd say I've had some experience smelling blood. Did I ever tell you I served as a canine cadet in the US Navy SEALs?"

As Roger would rather miss dinner than an opportunity to repeat his war stories, even a cat with the retention of a pumpkin could answer with reasonable certainty, "Somehow I recall I've heard that somewhere."

"Blood, eh? . . . Say, who would kill a harmless old lady cat?"

While they were sitting there staring at Skunk Cat's body, the human mother walked into the living room carrying a book. She turned on a reading lamp, which cast a pool of yellow light.

"What happened? Skunk Cat, are you all right?" She started to pick her up, but Skunk Cat's head lolled over and she saw the blood oozing from several needle-like tooth holes in the animal's neck. "Oh, my God." She looked at Roger and the cat. Roger sat down and whimpered. The cat waited.

The human mother cradled Skunk Cat gently in her arms and carried her out of the house. The cat followed. She put Skunk Cat down at the edge of the lawn and walked to the barn and came back with a shovel.

The cat watched her dig a hole.

Vanilla came from behind the barn, yawning. Then she stretched magnificently, sending a fine ripple of muscle from head to tail. The human mother saw her and shouted, "Get out of here, you miserable cat. Go away!" She flung a grass clod at her. Vanilla looked around, confused. The human mother pulled off one of her shoes and threw it at Vanilla. "Go away, murderer!"

Vanilla ran.

The cat ran after her.

She ran behind the barn and when the cat got there he saw her climbing the rough, red wall. He followed her up the wall and onto the roof and up the roof, over the peak, around the big air vent, and down the other side to the gutter. The barn was taller on this side and stood a full two stories above the sloping ground. Vanilla leaped into thin air.

The cat landed beside her on the pig house roof. She looked surprised that he had caught up so quickly.

"Why are you running?"

"She's throwing shoes at me."

"You knew Skunk Cat, didn't you?"

"I couldn't believe she followed me here. She was so ugly."

"Who killed her?"

"How am I supposed to know? I was sleeping."

"The human mother thinks you killed her."

"Well, I didn't—Why would I kill her? She was my mother."

"Your *mother*? Oh . . . I'm sorry."

"What for?"

"That's she's dead."

"I'm not."

"You're not?"

"She followed me everywhere. I hated her. Every time I'd find a good house, she'd show up yowling. She was such a sloppy mess. I'm glad she's dead. About time."

"Hey!" yelled the pig through his roof. "Can't anybody get any sleep around here?"

The cat leaned over the eaves and called, "Pipe down," to the pig glowering sleepily from his door.

"Good-bye," said Vanilla.

"What? Where are you going?"

"I can't stay here. They all think I killed her." She walked slowly down the slope of the pig roof. "All I wanted was a home . . . and family . . . a real family. . . ."

"Wait," said the cat. "Wait a little while."

The pig let out an angry grunt and shook the roof by rubbing against his doorway. Vanilla took the opportunity to scramble off the back of the pig house and disappear into the cornfield.

"Just wait a little while," the cat called after her.

From deep in the thick-growing stalks came a plaintive, "Maybe."

The cat thought hard. Had Vanilla snuck past him into the house, while he slept?

"You look," said the pig, "like you've got a problem."

How could he have slept through Skunk Cat's murder in his own house?

"It worries me," said the pig. "Distraction is a dangerous state for a creature that must be alert to the many who would step on it, drive over it, or bite it."

"Pipe down," said the cat. He had several pig acquaintances around the county. They were all worrywarts, but this one fretted in many more words than were needed. False fretting at that: High on the list of the many who would bite him were pigs—not out of malice, but they would snack on anything that couldn't get away.

"Tell me about it," said the pig. "I'm a good listener. What's your problem?"

There was a bull the cat would confide in—a great mountain of an animal, far away on another farm, who would listen in a silence broken only by the occasional rumble of sympathy. But who could talk to a worrywart of a pig? And yet, how to explain why he was troubled that Vanilla would be banished for killing her mother, even if, as she claimed, she hadn't? He liked the idea of keeping Vanilla around. Even if she had moved in on the human mother. Even if Vanilla was probably not a cat to turn his back on.

He said, "I'm trying to figure out who snuck into the house and killed an old cat in the living room. Bit her right in the throat."

"Who would want to?" asked the pig.

The cat thought. "The mink in the maple tree."

"Did the mink eat the cat?"

"No."

"So why would he risk his life sneaking into the house just to bite her?"

"That damned Jack Russell across the road could have bit her."

"You better look out for him."

"Thanks for the warning."

"What about that beautiful white cat I saw you mooning over?"

"What about her?"

"She's got trouble written all over her," said the pig.

"No, she's the old cat's daughter."

"I'd bet on the daughter," said the pig.

"No."

"There's stuff goes on in families that would curl your tail," said the pig.

"No way," said the cat.

"No one gets madder than shared blood. No one cares more. No one hates more."

"No."

"You know why?"

"No."

"Because family reminds us of ourselves. At our worst. Think back on how mad you could get at your mother."

"I never had a mother," said the cat. "Except the human mother, and she doesn't count that way."

"Well, I wouldn't turn my back on *my* daughter," said the pig. "Which is all I have to say on the subject."

"Thank the moon for small favors." The cat jumped off the roof onto the pig fence, where he swayed, as if to fall into the trodden mud. Every muscle in the pig swelled with anticipation. "Just testing," said the cat, and leaped to the grass.

He trotted to the house, curious. He could not believe that anyone could have walked past him and through his cat door even when he was sleeping under the pickup truck.

He walked around the house and climbed onto the front porch, where no one ever went. There was a hole in the screen door.

The big door behind it was open to let the breeze into the living room. The hole had been pushed in by something very strong. Something afraid to use his cat door, but strong enough to push the screen loose from one corner. A mink-size hole. Or a Jack Russell–size hole. Or a Vanilla-size hole.

He sniffed the screen. It smelled of cat. Female cat. But when he had female cat on his mind everything smelled of female cat. He was thinking that over when he realized there was another smell, too. Mink? Maybe. And dog. He was pretty sure he smelled dog. But his nose, unfortunately, was not the equal of his superb ears. He backed away, his brain disintegrating from overload, and plodded down the steps. Suddenly, his hackles rose and his ears lay flat. Something was lurking in the flower garden beside the front porch steps. He peered into the shadows. A white face peered back from the dahlias. It looked vaguely familiar. A sharp white face with beady dark eyes. The cat growled.

The white face growled back, revealing many, many teeth. He had never seen so many teeth. But he had! Fifty teeth.

The cat worked his way down the steps and cautiously into the flowers, not believing his eyes. As near as he could recall, he had eaten half his possum before the mink took it away from him. This would take "playing possum" to unprecedented extremes. "Possum?" he asked.

"Opossum, to you, you murdering feline."

Different possum. Much bigger.

"What's up?" asked the cat. He had never seen such a big possum. Twice the size of the one he and the mink had lunched on. He gathered his back legs, ready to fight if he had to, but strongly inclined to conduct an immediate tree search.

"I'm trying to find my son," said the possum.

"Oh."

"Seen him?"

"Ummm, no, I don't think so."

"A little guy about your size."

"Oh, him," said the cat. "Yeah, I saw him."

"Where?"

The cat stared at the mulch-covered ground. "I don't know how to tell you this."

"What?"

"Last I saw, the mink had him in the maple tree. . . . Sorry."

Opossum hunkered down sadly. "Damn mink."

"Did you happen to push your way into the house?" asked the cat.

Opossum looked away. "Why would I do that?"

"Looking for your son, maybe?"

"What if I did?"

"Did you push that hole in the screen?"

"A mother has a right to look for her son."

"All I'm asking is did you push that hole through the screen door?"

"Well, I'm not the sort to barge into human houses."

"I could tell that right off," said the cat. "But maybe you made an exception this time. You know the saying, a mother has a right to look for her son."

"So true, so true. . . . Yes, I pushed through the screen."

"What did you find?"

"Nothing but a bag of bones cat."

"Did you ask the bag of bones if she'd seen your son?"

"Of course."

The cat was pleased with his cleverness. He had established that Skunk Cat was still alive when the big possum pushed the hole in the screen. Now to find out if the possum killed Skunk Cat. "What," the cat asked, "did she say?"

" 'eeeYOOOWWrrr.' "

"Is that why you killed her?"

"Why would I kill a poor old bag of bones?"

"I would have killed her to stop that awful noise," confided the cat. The implied intimacy, calculated to make the possum confess, sailed right over the grieving animal's head.

"I was looking for my baby and it was obvious to me that that poor old bag of bones could not have hurt my baby," said Opossum, and waddled away, its pink-bottomed feet flopping skyward with each unhappy step.

The cat remained under the bushes thinking about what he knew. Then he walked around the barn and past the pig house and into the corn, where he walked between the dusty rows calling, "Vanilla. Vanilla. Vanilla."

"Quiet!" she hissed in his ear, and there she was camouflaged by a white shaft of sunlight that penetrated the stalks. Field mice scattered. "Thanks a lot," she said.

The cat whipped one from under a leaf and dropped it at her feet. "I just thought you'd like to know that the possum didn't kill your mother."

"Don't call her that."

"The possum made a hole in the door, which some other creature used to enter the living room and kill Skunk Cat, your mother."

"The human mother still thinks I'm that creature." She stalked off, white against green, white against brown, gone in a shaft of sunlight. The cat retraced his steps out of the cornfield and went and sat under the sugar maple where the mink lived.

He waited an hour, but did not doze off. He was not in the habit of sleeping during moments of life and a death. Finally, bored, he yelled up the tree at the high cavity the mink called home. "Hey! Mink! Wake up!"

Its bright, dark eyes appeared suddenly in a knothole that was situated much lower to the ground—and much, much closer than made the cat comfortable. It regarded him with the same studied nonchalance as he himself might appraise a fat vole.

"Did you by any chance go into the house recently?" the cat asked.

The mink appeared vaguely interested, vaguely curious, vaguely amused. But when, instead of answering that simple question, the mink quite suddenly made up its mind to kill him, the cat saw nothing in its expression but a cold confidence that in another instant one of them would be dead and it wouldn't be the mink. He might have wondered if the helpless chill that pierced his heart was akin to the chill that would shiver a vole, but he was too busy trying to stay alive.

The mink erupted from the knothole as if the tree had squeezed it out, and landed on the ground between the cat and the house, leaving the cat only the cornfield, the woods, or the barn to hide—in each of which place the mink was as capable as he. When the cat turned toward the pond, the mink fairly howled for joy. Water was its favorite and it was such a good swimmer, it regularly dined on fish. The cat doubled back and bolted for the front yard and the road.

The mink came after him in a flurry of teeth.

The cat fled across the lawn in ten foot leaps and ran blindly into the road, the mink inches behind him. He crossed the road and leaped the dusty rut that the Jack Russell terrier had worn in the grass. Instinct whipped the cat's tail alongside his heaving flanks and he heard the mink's jaws snap where his tail had been.

"Jack!" the cat yelled. "You misery. I'm in your yard."

"Ain't no Jack gonna help you," the mink laughed. "You dreamin'."

"Jack! I'm inside your electric fence."

At last, Jack came stumbling out from under the antique sled the new people had put on their lawn.

"Whoa!" said the mink and started to turn away. But Jack was on him in a flash, bit down on his spine, and snapped it with a shake of his head. The cat ran, outside the fence and across the road and halfway to the house. Exhausted, he looked back to watch Jack eat the mink.

"*Yaaaaaaaaaa!*" screamed Jack, and the cat nearly died. Instead of sitting down to eat the mink like any respectable hunter, the dog had leaped the fence, taken the zap in the throat, and was now coming after him with all four feet.

There was one tree, a hair closer than the house. And his cat door was all the way around the house in the back porch. He started for the tree and was almost to it, with Jack snapping at his tail, when he saw Vanilla watching from the cornfield. She looked like she enjoyed a good chase. The tree was still closer, but in an instant of blinding clarity the hoped-for pleasures of Vanilla and the ongoing misery of Jack collided like meteors in the black hole of his brain. He turned toward the house, instead of the safety of the tree.

Jack howled in joyous anticipation of breaking his spine.

The cat ran with the last of his breath for the front porch, up the steps, dove through the hole that the possum had made in the screen door and into the dim living room, through the dining room, and into the kitchen with the Jack Russell terrier clattering behind him. He skidded past the human mother at the sink, dove out his cat door, cleared the porch in a leap, and ran between the pillar-like legs of the human father.

"Stop that dog," cried the human mother. "It killed Skunk Cat and he's going to get ours."

The human father, who had his uses, plunged down with his pitchfork, catching the Jack Russell terrier between the tines and pinning it to the lawn, where it squirmed, snarled and snapped. The cat collapsed in a heart-heaving heap and watched as the human mother ran up with a blanket. A moment later, Jack was thrashing around inside the blanket with the corners gathered to form a sack.

Still too exhausted to move, the cat watched his humans drag the sack of Jack down their lawn, across the road, up the new neighbor's lawn to their front door, which they knocked on loudly.

• • •

THAT evening, a black truck with barred windows pulled up to the neighbor's house. A sign on the side read:

JACK RUSSELL TERRIER RESCUE
&
ADOPTION

The cat and old Roger sat on their lawn, side by side in companionable silence, and watched them load the Jack Russell terrier into it. After a lot of barking and yapping the truck pulled away.

"Good-bye, Jack," said the cat.

"Do you hear what Jack's yelling?" asked Roger. Jack was barking like crazy through the bars.

"No."

"Can't you hear him? 'It's a frame. It's a frame. They set me up.' "

"Roger, your hearing's shot. Must have been all those SEAL guns. He's saying, 'I'll get you, I'll get you.' "

"*Now* he's saying, 'I'll get you, I'll get you, I'll get you.' A second ago he was yelling he was framed. . . . Wonder who he's threatening to get. . . . Actually, all he's ever going to get is adopted far from here. . . . If anyone'll have him."

The cat turned his gaze to the pickup. The doors were open. Vanilla was sitting on the forbidden-to-cats driver's seat. The human mother was feeding her slices of liver while cooing, "Forgive me, Vanilla, for doubting beautiful Vanilla."

The cat felt great pleasure.

"You know something?" rumbled old Roger.

"What?"

"I had a good look at the bite marks on that old cat.

Those needle holes in Skunk Cat's throat? They weren't Jack Russell bites."

"Is that a fact?"

"Terriers grab a cat from above, snap the neck or back. Those bites were on the throat. Like a mink would kill. Or a cat."

"Or a mink."

"But a mink would have eaten her, don't you think?"

"Maybe the mink wasn't hungry."

"Could have been a cat that killed her," said Roger.

The cat looked up at his old housemate and repeated, "Maybe the mink wasn't hungry."

Roger said, "All I'm saying is a friendly warning—I've known you since you were a kitten, for moon's sake; you used to sleep on my head—and I'm telling you that Vanilla's not a cat to turn your back on."

"Roger, why would I turn my back on someone so beautiful to face?"

Roger ruminated on that awhile, silent but for his rumbling belly and wheezing lungs. At last, he looked sternly down his long nose and said, "But either way you look at it, that truck that took Jack took the wrong animal."

"I won't miss him," said the cat.

RONALD, D———!

Peter Straub

T HEY were a rugged bunch, the old originals, Chewey
thought. You could say those guys wrote the book, invented the rules, laid down the laws, set the mold. The
pioneers, they did it all. For four decades, showbiz was their
playpen. In the twenties they danced their legs off; in the
thirties they did boffo business at the box office; in the for-
ties they got so big, the Cagneys, the Grants, the Hay-
worths, the stars of the other Hollywood, begged for cameos
in their pictures; in the fifties they really hit their stride and
got into the merchandising, the theme parks, the licensing
business, the stuff that went on spinning off money long
after their end of the industry faded away to nothing. *No
limits*, that was the deal. Ten–twelve hours straight in the
studio, then a little cavorting in their kidney-shaped pools,
a few drinks with the girls at their favorite getaways, pub-
licity photos at Chasen's, an assignation in the back room
at Musso & Frank's, a quip for Louella at Mike Romanoff's,
a cigar at the Brown Derby, a little steam at the Beverly
Hills or the Wilshire, a nap and a pick-me-up back home
in the Hollywood Hills, then back into the studio for an-

other ten hours of mayhem. Every day a laff riot, every day a payday!

When the industry changed, which was a damn shame in Chewey's opinion, and never would have happened if every little project hadn't started costing forty mil and up, the old comic books vanished right along with the cartoons, and a whole new generation came in. Mutants and malcontents, most of them, Chewey thought. The ones who managed the crossover into film never panned out; they used violence and darkness as their hooks, but good old Tom and Jerry put violence right in your face and made you laugh at it. Crow, Judge Dredd, the X-Men, what were they but empowerment fantasies at heart? Say what you will about Uncle Ronald, he always had the sense to turn his temper tantrums into self-mockery, not bloodbaths. Besides, the new generation got everything wrong from the start—they dealt from weakness instead of strength and got the crossover ass-backward. Even a banged-up couple of old vaudevillians like Sylvester and Tweetie Bird, a one-joke act if ever there was one, knew enough to start in the movie houses and then go into comic books, not the other way around!

The problem was, no one had ever bothered to think about what these guys were supposed to do when they stopped performing. Of course they hadn't. Everyone imagined they would simply go on forever, rioting through movie houses, across lunch boxes and the funny pages, turning the tap that released a flood of golden coins day after day, month after month, year after year. Doesn't everyone, don't even *people*, think their present conditions, whatever the hell they are, will probably endure and endure . . . until they get even better? And isn't this dopey optimism endlessly, witlessly reinforced by TV and the movies? Case in point: *All Dogs Go to Heaven*. If that were true, would you want to go there?

Ask a former child star if all dogs go to heaven, Chewey thought, and after you hear the answer drive, if you can still

drive, over to your local Chewey D————'s Ducks Unlimited (one in Century City, one on Hollywood Boulevard, one
in Boca Raton, and one in Orlando), slide onto a bar seat,
and drink until you forget it. On the menu today: "Foofy's
Own Private Mudslide," $5.50; "Jinnie's Champagne Cock-
tail," $7.00; "Boodle Boys' Stolen Summer *Weissebrau*,"
$3.50 the glass, $14.00 per pitcher; plus the usual golden
oldies. Never mind that Foofy got so deep into LSD in the
sixties that he now speaks entirely in psycho-babble; never
mind that Jinnie died of Alzheimer's; never mind that the
Boodle Boys went straight about a million years ago and
now serve on the board of the Stooge McD———— Foundation. In Chewey's opinion, his great-uncle Stooge probably came out of the collapse better than anybody—the guy
had no family to worry about, and he was old enough to
have acquired some sense.

And of the children's generation, he had managed the
transition better than most. Some of Chewey's peers felt that
it was in poor taste—well, appalling taste, for a D————
to own a chain of duck restaurants, and some were offended
by his menu's "exploitation" of the family and their old
friends. The first time Screwy D———— had seen the menu,
he threw it on the floor, stamped on it in a fit of unintelligible obscenties worthy of Unka Ronald at his most irate, and
stormed out, swearing never to speak to Chewey again, a
vow it took him most of a year to break. At the time, Screwy
was ekeing out a living as a street mime, which had led
Chewey to the conclusion that only the very rich and the
very poor could afford to be proud.

The others had adjusted as well as they could, given that
most child stars do not make it even to, so to speak, purgatory. Screwy spent the time left over from his telephone
sales job on acting classes and auditions, and Bluey taught
second grade at a small private academy in Santa Monica.
Bluey's wife, Sharon, always felt a little insecure around
Cosima, Chewey's wife, but that was mainly a class thing.

Although Screwy never accepted his eldest brother's business, Sharon had finally managed to persuade Bluey that D———s were of another species entirely from the creatures they resembled.

Thank God for Sharon. Later, she confided that she had simply worn her husband down with relentless questions: *Do those ducks have jobs? Can they talk? Drive cars? Have you ever seen one of those ducks smoke a cigarette, Bluey, while you smoke at least a pack a day of Unka Ronald Ultra Lights? Ever seen one go to the toilet, Bluey? Or pick up a fork? And how about the whole question of food—do you think those birds in the park can eat stuff like chili dogs and steak and asparagus and your own personal favorite, choucroute garni? Well, if they can, why don't people feed them meals like that, instead of lousy old bread crumbs out of a paper bag? And why don't they complain? When some fool comes up to the side of the pond with a paper bag in his hands, why don't they yell FORGET THE BREAD CRUMBS, GO BACK HOME AND GET ME A NICE, JUICY VEAL CHOP? And how come they don't get arrested, going around naked all the time? You would, wouldn't you? They don't even own clothes, and you own five suits and four sports jackets! Your Uncle Ronald has six whole walk-in closets filled with suits. But what about those naked lady ducks, Bluey—do they turn you on? No? You don't even get a little tingle down there when you see them diving underwater for a bite of kelp? Are you sure, Bluey? Yes? Well, if all that's true, what's keeping us from getting a baby-sitter and going over to one of your brother's restaurants now and then for a free meal that I don't have to shop for, cook, or clean up afterward?*

A free meal, that was the real issue. Chewey had never minded the idea of comping members of his family and others from the old crowd. He even welcomed the Mick's kids and grandkids and let them stuff their faces gratis, although Mick and Jinnie had completely spoiled Burlie, Toodles, and Stacy-Wacey. Those three were so rich, they bought new luxury cars every time they wrecked the old ones. The fortune that came in from the Mick, why should they sweat over a little thing like a smashed-up Lexus? Mick didn't give a damn, that was for sure. Sour old guy, spent all day shuttling between Palm Springs, the Friars' Club, and the various houses he had bought for his mistresses, still hot to show off what rumor claimed to be the most remarkable endowment since Trigger's. Chewey could remember a party at Unka Ronald's and Aunt Maizy's house in the late fifties, someone playing the piano, the Mick's bratty kids shoving people into the pool, and the Big Guy motioning him aside, pointing to the area south of his big white buttons, and saying, "Well, Chewey-baby, I know you've heard about it, but how'dja like a little peek?" When Chewey declined, the Mick waved him away, saying, "In my day, people were gracious enough to show a liddle *cur-ee-oss-iddy*."

Which, at least in Chewey's mind, demonstrated another important point about the entertainment industry, namely that the same people who expected things to get better and better always felt as though they were getting worse and worse—day by day! Chewey had put in enough schmooze time at the Friar's Club to know that if you were in the mood to listen to a world-class whiner, all you had to do was sit down next to someone like Dick Tracy, that poor shlub. Every single time Annette Bening pops another kid, he sends her a dozen long-stemmed roses, good stuff, top of the line, but does Warren Beatty ever take a minute to call?

• • •

MOST of Chewey's time in the Friars' Club barroom had been served in the year after Aunt Maizy's unexpected departure for a better world, wherever that was. One day a hacking cough, the next day a raging fever, a night in the Danny Thomas wing at Cedars, and before you know it, you're slipping the preacher a couple of Franklins and thanking him for giving such a beautiful eulogy. That's how it went with Maizy D———, one, two, three—the cough, the fever, the funeral service. Caught Ronald completely by surprise, caught him flatfooted, knocked him stupid with surprise. No time to prepare or learn his lines, bang, deer in the headlights time. We're ready for your close-up, now do grief. Do mourning. Do heartbreak. Give us your pain, baby, you're an old trouper, give us your tears, your sleepless nights, your aimless days. If your dead wife doesn't do it for you, think of your dead puppy—you an innocent six, him a bloody smear on the highway. *That's* the heartbreak we want, the dead-puppy heartbreak, the I'm-all-alone-in-the-world-and-I'll-never-be-whole-again shtick. Your family, your friends, they all have these demanding expectations, they want the dull eyes and the unwashed hair and the unmatched socks. At the same time, and here comes the old double-shuffle, these very same characters, who of course happen to be your nearest and dearest buddy-roos, suppose its your duty, male and female alike, to overcome your personal and individual sorrow for the sake of the social tone that prevailed so happily in the days before the unfortunate loss, for it was that very tone that defined your relationships with these characters, and without it you risk being considered a loser and schlemiel, the kind of guy who won't let *you* get over *his* unhappiness.

In the above circumstances, a place like the Friars' Club barroom naturally comes into its own, you might say, being a convivial yet highly protected environment on its good days practically bulging with cynical hard cases and skirt-chasers firing off their best, roughest, most heartless lines at one another in a perpetual atmosphere of masculine camaraderie, and Chewey never minded, at least not much, the implied obligation three or four days a week to drive his grieving uncle over there for lunch followed by half a dozen afternoon Bombay Sapphire martinis in the form of three doubles. In the figurative embrace of his fellow-originals, Ronald found it possible to relax. When the Mick, the Big Guy, turned a rheumy, reptilian eye on him and growled,

"Sorry about Maizy, kid—best piece of duck's ass I ever had," and reliable old Porky, sweetest guy in the world, chimed in with, "Wrong, you asshole, you're th-thinking about her m-m-mother," Ronald could breathe easy.

When had Sylvia D——— first entered the scene? Chewey had never been able to pin that event to a specific date. Sylvia D——— had first appeared as a kind of sexual radiance, an erotic shimmer glimpsed in the bandinage at the Friars' and on the fairways of the clan's favorite golf courses. She had come in from Aspen, New York City, and Nice, where she owned houses; a marriage to an obscure Midwestern D——— had left her with a modest fortune and a beautiful daughter, Lizzie, for whom she might almost be mistaken; her father, Gaylord D———, a figure of immense rectitude in his mid-nineties, continued in his life-long capacity as lawyer and financial manager to several unnamed but fabulously wealthy families located in the Boston area. Chewey first heard the old hard cases and skirt-chasers begin to gossip about this mysterious creature nine or ten months after Ronald became a widower. She had emerged from Aspen, New York City, and Nice to attach herself to a friend and distant cousin of Ronald's named Myron D———, a retired doctor, in whose infatuated company she was seen, though never by Chewey, at many and many a party and charity event. The old boys adored the new arrival. Sylvia made them think of Cole Porter lyrics. She was a Bendel bonnet, a Shakespeare sonnet, she was . . . "Hell, I wish she *was*," Chewey heard the Big Guy mutter to poor old Joe Palooka one dim afternoon at the club. "I'd spend the whole day trying to figure out which to grab first, my tits or my ass."

In his role as his uncle's grief counselor and support system, Chewey was privileged to overhear step-by-step reports on the progress of the great Myron-Sylvia *amour*. Myron had proposed, and Sylvia had rejected him; they patched things up at a resort on Virgin Gorda; they spent Christmas in a suite at the Crillon; Sylvia had taken over Myron's exercise program and had him playing tennis twice a day; with the aid of a humongous diamond from Tiffany, they were at last engaged; the awesome Gaylord gave his blessing; the love-birds sailed first-class to Europe on the QE2, the wedding date still up in the air due to the conflict between Sylvia's desire for an appropriately lavish ceremony in a suitably *luxe* venue and certain unfortunate business obligations of Myron's. Then came news of the tragedy, which took place on a tennis court in Jerusalem on a blistering afternoon just as the prospective and still-overweight bridegroom blundered toward the net to hammer the pro's diplomatic return of serve.

Sylvia flew back alone and sequestered herself, apparently, in her father's mansion. As no one in the group knew Gaylord's address or telephone number, both of which were of course deeply confidential, likewise the same information for his great business enterprise, her whereabouts were uncertain. In the old boys' tasteless jokes about "Jewish tennis," many of them based on the vaudeville turns they had witnessed in their youth, could be detected a strain of melancholia distinct as—as the Mick put it, "the kiss of a four-bit stogie."

A month later, Ronald dropped into Chewey D———'s Ducks Unlimited for lunch on a day when Chewey was out shopping for a heavy-duty insecticide, and who happened to be seated alone at a booth in the back corner, perusing the menu with the aid of a Jinnie's Champagne Cocktail, but the ravishing Sylvia D———, his sister in grief, the all-but widow of this widower's distant cousin? Five weeks after that, Ronald called Chewey to inform him that the thrice-weekly visits to the Friars' barroom and the six Bombay Sapphire martinis in the form of three doubles were a thing of the past. "Kid," his uncle said, in the Borscht-Belt rasp that is the trademark of the showbiz original, "much as I love ya, there are certain needs common to

a D———— of my age and position in the world that no
nephew, no matter how great he is, and you are, kid, you're
the greatest, could never in his whole entire life supply the
answer to. Let's put it this way, all right? You with me?
Let's put it like this—I've never exactly been a God-fearing
D————, but right now at this point in time I am almost
tempted to think that cousin Myron, may he rest in peace
and all that, died for my sins. Because from the way I'm
feeling, I guess I musta gone to heaven." Sylvia D————
had moved into the quirky old house in the Hollywood
Hills.

So that was what happened to a guy like Uncle Ronald
when he had to stop performing. He lost his mind and fell
in love.

· · ·

IT was only a short time after the conversation in which
Ronald spoke of Myron dying for his sins that each of the
nephews received a call from their famous uncle inviting
them up to the house on King's Road to meet his beloved
and, he wished them to understand, bride-to-be. Cosima,
Sharon, and Pinkytoes, the wives, were invited, but Wolf-
gang, Truffles, and Afterburn; Acey-Deucey and Trinkle;
and Botswana-Infidel, the children of the three couples, were
not. Sylvia had let it be known that, generally speaking, she
found children unbearable, except of course for her darling
daughter, the incomparable Lizzie, who so greatly resembled
her.

At six-thirty P.M. on the appointed day, Chewey, Bluey,
and Screwy, side by side with their respective wives, appeared at the charming house on King's Road, Chewey at-
tired in a dark gray wool-silk blend from Armani, Bluey in
an only slightly chalkstained old tweed jacket with reinforced elbows from the more respectable end of his closet,
Screwy in black jeans, a black T-shirt, and a black leather
jacket from Melrose Avenue that went nicely with his goatee

and piercings. The ladies also had dressed according to their conceptions of suitability, with Cosima dignified and stunning in a little black Chanel, Sharon maternal and sensible in a pretty Laura Ashley dress, Pinkytoes sultry and disdainful in what appeared to be several layers of undergarments.

A glowing Uncle Ronald in a brand-new smoking jacket answered the door and embraced them each in turn. This was great, the whole family together again—apart from the children, Chewey silently noted—just wait until they met Sylvia, she was the best thing that could have happened to him, honest to God, sometimes you just got lucky, yep, he was a new man, on top of the goddam world, felt thirty years younger. Maizy, God bless her, woulda wanted him to have this happiness, didn't they agree? Hell, what were they doing standing around outside, let's go in so they can meet the goddam light of his life, and he meant that sincerely. He led them through the door and halfway up the hallway, bawling his beloved's name as if he suspected her of having fled from the room where he had left her.

But there she was, safely ensconced in the curve of the old Art Deco sofa with her ankles prettily crossed before her, her back ever so slightly turned to the decorative but unnecessary blaze in the fireplace, above it the impressive portrait of Maizy specially commisioned from Mr. Burl Karks and the urn containing her ashes on the mantel. Whitegloved fingers held her place in a little book and her lovely profile gazed through the great wall of windows upon the hazy panorama of greater Los Angeles. She seemed lost in her thoughts, these perhaps occasioned by the contents of the little volume, which, Chewey observed, was the *Selected Poems of Emily Dickenson*.

The sense that this tableau was all too literally a "scene" and had been stage-managed for maximum effect vanished the moment Sylvia turned her charming head, took in the company before her, and gave a palpable start of surprise.

In Chewey's breast, and no doubt in those of his brothers as well, happiness for his uncle's good fortune struggled against a primal form of envy—Sylvia was radiance itself, a creature seemingly made of sea-foam and moonlight. Unlike the commanding beauty portayed by Mr. Karks, she seemed inherently fragile, in need of protection from the cruder, more vulgar world lurking without. Her voice floated on a gasp of wonder: Were these three handsome fellows actually the wonderful nephews of whom she had heard so much? And Chewey, of course, she recognized him immediately, he who had done so much for dear Ronnie in his time of need.

Ronnie? Chewey asked himself.

The question disappeared before the spectacle of Sylvia D——— drifting up from the Art Deco sofa in an extravagant tumult of ruffles and drapery that yielded a momentary glimpse of a tender leg and a sumptuous bosom. Chewey felt as if he were levitating a few inches off the ancient Kirman rug. Like his brothers, he was infatuated on the spot.

It was to be the last time he took her at face value.

Sylvia deposited the book on the end table with a pat of fond regret. Surely, this was a moment worthy of celebration, was it not? A beaming Ronald, or Ronnie, rushed off to fetch a magnum of Dom Perignon, and while he was gone his heart's darling made a comic complaint of such a showbiz legend doing his own fetching and carrying. Yes, the boys agreed, that was the silliest thing, it was indeed, when "Ronnie" could so easily afford a manservant, not to mention a cook. Growing up in Gaylord's great manor house, the child Sylvia had enjoyed the attentions of four full-time servants, yes, those were the days, darling, no one expected such treatment now, but surely the boys thought it absurd that a figure of "Ronnie's" stature should, at his age, have to carry a heavy tray laden with drinks all the way from the pantry, or the scullery, or whatever that odd little room off the kitchen was called. In Screwy's hesitant affirmation Chewey thought he saw a trace of concern for little Botswana-Infidel's eventual inheritance. Well, *Ronnie* had millions, didn't he, literal millions, truth be told thanks to licensing agreements, more millions even than his uncle Stooge, and Chewey had no fears for the financial security of the next generation, even if Botswana-Infidel's bohemian father displayed more interest in spending money than earning it.

The sleeves of his jacket slightly dusty from the wine cellar, Ronald returned, staggering only slightly under the weight of the silver tray, on which rode the huge bottle within a huger ice bucket, eight champagne flutes, a bowl of yummy salted almonds, a double Bombay Sapphire martini on the rocks for the host, a bottle of Rolling Rock beer specifically requested by Pinkytoes, and a crystal ashtray roughly the size of a manhole cover. The question of who might use this last item, since Mr. and Mrs. Chewey did not smoke, neither did Mr. and Mrs. Bluey, and Mr. and Mrs. Screwy, as far as one knew, smoked only those exotic cigarettes made from a forbidden weed, was answered when the panting Ronald, "Ronnie," thrust one hand into a pocket of his splendid new garment and produced a pack of Pall Malls, one of which he tucked into his bill and another into his sweeheart's, then ignited both with a pass of a slim golden lighter. The old legend grinned at his dumbfounded nephews and their spouses. "Before Sylvia gave me this smoking jacket, I hadn't had a puff in forty years," he said. "But I don't want my honeybunch to smoke alone, do I? And at my age, it's like Sylvia says, you gotta give yourself all the treats your heart desires."

That afternoon, Ronnie's honeybunch regaled the nephews and their mates with piquant tales from an adventuresome life: She had grown up in Boston and Paris, gone to school in Switzerland, and spent a few years in her late teens as a starlet in the Roman film industry, now a wisp of its

former self, so sad, but as a result her French was *fantastique*
and her Italian *molto bello*. She had married young, but the
marriage didn't have a snowball's, the two of them being
babies still finding out who they were. Soon after sweet darling Lizzie's birth they parted never, alas, to meet again, for
the bereft hubby came to a mysterious end in Calcutta, she
thought it was, and with the kindly aid of his estate mother
and daughter traveled the world, never failing to appreciate
the finer nuances and subtler tones. Oft had they wintered
in delightful little Aspen, CO, where the amusing, in fact,
highly amusing, actor Jack Nicholson many times squired
them down the expert's slopes and feted them with his
homemade spaghetti bolognese and garlic bread; in Palm
Beach, they had been houseguests of the dashingly handsome, tragically misunderstood George Hamilton, who was
so much cleverer than anyone gave him credit for.

With all her experience of the world's rarest textures and
fabrics, Sylvia had of course been asked, as a personal favor,
to decorate if not virtually to design a great number of splendid houses and apartments owned by aristocrats, financiers,
and film royalty, work that had brought her if she might be
permitted to say so herself a nice degree of acclaim, of rec-
ognition, which is all we *really* need, isn't it? Oh yes, she
had turned professional, all her friends had insisted on it,
and by then it was time for darling Lizzie's education in
Switzerland, so Sylvia had accepted the challenge, what a
whirl, Paris Bonn Dallas New York Seattle St. Moritz
Cannes Frankfort Singapore Denver Boston Tokyo, heavens,
a girl had to get off the merry-go-round and find some peace
and quiet in her *own* space or just go crazy, and that was
when she met the divine Mr. Myron D——— and thought
he was meant to be her salvation, but it turned out Myron
had another role entirely, one that he performed beautifully,
like the gentleman he was.

"Don't laugh now, you little pricks," said Uncle Ronald,
lighting another Pall Mall and inhaling to a luxuriant depth,

"because what I'm about to say is a spiritual kinda thing. You could call cousin Myron, who was a guy I never paid a lotta attention to when we were coming up, if you want to know the truth, you could call him our Cupid. Sylvia's and mine. He was our goddam Cupid, that's what he was, and I pray that he may rest in peace, and all that good stuff."

A huge, transparent tear with the density of glycerine stood at the outer corner of each of his darling's rapturous eyes.

The impression Sylvia made on her fiancée's family was neatly summarized in the remarks uttered by the nephew's wives as the visitors passed through Unka Ronald's gate and hesitated a moment before separating into pairs for their homeward journeys.

Cosima said: "She's at least forty years younger than he is!"

Sharon said: "And she isn't trustworthy!"

Pinkytoes said: "And on top of that, she's an evil bitch!" From Pinkytoes, this may have been a compliment.

• • •

Two weeks after Sylvia had made her great impression upon the women of the middle generation, Chewey's uncle called him with an unusual request. It seemed that the awesome Gaylord, informed of his daughter's desire to remarry, had refused to grant his approval until he could "Look the fellow square in the eye," as he put it, and "judge the cut of his jib." The provenance of this last phrase was more financial than nautical, for by it Gaylord D——— had expressed his insistence upon reviewing his prospective son-in-law's account books, brokerage statements, income tax forms, and the like. He wished to do so in the privacy of the suite he had reserved at the Bel Air Hotel, and he wished to do so alone. Gaylord was to arrive late that afternoon, and Sylvia had borrowed Ronald's car for the purpose of driving to the local Mercedes dealership, there to purchase, as a kind of pre-wedding present, an appropriate means of transportation for herself. Would Chewey be so kind as to pick up his uncle, drive them both to the accountant's offices on Wilshire Boulevard to collect the crates of documents, then deposit them at the Bel Air?

A series of interlocking obligations involving an ineffective exterminator and a harshly worded document from the Health Department delayed Chewey's appearance at the house on King's Road until nearly four o'clock, and when he pulled up in front of the gate he noticed a FOR SALE sign halfway up the path to the front door. Half-crazy with impatience and anxiety, his uncle came rushing through the door, too rattled to say any more than that Sylvia could do nothing with his funny old house, nothing at all, it seemed the house had long ago outlived the charm of its eccentricities, and both he and his darling girl felt she deserved a canvas more worthy of her magnificent talents—that is, a house large and luxurious enough to bring out the best in Sylvia. Somewhere in Beverly Hills, they thought, something a bit off Mulholland Drive, on or near the crest of the hill. But couldn't Chewey please concentrate on what they were supposed to be doing and get to Wilshire in less than, say, an hour, or was that too much to ask?

Stung, Chewey raced like a madman to the accountant's office, where three large cartons filled with documents awaited him. Two of the cartons filled the trunk, so the third rode on the backseat as Chewey shot down the crowded avenues and byways that took him to the serene world guarded by the gates of Bel Air. His uncle kept glancing at his watch and firing off colorful obscenities. Chewey's attempts at reassurance backfired, badly. When he mentioned that all of this seemed entirely unnecessary, since Sylvia's first husband had clearly left her a good deal of money, Ronald groaned and said he was all wrong. The first husband, that bum, when he had that funny accident in Calcutta, or wherever it was, he had betrayed both trusting Sylvia and her doting father by leaving an estate half the size he had claimed. Damn near left the poor kid and her little girl without a dime to their name. Chewey'd heard about the house in Aspen, the house in Nice, that apartment in Manhattan, hadn't he? Too bad, they were long gone, no more, kaput. Why did Chewey think that the father was taking such pains now? Was Chewey a *complete* idiot? And when Chewey pointed out that Ronald after all possessed one of the world's best-known and most famous faces and had amassed a great fortune besides, his uncle's scornful response silenced him for the rest of the careering journey.

D———s like Gaylord cared nothing for fame, didn't Chewey understand even that much? D———s like that thought fame was vulgar. They thought fame was a *disgrace*, those old-time New England D———s! They'd rather be caught *dead* than have their pictures in the paper. Geez Louise, didn't kids know anything anymore, were they all blockheads? Gaylord and the Gaylord-clan, they represented culture, good breeding, good manners, hell, they went to the top schools in the country, and Ronald had never actually gone to school at all, had he? Out there busting his gut to get a laugh more or less from the moment he was born, how could he know anything about art, like paintings and statues, which were ordinary, everyday things to Gaylord and his pals, who had so many statues, they used the small ones for hat racks! And when it came to money, Chewey had it all wrong, kiddo, he had it arsey-versey, because Gaylord and those type of guys, money ran down the street just to jump into their pockets.

So on the one hand, Sylvia could barely afford her next six ounces of caviar; and on the other, she couldn't put her hands in her pockets without pulling out a fresh wad of bills. Chewey supposed his uncle had good reason to be worked up.

Then catastrophe, or what seemed to be catastrophe. A uniformed driver was opening the rear door of a black limousine as Chewey pulled up in front of the hotel, and from the dark interior emerged an elegant, white-haired, beautifully-attired D——— with an aristocratic profile and a cultured New England bearing. It could have been no one but Sylvia's regal father. "*!#@&!,*" Ronald muttered. The immensely uniformed doorman was already gliding forward; an eager bellhop followed the chauffeur to the back of the limousine and began stacking up a great number of suitcases. Uncle Ronald slid down in his seat and peered over the dash until the doorman had safely escorted the gentleman inside.

Chewey asked his uncle if he wanted to turn around and come back later, maybe.

For a short time, Ronald muttered to himself, throwing in an occasional *!#@&!* Then he straightened up, said, "No East Coast snob is gonna intimidate Ronald D———," and was out of the car before the doorman returned. Chewey explained that he and his uncle were dropping off some documents for Mr. Gaylord D———, and while the doorman and a second bellhop unloaded the boxes, he rushed inside to witness the awful donnybrook.

No curses or sounds of fisticuffs came to him from the reception area; no feathers floated in the air; no security men were hurrying toward the desk. All had the calm of a Christmas carol: the attractive young men and women behind the long desk, the upright, attentive figure of the concierge; the two elderly D———s engaged in friendly conversation beside a cart piled high with luggage. In fact, Chewey noted, the great, the ideally handsome, ninety-year-old Gaylord D——— appeared to be no more than sixty-five years of age. A smiling Uncle Ronald beckoned Chewey forward and introduced him to the great man, who displayed no irritation whatsover at the last-minute apppearance of the documents he had requested, who in fact regretted the necessity for such measures and hoped his new friend and future son-in-law would understand that in these sorry times it was a

father's unfortunate duty to ensure his only child's marital
well-being, especially since they had been so horribly misled
on a previous occasion not to be mentioned again. And
would these two fine chaps join him for a drink, perhaps in
that nice secluded corner of the lobby?

What seemed to Chewey a great number of bills were
distributed all around, and the three of them repaired to the
secluded corner, where they were promptly joined by an
obsequious waiter. Drinks were ordered and, with fawning
servility, delivered. The ageless Gaylord revealed his admiration for Ronald's splendid career, and over several Bombay
Sapphire martinis in the form of half as many doubles, the
charmed Ronald was induced to impart some of his favorite
tales of his industry's glorious Golden Age, along the way
and for the benefit of his new pal making clear that succes-
sive tidal waves of moola had washed his way, can you say
halleluja? The afternoon drifted into evening; the ever-more
worshipful waiter glided back and forth from the bar; suc-
cessive parties of guests checked in and out of the hotel.
Gaylord D———, who nursed two small glasses of sherry
throughout the entire conversation, expressed himself overjoyed with his daughter's good taste and good fortune,
which of course would be confirmed, he had no doubt, by a
jiffy little ramble through the papers now in his suite. To
Chewey, who drank only club soda, the great man's voice
seemed now and then to wobble off its New England axis
and tilt in a more westerly, Chicago-ish direction, but he
was in the food business and could not entirely trust his ear
for regional accents.

Only a single discordant note entered the long conversation, and only Chewey seemed to remark it. It was not
Gaylord's suggestion that Ronald might perhaps entrust
him with the handling of a portion of his holdings, specifically the money frittering itself away in mutual funds, for
the purpose of investing it in places no less safe but from
the financial viewpoint far more exciting. After a couple of

hours, Ronald had offered a clumsy hint that he would be open to just such a proposition. And Chewey supposed that Gaylord D——— knew what he was doing when it came to investments, even if his streetcar to Boston had experienced a long layover by the shores of Lake Michigan. The dissonance Chewey thought he had perceived came in when the great financier asked his future son-in-law, the world-famous comedian, if he ever enjoyed the sport of hunting.

Hunting? Chewey said to himself; and his uncle said, "Hunting?"

Didn't everyone know that characters like Ronald D———— and the Big Guy and their companions at the Friars' Club never went hunting? They played cards, they sometimes still rolled dice; they meandered across golf courses and played a little tennis. In pools, they floated rather than swam. Most of them disliked any activity that brought them out into actual daylight. Jeepers, Chewey remarked to himself, this guy doesn't have a clue.

"Hunting, yes, of course," Gaylord said. "Fellow like you, fellow with your experience, could handle a shotgun like nobody's business. Great fun. Get up before dawn, get rigged out in the proper gear, spend a couple hours banging away in the blind. I have a little place in Virginia. You ought to join me there sometime."

"A blind?" Chewey asked. "Like a duck blind?"

"That's the only kind I know," said the financier. "Tell you what, whatever we shoot, we give to you. Serve 'em as specials in one of your restaurants. You have wild duck on the menu now and then, don't you?"

Chewey shook his head. "I get my ducks from a farm on Long Island."

"Better taste, wild ones," Gaylord said. "Tang of genuine game."

Chewey's old enemy, heartburn, geared up to do its work.

• • •

A week after Gaylord D——— left town in possession of a handsome check representing the value of Ronald's mutual funds, Sylvia called everyone with two exciting bits of information. She and her honey-bunny had decided to skip all the fuss and bother of a big wedding and had been married the day before in a quiet civil ceremony at the L.A. County Courthouse. She was sorry none of the nephews had been invited, but they hadn't missed much, since the wedding had taken less than five minutes. And one family member had witnessed the event—the witness! At Ronald's insistence, her daughter, Lizzie, had flown in from Hawaii to have her baby where her mother could look after her.

Sylvia must have been guarding her daughter's health with the ferocity of a wolverine, for none of the nephews so much as glimpsed her until after the birth of her child, which followed the wedding announcement by two weeks. During those weeks, Ronald and Sylvia were preoccupied by some mysterious errand, some unspecified task that occupied most of their days and evenings. Chewey left half a dozen messages on their answering machine, none of them answered. On the fourth day of silence from the newlyweds, Chewey took a break from the restaurant and drove up into the Hollywood Hills to see if some disaster had occurred. He feared that he might come upon a smoking ruin, or three corpses eviscerated by wandering madmen.

On King's Road, the house stood intact, altered from his last visit only by the absence of the real estate agent's sign. Ronald had talked his bride out of selling the place, anyhow, good news to faithful Chewey, who loved the funny old house and saw no reason why his uncle should spend upwards of five million for a place off Mulholland. Mel Tormé used to live up there, but Mel Tormé was dead, and why would you want to live in his neighborhood anyhow? Chewey rang the bell, pounded on the door, peered in through the windows, all to no effect. One car, a two-seater Mercedes convertible, was visible through the windows in the garage door, but not his uncle's old runabout or Sylvia's new Mercedes sedan. That night Chewey called and left another message. Late the next afternoon, Bluey telephoned him at the restaurant and said that he, too, had driven up to the house and found it empty. At a family dinner the following evening convened expressly to discuss the Ronald problem, the three brothers were startled by the vehemence of their wives' dislike of their new aunt.

Cosima said: "She's a gold digger, and I don't trust her for a second."

Sharon said: "She's a gold digger, and a conwoman, and I don't trust her father, either. He's supposed to be ninety years old, but didn't Chewey say he looked sixty-five? I bet he isn't even her father."

With her usual candour, Pinkytoes said: "She's a gold digger, he's a conman, and do you think that this Lizzie is really her daughter? They've already stolen something like half a million in mutual funds, what's to stop them from killing Ronald to get all the rest?"

Two days later, Uncle Ronald strolled into Dewey D———'s Ducks Unlimited and apologized for having dropped out of sight. He looked healthy, serene, and in a blissful mood. Dewey could have kissed him on the spot. Oh, Ronald was sorry if the kids had been anxious about him, but they oughtta loosen up, y'know?, oughtta get some fun outta life insteada worryin' about an old coot like him night and day. Hell, the old coot was having the time of his life, no kidding. Sylvia, his bride, made him happier even than he had been in the days when everybody made a living outta going crazy. Couldn't believe his luck. Do anything to make that woman happy.

Chewey's heartburn kicked in again. What had the lovely bride required to make her happy over the past two weeks?

The darling kid was never happy in the old house, Chewey knew that. Forget about it being too higgledy-piggledy to allow the girl to express her natural talents, how could she ever be happy there, how could she feel at home? If he weren't such an insensitive old fool, he'd've understood the deal right away—you can't expect one woman to live in another one's house. So, like Chewey knew, they put the old place on the market. Whaddya know, sold right off the bat. And the very next day, their agent had shown them the perfect place. No kidding, perfect. Square feet up the wazoo, lotsa wall space, billiard room, library, four bedrooms, four baths, tennis court, big big pool, and best of all, the same great view he had before but even better. Amazing! Where was it? Oh, that was perfect, too. Just off Mulholland Drive, Drake Lane, on the crest of the hill. Mel Tormé's old neighborhood, did Chewey know that?

"I hope you'll be very happy there," Chewey said.

Happy? If his bride was happy, Ronald was happy. She *loved* the new place, walked around all day with a grin on her face. The kid loved decorating, and that's what had kept them so busy over the past coupla weeks. In and out of furniture showrooms, design centers, rug warehouses, art galleries, the studios of guys who made stained-glass windows and marble mosaics and art plumbing fixtures. . . . Did Chewey even *know* there were guys who made art plumbing fixtues? Of course on toppa all the decorating, she had Lizzie's baby to perk her up. Her first grandkid! By the way, Lizzie flipped when she saw the new bunkhouse. Got her room already picked out, and it'll be ready by her next visit! He hadda say one thing, Sylvia was right when she said her daughter was a beauty, that was for sure. Those two, you could almost mistake 'em for sisters. And Sylvia said the funniest thing when Lizzie had her baby. They walked into the room, see? About half an hour after the birth, this was. Well, Sylvia goes up, kisses her daughter, and picks up the little baby. Then she says—get this—she says, *You know, I've never seen one of these before.* With her own daughter lying right there in the bed!

"That's funny, all right," Chewey said. "Uncle Ronald,

why didn't you invite us to the wedding? We would have loved being there."

Oh hell, there was hardly enough room in that judge's little chamber for Lizzie's belly, much less the three nephews and their wives. And they had to have Lizzie there, poor kid was only days away from the big event, and no insurance, of course, because kids never had insurance these days, they couldn't afford it. So Ronald was happy to cover the medical bills. What was he supposed to do? Let the kid give birth in an emergency room? A man has responsibilities, after all. That's why he put the new house in Sylvia's name.

Reeling, Chewey barely heard his uncle say that he was sorry to break up the happy confab, but he had to pick up the girls and the baby and drive them to the airport. Lizzie was going back to Hawaii on the afternoon flight.

Were there afternoon flights to Hawaii? Chewey said his car was bigger than Ronald's old runabout, and it was parked right out in back. Could he spare the time? Of course he could. In fact, he had to leave the restaurant anyhow—a new, nearly radioactive roach powder had come on the market, and Chewey wanted to see if it worked as well as it was supposed to. Ronald said, Great, this way you get to meet Lizzie. Whatta peach.

On the way to the old house, Chewey realized that he had no idea if the baby was male or female, or what its name was.

"Uncle Ronald, what name did Lizzie give her baby?"

Ronald wasn't sure if he'd heard the baby's name. On the whole, he didn't think so. Maybe Lizzie hadn't named it yet.

"Well, is it a boy or a girl?"

Ronald wasn't certain he'd heard that, either. It was one or the other, though, that was for sure.

When they pulled up in front of the house on King's Road, Ronald jumped out of the car and ran up the walk before Chewey's feet hit the asphalt. Chewey came around the car and started up the walk toward the open front door.

He could hear his uncle calling his wife's name, as he had on the afternoon when the nephews and their wives had been introduced to her. Chewey went through the doorway and stood in the hallway, listening to his uncle yell "Sylvia!" from the direction of the kitchen. He walked into the living room where Sylvia had so becomingly adorned the Art Deco sofa. Today the sofa was empty, and no fire burned in the fireplace. Above the mantel, a pale rectangle showed where Aunt Maizy's portrait had hung. Quick footsteps began to mount the stairs in the hallway. Ronald yelled "Sylvia!" again. Chewey's eyes moved back to the mantel—her ashes were gone, too. What had happened? He banished his sudden vision of Sylvia throwing the portrait into a blazing fire and following it with her predecessor's ashes.

From upstairs came a clamor of voices that quickly softened into whispers.

Sylvia's voice called out, "Chewey, are you here, darling?"

Chewey allowed that he was there.

"And are you really going to be a sweetheart and drive us to the airport? You don't have to, you know."

Chewey insisted on driving them to the airport.

He went out into the hallway and looked up the staircase. A low rumble of conversation came through the door to the guest room. The door flew open, and Sylvia came rushing down, followed by Uncle Ronald and a slim young woman carrying a baby basket. Sylvia ordered him out of the way. The plane took off in an hour, they had to get out there right away, so get in your car, Chewey, and show us how fast you can drive. Chewey jumped aside, and Sylvia hurtled past him and out the still-open front door. Ronald came rushing after, a small overnight bag swinging from his left hand. Lizzie flew past so quickly, he hardly took her in: He had a blurry impression of gypsy-ish hair around the hard but attractive face of a woman not far from thirty. He could not see the baby at all.

Sylvia and Lizzie had climbed into the backseat before

Ronald was finished locking the door. Sylvia motioned them forward with a furious wave of her hand.

For the first ten minutes of the journey to the airport, the two women huddled together and spoke too softly to be heard. Ronald told a long, pointless story about Joe Palooka, that poor bastard. The baby did not utter a peep. Looking into his rearview mirror, Chewey saw the two heads, blond and dark, move apart. Sylvia leaned forward and patted Chewey's shoulder with a delicate porcelain hand. It was so nice of him to do this, wasn't Chewey being sweet, Lizzie?

"We better get there in time," Lizzie said. "You know what I mean."

Chewey asked about the baby's name.

"It doesn't really *need* a name yet, does it?"

He asked if her husband was picking her up at the airport in Hawaii.

"*Hawaii?*" she asked, then immediately said, "Oh, yeah. No, he's not. He can't. The stupid jackass is dead."

When he found her face in the rearview mirror, it was shadowed by her dark tangles of hair.

"Fell off a mountain, the dope," said Sylvia. "Right outside Calcutta. Calcutta's where the bad husbands go."

For the rest of the journey, Ronald rambled cheerfully through memories of the golden days. The child never made a sound.

Chewey pulled up in front of the enormous terminal and began to open his door. Again, Sylvia's slender fingers tapped his shoulder. No, he shouldn't get out, he'd done enough, she would just run Lizzie to her gate and say goodbye, don't be a silly old silly.

Protesting that at least he had to give a proper farewell, Chewey ignored the grip on his shoulder and got out of the car. "Me too," Ronald said, and got out on the other side.

"As long as you're out there, hold this." Lizzie thrust the baby basket at him through the open door. Startled, Chewey looked down into the depth of the blankets and saw a pink, immobile face that might nearly have been made of plastic. Lizzie scrambled off the backseat and snatched the basket away from him. Then Sylvia was before him, giving him an air kiss. She gave another to Ronald. Her head turned toward the glass doors, Lizzie stepped sideways. Chewey moved with her and again peered into the baby basket. A wide blue eye stared upward, though not, apparently, at him. Very slowly, a broad pink lid swam over the blue iris and swam back up.

"Nice to meet you, I'm sure," said Lizzie's voice. The blue eye, the perfect skin, and the blankets disappeared. He straightened up to see Lizzie's back fleeing toward the glass doors, her mother hurrying along in her wake.

• • •

THE new radioactive insecticide worked like a wonder, but for two days after it was administered, every duck that came out of Ducks Unlimited's kitchen tasted like a chemistry set. Chewey was forced to go on the Internet. He consulted search engines and searched for newsgroups that might discuss his problem. Alt.restaurants.infestation sounded promising, but turned out to be a forum in which food service personnel griped about their customers. Alt.burning cockroaches.zone, which he tried on a lark, brought a loose, baggy critical perspective to the problem of head lice. Alt.foodies and alt.kitchens missed the mark completely. Chewey spent so much of his evenings at his computer that Cosima grew sulky and the baby, Afterburn, screamed when he picked him up.

He was just investigating a group called alt.insects. demonic.entities when he answered the telephone and heard Sylvia's silken voice, beginning as usual without preamble, telling him something about travel plans. He wanted to hang up; he wished he could find a newsgroup that would tell him how to rid the world of Sylvia; what he said was,

"Excuse me, my mind was wandering. Could you repeat that?"

This was three days after Lizzie's typhoon-like exit from Los Angeles.

Chewey should really take something to aid his concentration, Sylvia said, but all right, she would start over. Without Lizzie around, the house in the Hollywood Hills seemed intolerable. She was sorry, but she couldn't stay there another day. Sylvia's mental well-being, in fact, the state of her health in general, compelled her to go off on a nice little journey somewhere until the house on Drake Lane was ready for her "touch." Some distant cousins in the Cotswolds had been literally begging her to come for a nice long visit, and she thought this was the perfect time to answer their wish. Ronnie understood completely. He *wanted* her to go. Well, Chewey knew how his uncle Ronnie felt about family. It was *everything* to him, simply *everything*. But Sylvia could not help but feel guilty anyhow, leaving Ronnie all alone like that. Would Chewey please look after the darling, would he try to keep him entertained in the absence of his honey-bunch? She would also call her father, the splendid Gaylord, to see if he could think of some little project the two of them could do together. Wouldn't that be the sweetest thing, Sylvia's two darling men having guy-type fun together? Anyhow, Sylvia wanted Chewey to know that she had booked a flight to London for the afternoon of the following day, so maybe he could be a very, very good boy and invite his uncle for dinner tomorrow night?

"Sure thing," Chewey said, and went back to his research. By the time he came across alt.bugs.goodriddance an hour later, he had forgotten all about his promise. The things he saw as he wandered through newsgroups blotted out everything else, and he did not get to bed until two in the morning.

Soon after he arrived at the restaurant the next morning, he saw something disappearing under his gas range that made him want to turn around and walk back out. It could not have been a roach; although he had never seen a rat that large, there was a faint possibility that it was a rat. A rat the size of a Border collie, with insect-like hind legs. Wishing that he were holding a .357 Magnum, Chewey got on his knees and looked under the range. The thing had gone somewhere else, perhaps into the walls. He could see no big holes or openings, but a thing like that probably had the power to slip through cracks. For some reason, he remembered the expressionless blue eye that had winked at him from the depths of the baby basket. For a moment his head swam and his stomach threatened to turn inside out.

He stretched out on the floor in front of the gas range, breathing in big, noisy gulps. The dizziness and nausea passed. He got to his feet and went to the front of the restaurant, where his manager was punching figures from an account book into an adding machine. Chewey told his manager to call the staff and tell them not to come to work for three days. Then he told him to go to the discount store and come back with a dozen boxes of the radioactive roach killer. The manager said Chewey looked sort of funny, was he feeling all right?

"Not really," Chewey said. "Get that stuff, okay? Buy their whole stock. Buy every box they have."

His manager told him he ought to go home, and not to worry about the radioactive bug powder. He would put it in all the right places, now you go home, Boss, you look like you need some rest.

Chewey saw that mechanical eye winking up at him.

Uncle Ronald! he thought.

The manager picked up the telephone and began speed-dialing the chef and the headwaiter, who would then notify their men of the three-day closing. Chewey waved a sketchy good-bye and went back through the kitchen, being careful not to look too closely at anything, through the rear door, and into the alley, where his car baked in the sunlight.

When he drove into the street, he took his cell phone from his pocket. Uncle Ronald picked up on the second ring.

"Uncle Ronald," he said, "I just remembered that I talked to Sylvia last night, and she wanted me to ask you to dinner. Why don't you come over about six? Cosima's always asking about you, and the kids would love it."

Well, said Uncle Ronald, he'd love it, too, but he was afraid he couldn't make it that night. As a matter of fact, he was going to be out of town for the next four or five nights. That Sylvia, she was really something. You'd think a guy was in danger of falling apart, the way she worried over him. So she gets up and goes to visit her cousins in the Cotswolds, so what? Is he going to break down and go nuts just because he's on his own for a coupla weeks? Does he need baby-sitters now, do people have to put him to bed at night? It was ridiculous, but he loved her for it.

"Uncle Ronald, it's just an invitation to dinner," Chewey said.

Yeah, but see, here is Sylvia coming at him on two fronts, get the picture? Not only does she call his favorite nephew, she also goes and calls her daddy, good old Gaylord, and whaddyaknow, Gaylord loves the idea, he got right on the phone with him, worked out all the details right there on the spot.

"What details?" Chewey asked.

For the trip, dummy. What did he think, a man could get organized without making *arrangements*? Gaylord got his plane tickets, set up a car to take him to the airport. Actually, the car was due now, that's why he picked up so fast—he thought it might be the driver. Everything else he needed, Gaylord would have waiting for him.

"You're going to Boston?" Chewey asked. "You're going to stay with Gaylord?"

Hell no, Boston? *Boston?* Gimme a break. This was gonna be an adventure, what kind of adventure could you have in Boston? No, Gaylord was in *Virginia*, he was inviting him to *Virginia*, where he had this like duck-hunting camp or something, been in his family for like three generations, everything first class, no discomfort, even the ducks are like trained to fly where you aim the shotgun, piece a cake. Just the two of them, the dogs, and the ducks, plus a cook who comes in at mealtimes.

"Uncle Ronald, I don't think you should go," Chewey said. "I mean it. I don't even think duck hunting is legal in Virginia." But he heard no companiable hum in the receiver; his connection had been severed. When he redialed, Uncle Ronald said, "Hel. . . . Chewey? . . . Darn phone . . . Hate these blasted . . . Hey, the driver's here." The line went dead.

HOLE IN THE HEAD

Whitley Strieber

I didn't notice it at first. I'd heard nothing, certainly felt nothing. Some people probably notice right away. You'd assume. Me, I did not notice for quite some time that I was dead.

I had been in the living room watching television. In fact, I was watching a Yankees game. Third inning, Yanks are up, Jeter is on second, one out. O'Neill comes to bat. He's hitting .278, so there's somewhat of a reason to be interested. I was watching the at-bat, thinking about how much Muziak looks like a gorilla, when I noticed that Muziak *was* a gorilla. I blinked my eyes. Nothing. He was still a gorilla.

This fascinated me. Dan Muziak had become a large ape in a White Sox uniform. This was what I saw. What I did not see was the gun. I did not hear the shot. I felt absolutely nothing. It's called being killed instantly. So I watched the ape pitch O'Neill out. I wondered if the umpires would be upset that the Sox had fielded an actual gorilla. This is what happens to us dead men: Dream and reality meld into one seamless whole. Kind of confusing. Things keep appearing.

All of a sudden I was in my boyhood room at home, taking pictures of Kelso, my dachshund. Then I thought, I'm asleep and I'm dreaming of when I was taking pictures of Kelso. Then I thought, this is the most vivid damn dream I've ever had. Kelso had the distinction of being run over by the 104 bus twice and living through it both times. He died of "generalized organ dissolution" two years after the last time the bus driver, Mario Johnson, tears streaming down his face, brought him up to the apartment.

What the hell got me thinking about Kelso, I was wondering, when I saw that somebody was coming slowly up the walk, coming to the house. I heard the doorbell ring. And all of a sudden, my boyhood is gone back into its keepsake drawer. My good friend Rollo Winter is here. He's got a bottle of champagne. What the hell is this? I go to the door but Joanie is already there. She lets Rollo in and he goes into the living room and looks down at my chair.

"Ding dong," he says, "the old shit is dead."

I chuckle, nodding as I follow him into the room. "Not quite," I say. But I also know that the chair is not empty. There is somebody in the chair. And I know, also, who that somebody is. But we don't think about that, do we? We don't think about death, not on a peaceful Saturday afternoon when you are in the silver of middle-aged health. Late middle age.

Joanie says, "It was just so easy, once I got up the nerve, it was just so amazing, all of a sudden it was almost—oh, automatic." She went twirling around the room, her skirts flying. "Ding dong, ding dong," she sang. Then she danced up to Rollo. "How do we get away with it?"

"You."

"Me?"

"Shot him. I didn't. I wasn't even here. I was shopping down on Front Street."

Shot? Shot who? And then it hits me, hits me very hard——if the guy in the chair is me and I am standing here in the living room watching my wife sail around singing "Ding dong, ding dong" then what in the world is up?

I went over to the chair, looked down. It was me, okay, with a neat hole right in the top of my head. It had bled, and there was a good bit of blood on my neck and down my back. She'd come up from behind and shot straight down into my brain. Killed me so fast I didn't feel so much as a whisper of breeze as the bullet penetrated.

Then Rollo picks up something from the floor. He carries it in a handkerchief. It is a little blue pistol that I have never seen before. Now, what does this mean? I can see, I can hear. In fact, I am here, definitely here.

Okay. I am falling apart. Nervous. Yeah, let's say that I am a little nervous. Rollo has the hand of the me in the chair. He is putting the gun in the hand. A glance at the television: The first-base umpire is a hippo in a blue suit. You try and figure that out.

Rollo says, "Joanie, you're an idiot."

She stops dancing with the champagne. She stops and stares at him. "What?"

"This is not a believable suicide you got here."

"Why not?"

Rollo manipulates my arm with the pistol in it. "It'd be, like, some kinda yoga thing."

Joanie puts her beautiful, tapered fingers on her smooth, softly blushed cheeks. "Holy shit," she says.

"That's right. He couldn't have done this to himself. Not a shot like—goddamnit, why would you *ever* think to shoot him in the one place he could not shoot himself."

"I didn't want him to see me."

"Oh, great. That's just great. Now we got a murder investigation to get through. Oh, nice. Very nice."

A giraffe is running the bases. Has Michael Jordan gone back into baseball? "Turn off the TV," I say. There is no response at all. They are entirely concentrated on the gun. Damn thing. Where did she get it?

And then I see her: She's going into Nadle's. It's last week. She is looking at the rows of pistols under glass. Nadle's Gun Shop. I've passed it a thousand times on my way down to the office and back. Never stopped there, though. I am looking at the rows of pistols. Obsessing.

"I want a gun for my purse," she says to a wide, grinning man who is probably Mr. Nadle.

"That would be a pistol," he says. "I have a very nice little number right here." He calls it a "number." It's a scene circa 1956. In fact, I could believe that the whole gun shop is circa 1956. And it is, because now it's my dad buying a pistol. He's buying a slightly larger "number" from the father of the current Mr. Nadle. It is the pistol that will blow his brains across the mudroom just six days from now, the pistol that will be in both of my eleven-year-old hands.

Thunder rumbles, the first sound I have heard since I was killed. It rumbles across the sky, through the living room, the whole house, a great, bellowing, echoing blast of thunder. Outside, things are changing. Wind is blowing the blossoms off the trees. Huge, bulging clouds tower into the sky. An old tramp is walking down the street, his collar turned up against the wind, his hat pulled down in anticipation of the rain.

I know that the old tramp is dangerous, that he must not see me, that if he does see me I will be in great peril, in peril of my soul. For that old tramp is my father, who has been walking the pathways of heaven for forty years, looking for the boy who took his life.

He passes, though—miraculously, it seems to me. He takes his storm with him, and now there are robins on the lawn. They have gossamer wings, the wings of fairies or damn big bugs. I see a hamburger on the TV. Rollo and Joanie are struggling and yelling themselves hoarse over the placement of the gun. What will they do? How will they explain that I, who already have short arms, have managed to reach up and fire a .22 hollow-point bullet down into my brain from directly above?

How long, I wonder, did she stand back there? The whole first half of the third inning? Longer? I guess that the moment of my death was marked by Muziak turning into a gorilla. He's still a gorilla, now that we are back to the game. A hippo and two warthogs are umpiring. The teams consist of a pack of apes and a pack of dogs, except for Paul O'Neill. But why a giraffe? He's not that tall.

Oh, I see. I am seeing right into their minds, and in his secret self, Paul O'Neill would *love* to be a giraffe.

My God, but Joanie is beautiful. To think that I can bed that dream of a woman anytime I want.

She is in the kitchen drinking coffee with Jim Beam in it. I don't believe in expensive bourbon. It's no better than Jimmy, nothing is. Okay, so I'm a brand freak. My bourbon is Jimmy, my scotch is Johnny Blue, my cigar is the H. Uppman No. 2, the richest, roughest, sweetest smoke ever rolled by the hand of man. My friends Hoy and Benno bring them in from Mexico. They supply all sorts of people. They are basically cigar smugglers. May they be praised before the throne of God.

I go into the den. My den. Open my humidor. Only, that does not happen. I am fascinated, disturbed. I can't open a humidor? What can I do? Anything? Nothing? My father wanders the byways of the world, looking for the boy who took his life.

I slipped, you see. I did not mean to . . . but, uh, well, I sort of—no, I *did not!* I hear the mechanism clicking and ticking as various parts of it are engaged. My fat boy's hand is the motive power, the muscles being commanded to fire by my brain, and the energy in my brain comes from—oh, dear. Oh, dear. It is not an accident. No, I have always known this. It was no accident that I killed Dad. I just plain shot him. I shot him, and now I see the bullet coming out of the barrel. It's spinning fast, moving slow. We are in another phase of time, me and the bullet. It comes slowly out of the billow of gases that surround it, traveling into the clear air.

I am not going to miss. That's what I think back there in the sun-flooded mudroom at the age of eleven. I am not going to miss. But I tell myself—I *tell* myself—that it's all automatic, it's just the gun, it's just a game, it's just just just—murder.

Murder! I murdered him. Patricide. Is that it? I murdered him with malice and I got away brand spanking clean, a scared little boy in a big room saying, "It just went off all of a sudden and I killed my daddy and and . . ." Inside I am going, *"Owheeeeeeiiaaayyyy!"* So they send me home to my quiet house and Mom and Missy, and we are all quietly happy for many, many years.

He walks these hills in a long black mood, looking for the boy who took his life. He has been looking for forty years. He never stops, not day nor night, striding up and down the streets in the storm without end, the slashing rain, the wind bowing the trees, the lightning that shatters the air. He wants my soul. He is going to put me in a cage and hang me in a window, and I am going to be there for a long, long time.

And here I got murdered myself. I got shot. Oh, hell, I am shot! I race through the halls of the house, my feet not pounding on the floor I don't feel. She murdered me. Oh, damn, I am dead. I am dead, it is just now really hitting me. Oh, hell, I am dead, I can't get back in my body because nothing I can do will make it move or change in any way.

My body is sitting there with a gun in its hand and a bullet hole right in the top of the head. Now, isn't this going to be an interesting conversation we're going to have with Officer Sneed? He is our town police chief, who will be the officer who comes.

They haven't called him yet. They are running around like two chickens, clucking and scratching and squawking at each other. A terrible botch has been made of the crime. It would be obvious to anybody that murder has been done. Obvious, certainly, to Officer Sneed. Bill Sneed, who has a smoking problem and a drinking problem and every Saturday gets a spanking from his wife.

Now, can you beat that, that big old pale hulk of a man drooped over the lap of his old lady, and she pounds away with a bath brush while reading *Cosmopolitan*. This ritual has been part of their lives for forty years. In fact, he asked her to do it when they were blushing and young, and she did it because she thought, It is such a strange request that he will marry me if I agree to this. And so he did, and they have been happy enough ever since. He looks forward to his Saturday thwacking, and she to the rump-bump that ensues thereafter.

How wonderful are the ways of the world. And we dead, we see it all.

OH MY GOD HOW I CAN *SEEEEEEEEEE*!

Way away to the horizons of time, the beginning and the end, alpha and omega. I see it all, from the first muddy worm to the last, the whole whooping, crawling, roaring, flying, snarling, singing journey of the living from the first heaving of the mud to the long autumn beneath a restless future sun.

How boring. How claustrophobic. Is there no way out of all this knowledge?

Well, I can watch the little play play out here in the House of Mirth. In fact, I must. Because if I go outside, I am going to have to face the Master of the Storm, and he is going to punish me very hard for the crime that I got away with so squeaky clean.

I got trauma counseling—Dr. Jim Fisher, Jimbo, who was basically into fishing. We talked fishing. Later, we went fishing for bass with flies we had made under hard light. Jimbo was wise in the ways of the largemouth bass. He had a mastery with the cast of the line, and it drops again upon the still water, lying out behind the fly just as softly as the skate of a water spider. Oh hell, I am killed!

Why? Joanie baby, *why?* My God, it's happened. I'm dead. I'm a damn dead man! And hayleelooya, we *do* go on. *Hayyaloola lawd!* I race around the living room, circling that old dead me in the chair with the gun pushed down against the top of his head—oh, laylooya we *do* go on! Hip hop, I can jump up to the ceiling and then just settle like a leaf. Rollo you bozo, I see what you're thinking. You're thinking about the million dollar policy. She doesn't know that all the dough goes to the partnership and thus to you.

Damn, Mike Splitt's in it with you! Oh, hell, Mike, you suckin' fuckin' dickhead of an accountant. You silver tongued frog prince. O you did pull the wool. Hey, *sucka,* you wanna get it on? Telling me it was a tax advantage to will my partnership residue to that damn trust.

My God, Rollo, Rollie boy, hey, you are one sinister son-embitch. She's gonna get her ass arrested and you want that, you want it. Cause my ladybaby is gonna go to jail and you are gonna haul tail to Mexico and live it up-o. Oh.

Clever boys. You've been planning and plotting and here comes Mike with tears in his eyes, followed by Arnold German, our lawyer, who wastes no time in saying, "My God, hon, you killed the bastard finally."

"He just shot—shot—oh, Arnie, is that what it looks like?"

"You don't shoot yourself in the top of the head."

"He did! Didn't he, Rollie?"

"There was a family dispute, Arnie."

"Rollie!"

"Have the police been . . ."

All eyes to the front. The door swings open. In comes a whole clown college composed of cops, followed by Officer Sneed, who got his gun butt caught in the door handle of his brand-new cop car and so was slowed. But here he comes, pot pouring out across his Big Tex belt buckle. Sneed's dream is to be called Big Tex.

And then the bastard goes up to Joanie and whispers, "Did we get him?"

"Done," says Joanie, "with a wrinkle."

"Oh, Jeez, guys," says Big Tex, "I can't certify this a suicide with a hole *there*. Who shot him?"

"Her." Arnold tosses his chin in the direction of her flouncing wiggery. "Smartie over there."

"Jerusalem."

The younger cops have trooped into my den to steal cigars, which they are doing with blasted abandon. Come on, Joanie, wake up! The bastards are breaking into my humidor! I get killed and the cops who aren't in on it are only interested in loot. Shoot!

Okay, let's see. There's Joanie, guilty. Rollie, guilty. Arnie as sin, Mikey as sin, Big Tex as sin. Wow. I was murdered by a damn committee. And all for a lousy million.

Except . . . no, look at them, look at their minds. They're dancing with delight over all the money! God, they loaded me with insurance, dammem. Four mil, no five. Five million dollars on my head and I didn't even know it.

And here comes Lucia Cadwallader in her too-old Merc and her live-in hair. Look at her smiling, all cheer and goo. My insurance agent's in on it, too! Lawsy me, everybody's guilty.

I feel bad. I'm gonna miss bein' alive. Miss my den with my Internet porn and my fat Cubans, miss my slick Beamer and my pretty forty-footer *Miss Smith,* sailing her in the sun, and I'm gonna miss you, Joanie, oh, because you see, I really am in love with you. Oh, I used to lie in you and on you, and gain my soul's joy in the whispers and slick of you. And you, you just lay there with your button eyes and your actor's sour heart, you traitorous little sowlet. Dincha? Dincha? Oeeeeee! I'm gonna *haunt* you. I am gonna haunt you so damn hard.

Thing is, how? I mean, I don't see any haunting school around here. In fact, all I see is what I've always seen, my living room around me, my car outside, the sprinkler I set at dawn still twinkling in the noon sun. In fact, being dead is just like being alive except they can't see you and they can't hear you and you can't do nothin' but whine and wail in your own damn soul.

Except there is one thing that is new. Down in the street, Dad goes back and forth, for dad is conducting this whole thing like Stokowski conducted the Phil. It was Dad who came to her like a breeze in the afternoon and said, "Murder him, Joanie. . . .'Cause if you do, you'll be rich and he'll be . . . oh, how fine that would be." Dad whispered and tempted and made her mind fly from the port of ordinary thought, into the storm of danger and murder.

So she did it all, all right, except for the top of the head bang you're dead thing. Now what're they gonna do?

Cut her out, sacrifice her to the stone of the court, that's Rollie's notion. Big Tex would like to get away from his paddlin' frump and take a little a that Joanie medicine instead. Arnie and Mikey, they don't care about Joanie, just the money. Moola is what Arnie calls it in his mind. Moola, he keeps thinking. And we went fishing, we two, up on the Monster Coulee where the largemouths live in the deep eddies, and yes, we did a little thing there—oh, hell, it was nothing. I mean, just a guy thing. We got over-excited from killing fish. Somethin' about all that wet, slick skin and all of a sudden—gee, a balding accountant and a cigar-chomping import huckster? No accounting for taste, is there? But he did a sweet thing, Mikey, that now I am grateful for.

In death, you cannot taste, you cannot feel, you cannot touch. But everything is so vivid, so rich-looking, so . . . oh. Joanie just damn killed me and what do I want? To insert my memory of a hard-on into the wonder of her. But also, there was a little finger of desire in me for the rougher tucks of a guy riding my back, and Mikey did that. Afterward, we made bass poached in white wine in that rough cabin, and sat on the porch and ate our bass and drank the vino that was left.

So I have that. I possess it. My memories are, like, in a kind of backpack or figurative pocket.

Joanie, damn you. DAMN YOU!

Why did I murder you, Dad? Or did I? Yeah, I did. I did it because I just sorta kinda . . . could. You flew. You flew all the way across the mudroom with your lips slack and flopping and your hands spread against me like you'd seen the evil eye. You flew backward and hit that wall with all your weight and threw up everything you just ate, the sausage and the french fries and the coffee and then came the blood, a rather magnificent gusher of it that made brief rivers and was gone through the floor.

Mom had you cremated. I lost the ashes in some move or other, that little box we kept in my room, in the first house on my mantel, in the second on my sill, and in the third . . . well, I sold your ashes to Paul Moon, who wanted to do a ritual with them in hopes of interesting Satan.

Fifty bucks, and then I see the tape, they have pissed in you and are smearing you black and wet upon their naked bellies and their tongues.

Their idea: Get Satan to pick stocks for them. We were younger then.

There are ancient codes that the living forget, but Dad has not forgotten. Smeared on his forehead like Ash Wednesday ash is ash from that night, still wet with the piss of teenagers. "You sold my ashes for fifty dollars. Desecration, desecration."

The power of the father matters here. We know ourselves in terms of the long blood and the long home of the soul, the ancient days through which we have wandered.

I got murdered, damnit! I want to drive my car. I want to play golf on Saturday. I want to be heard and to care, and to be made whole by whatever wholeness may still pertain to me. But I think that I must wander here longer, for I murdered and was murdered and there are scandalous knots to untangle.

"We better get him buried fast," Big Tex says in a new, growlly tone I haven't heard before. He jots something on a piece of form paper. "Hopefully the coroner won't look too hard."

Nah, he'll look. He's *got to look*, because if he doesn't then I am tossed off like a broke-down old tiger. I watch them moving me and that is a very strange thing. I tell me to scream. Nada. I tell my hand to fist, my arm to bash. No. I try to get in. Inside, it's as slick as mercury. I just slide out. All of the attachments of the body are closed.

I'm in the living room, but when I look down my front I see only the floor. When I try to feel myself, nothing feels as nothing.

So where am I and what am I and who am I now anyway? I don't know where to go. Is there no heaven? And what about that light you're supposed to go in? That's nowhere around here.

I am getting very pissed off here. What am I going to do with myself, floating around unable to talk or to do anything, just basically looking over the shoulders of my own murderers until I—what?

Oh, God. What if this is eternity? It's this—just hanging around watching, nothing to do, nobody to talk to, nowhere to go. Oh, God. When I was a boy—a Catholic boy—I used to commit mortal sins on purpose because heaven seemed so dreadfully dull. Who wants to spend even ten minutes praying, let alone all eternity? But this—watching the damn roses forever. Help.

Help me. I'm dead and I'm scared, I'm real scared. I got to go out there and face my dad. But at least he's company. Plus, the day is getting on. It's going to be night soon. What do I do then? Do the dead sleep? I'm not tired but I remember how nice it was to be tired. I'm not hungry but I remember meatball sandwiches and Thai spring rolls and Dr Pepper and Pacifico Beer, oh yowsa. Oh, yes, the steaks at Sparks in Manhattan.

Why am I scared like this, scared of the night, the on-coming bloom of darkness? I know something in my deepest instincts about the night. The dead are different in the dark. Something is going to happen. Out front, Dad waits. For the first time, I hear him. Or rather, feel him: "Why did you kill me? Why did you take my life from me?"

An agony like a twisting, burning knife goes through me. Why did I? Dad, I don't know. I just did it. I shot you through the heart because I could shoot you through the heart. And no, you never did any awful thing to me, you always tried to give me a good home and all of that. I took your life, Daddy, and I don't know why.

But at least Joanie, you know.

I'm on a silver table. How did this happen? I am in the living room and in the hospital at the same time. The coroner is a kid from some Asian country, a kid with curly hair and deep eyes and he is thinking about a girl too tall and exotic and so soft and smooth that she is like an altar. You want to go to heaven, little coroner, go in her arms. There is heaven and God in the woman.

Damn, where's the light that is supposed to take you into ecstasy? Damn, I need it because he is cutting me open and I am watching my insides get taken out and weighed. I am butt-naked in front of him and a woman and another guy. They don't even treat me like meat.

"This man was murdered," the coroner says. He writes on a form. Then they dump my organs back in—oh, there's my liver, it is pale pink. There's my guts, they are knobby and probably still full of shit. There is my jaw and I do remember a pain on dying: It was in my jaw. Yes, a sort of tight twisting back behind my throat. The bullet blasting down through my brain and into my neck, I suppose.

The piece of paper goes into an out box. For me, that piece of paper is marked by golden light. You see, when you are wronged like I was wronged, you want them to be punished. At first, this feels like revenge. But later, you find out something different.

So. So? Wasn't the deal that there was this huge, warm light and the drill is, you go into the light. Or you go before St. Peter to be judged? I mean, I was a little boy when I kilt my dad. I was not by the law responsible. And he laughs, "Heh heh heh." And then he says, "By the *law*," with such utter scorn in his voice. He says, I was a good father, son. I was so in love with you. When I saw that pistol rising, a hurt went through my heart, son. I sang you to sleep, son, remember "Papa's gonna give you a diamond ring," o my son?

He's coming up the walk in a long black coat, his hat pulled down over his eyes. He's singing. Why not, he's happy, happy at last. My God, he can't sing a note. "My oh my, what a wonderful day." Maybe that's why I shot him. He comes closer and closer. We are face-to-face now. The pupils of his eyes are compound, as if they've been dissected off the face of a fly. His skin—the skin of his soul—is compiled of what look to me like millions and millions of insect wings. His is the most profoundly lifeless face I have ever beheld. To see him moving, to see his hideously bright smile, makes me feel as if I am ice itself, the very glacier at the bottom of the world. "Want a cigar," he asks and his voice—his *voice*—ripples like a brook that we loved, out behind the old house in Stamford, when I was very young. The words penetrate to the heart of my heart, and I must tell you, I never knew that I had such feeling in me. Remorse does not begin to describe it. I feel as if I have stolen the best thing in the world from the most innocent creature ever born. And he says, "Light?"

I realize that he's given me a fabulous cigar. It's not branded, but I can tell instantly that it's very, very good.

The ever so slightly moist coolness of the wrap, the firm pack of the leaf inside, the dense aroma of cured tobacco—I know a good cigar. A glance tells me that it's already cut. I put it to my lips. He lights me up. I draw.

The smoke is moist and warm, promising a legendary richness of flavor. But there is no flavor. There is only the barely perceptible presence of the heat. And he says, "Nice, eh?"

"Yeah. Oh, yeah."

He drops his arm over my shoulder. "Pal," he says, "I don't think there's any easy way to tell you this. But I'm here to take you to—"

"I know I'm going to hell."

"Hell, hell. You're goin' to heaven." He pronounces the word with a sepulchral grace.

"But I sinned."

"Shit, it don't matter with him. You could be old Hitler himself, he likes your singin' or thinks you look cute in them damn wings or for whatever reason, up you go."

"But is it . . . bad?"

"My boy, it's worse than that. You see, the problem with heaven is God. God's kinda nice. And heaven is kinda nice. And that kinda goes on for all eternity."

I was confused. Disquieted. This was all sort of—well, it was right, in that names like heaven and hell were in the correct usage. But I was being told that heaven was so nice that it was, essentially, terrible, and that, somehow, added up to two wrongs making a right. Or did it? No, it was the opposite.

"At least, as a denizen of the night, you'd be able to fuck up your wife in some very satisfactory ways."

"Like, how?"

"Oh, get her audited every year, for starters. Lotta shitty luck. She'll marry Rollie, he'll come down with acromeglia right away."

"Which is?"

"Bones don't stop growing. You look like Abe Lincoln. Beyond that, the Elephant Man."

"You've been out there messing with me like that, all along?"

"It's been fun."

"Dad, I'm sorry. I don't know what came over me. I just—"

"Pulled the *goddam trigger*."

"Ah, yes, that."

He thrust his hand into my chest and I felt that. He drew my heart out, and I felt that. And he squeezed it until pus came out between his fingers, and that felt like it was being stepped on by an elephant.

He tossed it to the ground. I looked down at it, still beating, his fingermarks white scars in its pinkness. "Here's a mystery for you," he said in a wheedling tone. "Why aren't you dead?"

"I am dead."

"Nope. You're just dreaming. This is just one whale of a fucked up nightmare. I am not your father. I am a demon called Borak. I have purchased the right to torment you from a torture store called Mephisto's Waltz. But, unfortunately, your body chemistry is working against me, and I must now depart, as you are going to wake up just in time for the seventh inning stretch. But this is also a warning. The gun—"

"The gun?"

"Take me out to the ball game . . ."

I choked back my spit and pitched forward in the chair, grabbing for the top of my head. Joanie said, "What the . . . ?" She came to her feet. "You okay?"

"Yeah! Yeah, I—oh, good Lord. Whoa." I gargled and choked. My eyes watered, my throat closed.

I heard her say ". . . heart attack" and I shook my head. She conducted me to our big old mahogany bed. I sat on it, then lay down. I coughed some more.

"I don't want to be a bore," I murmured.

She sat beside me, crossed her smooth and gleaming knees. "You're hardly that, honey. But you're sore, look at the way you're holding your chest. I think you *did* have a heart attack."

"At forty-eight, that's a little hard to believe."

I remembered Borak as if I had seen him in an aquarium. I remembered the gun. She was smiling down at me. Oh, how fetching she was. How very fetching. I reached out and she took my hand. I kissed her smooth skin, smelling faintly of soap and Chanel. "We can't do it *now*," she said. "I don't want you to end up dead." And there came then a glimmer in her eyes, a sort of flicker, quick as the green flash on a tropic night.

She left me then, to whatever plight or grim adventure of the mind had invaded me. There was no talk, I noticed, of the emergency room or calling Dr. Lauter, and I thought that perhaps there was indeed a danger to me here, something I really needed to see.

I thought that the dream was true: that my wife, more or less out of the blue, was planning to kill me. Outside, the bluebirds sang in their nests, the phoebe spoke her note and the afternoon wore down the sky. I decided to become a sort of spy in my own life, and began by searching her lingerie drawer. I went then to the blouses, then the sweaters, then the shorts, not stopping till I'd gone through all four.

No gun. What a bore. I thought it had to be here somewhere. So I went to the closet, searched there. Nothing. The bathroom—of course, in the toilet tank. No thanks. In that little door in the side of the tub, that led to the pipes, put there lest they leak. Not there, either.

Her car, then? I pulled on my sneakers and padded down the back steps. Glove compartment. Not that department.

Space under the cup holder, no closer. Try the trunk, maybe in among the junk.

And then there it lies, right before my eyes, along the edge of a board up near the ceiling, just below where the paint is peeling. I can't believe it: It's even blue, a twenty-two. I'm tempted to get it but that'd tear it, wouldn't it? She'd act then, no matter what was said. If she knew I'd seen the gun, that'd be the end of my fun.

The funny thing was, I experienced an explosion of desire. I'd never wanted her so much in my life. Despite all the strife in our marriage, she was still my wife, and I'd married for beauty, after all.

What had happened over the past fourteen years was that any slight awkwardness of girlhood had lost focus. She was all curves and smooth expanses, with green, frank eyes and a nose that needed to be kissed, with skin you thought must taste of paste and perfume, and did, and lips that slipped and slid against yours when you kissed her, and a tongue, too, that she knew how to use.

What a woman she was, striding the garden with her secateurs, naked as a stone, her basket packed with roses. Or swimming in the nude, the moon upon her soaked breast as soft as angel's breath. And when I made love to her, my heart whispered, God, my boy, is a woman.

God is a woman. So devoted to her I was, so used to the role of the supplicant, that I actually thought first of how she would get away with it, not of how to get away from her.

Why was she killing me? Not hard to see. Or was it, really?

There were a lot of other reasons to have a cruel little pistol in the garage. Maybe she'd seen some rats. Or a snake. We'd had a snake in here once, a black snake that had raised its head and then sped down a crack in the concrete as quick as a shadow.

She came out, her eyes wide with concern.

"I thought I'd ride over to the emergency room," I said. "Just to be certain."

"That's a great idea." She glanced toward the gun, so quick, it was like a pedo sucking the sight of a boy. In that green glance there was a rich trove of perversion. And I knew then for certain that I was to be murdered with the gun. No look could contain that much that was twisted and filthy and wrong, and yet be so quick, that was not the glance of a murderer.

I thought—I actually thought—as we drove through the wide shade of early summer, that I ought to do it for her, save her the danger. No matter me, I wanted her to be safe.

A gun in the mouth—how would it taste? And a twenty-two—would it blow enough of a hole, or would I just be Reeved? Such a sad irony, that Superman would end up living in a tin can. And him a wonderful man. Nobody would want to kill him but him. And me? I had no desire to die. I just wanted my Joanie to be safe and happy.

And then I wondered, am I at the center of a plot? Was the whole dream real, or not? I'm a pretty rich man, I've got a fair amount of cash on hand, not to mention bonds and, better, letters of credit drawn on Credit Suisse, collectively worth five million dollars.

She might see a world beyond me, without me, with me dead. She'd be head of firm and family. She'd be profoundly free.

The emergency room doctor took an immediate interest. You didn't fool around with a guy coming in with chest pains. But the EKG drew a neat and unvarying line. I was fine. So we returned home, with both of us, I suspect, thinking only of the gun.

The next day was Sunday and I invited Rollie out to golf. We had a good time on the front nine at the club, and I went home thinking he wasn't in it. So I took Mikey to lunch on Monday, and described a story I was thinking of writing, just like the story I'd been dreaming when the demon showed up. Unless, of course, the dreaming had *been* the demon.

He thought it was a pretty good yarn, there was no more than that. Still, I could not forget the gun. I kept thinking—maybe I should just use the damn thing, get it over with.

Thing was, I had shot my dad. Shot him right through the heart with a pistol we had unloaded together. There was a lot of guilt, still, and I guessed that I had seen my father's kindly warning to me through the medium of that guilt. Behind the appearance of the angry man was a lost father who had been guarding his son for years.

Killing him had nearly killed me. It had defined my life. An accident, though—horrible then, horrible now. Dad had come. Dad had warned me.

Then, on Wednesday, the gun was gone. Just like that. So I knew she knew it was there. And I had to think, it's all real, the thing is happening. But life continued, we ate our supper and watched some TV, then I decided I'd ask her to dance. So we danced on the terrace by yes the moonlight and yes I rubbed her to the music of Harry Connick, Jr., "Begin the Beguine," and then we went to the shadowy end of the terrace where the couch on springs sits and stripped and made a kind of pale sense in the jasmine scented night. I wanted her to love me or give me a reprieve at least, and so I kissed her in all the slow places, upon the hills of her magic and in the low oyster of her. She sighed some, and then said something I didn't catch.

We made love with the care of an established couple. She had such a capacity, did Joanie, to make me feel naked. But again in the moonlight there was something in her eyes of the serpent, that careful glance, horribly empty and concealing.

That night late, I found the gun again. It was as if it was stalking me, that little fist of a pistol. Loaded, I checked that. It was in her third drawer, back behind the gym shorts.

A day passed like a day in creation, and I felt the skill of God in every drop of a leaf or water. When I ate my food, I experienced a series of surprises, as if each bite had conducted me to a new galaxy.

And then the gun was in her bedside table, hidden beneath her glasses case, like a thing from some dark fable.

I realized that I had only days to go. My wife would take my life.

Knowing that she desired my death made me mad but also made me want to accommodate her. When we first met and I used to date her, I always tried to open doors and step aside, and treat her as if she was a lady. I did that again, and again thought maybe I ought to get down *Gray's Anatomy* and see if I could find a foolproof point of penetration, that would leave me no chance of leaving her with a vegetable instead of a buriable.

But I didn't do it. Instead, I talked to her. I talked of our early days and special ways, and all the fun we'd had. She responded with her own stories, and I sat with my eyes wet, and noticed that hers were not. I tried to catch her in calls to Rollie or anybody, but there was nothing wrong, nothing except the slow embrace of the gun.

Saturday came, and it was no longer in its drawer. I went in to watch the Yankees game. I was so scared that I was ready to piss myself. I drank like a machine. Muziak was pitching again. Or no, last week it had been Cerniak. In fact, it hadn't been the White Sox but the Red. And the Yanks had won six to one, another one for old Steinbrenner. The third inning came. I watched Jeter at bat get a hit and trot into second. Then O'Neill came up. He gave a few practice swings, and I felt above my head a breath of breeze so slight that it almost wasn't there. But I knew that my passion and my love, for reasons I could never fathom, had come again to kill me, and again she committed the sin, and again I felt the fist plunge into my throat, and saw myself pitch forward like a blown scarecrow, and saw her draw back the gun and shake her blond hair in a shaft of sun.

She turned then and made the call, and here they came, all the players in the game. It was just as I had dreamed it, the instant death and then the frantic, bodyless swimming as they wailed and chanted about the hole in the top of the head.

My father came mourning as he had, no longer a demon but still damn mad. "You're a fool when it comes to guns, boy," he said. "Always have been, always will be."

Yep. And for all eternity.